"There's no way of guessing who's going to do well and who's not," Danielle explained.

"It's interesting you say that," Erin responded. "About an hour before she went into labor, I accidentally walked into Mrs. Allen's room. She was sleeping so peacefully. She looked fine. I think I scared the nurse who was in there."

"Do you mean Pat?"

"I guess so. . . . I only saw her for a few seconds."

"Pat's a guy," Danielle informed Erin.

"I know I'm getting older and my vision is staring to fail, but the nurse I saw in Mrs. Allen's room was definitely a woman."

"No, that's not possible. There are only two RNs on duty in the evening. It must have been Pat who you saw."

Erin took a step forward and placed her hands on the desk. "The person in the room was a woman," she said firmly. "She was adding a medication to the IV. I'm sure of it."

Danielle looked up quickly and then slid the final chart back in the rack. "It was nice talking to you, Erin." She grabbed her stethoscope from one of the drawers, stood up and headed down the hall.

Erin immediately felt her pulse quicken and a knot form in the top of her stomach.

FINAL
Diagnosis

GARY BIRKEN, M.D.

BERKLEY BOOKS, NEW YORK

FINAL DIAGNOSIS

A Berkley Book / published by arrangement with
the author

PRINTING HISTORY
Berkley edition / December 2001

Visit our website at
www.penguinputnam.com

ISBN: 0-425-18269-X

BERKLEY®
Berkley Books are published by The Berkley Publishing Group,
a division of Penguin Putnam Inc.,
375 Hudson Street, New York, New York 10014.
BERKLEY and the "B" design
are trademarks belonging to Penguin Putnam Inc.

PRINTED IN THE UNITED STATES OF AMERICA

10 9 8 7 6 5 4 3 2 1

This book is dedicated to Melissa Lurz. Fighting on with endless courage, dignity and tenacity, her indomitable spirit and love of life helped her face the tide of extreme adversity.

Acknowledgments

By the time a story writer has completed a novel, the list of people to be acknowledged has almost taken on a life of its own. To begin with, I wish to thank Ross Browne for helping me to acquire the basic knowledge and skills of fiction writing.

I would be remiss not to recognize Joan Sanger's enormous contribution to this book. A gifted editor, her insight into character and plot development were invaluable. What began as a professional relationship has now blossomed into a cherished friendship.

Loretta Barrett's role in my career has been both essential and unique. Patient and astute, her advice and guidance along the way have made some very tough decisions seem easy.

I would also like to thank my editor at Berkley, Natalee Rosenstein, who was always available and genuinely willing to help through the entire publishing process.

Many of my friends, relatives and associates were kind enough to read the manuscript and offer criticism. They include: Barbara Gianos, Linda and Jay Fabrikant, Alison Birken, Udyss Romano, Sharon and Lucien Lallouz, Linda

Winrow, Margo Young, Denise Causa, David Drucker and Cathy Burnweit.

A special thanks to Frank Sacco for his creative suggestions in the development of this novel.

Prologue

The operation to save Maggie Daniel's unborn baby lasted nearly four hours. Still under the heavy effect of the anesthesia, she lay quietly in her dimly lit hospital room. A continuous infusion of intravenous morphine helped ease the constant pain from the long incision that ran across her lower abdomen.

Maggie's vision was faintly blurred and she barely noticed when the silhouette of a thin woman dressed in a white uniform moved silently across the foot of her bed. Turning her head on the pillow, Maggie watched as the young nurse removed a syringe from her pocket, inserted the needle into the rubber port of her IV and slowly injected its entire contents.

"I'm giving you something to help you sleep," the nurse whispered.

Consumed by a deepening sense of tranquility, Maggie nodded, managed a brief smile and then closed her eyes. Her breathing slowed and then became more rhythmic as she drifted into a restless sleep. The nurse watched carefully as tiny drops of saline fell in perfect synchrony into the clear plastic tubing that twisted and curled until reaching the IV in the back of Maggie's hand. When she was quite confident the drug was coursing through her bloodstream, the nurse removed the needle and quietly left the room, leaving the gentle rush of air that inflated the blood-pressure cuff as the only sound that disturbed the silence.

It took several minutes for the steady ooze of warm blood and clots accumulating between Maggie's legs to awaken her. Just as she began pushing herself up in bed, the first contraction rocked her. Her only thought was to grab her belly and push back against the overwhelming pressure of the uterine spasm. In spite of her efforts, the pain only intensified. Desperately trying to recall what she had learned in Lamaze class, she opened her mouth, took a deep breath and then blew it out in short, rapid bursts. She reached down, hoping to locate the nurse's call button, but it had become lost in the covers. Just as she was about to give up, the main lights came on and two nurses raced to her side. Cheryl Quinton had been a charge nurse for five years and had become an expert in the care of women who had undergone fetal surgery. While Cheryl reset the blood-pressure device, the other nurse, Mike Murphy, moved around to the foot of the bed and gently lifted the blanket above Maggie's knees.

"We have a lot of clotted blood here," he whispered to Cheryl.

"Hang on, everything's going to be okay," she told Maggie in a reassuring voice while she waited the last few seconds for the digital readout on the blood-pressure machine. When it finally came, she turned to Mike. "Her pressure's low."

"How low?"

"Eighty over fifty," she said.

"What about her pulse?"

Cheryl paused for a moment before answering. "It's a hundred and sixty."

"How far along is she?" he asked.

"The last ultrasound was consistent with a twenty-six-week pregnancy."

"What operation did she have?" Mike asked as Cheryl handed him three empty blood tubes to hold.

"The baby's urinary tract was totally blocked. They made an opening in the bladder to relieve the pressure." Cheryl reached down and placed her hands on Maggie's abdomen. "She's in labor," she told him softly. "Go to the desk and page the doctor." Mike nodded, cast a final glance at Maggie and then headed for the door.

"Is my baby okay? Please don't let anything happen to him," she begged as she tried to push the covers back below her knees.

"We're calling the doctor now. Try and stay calm. It's very important," Cheryl said evenly while glancing up at the fetal monitor. "The baby's heartbeat is very strong."

"Call my husband," Maggie pleaded. Her face was desperate from the constant waves of pain rolling across her lower belly. "I can't stand the pain," she moaned, turning her head from side to side on the perspiration-soaked pillow.

"Your blood pressure's a little low. We have to be careful about how much pain medication we give you."

"I don't care . . . just please give me something."

Cheryl placed a tourniquet around Maggie's upper arm and prepared to draw a blood sample. Her breathing was considerably more labored and her skin had become mottled and cool. Just as Cheryl was about to summon Mike back to the room the fetal monitor suddenly alarmed. The high-pitched warning, indicating a slowing heart rate and impending fetal distress, became louder and louder.

"We have to move her down to the intensive care unit right now," Mike announced as he came through the door. "Dr. Hannigan's on his way in. He said he'll meet us there. He wants her to have a bolus of Ringer's lactate and start on Terbutaline and a magnesium drip stat. I called the ICU. They're sending us some help."

"Something's happened to the baby. I know it. The surgery didn't work," Maggie said in quiet desperation just as a burly orderly in rumpled green surgical scrubs pushed a stretcher through the door.

"You're experiencing premature labor," Cheryl explained to her in a guarded tone as she helped the orderly snug the stretcher alongside the bed. "Just to be on the safe side, we're going to take you down to the intensive care unit."

Maggie's face was now the color of chalk, her eyes sunken and hollow. "Oh God, this can't be happening."

With Mike's help, the orderly transferred Maggie slowly onto the stretcher. Cheryl fitted an oxygen mask over her nose and mouth, checked the fetal monitor for the last time and then watched as Maggie was wheeled out of the room. She glanced down at her watch. It was a few minutes past midnight.

Cheryl walked slowly toward the door, stopping only for a moment to study a framed photograph of Maggie and her husband that sat on the night table. She shook her head, offered a silent prayer for Maggie Daniel's baby and then turned out the lights.

It was nearly six a.m. when Cheryl finished up her charting. She took off her half-moon reading glasses, reached for the phone and called the ICU nurse caring for Maggie. After a short conversation, she thanked the nurse and slowly hung up the phone. Her daunted expression betrayed the evening's ordeal.

"What's going on?" Mike asked.

"She's stable."

"That's great news," he said.

"I just don't understand," Cheryl muttered more to herself than to Mike.

"What do you mean?"

"When we got the report from the operating team, they said the surgery went fine."

Mike shrugged and then furrowed his brow. "But that doesn't always mean that things are—"

"They said she had absolutely no hint of premature labor

either during the case or in the recovery room—I just don't understand," she repeated.

"What about the baby? How's he doing?"

Cheryl stood up and shook her head. "There was too much bleeding. They couldn't save him."

PART
One

Chapter 1

"Fetal surgery has come a long way," Dr. Marc Archer told the woman sitting across the desk from him. Claire Weaver edged forward in her chair and squeezed her husband's hand just a little tighter. She was an attractive woman, almost regal looking, who had managed to maintain a certain willowy appearance even in the face of a difficult pregnancy. Her large hazel eyes were slightly watery but remained watchful. She was dressed simply in a wheat-colored, neatly pressed cotton maternity dress.

"I've heard nothing but wonderful things about your hospital, Dr. Archer," she told him as she took another look around his impeccably decorated office. The plush royal-blue carpet was immaculate and the floor-to-ceiling hand-crafted wall unit with thick hung-glass shelves lent a scholarly atmosphere.

He smiled briefly from behind his mahogany desk. "It's not exactly my hospital, Mrs. Weaver. But I feel very fortunate that I've been part of assembling the best physicians, medical technicians and research scientists in the country to help advance the surgical treatment of fetal diseases." He renewed his smile and added with an obvious sense of pride, "I think it's safe to say we've become a very important part of Miami's medical community."

"It's all very impressive."

"Well, we've made tremendous strides since starting this project almost twenty years ago as one small building on the Jackson Memorial Hospital campus. We barely had enough money to pay the electric bill, but thanks to an incredibly dedicated group of fund-raisers, we grew faster than anyone expected. Finally, in 1992, we moved into this complex on Key Biscayne."

"Are most of your patients from Florida?" Claire asked.

"Not really. Actually, we take care of patients from all over the world."

Archer's drab brown hair fell at an oblique angle across his prominent forehead. His lean, six-foot-two frame and smartly cropped beard made him look younger than his fifty-two years. Dressed in gray cuffed slacks, a button-down white shirt and a striped navy-blue tie, he was pure Ivy League.

"How many fetal operations have you done?" Claire asked.

Archer thought for a moment before replying. "Almost two hundred. We're now able to surgically treat more and more major birth defects before these infants are even born."

Claire cleared her throat. "What can you tell me about my baby's illness, Dr. Archer?" She watched him carefully as he rocked back in his black leather manager's chair and gently stroked his beard.

"I'm sure a lot of what I'm going to say you've already heard, so please indulge me."

"Of course," she said.

"You're twenty-three weeks pregnant and it appears fairly certain from your ultrasound that your baby has a congenital cystic adenomatoid malformation of the lung." Archer paused for a second, studied Claire's blank expression, and added, "For simplicity we just call the disorder a CCAM."

Her husband, Alex, who had remained uncharacteristically

silent, moved to the edge of his chair and asked, "We've spoken to so many doctors in the last few weeks who have given us an awful lot of information. Would you mind just going over. . . ?"

"Of course," Archer answered. "CCAMs are large masses of tissue attached to a baby's lung that can cause a number of problems, the worst of which is blocking the normal growth of the lung."

Alex asked, "Why can't the baby just have an operation after he's born to remove it?"

"In some cases we can do that. But your baby's already showing signs of accumulating fluid in his body, which is an ominous sign and puts him in a very high risk group." Archer moved a stack of medical journals a little farther over on his desk before continuing. "The good news in your baby's case is that he does not appear to have any other major problems."

"Does that really make that much of a difference?" Alex asked with a measure of gloom in his voice.

"It makes an enormous difference," Archer explained. "In those cases where a baby has a major associated problem, such as heart disease or a severe genetic disorder, well . . . I'm afraid he or she wouldn't be a candidate for fetal surgery."

"But I still don't understand why we just don't wait and—"

"If the problem's allowed to continue through pregnancy, there's a good chance the baby will be born prematurely and very sick."

Claire sat in silence studying Archer's expression. When it changed to an even more solemn one, she said, "There's something else, isn't there?"

"I'm afraid so. There's a very high probability that we could lose the baby even before he's born."

Alex, who was practical and unflappable by nature, put his arm around Claire's shoulder. He was a deductive thinker and a man who disliked fanfare in any form. His handsome appearance had changed very little over the years. His hollow cheeks and slate-gray eyes complemented his sunburnt complexion. Being a former college rugby player and dressed now in a faded maroon flannel shirt and jeans, he looked more like a lumberjack than an airline pilot.

"Dr. Archer, it took my wife three years to get pregnant with our first child. Claire was an infertility patient. She's already endured more than most women could have."

Archer waited until he was sure Alex was finished. "I can appreciate how you must—"

"She loves kids," he pressed on. "Everyone who knows her will tell you she's the best damn kindergarten teacher in Virginia." He stopped for a moment and gazed over at Claire. "When our first baby died in the delivery room, it was almost too much for her to handle."

"I fully understand, Mr. Weaver. Many of our patients have had similar experiences."

"What are my baby's chances without fetal surgery?" she asked in a cracked voice barely above a whisper. "I just can't bare the thought of losing another baby, Dr. Archer."

"We're going to do everything possible," he said to her, and then slid a box of tissues across the desk as inconspicuously as possible. "The first thing you have to do is consider your options. There are three."

"What are they?" Alex asked before his wife could.

"Well, you can opt to terminate the pregnancy."

Claire crumpled one of the tissues in her hand and looked directly at Archer with an obvious resolve in her eyes.

"I'm a practicing Catholic, Dr. Archer. I'm afraid termination's not an alternative."

"I understand perfectly," he said.

"You mentioned there were three options," she said.

"You can decide to carry the pregnancy as far as it will go and deal with the problem after the baby's born."

"But I thought you said that without fetal surgery there would be a strong possibility that our baby might die before he's born?"

"I'm afraid that's true."

"What about with fetal surgery? How much will that improve the odds?" Alex asked.

"Our survival rate in treating babies with CCAM with fetal surgery has been almost sixty-five percent," Archer answered.

Alex stared across the room at an oil painting depicting a tranquil Mediterranean harbor at dusk. He lowered his eyes and then pulled his wife closer. When he did, she let her head rest on his shoulder. He whispered something in her ear and then, with her head still against him, she nodded.

"Dr. Archer, a lot of what you've told us today we already had an inkling of. Claire and I are in your office because we're convinced our baby's best chance is here." He looked up for a moment. "Will you be the one doing the surgery?"

"No. I'm afraid not. Over the years, my administrative duties at the institute became so overwhelming I was forced to give up my clinical practice. Dr. Noah Gallagher is our chief of surgery. He'll be in charge of your wife's care."

"I see," Alex said with a hint of disappointment. "When do we get started?"

"Actually, Mr. Weaver, we already have. We received Claire's medical records from her obstetrician several days ago. I'm going to make arrangements for her to be admitted tomorrow morning for a few days. We'll need to do several more tests before surgery."

"Do you have any idea when the surgery will be?" Claire asked.

Archer reached for a large leather journal on his desk. He flipped it open to the middle and then studied the page for several seconds.

"Assuming there are no problems, I think we should be ready to operate in about three weeks."

"We want to thank you for everything, Doctor," Claire said.

Archer stood up. "My secretary will give you all the instructions. I'll stop in and see you tomorrow afternoon. We have a lot more to talk about. You're going to be a busy lady for the next few days, Claire. Try and stay calm. We're going to walk you through the whole process one step at a time."

Claire and Alex stood up. "When will we meet Dr. Gallagher?" she asked.

"I'll inform him you're here. I'm sure he'll want to meet with both of you as soon as possible."

Claire managed a half smile through pursed lips, took her husband by the arm and waited for Dr. Archer to come out from behind his desk and escort them out.

"I'm not sure I'm ready for all this," she whispered to Alex.

"Sure you are. You're the toughest lady I've ever met. Anyway, we're going to do this thing together," he assured her, covering her hand with his and then hugging her.

When she felt his shirt becoming moist from her tears, she turned her head to the side, smiled and told him she was ready.

Chapter 2

As the aging yellow cab coughed a thick cloud of charcoal exhaust and sped away from Miami International Airport, a grateful Erin Wells never looked back. Ever since her first plane ride as a child, the mere sight of an airport made her cringe with anxiety. The moment she set foot on an airplane, her mouth became dry and an awful fullness settled in her throat that made it almost impossible for her to swallow. If there was a negative aspect of being a medical reporter for the *AMA News*, it was the requirement to travel.

Gangly and self-conscious as a teenager, Erin Wells had become more attractive with each passing year. She was wearing a smartly tailored pale gray jacket with a matching skirt. Her skin was radiant, her nose just slightly upturned and her eyes a deep sapphire blue. Her daily workouts were inviolate and emblematic of her resolve to maintain a wispy figure. Creative and at times unconventional, there was generally a method to her madness.

It was about two in the afternoon and the traffic was light. Erin stared out the window and watched the large leafy palm trees that lined the Julia Tuttle Causeway glide by in a blur.

The beaches were sparsely occupied with sunbathers but dozens of jet-skiers buzzed up and down Biscayne Bay, shooting enormous spouts of water high into the air with each sharp turn.

Typical of South Florida in the fall, it was a cool, cloudless day with shifting gusts of wind, and as the causeway gently arched over the water, she could see the modernistic Miami skyline in the distance. Erin let her head fall back against the top of the seat and listened as the cab's noisy air conditioner droned above the Latin music coming from the two front speakers.

"First time in Miami?" the cab driver asked. Erin glanced up and caught him peering at her in the rearview mirror. He was young with a gangly neck, bushy eyebrows and a rounded forehead. The collar on his tan shirt was worn and tattered.

"I've been here before," she answered with a quick smile.

"Here on business?" he asked as if they were old friends.

Erin pulled her leather carry-on a little closer, shook her head and wondered why she always wound up with a talkative cab driver.

"I'm here to visit a friend. She's a patient at the Fetal Institute," she answered politely, hoping to satisfy his curiosity and be left in peace.

"The Fetal Institute. That's quite a place," he said and then followed with a long whistle. "It's in the newspaper all the time."

Erin took a moment and gazed out the window. She thought about Claire Weaver and all the hard times her best friend had been through with her pregnancies. Since enrolling at Penn State, they had shared the good times and the bad, although recently it seemed like the bad far outweighed the good for Claire. The recent loss of her baby was devastating and almost proved too much for her to shoulder. Alex Weaver was a supportive and compassionate husband who was genuinely dedicated to his wife, but when times were particularly bad, it was Erin who emerged as Claire's emotional lifeline.

When Claire and Alex asked her to come to Miami for moral support, she never hesitated.

The remainder of the ride to her hotel took only about twenty minutes and much to Erin's relief passed in silence. She pushed open the door and asked the cab driver to wait for her while she checked in and dropped off her luggage.

Erin quickly crossed the ornate lobby. Fortunately, there was no line and the entire registration process took no more than five minutes. The polite young man who handled the check-in assured Erin her bags would be taken to her room immediately.

Returning directly to the cab, Erin climbed in the back and relaxed for the short ride to the Fetal Institute. A large circular driveway scalloped with multicolored impatiens accessed the main entrance of the hospital. Before the driver could open the door for her, Erin was out of the cab. After taking a few deep breaths and stealing another peek at the Miami skyline, she looked up at the building.

The institute, constructed of sharply cut stone, was a freestanding four-story structure with edged corners. The research facility was a separate building that joined the main hospital by way of an ornate breezeway. Located on Pine Tree Drive and overlooking Biscayne Bay, the facility was an impressive addition to the unique architecture of Miami.

Erin walked under a large royal-blue canopy and into the lobby. It took her only a moment to spot the information desk.

"Can you help me, please? I'm looking for Claire Weaver's room," Erin said.

A girl with a long ponytail and a red-and-white pinstripe volunteer uniform, who Erin guessed was in her late teens, smiled and ran her finger down a computerized list of patients.

"She's in two-eleven," she said, pointing down a long hallway. "The elevators are right over there."

She thanked the volunteer and headed straight for the elevators. Once on the second floor, it was a simple matter to locate Claire's room. The door was slightly cracked and she decided to give it a gentle push instead of knocking in case Claire was asleep. The bed was empty. Looking across the room, she saw her friend sitting in a beige recliner gazing out the window.

"Excuse me. I'm looking for my long-lost college roommate. I understand she swallowed a basketball and they had to admit her to this hospital."

When Claire heard her friend's voice, she immediately became wide-eyed with joy.

"I'm so glad you're here," she told Erin as she slowly maneuvered herself out of the recliner. "I was so excited I called the airline to make sure your flight was on time. You're the best." The two women met in the middle of the room and hugged.

"This is some classy place," Erin said, looking around. "I wasn't sure whether the cab had pulled up to a hospital or to some snooty spa for the rich and famous."

"Technically, it's an institute . . . which I guess is just a fancy name for a specialty hospital."

"Well, excuse me," Erin teased, covering her cheeks with both hands as if she had just said something unforgivably stupid. In the next moment, she dropped her hands slowly, revealing a more serious expression. "How are you feeling?"

Claire frowned and then shrugged her shoulders. She was wearing a light pink chenille robe, very little makeup and white kneesocks. Erin immediately noticed her eyes were just slightly sunken.

"I feel okay, I guess. They've been doing a lot of tests. The whole thing is exhausting . . . and kind of scary."

Erin hugged her friend again and whispered, "You're a good person. Bad things don't happen to good people. You'll be fine."

"I wish the doctor would get here. I've been waiting for him all day," Claire said with a touch of impatience.

"I'm sure he'll be here soon. Where's Alex?"

"He just left to get something to eat. He'll be back in a bit."

"So, tell me what's going on," Erin said.

"There's not much to tell. If everything checks out okay, surgery should be in a few weeks."

"That . . . that sounds great," Erin said.

"I guess so," Claire whispered, reaching for a tissue. "Never mind me," she continued. "What's new? How's life in Washington?"

"Well, let's see. Where do I start? DC is a great place to live. I'm still dating Will. . . ."

"And . . ."

Erin shrugged and said, "I keep waiting for the earth to move, but so far . . . not even a minor tremor."

Claire grinned affectionately. "Still waiting for the fireworks and harp music, I see."

Erin puffed her cheeks. "What can I say? I'm an incurable romantic. I guess I never got over spending my junior year in Paris."

"Yeah, I remember that. I was always jealous of you winning that scholarship. What about your new job? Do you like it better than nursing?"

"Claire, I love writing about medical issues, and being a reporter for the *AMA News* has been incredible. I think I've finally found the perfect job."

"Do you miss nursing?"

"Not for a moment," Erin said without hesitation. "But I don't regret getting a nursing degree because it has really made me a better medical reporter."

"Which reminds me," Claire said. "What happened with your idea to write a story about the institute? Did you ever get permission?"

Erin immediately nodded. "My editor thought it was a great idea. He approved the project the same day I put the proposal on his desk. I then called a Dr. Archer here at the institute." Erin stopped when she saw her friend smile broadly. "Have you met him?" she asked Claire.

"Alex and I talked with him yesterday. He's quite a guy," Claire said, beaming. "He made Alex and me very comfortable. When I was sitting in his office I checked out his diplo-

mas. He went to med school at Harvard and then did his pediatrics residency at Boston Children's Hospital. He's also a
board-certified neonatologist."

"That's pretty impressive."

"So, what did Dr. Archer say about the story?" Claire
asked.

"It was a bit of a tough sell, but he finally agreed to let me
do it."

"When do you start?" Claire asked.

"Actually, my first interview's tomorrow. It's with one of
the physicians . . . but I can't remember his name. Wait a sec,"
Erin said, reaching for her purse. She pulled out a small spiral notepad, flipped it open and ran her finger down the page.
"Here it is. His name is John Freeman. He's the director of the
research laboratory. It should be interesting," she said, closing
the notepad. "I just hope he's not one of those academic
eggheads who are impossible to interview."

"I'm sure you'll have him eating out of your hand in no
time," Claire said. "Nobody can charm the birds out of the
trees like you can," she added, shaking her finger at Erin as if
she were scolding a toddler.

"Me?" Erin asked with affection. "What about the way you
could always wrap kids around your little finger and make
them love you? I was so jealous." Erin giggled along with her
friend and then noticed Claire staring over at the recliner. Erin
gently took her by the arm. "C'mon, let's sit back down."

Claire took a deep breath, looked again at the inviting chair
and nodded. "That doesn't sound like a bad idea."

"I wonder how many students in college had the same
roommate for all four years?" Erin asked as she helped Claire
back into the chair and then made sure her feet were squarely
on the footrest.

"I don't know. But having to listen to your crazy stories
about all those boyfriends . . . now that was a trick. And your
thirtieth birthday last spring. I didn't think you'd ever get over
the emotional trauma of that transition."

Erin smiled. "Well, we can either keep reminiscing about

the old days or you can tell me what's going on with my god-child."

Claire became circumspect. "It's been a crazy day. They're running all kinds of tests."

"And?"

"Who knows? They haven't said very much."

Erin said, "They must be telling you something."

"Only that they're waiting for all the results to come in." Just as Claire was about to continue, Noah Gallagher knocked on the door. He was dressed in his royal-blue surgical scrubs covered by a perfectly pressed white lab coat with his name monogrammed over the pocket.

He looked at the two women. "My name is Dr. Gallagher. I'm the chief of surgery and just wanted to introduce myself." He cast a polite glance at Erin. "But if this is a bad time, I can come back later."

"Not at all," Claire insisted. "This is Erin Wells. She's an extremely close friend. We have no secrets."

Erin smiled and then looked away when she caught herself staring just a little too long at the handsome doctor. She walked across the room and shook his hand. Apart from his watch, he wasn't wearing any jewelry.

"Has Dr. Archer already gone over the basics with you?" he asked Claire.

"Yes, and he was very reassuring." Claire looked toward the door and then over at the small digital clock next to her bed. "Something just occurred to me, Dr. Gallagher. My husband should be back in about an hour. I'm sure he'll have a million questions. Is there any chance you might be able to . . ."

"Absolutely. I'll be tied up for the next hour or so but I'll stop back later."

"Thank you very much."

Noah looked over at Erin. "It was nice to meet you, Ms. Wells."

"It was nice meeting you too, Dr. Gallagher." Erin waited until the door closed behind Gallagher, looked over at Claire with raised eyebrows and let her mouth drop open. "Now there's a cute doctor. I wouldn't mind being one of his patients."

Claire shook her head slowly. "I think he mentioned something about being a fetal surgeon. You might not exactly fit his patient profile."

"For a date with him, I'd definitely consider returning to the womb."

Claire laughed. "You haven't changed a bit. I saw you checking him out for a wedding band. Could you be any more obvious?"

"It never hurts to keep your eyes open."

"I thought you were dating somebody," Claire said.

"Dating, yes. In a love coma, no." Erin glanced toward the door and then said, "I'll be right back."

"Where are you going?"

"Don't be so nosy."

"Poor Dr. Gallagher," Claire said in a voice just loud enough for Erin to hear.

Erin walked out into the corridor and spotted Noah at the nursing station. His head was down and she assumed he was making an entry in one of the patient's charts. As she approached the desk, she saw him looking at his pager. A frown came to his face. He replaced his beeper on his belt and then reached for a phone. He listened for a moment, then she heard him order a chest X ray and watched as he hung up the phone.

"Dr. Gallagher, do you have a moment?"

Noah looked up. "Of course, Ms. Wells."

"I didn't mention it before but I'm a reporter for the *AMA News*. My editor contacted Dr. Archer last week and he was kind enough to invite us to do a story on the institute. When the assignment was offered me, I jumped at the chance."

Noah's expression became slightly wary. "I thought you were here to visit Mrs. Weaver."

"That too," she assured him. "I'm kind of mixing business with pleasure. I was hoping when you had some time we might be able to talk. You mentioned that you're the chief of surgery and I thought—"

"I'm not much for the limelight, Ms. Wells." His tone was polite, not dismissive.

"Please call me Erin. To be honest with you, Doctor, we're not exactly a supermarket tabloid. I think we can do a nice story and still guarantee you that you won't have to wear a baseball cap and dark glasses every time you feel like stepping out into public."

"I'll give it some thought," he promised with a smile.

"You surprise me a little," she said, hoping his curiosity would spark a request to elaborate.

Noah tucked the chart under his arm and asked, "Why's that?"

"Most surgeons I've run into couldn't wait to talk about their accomplishments. How come you're not interested?"

"I guess I'm not most surgeons, Ms. Wells," he confessed with a bit of a blush.

"There you go again."

"I beg your pardon."

"You called me Ms. Wells again," she pointed out as she walked around to the other side of the desk and sat down beside him.

A little miffed by her bold gesture, he pretended not to notice her seductive eyes, attractive figure, and the more than subtly provocative scent of her perfume. He actually found the feeling a little refreshing, causing him to wonder if an ember of hope of meeting the right woman still flickered.

Since his divorce eight years ago, he had been out on an infinite number of first dates, but could count on one hand the number of women he had taken a serious interest in. Making matters worse, his parents, who were still married after forty-eight years, could not understand why their only son had abandoned his marriage.

"May I ask you a question?" Noah asked, replacing the chart on the desk and then turning toward her.

"Now you sound like a reporter," Erin joked. She waited for him to respond but his businesslike expression never

changed. *Great, another doctor without a sense of humor.*
"Sure," she said. "What's your question?"

"Mrs. Weaver mentioned you were close friends. I saw
from her medical records that she's already lost one baby. She
seems quite composed under the circumstances."

"Claire's an incredible lady. Probably the most gentle,
even-tempered person I've ever met. She has the faith of a
child and doesn't deserve any of this." Erin turned her chair,
shook her head and looked back toward her friend's room.
"You said you had a question."

"Uh . . . yes. I was wondering why Mrs. Weaver selected
our facility? She lives in Virginia. There are two other centers
that are closer."

"Well," Erin started cautiously. "As I'm sure you know,
there are only seven hospitals doing fetal surgery in the country. Yours is the only one that does it exclusively and your survival statistics seem to be better than the others."

"It sounds like the Weavers did their homework. I'm not
sure our results are really any better than the other fetal
surgery centers, but it's certainly nice to receive the vote of
confidence."

"I'm going to be conducting quite a few interviews while
I'm here, but I'd also like to get a feel for the actual operative
procedures," she said. "I don't know if I mentioned it, but I
have a nursing degree. If it's at all possible, I'd really like to
observe you in the operating room."

"A nurse? How does one go from being a nurse to a reporter for the *AMA News* . . . if you don't mind me asking?"

"Not at all. Actually, I kind of got pushed into nursing by
my mother. My minor at Penn State was journalism. I realized
after my freshman year that my true passion was writing. I
guess I never got it out of my blood. Anyway, after spending
a few years as a clinical nurse, I decided it wasn't for me. I located a headhunter who hooked me up with the *AMA News*.
The interview went great and . . . well, the rest is history."

"That's incredible," he said with the first bit of emotion
Erin had detected. If she were any judge of people, she would

say there was a touch of envy in Dr. Gallagher's voice. "I love what I do," he said, "but I sometimes wonder what it would be like to make an abrupt career change."

"Well, anytime you want to talk about it, I'm the expert. I've been there, done it and have the T-shirt. Believe me, it's possible to have more than one passion in life," she said confidently, not really thinking he was the type of person to switch horses in midstream. He seemed way too structured for anything that capricious. "Uh . . . what about observing you in the OR?" she reminded him.

"To be honest with you, I'm not quite sure what the hospital policy is. I'll have to check with Dr. Archer and get his approval. Can I get back to you?"

Erin was disappointed. "Sure, that will be fine."

Noah looked down at his watch, fidgeted with the band and said, "I must have lost track of the time. I really have to get going."

"An emergency?" she asked skeptically.

"Actually," he said, looking from side to side. "I have an appointment to get my hair cut."

"Approved by Dr. Archer, I assume," she said just above a whisper.

Noah frowned to cover up the spontaneous grin. "You have an interesting way with people, Erin. Did anybody ever tell you that?"

"Only my first four therapists. So, what do you say? Can I call your office to set up a meeting? I'm still really interested in—"

Noah extended his hand. "As hard as it is for me to say this, I'll have to clear your request with Dr. Archer. After I've discussed it with him, I'll have my secretary give you a call."

A little dumbfounded, Erin watched Noah stroll away. She then returned to Claire's room, where she spent another twenty minutes or so trying to cheer her friend up. After a lengthy good-bye filled with words of encouragement, she left the institute and hailed a cab. Erin had only been in Miami on one other occasion. Instead of listening to the loquacious cab driver rambling on about local politics, she gazed at four luxury cruise ships docked in a perfect line just on the other side of the causeway.

She thought about Claire and then wondered about her conversation with Dr. Gallagher. As a surgeon, he seemed quite competent, and to his credit, he seemed to lack the pro-totypical arrogance that she was so familiar with. But his aloof nature and questions regarding Claire and Alex's choice of the institute were certainly unusual, to say the least. But more than Dr. Gallagher's guarded nature, she was truly per-plexed by the autocratic way that Marc Archer obviously ran the hospital. Most experts in health care would agree that the days of the one-man-show method of running a hospital were long gone, and that the delivery of excellent patient care re-quired a team approach consisting of many individuals with varied expertise. She wasn't quite sure why, but her first im-pression of the Fetal Institute was one of uncertainty and per-haps a little apprehension.

Looking toward the front seat, she frowned at the meter as it clicked along like a slot machine out of control.

By the time her cab pulled up to the Hotel Inter-Continental, a subtle and disquieting feeling had overtaken her, and she found herself pondering whether Claire and Alex Weaver had indeed selected the best hospital for the care of their unborn baby.

Chapter 3

Dr. John Freeman, the director of the research laboratory at the Fetal Institute, sat in his brightly lit office staring at the phone. Largely the result of his unflagging efforts, the lab had become a nationally renowned and highly respected facility. During the last five years, data generated from scientific experiments carried out there had appeared in several prestigious medical journals.

The laboratory was divided into two work sections separated by a wide central corridor that led to the administrative offices. Several large banks of complex scientific instruments were positioned flush against the two far walls. Four lab benches covered with computer monitors and other research instruments left little space for any additional apparatus.

It was nearing five p.m., and apart from a couple of cleaning personnel and one security officer, the lab was empty. Freeman picked up a stack of papers, leafed through them quickly and then tossed them back on his desk. He closed his eyes for a few moments and then softly rubbed the bridge of his nose where his eyeglasses had left their imprint.

Dr. Freeman was a well-recognized and brilliant research

scientist. A bit eccentric and an incurable control freak, he had insisted upon an office with a large bay window, which allowed him to keep an eye on the lab at all times. Being totally oblivious to current style, he dressed as if he hadn't set foot in a men's store for twenty years. He was of short stature, average looking, and sported a sparse mustache that always looked like he was still in the process of growing it. Rapidly approaching his fiftieth birthday, he closely guarded his privacy and rarely socialized with any of his fellow workers.

Freeman looked down at an eight-hundred number scribbled on a small piece of scratch paper and then slowly reached for his cell phone. Feeling his heart start to accelerate, he froze in place. He looked at his watch for several seconds, assuring himself for the third time that there was no time difference between Washington, DC, and Miami. Just as he was about to tap in the number, he heard a loud rap at the door. He removed his reading glasses, leaned forward and peered at the attractive young woman smiling at him through the window.

"Just a moment," he said, grabbing a stack of papers on his desk and hurriedly shoving them into the top drawer. He took a second look at the woman and then crossed the room.

"Can I help you, miss?" he asked as he opened the door.

"I hope so. Are you Dr. Freeman?"

"Yes, I am," he answered.

"Well then, I believe we have an appointment. My name is Erin Wells. I'm a reporter with the *AMA News*."

Freeman appeared completely befuddled as he fumbled for a three-by-five card that he always kept in the top pocket of his rumpled lab coat.

"Yes, you're quite correct," he said, tapping the card with his index finger. "I have it right here on my schedule. Erin Wells, five p.m. Won't you come in?"

"Thank you."

As soon as Erin was in the office, she had a good look around. The habit had become an important part of her interview routine and frequently offered her an advanced insight into her subject. Freeman's office was more than a bit disheveled. His desk was scattered with half-opened mail, piles of paper and scientific journals. Three metal bookcases, which were turned caddy-corner instead of being neatly aligned, were a hideous shade of dark green and badly scratched. On the top shelf of the middle one, Erin noticed several coffee-stained Styrofoam cups.

"Dr. Archer mentioned that you had requested an interview," he said politely. "I guess I just forgot." He looked down at his watch and then added, "I wonder if I might impose upon you to delay our talk for about forty-five minutes. I've planned my day poorly . . . and, well, frankly, you've caught me at a bad moment."

Erin smiled. "The same thing has happened to me a million times," she said. "Supposing I come back at about quarter to six?"

"Uh . . . why don't we meet in the administrative conference room off the main lobby?" he suggested. "It's much more comfortable than this dismal office."

Erin took another look around. "I'll be there," she said, not anticipating any problem finding the place.

John Freeman escorted Erin to the lab's main entrance and thanked her again for her indulgence. As soon as he returned to his office, he walked over to the refrigerator, removed a carton of orange juice and then returned to his desk. He glanced down at the eight-hundred number, trying to build his confidence, and then took two long swallows of the juice.

Anticipating a long and difficult call, he picked up his cell phone and dialed the number. He took in a full breath and let it escape slowly. Pressing the receiver firmly against his ear, he paced up and down in front of his desk, listening impatiently as one ring led to the next. When he was just about to hang up, the call was automatically answered. The monotone recording droned on, but eventually informed him the offices were closed.

John Freeman slowly replaced the phone in his briefcase and gazed through the bay window at the laboratory he had poured his soul and life's blood into advancing. He pondered the phone call he had just made and had to confess he was relieved that he now had some extra time to think things over a little more carefully.

After a few more moments of thought, it suddenly occurred to him that he now had forty-five minutes to kill before meeting with Erin Wells. With nothing to keep him in the lab, he took a final long gulp of his juice, grabbed his briefcase and decided to go to the hospital library to complete a literature search on his latest experiment.

Frank Grafton watched carefully as Dr. Freeman locked the laboratory and quickly disappeared down the main corridor. Grafton had been chief of security at the institute for seven years. He was of average height, with convex but broad shoulders. His head was boxy and he moved with a slight stoop in his posture. His facial features were plain with skin that had been potted since late adolescence. Before accepting the position at the institute, he served two tours in the Marine corps as a gunnery sergeant. He made no secret of the fact that he'd seen action in Desert Storm, claiming to have killed dozens of Iraqi soldiers and single-handedly taking out two enemy tanks. Following his discharge, he continued to live by a strict military code of discipline and honor, which mattered to him as much in civilian life as it had in the Marines. Living alone, he shunned all serious relationships with women, writing them off as an unnecessary distraction, but enthusiastically cultivated involvement in several veterans groups and discrete right-wing organizations.

With Dr. Freeman now well out of sight, Grafton unhooked his key ring from his belt and opened the main door to the lab. He moved quickly down the corridor until he reached Freeman's office. After a few seconds, he found the light switch and flipped it on. He looked down at the desk and shook his head at the lack of order.

The only sound in the room came from the dull hum of the

refrigerator. Grafton looked down and picked up the small piece of yellow paper and read the number a couple of times. After a quick look around, he pulled out a small blank card, copied the number down and replaced the piece of paper exactly where he'd found it.

The air-conditioning kicked on and Grafton looked up as a jet of cool air grazed the back of his neck. Making his way over to the water cooler, he reached up and opened the cabinet. The only other thing on the shelf besides a bottle of Tylenol was a Yellow Pages and a large manila envelope, which he immediately slid out and unclasped. The report he found inside consisted of about ten pages of data printouts, graphs and complicated computations. He turned to the first page, which appeared to be a letter, and read it twice. He scratched his head, wondering why Freeman wasn't a little more creative in his choice of a hiding place.

He walked over to the small photocopy machine in the corner and turned it on. As soon as he completed making a copy of the report, he slid it back into the envelope and returned it to the cabinet on top of the Yellow Pages. He stopped for a moment and studied Freeman's diplomas and certificates on the wall. They were all identically framed in dark wood but hung in a random display.

Taking a seat behind Dr. Freeman's desk, Grafton leaned forward and opened the top drawer. Knowing exactly what he was looking for, he reached all the way toward the back. As soon as he felt the small leather case, he pulled it from the drawer and unzipped it. Amongst several sealed alcohol swabs he found a small plastic bottle, which he promptly removed and tucked away in his front pocket. Then, from his other pocket he pulled out an identical bottle and slipped it in the case.

Confident about the results of his mission, he closed the drawer, walked back to the door and, after taking one last look around, turned off the light and left John Freeman's office.

Grafton returned directly to the institute's central security office. The automatic coffee machine, located on a small table next to the central monitoring area, was still on. Pouring himself a mug, he was quite confident that none of the other security officers on duty had seen him in Freeman's office. He took one sip of the coffee, cringed at its stale, bitter taste and tossed it in the sink. He placed the mug on the countertop, sat down at his desk and began reviewing the monthly performance evaluations of his staff. He paused for a moment and thought about the report he had just copied in Freeman's office.

"Things should really start to get interesting around here now," he said confidently, as if someone were listening to his revelation. He reached into his back pocket and pulled out a small cell phone and tapped in a number from memory.

"Yes."

"It's Grafton. I've had a look around. I'm afraid your suspicions were correct. He's put a report together that could prove rather embarrassing."

"Do we know if he's sent it out yet?"

Grafton pulled out the documents and scanned the first page. "It's dated yesterday and there are several handwritten corrections and scratch outs. This looks like an edited copy so I suspect we're still okay."

"That's assuming he hasn't spoken to anybody," came the response.

Grafton, frozen in thought for a moment or two, finally said, "All the more reason to act as quickly as possible." Grafton heard a low moan and then a snicker.

"Your impatience is showing again, Mr. Grafton. Let's just keep an eye on things—shall we?" Grafton looked toward the ceiling, not at all surprised by what he had just heard. Another example of the civilian versus the military mind.

"But the way, it's my understanding we have a reporter snooping around," Grafton mentioned.

"You're half right. There is a reporter on assignment at the institute. She's not writing an investigative piece and our expectations are that it will be a flattering article. She's a friend of one of the patients, Claire Weaver."

"The one who was just admitted?" Grafton asked.

"Yes, but I don't expect either of them will be with us very long. Mrs. Weaver should be on the operating schedule in about three weeks. Hopefully, by the time she has the surgery, Ms. Wells will be finished with her story."

"I thought we—"

"The numbers, Mr. Grafton. We have to keep a very careful eye on the numbers."

"And Mrs. Weaver?"

"Mrs. Weaver will do fine."

"And the—"

"The baby? Unfortunately, I can't be as optimistic. But Mrs. Weaver is young and healthy. Hopefully, her next baby will be the picture of health. Call me tomorrow." The line went dead before he could respond to the comment regarding the Weavers' baby. He didn't appreciate being hung up on but now wasn't the time to make an issue of it. Under different circumstances, it wouldn't be something he'd put up with.

Without giving a second thought to the fact that Claire Weaver's baby's fate had already been sealed, Grafton turned out the lights and left the office.

Chapter 4

Erin and John Freeman both arrived outside the administrative conference room at exactly five forty-five. After a brief joke about importance of punctuality they entered the room. In the center, a large oak conference table in the shape of a racetrack sat beneath a soft flood of halogen lighting. A dozen high-back chairs surrounded the table. The walls were wood paneled and the floor was a rich Travertine marble. Large oil portraits of past presidents of the hospital medical staff hung on the two far walls.

As soon as they were seated, Erin opened her purse and set a small tape recorder on the corner of the table. Just before flipping it on, she looked up and noted the subtle look of bewilderment on Freeman's face. "I'm sorry, I should have asked about the recorder. It bothers some people. Do you mind if I use it?"

"Not at all," he answered, waving his hand a few times.

"Good," she said, turning the recorder toward him. "Let's get started. How long have you been with the institute?"

"Since March of 1993."

"Have you always been the director of the research lab?" she asked.

"Yes, I was hired for that specific purpose."

"Tell me the most exciting thing you've worked on."

Freeman smiled. "That would be difficult, Ms. Wells. We have so many irons in the fire at any one time and all the projects seem exciting to me."

"I see. Well, is there any project going on right now that you think might be of interest to our readers?"

Freeman interlocked his fingers and placed his hands on the table. "Uh . . . not really. Most of our projects have been ongoing for years."

"Is there an area in fetal research that you have a particular interest in?"

"Tocolytic agents," he said. "It's always been a—"

"Tocolytic agents? I'm sorry, you'll have to help me out a little. I must have missed that lecture in nursing school."

Freeman grinned. "They are medications that stop premature labor. Probably more than anything, they've become the key to successful fetal surgery. If we can discover how to prevent our patients from going into labor, our infant survival rate will go way up."

"What about the medications the obstetricians are presently using?"

"They're okay," he said, adjusting his spectacles and then sliding a pile of papers off to the side. "In fact, they're the ones we're presently employing."

"Then why look for new ones?" she asked.

"Because they only work about half of the time," he emphasized with a strange intensity in his voice. "We need a medication we can count on, one that will predictably stop labor in all cases and without causing harm to . . ."

Erin waited for several seconds for Freeman to complete his thought. He looked vacantly across the room and then rubbed the back of his neck.

"You said without causing harm . . . and then you stopped. Did you mean to the mother?"

His eyes quickly refocused. "Yes, of course, to the mother."

Erin saw him swallow and then look nervously past her again. She switched to more neutral territory. "Are you working on any new surgical procedures?"

"Fetal surgery is probably the most dynamic field in medicine today, Ms. Wells. We're always working on new things."

"For instance?"

"Unfortunately, most of the projects we're working on are confidential," he informed her.

"Confidential?" she asked, wondering why he was being so evasive.

"Yes, I guess that's one of the prices we paid when we allowed corporate America to take over medicine and scientific research. They control the dollars, so they make the rules." His manner was polite, not brusque. His frustration was more than apparent.

"I see," she said. "Well, let's switch gears for a moment. What's it like working with these patients? Are the women anxious to participate in your research, and do you think they understand the importance of your work?"

"Actually, my duties are confined to laboratory studies," he confessed. "All of my subjects have four legs and rarely share their feelings with me. As director of basic research, I have no interaction with the actual patients."

"Why is that?"

"I'm afraid you'd have to direct that question to Dr. Archer. It's not my policy—it's his. Most research institutions coordinate the clinical and basic research efforts. Perhaps, if I had more to . . ." He looked over at Erin, stopped dead in his tracks and shook his head in silence.

"More to what?" she asked, leaning forward and tilting her head innocently to the side.

"Uh . . . nothing, it's nothing." He smiled at her nervously and then picked up a small paper clip and began bending it.

"Would it be possible for me to speak with some of the

women who have participated in the research studies?" she asked. "Perhaps they could—"

"I'm afraid that's not my department . . . but there are certain issues of patient confidentiality. If you're interested in talking to some of our patients, you'd have to clear it with Leigh Sierra and Dr. Archer."

"And where would I find Ms. Sierra?"

"Actually, it's Dr. Sierra. She's the director of clinical research. Her office is on the third floor of the main hospital."

"Do you think she'll speak with me?"

"I don't see why not, but you'll have to check with her," Freeman said.

"Do I also have to check with Dr. Archer?" she asked him.

"If you don't mind, I'd prefer not to answer that question."

"I see," she said, tapping on her spiral notepad and then folding her arms. "Look, Dr. Freeman, with all due respect, I'm not an investigative reporter. My sincere intent here is to do a positive story about the exciting and groundbreaking work the institute is doing, but I need some cooperation to do that. I don't quite understand your reticence."

Freeman was measured in his answer. "I'm not accustomed to being interviewed, Ms. Wells. You'll have to forgive me," he said in a strained voice. Without uttering another word, he got up and walked over to a small refrigerator that occupied the central portion of a large multipurpose wall unit. His hands were trembling when he opened the door. He reached in the back, pulled out a small bottle of apple juice and opened it. He tried to steady his hand but as he gulped down the juice, a few drops still managed to spill. He looked at Erin nervously, but she returned his glance with a smile, pretending not to notice the obvious tremor in his hand.

"You mentioned you're working on finding a drug that would reliably stop premature labor," she said. "How do you go about doing that?"

On his way back to the table, Freeman flexed and extended his neck in what Erin assumed was an effort to relax. "We fol-

low strict scientific protocols that were approved by the Food
and Drug Administration."

"Is that difficult to do?" she inquired.

"I'm not sure I understand your question."

"Oh, you know, jumping through all those government
hoops and wading through all that bureaucracy."

"No, actually they're quite reasonable," he claimed. "A lot
of it's based on their assumption that we're honest scientists
and will conduct ourselves with integrity."

"I'm interested in a comment you made before," she said,
noticing his hands were no longer shaking. "It was the confidentiality issue. Do you think that's right?"

"Do I think what's right?"

Erin tried to explain. "Well, should people be denied information about drugs under investigation because it's in the
best interest of a particular corporation? Should we trust our
government agencies or should the press be a watchdog?"

"Watchdog? That's a tough one . . . and I suspect beyond
the scope of your story." Erin watched as the corners of his
mouth came up slightly in spite of his attempt to prevent a
smile. "The relationship of the press to scientific research has
long been an interesting question. My father was the editor of
a small paper in New England. Of all the things he told me
about the newspaper business . . . do you know what the most
vivid one is?"

"I'd be guessing," Erin confessed as politely as she was
able.

He stopped for a moment, drew her in with his eyes and
said, "Never underestimate the power of the press." Freeman
then closed his eyes and rubbed the sides of his temple. "Ms.
Wells, I'm afraid I've developed a terrible headache. I wonder if we might continue the interview at another time?"

"Of course." Erin reached forward, clicked off the recorder
and stood up. "I'll give your secretary a call in a few days. I
hope you feel better, Doctor." When she shook his hand, she
could feel a slight tremor. His smile was strained and his palm

moist. "Why don't you just sit down," she suggested. "I can find my way out."

Erin closed the door quietly behind her and started across the lobby. She'd have to jog her memory, but off the top of her head, she couldn't remember an interview as strange as the one she had just finished.

Chapter 5

The cafeteria at the Fetal Institute was a small, nicely decorated dining area with polished wooden tables and a thick brown Berber carpet. An eclectic collection of photographs of scenic mountain vistas hung on the near wall.

Erin went through the self-service line, quickly picking up a small tossed green salad and a container of low-fat strawberry yogurt. She paid for her lunch and was headed across the cafeteria when she caught Noah Gallagher's eye. He was sitting alone at a small table toward the rear.

"Do you mind if I join you for lunch?" she asked in a casual voice.

A bit flustered, he cleared his throat, and then pointed to the chair across from him.

"Sure," he finally managed. "Please sit down."

"Thanks," she said, placing her tray down and pulling out one of the two empty chairs across from him. She couldn't help but notice his plate was still quite full. He was dressed in surgical scrubs and sporting a two-day stubble.

"How have you been, Ms. Wells?"

"You promised to call me Erin," she said, shaking her finger at him. "I know we talked about that."

"Forgive me. I guess I must have forgotten."

"I just left Claire's room. She seems exhausted. You guys really know how to put someone through their paces," Erin said, and then turned her tray around, picked up a napkin and placed it on her lap.

"We should be done in the next few days, but I can assure you the tests are all necessary."

"I never doubted it for a second," Erin told him, waving her fork in his direction and then poking away at her salad. He was talking to her like a patient, a situation she was hoping she could change. "But on the other hand, she's only been here for a few days and she's quite pregnant."

"She'll be fine," he promised. "She strikes me as a strong person."

"She wants to be a mom more than anything. And if you know anything about Claire Weaver, you know that when she puts her mind to something, she's going to get it done."

"It sounds like you know her quite well."

"When we were seniors in college, she decided to set up a magnet program in the elementary schools to identify the gifted math students."

"That sounds like an ambitious undertaking," he said, sipping his iced tea slowly. "My sister's an elementary school teacher. I have some idea of how tough a job it can be."

"Claire navigated her way through the local government, school board administration and PTA like a submarine commander dodging depth charges. Within a year the program was an enormous success and being expanded across the entire state."

"Everyone in the institute who's met her seems to like her very much," Noah added.

"Did you give any further thought to that interview I talked to you about?" Erin inquired.

"Actually, when I spoke to Dr. Archer, he told me that he would be approving and setting up all the interviews."

"Really? I'm a little surprised," she said.

"Don't be. That's the way things run around here."

An elderly woman in a drab olive hospital uniform walked by and stopped at the table next to theirs to pick up a couple of dirty trays.

"What's it like working here?" she asked in a nonchalant voice.

Noah looked up, twisted in his chair and stroked his two-day growth. "Are you asking in your professional capacity?"

"Nope. This is strictly off the record. I'm just interested," she said, noticing his soft brown eyes and wondering what it would be like to be in a candlelit restaurant with him instead of this boring cafeteria.

Noah nodded. "Okay . . . yeah, I like my job."

"Why?"

"Because we're the vanguard of fetal surgery. It's the most dynamic field in medicine today. It's exciting . . . and I think we're making a real contribution."

"Why did you become a pediatric surgeon?"

"Ever since I was in junior high, I wanted to be a pediatrician. During my third year of medical school, I did my general surgery rotation at Cook County Hospital. When the rotation was over, I was hooked on being a surgeon. I loved pediatrics, so combining the two was an easy decision." Noah stopped for a moment and stared down at his food. He seemed distracted. Erin leaned forward in her chair and noticed the vacant look in his eyes. An instant later, as if he had just been snapped back to reality by a hypnotist, he looked up.

"Where did you grow up?" she asked.

"In Skokie, Illinois. Have you ever heard of it?"

"It's one of the northern suburbs of Chicago, isn't it?"

"Yeah," he said with a grin. "I'm impressed."

"Claire and her husband have a lot of confidence in you."

"That's nice of you to say but I really don't think they know me well enough to—"

"Claire's always been a shoot-from-the-hip, first-impression-type woman. But she's usually right," Erin said.

Noah's complexion turned just slightly red as he picked up a fork and twirled his pasta.

"As I mentioned to you," he said, "there are several other hospitals doing equally fine work and—"

"There you go again," Erin said, using her fork as a pointer. "You're either the most modest surgeon I've ever met or—"

"Have you started your interviews yet?" Noah asked.

"Just one. I met with Dr. Freeman yesterday."

"He's a nice guy." Noah wiped his mouth and then took another swig of his iced tea before adding, "I'm a little surprised."

"What do you mean?" she asked.

"Because I'm sure Dr. Archer set it up and he and Freeman have been a little like oil and water the last month or so."

"That's interesting."

"That's also off the record, Erin."

"Okay, Noah," she promised, sarcastically emphasizing his name as he had just done to hers, and then raised three fingers straight up in the air. "Boy . . . is this place a hospital or a secret government installation?"

"A hospital," he said. "It's definitely a hospital. Why do you ask?"

"When I spoke with him, Dr. Freeman was more than just a bit cautious," she said.

"What do you mean?"

"Well, does everything around here have to be cleared by Dr. Archer?"

Noah set his fork down and thought for a moment. "Sometimes it's just easier to go with the flow," he finally said.

"You're dodging me."

"I beg your pardon," Noah said.

"I'm a people person. I can always tell when someone's holding out on me." The words were barely airborne before she regretted the comment. She already had him targeted as a key contributor to her story and the last thing she wanted to do was put him off by being too pushy. "Who owns the hospital?" she asked, giving him the out he needed to avoid the moment.

"It was originally a joint venture between a group of physicians and the Urbecom Hospital Corporation. Dr. Archer was instrumental in orchestrating the deal."

"Urbecom's a major player," she said. "I recently read an article that claimed they were the second biggest hospital conglomerate in America."

"That may be true, but there were too many chefs stirring the broth," he explained, pushing his chair back and crossing his legs. "It led to a lot of bickering and infighting and the hospital was eventually sold to a company called Neotech."

"When was that?"

"About seven years ago," he told her.

She shrugged. "I never heard of them."

"In comparison to some of the other hospital corporations they're small. But they've been very successful," he told her. "They buy up boutique hospitals doing cutting-edge medical research. There's a rumor they may be bought out in the near future."

"What do you mean by boutique hospitals?" she asked, taking the last spoonful of her yogurt. He seemed more at ease, speaking freely and losing his well-practiced doctor's voice. She studied his facial features as he spoke and had to admit he was even more attractive than she remembered from their first meeting.

"A boutique hospital is one that is highly specialized and committed to both patient care and doing upscale medical research." Noah looked down at his watch and shook his head. "I'm sorry. I've got to get going. I'm due in surgery." Erin watched as he quickly stood up and grabbed his tray.

Before she gave it any thought, she said, "If you should need me for anything, I'm staying at the Inter-Continental." Noah froze in place and looked at her with a blank expression. She considered herself a modern woman, and the comment was a little brazen even for her.

"The Inter-Continental? That's a very nice hotel," he said. "They have a great French restaurant there."

"I heard the same thing. But when I called, the maitre d' told me the minimum reservation they accept is for two."

Noah laughed. "You're an original, Erin Wells. I'll say that about you."

"I'll take that as a compliment,"she said.

"By the way, I got approval for you to observe in surgery. Just give my office a call so we can coordinate our two schedules."

"That's great news. I'm looking forward to it."

He waved good-bye and she watched as he crossed the cafeteria.

Erin picked at her lunch for a few more minutes. Feeling somewhere between petulant and boy crazy, she cautioned herself to act her age. But as she dumped her tray into a large black receptacle, she couldn't help but wonder again what it would be like to be out to dinner . . . and maybe even a little more, with Noah Gallagher.

Chapter 6

Exhausted from eight hours of endless tests, Claire had drifted off into a restless sleep. The first wave of pain was mild, caused her to stir, but did not awaken her. The second contraction came about two minutes later, gripping her abdomen with an intensity far exceeding the first. She blew out two quick breaths, grabbed her belly and immediately began pressing the nurses's call button. Several more seconds passed and the pain began to subside slightly. Just at that moment, Cindy Gonzalez, the charge nurse, came through the door. An experienced leader, there weren't too many problems she couldn't handle with speed and efficiency.

"How can I help you, Mrs. Weaver?"

"I think I'm having contractions," she answered with a grimace.

Cindy stepped closer to the bed, put her hands on Claire's abdomen and felt the boardlike rigidity of her belly. When she looked down and noted a few drops of blood just below the waist of Claire's hospital gown, she pulled out her portable phone and tapped in a three-digit code.

"Mary, I could use your help in two-eleven with Mrs. Weaver . . . and can you ask the unit secretary to page Dr. Gallagher?"

"What's happening?" Claire asked, breathing quickly through her mouth.

"I'm sure it's nothing," Cindy answered evenly. "You're spotting and having a few cramps. Until Dr. Gallagher gets here I just want to play it on the safe side."

Claire closed her eyes and again rubbed her abdomen. For the moment, the contraction had passed and she was in no pain. She opened her eyes. "Am I going to lose the baby?"

Cindy stopped what she was doing and reached for Claire's hand. "Of course not. This kind of thing happens all the time. The baby's going to be fine."

Claire's mouth was dry and as she tried to swallow, her throat tightened. Even though the fear of losing her baby was not completely unfamiliar to her, her heart still raced. She leaned forward, pushed her hospital gown to the side and saw the same drops of fresh blood Cindy had.

"Oh my God," she moaned in a cracked voice. "When will Dr. Gallagher be here?"

"We paged him a few minutes ago. He should be here any time."

"He's here now," came a calm voice from the other side of the room as Noah walked through the door. Claire tried to smile as she looked up at her doctor. "What's going on here?" he asked Claire in an upbeat tone. "Can't I leave you alone for even a few hours?"

"The baby seems to be confused about his birthday," she said, trying to joke along with him. "He thinks the party's today."

"Really," Noah said as he examined Claire's abdomen. "Well, I hate to be the one to spoil his plans, but this is one bun that has to stay in the oven a while longer."

"That's more than okay with me, Dr. Gallagher," she said.

Noah turned to Cindy. "Put a call into Dr. Halliday. I think obstetrics needs to be involved."

"I'll have him paged right now." Cindy again flipped on her cell phone, and as soon as the unit secretary answered, she gave her instructions to page Dr. Halliday. "We've already notified the pharmacy to send up the protocol drugs."

"Do you have the results of this morning's ultrasound?" Noah asked Cindy. "I want to make sure the placenta's in the right place."

"I'll have to check the computer."

"Fine, in the meantime put her feet up and keep an eye on her." Noah walked over and sat on the side of Claire's bed. "I'm going to ask Dr. Halliday to have a look at you. He's an excellent obstetrician and I'd really like his opinion."

"What do you think the problem is?"

"Well, it could be a couple of things. The most likely explanation is premature labor . . . but that doesn't mean you're going to have the baby now. We can almost always stop the contractions with rest and a variety of medications."

Claire glanced over at the small digital clock on her nightstand and then let her head fall back on the pillow. She was a little uncomfortable that Alex wasn't there but understood he couldn't turn down a request from his supervisor to fill in for a pilot who was down with the flu.

"I'm sure everything will be okay," she said with a strained conviction. "Alex won't be here until later. When will you be back to speak with me?"

"As soon as Dr. Halliday looks your chart over and examines you, I'll speak with him and then be back to go over everything with you."

An hour later, Claire was alone in her room. The only sound was the rhythmic cacophony of the monitors. Cindy had added another medication to her IV and the cramps were much milder and coming less frequently. Claire watched the tiny drops of the IV solution fall from the chamber into the clear plastic tubing. The effect was hypnotic and within a few minutes she fell into a restless sleep.

•   •   •

It was just after seven p.m. when Noah gently knocked on Claire's door.

"Come in," a man's voice responded, just above a whisper.

As soon as Noah pushed the door open, he saw Alex Weaver standing in the middle of the room staring at Claire. He was dressed in his airline uniform with his black jacket folded neatly over a chair.

"I guess I missed some excitement around here today," he said to Noah.

"Nothing we can't deal with. Did you have a chance to speak with the obstetrician?" Noah asked.

"Yes, he left a few minutes ago. Should we wake Claire?"

Noah glanced over at Claire and then moved to the head of her bed. Her hair was moist and stringy from perspiration. Noah whispered her name twice but she was obviously in a deep sleep. He smiled at her and then slowly pulled the blanket up to her shoulders.

"Why don't we let her sleep," Noah suggested. "She's already had a hell of a day. We can fill her in later." Noah pointed across the room to two chairs that faced each other across a small table.

They were barely seated when Alex asked, "How bad is it?"

"Well, actually, the ultrasound is normal. In fact, all of the tests have come back fine. Dr. Halliday thinks she has what we call a threatened abortion."

"What's that?"

"It's not an uncommon problem . . . especially in these cases. There's really not too much we can do other than treat it with medications, keep her at bed rest and watch things carefully. Most of the time, the contractions stop on their own and the baby is not harmed."

Alex nodded his head as Noah spoke. "And what happens the other times, when things don't go so well?"

Noah paused for a moment. "The contractions increase and the pregnancy can terminate in a spontaneous abortion."

Alex stood up, turned and stared out the window. His

shortly cropped hair and perfectly pressed shirt were strictly regulation. Noah's instinct told him the man had two loves in his life: Claire and flying.

"What do we do?" Alex asked.

"Keep her here where we can keep an eye on things," Noah answered, sensing Alex was struggling to stay calm and in control.

Alex turned around. "I assume that means we're not going home tomorrow."

Noah displayed no uncertainty when he answered, "Let's just see how she does over the rest of the weekend."

Alex covered his face with the palms of his hands and let his head drop forward. "She'd be happier at home."

"I'm not sure that would be wise," Noah warned. "You're a pilot, Alex. We've both been trained the same way—not to take chances."

Alex again looked out the window. "You're right. I don't know what I was thinking. We'll stay the entire three months if we have to. I love my wife, Dr. Gallagher. Nobody deserves a healthy baby more than she does . . . she has a gift with kids . . . a real gift," he added as an afterthought. "Between Claire being hospitalized and the airline layoffs, I don't know how things could be worse."

"Layoffs?" Noah asked.

"I just got the memo today. They're going to lay off about seventy-five pilots. I was just hired a few years ago, so I suspect I'll probably be looking for a job in the next few months." Alex shook his head and closed his eyes for a moment.

"What's the job market like?" Noah asked.

"I'm afraid there are a lot of good pilots fighting over a lot of bad jobs." Alex half smiled. "Something will come up eventually, but finances could get awfully tight."

Noah got up without making a sound. "Claire told me you're the best pilot since Charles Lindbergh. Things will work out. I'll stop in later."

Noah walked across the room, stopped for a moment and

studied Claire as she slept. Her breathing was rhythmic and peaceful. After taking one last glance at the monitors and checking the IV, he left Alex Weaver alone with his wife.

Alex sat down, unbuttoned the top button of his shirt and rubbed his eyes. He wasn't a religious man, but the thought of going down to the chapel for a few minutes crossed his mind. There was a grave injustice befalling the woman he loved and he was desperate to do something.

"What's going on?" asked a voice from the other side of the room. Alex looked up, forced a smile and walked over to his wife.

"Nothing, Dr. Gallagher just left. He said you're doing great."

She frowned just as he expected. "Why didn't you wake me?"

"The baby needed his rest. You didn't miss anything. It was mostly boy talk."

"Really?" she asked skeptically.

"Really. Dr. Gallagher did some flying during college. He was telling me about it."

"You guys talked about flying? And am I to assume my name never came up?"

"Of course it did," he said, sitting down on the bed beside her and gently rubbing the bottom of her belly. "He said you're doing great."

"I see," she said, placing her hand on top of his. "So does that mean I'm going home soon?"

"Actually, we talked about that very thing and . . . and Dr. Gallagher doesn't think it would be such a great idea. He thinks you ought to stay for a little while."

"I see. And what do you think?" she asked.

"Me? I'm a pilot, honey, not a doctor," he said slowly. "But I do expect my passengers to listen to me. So I guess it would be a little hypocritical if I tried to second guess your doctor." Alex leaned forward and kissed Claire on the cheek. "I love you. I'm sure he'll be back later to talk to you about all this."

"What are we going to do for the rest of the weekend?" she

asked as her eyes became a little weepy. "You're not even going to be here."

"That's where you're wrong. I traded trips with one of the guys. I'm going to hang out with you all weekend. We're going to play Monopoly, gin rummy and rent a bunch of romantic tearjerkers. I'll bring in some wine and we'll make love all night like a couple of college kids." His final suggestion hit the mark and the corners of Claire's mouth finally turned up into a warm smile.

With Alex at her side the entire time, the rest of the weekend passed uneventfully. Claire ate too much Ben and Jerry's ice cream, destroyed Alex in every board game they played and still found time to laugh tirelessly at his tired old jokes. During the entire time, she only experienced an occasional premature contraction. Erin visited frequently, trying every trick she knew to build Claire's confidence. By the time Monday morning arrived, Claire's spirits were finally a little more optimistic.

Chapter 7

Completely absorbed in trying to solve a glitch in one of his complicated enzyme experiments, John Freeman sat in front of the lab's mulitmillion-dollar electron microscope mumbling to himself. His all-too-frequent Monday-morning headache was already pounding. He hadn't accomplished much over the weekend, having spent most of his time going over technical reports and several new research proposals.

From time to time he looked up from the scope and jotted down a few notes on a white legal pad. Freeman wondered why the lab was so warm but was too engrossed in his problem to call plant engineering. His neck muscles felt tighter than a violin string and the pain from his head was now radiating down to his chin. When he tried to stretch his neck out by slowly rotating his head from side to side, he felt a ring of perspiration gathering just above his collar.

When he again looked into the scope, the field appeared blurry. Freeman removed his circular wire-rim glasses and wiped the lenses with a tissue. His chest felt heavy and congested, causing him some difficulty breathing. He forced himself to take a deep breath, which resulted in an immediate bout of deep coughing. *Great, that's just what I need now ... the flu.*

Carl Chandler, the assistant director and a senior researcher with both an M.D. and a Ph.D. in pharmacology walked by, took one look at Freeman and stopped dead in his tracks.

"You look like hell, John. Are you feeling okay?"

"I'm not sure," Freeman admitted with a nervous half smile, starting to feel as if there were a five-hundred-pound bag of concrete sitting squarely on his chest.

Carl took a step closer and reached out for Freeman's wrist. "For God's sake, John, your pulse is all over the place."

"I don't know what . . ."

Carl looked up and waved to one of the technicians. "Get a stretcher in here right now. We'll also need an IV setup and a cardiac monitor . . . and some oxygen . . . and page Dr. Gallagher stat. We need a clinician, not a researcher," he added in a whisper.

Less than thirty seconds had passed. Dr. Freeman's skin was cool and clammy. His face was rapidly becoming the color of chalk. As he struggled to breathe, the air hunger was frightening, reminding him of a time many years ago when a bunk mate at summer camp held him underwater too long.

The main doors to the lab flew open and two technicians rolled a cart through the door and over to Freeman. Together they gently helped him off the stool and onto the cart. Chandler placed a small pillow behind his head. A moment later Noah Gallagher, trailed by two nurses, raced through the door.

"What's going on, John?" he asked as calmly as he was able, placing a stethoscope over his colleague's heart.

"I . . . I don't know. The pain's incredible," he complained.

"Don't try to talk now. Everything's going to be okay," Noah assured him.

It took the nurses less than a minute to start an IV and strap on an oxygen mask. Not being equipped to take care of cardiac problems in adults, Chandler immediately called 911 to transport Freeman to the nearest hospital.

"His blood pressure is eighty," one of the nurses whispered to Noah. "We really need to get him out of here."

"The ambulance is on the way," Chandler piped in.

Freeman's eyes were closed. His face was now mottled and heavily beaded with perspiration. His heartbeat remained irregular but was now ominously slowing.

"I'm sure he's having a heart attack," Noah told Chandler in a voice barely above a whisper. "Do you know if he has a history of cardiac problems?"

"No way. He's one of the healthiest guys I've ever met. He's twenty pounds underweight, eats nothing but organic foods and works out five times a week. He could be the poster boy for the American Heart Association." Chandler shook his head in disbelief and added, "He's only about fifty years old, for God's sake, Noah."

Ten minutes later two paramedics dressed in navy-blue uniforms arrived. The men, who struck Noah as young enough to still be in high school, assessed the situation rapidly and immediately transferred Freeman to their own stretcher.

Noah took Freeman's hand and squeezed it. "Don't try to talk, John. We're going to take you to another hospital. Everything's going to be fine." Freeman turned his head just slightly and tried to nod.

"We'll take him to Southside," one of the paramedics told Noah as he placed a larger oxygen mask over Freeman's face. "We better get going, Doctor."

"Can I come along?" Chandler asked.

"Absolutely," came the response from the second paramedic.

Noah watched as John Freeman was wheeled out of the laboratory. He looked down at his watch and realized he was late for surgery. He knew Freeman lived alone, and hadn't the first clue who to call. After giving the situation a little more thought, he reasoned that Carl Chandler would handle matters. Noah made his way slowly toward the exit, still a little shaken by John Freeman's sudden illness.

It took Noah several hours to complete a difficult operation of placing a metal clip on the main artery to a large abdominal tumor in a twenty-eight-week fetus. The procedure had gone well and Noah was confident that total removal of the growth would now be possible soon after the baby was born.

He walked out of the operating room and made his way straight to the main desk. Just as he went to pick up the phone, Carol Singer, the charge nurse, covered his hand with hers. Her silence spoke volumes, her expression was somber.

"Dr. Freeman died in the emergency room at Southside. I'm so sorry. Dr. Chandler called about an hour ago with the news. I . . . I didn't want to disturb you while you were in surgery."

Noah closed his eyes for a moment and then shook his head.

"I can't believe it," he muttered and then grabbed his patient's chart from the desk, thanked Carol and walked slowly toward the recovery room. He threw his sweat-soaked surgical cap into a large circular laundry bin. The stress of this job is bad enough, he thought, but being reminded of his own mortality was not something he needed.

Chapter 8

Noah walked quickly through the lobby. It was the end of a long day and after almost two hours of rounding with the residents, he was tired, hungry and anxious to get home.

The news of John Freeman's death was still only hours old. But a colleague's death was different from a patient's. One was expected and oftentimes not preventable, while the other a stark reminder that disease offers no dispensation to the physician. Noah was typical of most doctors, having developed his own coping mechanisms for dealing with mortality. In John Freeman's case, he did not deny his death but viewed it without reference to time, making his friend's tragic passing seem as if it had occurred six months ago instead of six hours. It wasn't an absence of emotion or compassion, but more of an attempt to move on as quickly as possible.

Once outside, Noah strolled directly toward the parking lot, paying little attention to the woman standing at the edge of the curb.

"Dr. Gallagher? Is that you?"

Even though he had only spoken to Erin on a couple of occasions, he immediately recognized her jingly voice, stopped and turned around.

"Hello, Miss . . . uh, I mean Erin. How are you?"

"At the moment, a little frustrated. Somebody should write a letter to your mayor complaining about the shortage of cabs. I've been standing here for twenty minutes . . . and it looks like it's going to rain." Noah looked up to see a beautiful South Florida cloudless sky with enough stars to hold an astronomy class.

"Maybe even a hurricane," he said politely.

"Will you be needing a cab?" she asked. "Maybe we can share one."

Noah peered again at the attractive woman with the pitiful expression. "Actually, my car is right over there." He watched as she glanced in the direction of the parking lot and then hoisted her oversized purse a little higher on her shoulder.

"It's a lot easier to get a cab in Washington. I can tell you that," she said.

Noah took a step forward and, as he sometimes did when he was nervous, pushed his hands into his pockets. "May I offer you a ride to your hotel?"

Erin looked out at the main road that ran past the institute. "That's very kind of you but I think I'll be okay. I'm sure there'll be a cab along in the next few minutes."

"I wouldn't count on it," he said, wondering why she hadn't simply called for one. "You could be here all night waiting for a taxi. Come on. My car's right over there. I'll have you back to your hotel in no time."

Noah pointed to the parking lot, she thanked him and together they walked the short distance to his black BMW convertible. It took him only a moment to disable the alarm and open the door for her.

"How about putting the top down?" she suggested.

Noah slammed the door shut, walked around to the driver's side and got in. "I thought you said it looked like rain."

Erin stuck her head out of the window for a moment and then said, "I think it just blew over."

Noah laughed out loud and then lowered the top. "Are you enjoying Miami?" he asked.

"To tell you the truth, I haven't really seen too much of it. I spent all weekend with Claire trying to lift her spirits." Erin smiled and then shook her head. "If the three of us had played one more game of Monopoly or gin rummy, I would have jumped out of the window." Erin's smile changed to one of affection. "At least she didn't have any more contractions."

As they proceeded north, Noah politely listened to Erin's small talk, interrupting her from time to time to point out some of the more well known hotels and other sites. Even though the top was down, he couldn't help but notice the enticing fragrance of her perfume. Her cream-colored blouse was open down to the third button and he had to concentrate on maintaining eye contact when he turned to talk with her.

"It's called Knowing," she said directly.

"I beg your pardon."

"My perfume, it's called Knowing."

"I . . . that's very . . . I—"

"It seemed like you leaned over a couple of times. I assumed you liked it," she said and then flashed a smile.

"I didn't mean to—"

"The houses along here are so beautifully lighted," she told him.

"Most of them are Mediterranean revivals built in the twenties and thirties. They're very typical of this area of Miami. They usually have wide-open courtyards, Spanish tiles and arched doorways. If you keep your eyes open, there's a great old fountain about two blocks ahead on our right," he said as he pointed out her window.

Erin gazed over at Noah. "You sound like a tour guide."

"I've always loved buildings. The premed curriculum at Stanford was pretty dry. If it weren't for the history of architecture courses I took I would have died of boredom."

His enthusiasm appeared genuine and she didn't doubt for a second that he would have drawn upon the same energy and commitment in designing buildings that he did in medicine. "I have an idea," she said. "Why don't you let me buy you dinner? I haven't eaten anything since early this morning and it's the least I can do to show my appreciation for the ride."

Noah was presently in the throes of a major romantic slump. Tired of being fixed up and reliving each first date over and over again, he was fed up with the singles scene. He had even considered joining a singles' club, but after some thought had dismissed the idea as an act of desperation.

"Why not?" he finally managed. "But dinner's on me. I'm still a bit of a dinosaur and you'll just have to indulge me."

"It's a deal," she told him.

"What kind of food would you like?" he asked, assuming she would defer the choice to him. "There's a nice—"

"Italian."

"I beg your pardon?"

"Italian," she said again.

"Okay," he acknowledged slowly, casting a subtle glance of disbelief in her direction. "I like Italian . . . but you're in the stone crab and key lime pie capital of the world. Most people who come to Miami want to go to Joe's or—"

"No, thanks, Italian will be fine."

Noah scratched his head. "Great, Italian it is." He watched her looking out the window, seemingly enthralled with the local sites. "There's a small Italian restaurant just a little west of here. Nothing fancy, but the food's great."

"I can't wait," she said. "I'm starving."

It took Noah only a few minutes to reach Angelo's Trattoria. A plump young woman with a broad smile and bushy eyebrows greeted them as they walked through the door. The restaurant had an informal, neighborhood atmosphere, with bleached wood floors. The two far walls were covered with commercial watercolors of Florence and Naples. There was a neatly pressed red-and-white-checkered tablecloth on each table. The restaurant was only about half filled and they were seated immediately.

"This is a lovely place," Erin said, unfolding her napkin and placing it on her lap.

"I eat here at least once a week. The best thing about Angelo's is that I never run into anyone from work."

"Would that be so bad?" she asked, poking her head out from behind the menu.

"When I leave the institute at the end of the day, I like to leave it behind me."

"I guess that's understandable," she said. A barely audible Gilbert and Sullivan operetta played in the background. She put her menu down. "How long have you been in Miami?"

"I came right after finishing my pediatric surgery fellowship in Baltimore. That was about ten years ago."

"I thought you said the institute has only been around for seven years."

Noah nodded. "I was in private practice for a few years but it wasn't for me."

"Really?" Erin asked as she picked up the menu for a second time. "What was wrong with private practice?"

"The politics and brownnosing were beyond description. It seemed like the size of your practice was more related to whom you played golf with and the charity events you attended than your ability as a surgeon." Noah shook his head in obvious disgust.

"That doesn't sound like much fun," Erin said.

"It wasn't. There were no residents or students, so there was no teaching. After a while, my days were filled with the same menial tasks I did as an intern in Chicago." Noah stopped for a moment as if he had been reminded of a particularly awful nightmare. "I was already looking for another job when the institute approached me."

A young lady with short blond hair, who couldn't have been more than twenty, approached and placed a basket of assorted rolls in the center of the table next to an empty Chianti bottle with a candle in it.

"The waiter will be over in a moment," she said with a mild Italian accent. "May I bring you something to drink?"

"I'll have a glass of Chablis," Erin said and then looked over at Noah.

"Dewar's on the rocks for me, please."

The young lady smiled and walked away. Noah crossed his arms in front of him and leaned to the side. "I saw Claire late this afternoon," he began. "She mentioned she had just spoken to you."

"Really? What else did she say?"

"Only that you have a lot of spunk and would make someone a great wife."

Erin was incapable of blushing but her pupils dilated, and in complete exasperation her chin dropped, leaving her mouth agape. Claire had always been in incurable matchmaker, and it appeared she was up to her old tricks.

"If my friend were not a teacher," Erin began with a stern but affectionate inflection in her voice, "I'm sure she would have run a very profitable introduction service. Did she really say spunk?"

"I'm afraid so," he confessed.

"God, that's why my editor told me he hired me."

"Because you had . . . spunk?" Noah asked.

She let out a long slow breath. "That . . . and because I had a face nobody could say no to."

"How many stories have you written for the *AMA News*?" he asked as the hostess returned with their drinks.

"I just completed my ninth. My nursing background has really helped. It's mainly a people job . . . and I love being with people."

Noah smiled across the table, mesmerized by the brightness and animation of her eyes. He'd never met her editor but was starting to understand what he meant by a face that nobody could say no to. The warmth he felt was a fire starting to kindle, a feeling he hadn't experienced in quite some time.

"It sounds like you've won the lottery," he said.

"Not exactly, but I wouldn't trade my situation for anything. How long have you been divorced?" she asked without breaking stride.

"I beg your pardon," he said, his mouth just slightly agape.

"Your divorce. How long ago was it?"

"Did I say anything about being divorced?" he asked.

"Did you have to?" she countered, plucking a sourdough roll from the basket. "Would you like one?"

Noah waved his hand no and then swallowed hard. "How do you know I was ever married?"

"Weren't you?" she asked, putting a roll on his plate in spite of his gesture to the contrary.

"Yes, but that doesn't answer my question."

"I guess it's a little bit of instinct and a lot of observation," she said. "It must come from being a reporter."

"What kind of observation?" he asked, staring down at the roll he hadn't asked for, assuming one of the nurses or other personnel at the hospital had told her about his divorce.

"Well, in the first place, you admired my perfume but didn't flatter me with some lame compliment. Second, your choice of restaurant . . . and the way you talk to a woman." Erin frowned and then looked around the restaurant. "Where the heck's the waiter? I'm starved."

Noah grinned, looked around until he caught the waiter's eye. He was an elderly man sporting a bad toupee and an immaculate white apron that covered his pasta belly. He smiled and mouthed that he'd be right over. A minute or so later he arrived and flipped open his pad. They each ordered the same thing, the catch of the day. At Erin's behest, Noah ordered a bottle of Chianti. Waiting for the food to arrive, he lost track of time listening to the world according to Erin Wells.

"Let me ask you something," Noah said. "It's about something you said before."

"Okay," she said.

"How do you know my wife's not sitting at home right now waiting for me?"

"Because if that were the case, I wouldn't be here."

"Really. How can you be sure?"

"Not a chance."

"Why not?" he asked.

Erin interlocked her fingers, set her hands on the table and leaned forward. "Do you really want to hear this?"

"Forget it," Noah said before she could say anything more. "I'd probably never understand your explanation anyway. How about you? Ever been married?"

"Nope," she said.

"How come you never got married?" Noah asked her.

"Nobody who I ever wanted to asked me. It's that simple."

"I see," he said, hard pressed to understand how such a minor point would have stood in her way. "How close are you with Claire Weaver? You said you were college roommates?"

"We were more than roommates. There's nothing I wouldn't do for her. We were inseparable at Penn State. We lived together, worked together and shared our deepest, darkest secrets." She paused for a moment before adding, "You don't get many chances in one lifetime to form those types of friendships."

"I wouldn't know," he lamented. "I've always been kind of a loner. I lived alone in med school and most of my residency. After that much time you get accustomed to it. Maybe that's why my marriage didn't work out." He made the comment almost as if he were thinking out loud, forgetting for the moment that he wasn't alone. He quickly glanced across the table hoping he wasn't wearing his embarrassment on his sleeve. Erin's eyes were understanding, her expression sympathetic.

"I doubt that was the problem," she assured him. "Do you have kids?"

"No. Our marriage was never solid enough. It would have been a mistake. Hopefully, it's still in my future."

They ate slowly and, for the most part, kept the conversation light. Erin raved about the food, finished her main course and then ate the rest of his. Watching in awe, he wondered how she could consume so much food and still maintain such a trim figure.

He found her uninhibited nature and joie de vivre refreshing, especially when compared to the recent group of shallow pseudointellectuals he had dated. In one short dinner, she had recharged his dormant interest in romance. They had been dining for almost two hours when their third cup of cappuccino arrived at the table.

"I spend a lot of time at different hospitals," she said after thanking the waiter for the cappuccino. "I find yours a little strange."

"I'm sorry to hear that," Noah said, a little miffed that she had decided to mix business with pleasure. "But remember, I just work there."

"I heard about Dr. Freeman's death. Was he a friend?" Erin asked.

Noah remained straight-faced. His professional side took over, camouflaging his pain over his colleague's death. He had no interest in discussing the matter but didn't want to appear rude.

"I knew him, but not well," Noah replied. "I'm much more involved with patient care issues than basic scientific research. He was a dedicated and innovative man. I can tell you one thing, the field of fetal medicine has lost an important player."

"I interviewed him last Friday. To tell you the truth, I found him a tad on the strange side."

Noah didn't respond, but instead looked toward the front of the restaurant and listened as a gregarious patron thanked the indulgent hostess over and over again for a wonderful meal. "Strange? In what way?" Noah asked in a puzzled tone.

"He was very nervous," she explained. "He'd start to talk about something and then all of a sudden stop as if he had caught himself saying something he shouldn't have."

Noah forced a small smile. "I wouldn't make too much of that, Erin. Researchers can be strange ducks. They're usually pretty hush-hush about what they're up to."

"That hasn't been my experience," she said, raising the cappuccino to her lips. "They're usually quite proud of their work."

Noah picked up his spoon and rolled it between his thumb and forefinger. "The man was in the prime of his career and now he's dead. I'm not sure anything else is too important."

"I'm not sure," she offered. "But maybe you can help me out."

"I see," he said in a discouraged voice, placing the spoon down in front of him. "Is that what this was all about tonight? Your assignment, so to speak?"

Erin pushed her chair in a little and fiddled with her gold tennis bracelet. There were only three or four tables with people still left in the restaurant.

"No, my motives were more selfish than that. I wanted to spend some time with you."

"For personal or professional reasons?"

"Probably a lot more personal than my editor would like," she answered without hesitating.

"Okay," he said with a smile and then followed with a long, slow breath. "Okay. What's bugging you about the institute?"

"I'm not really sure. It just seems like nobody wants to talk about the place. The first time we met, you dodged me like I was trying to sell you life insurance. And then you gave me the distinct impression that you thought Claire should have chosen a different hospital."

"I'm not sure—"

"And what about Dr. Freeman?"

"What about him?" he asked.

"There was definitely something bothering him when I interviewed him," Erin said firmly.

"C'mon, Erin," Noah urged. "Did you ever think that maybe he was having a personal problem or something?"

Erin shook her head. "No way, not a chance. He was upset . . . maybe even a little scared, and I think it had something to do with the institute. Do you know if they'll do an autopsy?"

"I don't know, but there would be no medical reason to do one. He had a heart attack. I was there," Noah emphasized, but in a lower voice. "They can't do an autopsy on everyone who dies of a heart attack. You're a nurse. You know that."

"Okay, what about Dr. Archer?"

"What about him?" Noah asked, nodding as the waiter placed the check on the table.

"C'mon, Noah. He runs the place like a boys' military academy. It's like they're all Stepford doctors or something."

"I'm not quite sure I understand your drift," he said slowly.

"He has to approve everything. I can't even speak to anyone without his holiness's consent. And when I do interview them, it's obvious that they've been briefed." She plucked her napkin from her lap and tossed it on the table. There was only one other couple left in the restaurant. Noah removed his credit card from his wallet and placed it on the small black tray.

"The man is singly and totally dedicated to advancing fetal surgery," Noah offered in Archer's defense. "Without him there wouldn't be an institute. So what if he's a bit of a control freak?"

"A bit of a control freak? Gimme a break. The guy's ego's so big it needs its own area code for God's sake."

Noah chuckled at her comment and then busied himself signing the credit card receipt. He looked up, smiled at the hostess and they both stood up.

Noah's BMW was the last car in the parking lot. Their conversation was innocuous as they rode across the MacArthur Causeway. Erin again noticed three beautifully illuminated cruise ships docked just below them.

"Tell me I'm crazy about the institute, Noah."

He looked over at her with eyes that said it all. "You're crazy."

"This is not about the story, Noah. This is about my friend who deserves to have a happy, healthy baby."

"Your friend will do fine. You're letting your personal feelings for Claire interfere with objectivity."

"Maybe," she said.

They pulled into the wide circular entranceway of the Hotel Inter-Continental. A line of white stretch limousines was parked along the far curb and the entire area was lit up

like the Orange Bowl. Noah pulled up behind the limousines
and turned the engine off.

"I think you're getting carried away," he cautioned.

"I wish I was as sure as you are."

"You know, Erin. You may be a great reporter and have a
world-class instinct but you're not clairvoyant."

"I'm not?" she asked with a seductive look.

"No, you're not."

"Okay. In that case, the answer's no," she said evenly.

"What answer? I didn't ask a question."

"I know. But you were trying to."

"What are you talking about?" he asked.

"You were trying to figure out if I'd invite you up to my
room."

For the second time since offering Erin a ride, Noah found
his mouth dangling open. He shook his head and then cleared
his throat. He never would have suggested such a thing, but to
deny it hadn't crossed his mind ten or fifteen times in the last
hour would be stretching the limits of honesty. Jumping into
bed with near strangers had never been his style, but he was
very attracted to Erin and probably wouldn't have refused the
offer. Considering how brazen she'd been, he was actually a
little disappointed she hadn't suggested it.

"I don't recall asking you to bed," he managed in a formal
voice, trying to hide his bruised ego.

She laughed. "Body language, Noah. Have you ever heard
of body language?"

"I think . . . well, of course I have," he stammered. "It's
just—"

"It's a form of nonverbal communication." Without thinking he looked down at himself. "Not that," she said, howling
out loud.

"Well, maybe you've been sending out some of your own
vibes."

She put her arm around his shoulder and kissed him twice
on the cheek. "I don't doubt it for a second. But, remember, I

didn't say I didn't want to sleep with you . . . I just said I wasn't going to sleep with you tonight."

Before he could respond, she opened the door, got out and disappeared through the large revolving glass doors leading to the lobby. Noah put both his hands on the wheel, let his head fall forward and thought about the evening. After a few minutes he pulled away, thinking about Erin Wells and how much she intrigued him.

Chapter 9

Erin sat quietly in Claire's hospital room looking out at the bright spectrum of colored lights illuminating many of the Miami skyscrapers. The moon was full, making the view of Biscayne Bay with the skyline in the background spectacular.

Alex had left early that morning on a trip to Arizona and had asked Erin to stay with Claire until he returned at around midnight.

Erin turned her head for a moment and watched Claire sleep. Her breathing was rhythmic and calm. Erin stood up, tiptoed over to the door, stole a final glance at her friend and then slipped out into the hall.

Once in the hall, she went directly to the visitors' lounge, slid a dollar in the soda machine and listened as her Diet Coke tumbled loudly to the bottom of the machine.

After spending most of the day working on two stories with rapidly approaching deadlines and also trying to line up interviews with some of the key people at the institute, Erin was worn out.

Her cell phone was buried deep in her purse and she barely heard it ring.

"Hello."

"Erin, it's Noah Gallagher. How are you?"

"I'm fine," she said. "And it's not necessary to mention your last name," she said tartly. "I think I know who you are."

"Well, I . . . I was just—"

"The food was great last night," she said.

"I'm glad you enjoyed it. I . . . I just wanted to let you know that I had a really nice time . . . and was wondering if you . . . I mean if it doesn't interfere with your schedule . . . if we could have dinner again."

"I don't see why not."

"That's great," he said.

"Noah?" Erin asked after a brief silence.

"Yes."

"I think it's customary at this point of arranging a date to select a time and place."

"Absolutely," he agreed. "How about tomorrow night?"

"That will be fine," she said.

"I'll call you tomorrow afternoon so we can set up a time."

"I'll look forward to your call," she said before saying good-bye.

Erin stared in a daze at the soda machine thinking about Noah's call for a few moments. She was excited about seeing him again and actually felt a little irritated for being so boy crazy. She tried to erase the embarrassed grin she knew was on her face as she took the last sip of her drink and then tossed the can in the trash.

On her way back to Claire's room, she noticed the floor was quiet and dimly lit. She slowly opened the door and took a few steps inside. The only light in the room came from a small reading lamp on a corner table. For a moment or so, she was a bit disoriented because the window and recliner seemed to be on the wrong side of the room.

A nurse in a white uniform was attending to Claire's IV and didn't appear to notice that Erin was standing across the room. Erin squinted, leaned forward and watched as the nurse injected a medication into the IV bag. She was a thin woman with her hair pulled straight back in a tight bun. Erin took a couple of steps forward, looked at the patient's face and immediately realized she was in the wrong room.

"Oh, I'm so sorry," she said to the nurse, who instantly whirled around and locked eyes with her. "I must be in the wrong room. Please excuse me." Even in the poor light, Erin couldn't help but notice her startled expression.

The nurse turned back around, capped the needle and shoved the syringe into her pocket. "I'll be out of here in a moment."

"No, it's my mistake," Erin said, a little surprised at the nurse's nervous mannerisms. "I thought I was in Claire Weaver's room. Uh . . . what room is this?"

"Two-thirteen," she answered.

Erin took a deep breath. "I should be next door. It was dark in the hall. I guess I should have paid closer attention."

"It's not a problem, miss," the nurse said. She was now turned around with her back to Erin.

Feeling a little foolish for her careless mistake, Erin went back into Claire's room and again sat down in the chair. The bathroom light was on and the door was cracked just enough to cast a splash of light in the room. Erin took a brief look at Claire. She was sleeping on her back, breathing easily. Her face was tranquil and the contour of her enlarged uterus nudged the blanket up into a gentle curve.

Still a little embarrassed about her bonehead move, she suddenly remembered seeing the patient in 213 earlier that day when she was wheeled into her room. Her name was Sarah Allen. Erin was fairly certain she had undergone fetal surgery and was returning from the recovery room. She had overheard the nurses talking about her operation and recalled thinking she might be a good person to interview when she recovered.

Erin was just starting to drift off when a loud commotion in the hall startled her. She stood up, crossed the room quickly and stepped out into the hall. The corridor was now brightly lit and there was a stretcher sitting in the doorway of room 213. Two nurses stood in the hall while a gaunt orderly in hospital whites pushed the stretcher into the room. The nurse in charge, Danielle Carson, flipped through a patient chart. A young man in white scrubs wearing a stethoscope around his neck emerged from Sarah's room. Erin moved to the opposite side of the hall and then took a few steps toward the nursing station. The reporter in her was now in full gear, leaving her with an excellent view of the medical team at work and within easy earshot.

"Mrs. Allen has gone into labor," Bruce Harrison, the obstetrician on call, reported as he waved Danielle over. "At first, I thought they were just Braxton-Hicks contractions, but after looking at these tracings," he said, pointing to a long strip of monitor paper. "I think it's the real thing. She just had surgery today," he mentioned, tapping the front of her chart. "We're starting to see too much of this. I don't think the baby's going to make it. What time did you get her from recovery?"

"At about four," Danielle told him.

"Any problems in surgery?" he asked, giving the chart back to Danielle.

"None that they mentioned in the report. Actually, the operating team was quite encouraged."

"What was the procedure?" he inquired without taking his head out of the chart. Erin watched the young doctor as he worked. His voice and manner were quite clear and confident. They removed a tumor from the baby's lower spine."

"Did she receive pre-op Indomethacin?"

"Yes," Danielle said without having to check the chart.

"And have you started the nitroglycerine? I still think that's the best drug we have for stopping labor."

Danielle nodded. "We hung it ten minutes ago per the protocol."

"Well, let's get her over to the ICU. I'll recheck her once she's over there."

"We've already called for an ICU bed. They're expecting her."

"Make sure Dr. Sierra in clinical research knows about what happened," he said. "I'm sure Mrs. Allen's on the study."

"She is."

"What about her husband?"

"We called him. He's on his way in. I'll send him to the ICU as soon as he gets here."

Erin was pleased that nobody appeared to notice her. She watched as the orderlies transferred Sarah Allen to the stretcher in preparation for taking her to the ICU. Erin could easily see her face. It was ashen and contorted. Moaning in pain and holding her abdomen, Sarah flipped her head from one side of her pillow to the other. Erin took a deep breath and then swallowed hard. Her eyes felt weepy.

"The IV bag is empty," Danielle told Dr. Harrison. "Give me a sec. I'll hang a new one."

Having done it a thousand times before, it took Danielle only a few moments to put up a fresh bag of IV solution.

Erin continued to watch as the cart carrying Sarah Allen went flying by. And then, as quickly as the excitement had begun, it was over. Erin peeked back into Claire's room, hoping she'd slept through all the excitement. She heaved a breath of relief when she saw her friend was fast asleep.

After a few minutes of discussing Sarah Allen's unexpected turn for the worse, Danielle and the other nurses returned to the nursing station. Erin followed and waited for Danielle to replace one of the patient's charts in the large rack that rotated like a lazy Susan.

"Is it always this exciting around here?" she asked Danielle, more as a reporter than a curious bystander.

"Not always," she answered in a polite but guarded voice.

"My name's Erin Wells. I'm visiting Claire Weaver. I'm a nurse."

Danielle looked up and extended her hand. "Really, what kind of nursing do you do?"

"Actually, I haven't practiced in a few years. I worked in the Neuro-Rehabilitation Unit at Grady Memorial for five years taking care of patients with severe head trauma."

"Grady Memorial in Atlanta?" Danielle asked.

"That's the one."

"I've heard of it. That's a pretty prestigious unit. Why did you give it up?"

Erin shook her head. "I'm not sure. It just got too hard, I guess."

"I know the feeling," Danielle said with a sigh.

"Do you think she'll be okay?"

"It's hard to say. Each patient seems to react differently."

"How do you mean?" Erin asked.

"There's just no way of guessing who's going to do well and who's not," Danielle explained. "There's just no rhyme or reason to it."

"It's interesting you say that," Erin responded. "About an hour before she went into labor, I accidentally walked into Mrs. Allen's room. She was sleeping so peacefully. She looked fine. I think I scared the nurse who was in there."

"Do you mean Pat?"

"I guess so. It was kind of dark. I only saw her for a few seconds."

Danielle laughed and then covered her mouth. "Then it must have been real dark."

"What do you mean?"

"Pat's a guy," Danielle informed Erin.

"Oh." Erin hesitated for a moment, tilted her head to the side and continued, "I know I'm getting older and my vision is starting to fail, but the nurse I saw in Mrs. Allen's room was definitely a woman. Could it have been someone from the pharmacy?"

Danielle answered immediately, "No, that's not possible. We do all the meds and IVs. There are only two RNs on duty in the evening. The only other person working is a nurses' aide and she's been in the same patient's room all night. It must have been Pat who you saw."

Erin took a step forward and placed her hands on the desk. "The person in the room was a woman," she said firmly. "She was adding a medication to the IV. I'm sure of it."

Danielle looked up quickly and then slid the final chart back in the rack. She took a few steps to her right, gathered up a few clipboards and hung them each on the wall.

"Well, I'm sure there's a logical explanation. Now that I think about it," Danielle said as she tapped her lips with her finger, "I was in Mrs. Allen's room earlier this evening. It was probably me that you saw."

Erin took a long look at Danielle's short, curly blond hair and dark blue sweater. She had defused enough situations and pacified enough patients and family members in her career to know when she was getting the same treatment.

"You're probably right. It must have been you," Erin finally said.

Danielle looked down at her watch. "I have to take eleven p.m. vital signs. It was nice talking to you, Erin." Danielle grabbed her stethoscope from one of the drawers, stood up and headed down the hall.

Erin remained at the nursing station for a few minutes, crossed her arms and stared down the hall toward room 213. She left the nursing station and walked down the hall. When she reached Sarah Allen's room, she stopped and looked in. The room was empty and still messy from all the activity. The bed hadn't even been stripped yet. Scanning the room, Erin noticed the empty IV bag hanging over the side of the trash can.

She immediately felt her pulse quicken and a knot form in her stomach. She took a fast look down both sides of the empty corridor. There was no one in sight. Without a lengthy deliberation, she slipped into Sarah's room, grabbed the empty IV bag off the waste can and immediately returned to the hall. Feeling like a shoplifter at the mall, she shoved the empty IV bag into her purse and returned to Claire's room. She was just about to pull the bag out and have a closer look when Alex walked in.

"How's she doing?" he asked anxiously, placing his black flight briefcase down. He had already removed his tie and opened the top button of his white dress shirt. "I've been worried about her all day." He walked over to the bed and gazed down at his wife. "I guess I was a little distracted. I'll tell you, if any of my passengers knew how lucky they were to arrive in one piece today, they'd probably never fly again."

"That's a little scary, Alex. I think from now on I'll interview my pilots before I fly." Nobody knew better than Erin how much he loved Claire. They had been best friends from the day they met and were totally devoted to each other. They meshed perfectly. She added the creativity and spontaneity to the pragmatic part of their relationship. Alex, on the other hand, handled most things as if he were filing a flight plan. From the beginning, he had been a major player in her infertility problems, sharing every step of the process and never once harboring a particle of resentment.

"Did everything go okay today? Did she have any more contractions?" he asked.

"No, she's doing great. Listen, I'm beat. If you don't need me, I think I'll get going."

Alex put his arm around her shoulder. "I don't know how I'll ever be able to thank you for all this. I can't tell you how much it has meant to Claire and me to have you here."

Erin felt her face flush from his genuine display of emotion. "She'd do the same for me, Alex. You know, when I was growing up, it . . . it was only me and my little brother . . . and then, when he died . . . well, it was so hard to . . ."

"I understand, Erin."

"Claire's the closest thing I'll ever have to a real sister."

She kissed Alex on the cheek and headed straight for the elevator. Within seconds of hitting the button, the twin doors rumbled open. The car was empty and she stepped on. Erin watched the digital display over the door jump from "2" to "L" but her mind was elsewhere.

"I must have been out of my mind," she said in a whisper, opening her purse and looking at the IV bag. In spite of her stupid act, she was at least reasonably certain she hadn't been seen in Sarah's room.

A lone cab sat in front of the institute with only its yellow parking lights on. It was a starless night, a little cool and airy. Relieved when she saw the off-duty light wasn't on, she hurried over to the taxi.

The cab driver was a quiet man, which to Erin was a blessing. Leaning back against the uncomfortable vinyl seat, she closed her eyes and tried to collect her thoughts. She was reminded of Noah's comments about her imagination. As hard as she tried to be logical, by the time she arrived at the Hotel Inter-Continental, she was more than just a little worried about Claire Weaver.

Chapter 10

Claire had already finished her breakfast when Erin came into the room. She had just stepped out of the shower and was wearing a baby-blue terry-cloth robe that Alex had given her for Christmas. Her hair was still damp and she hadn't started her morning ritual of putting on her makeup yet.

"You don't look too shabby," Erin said as she put her purse down on the night table. She was wearing charcoal-gray cargo pants and a white cotton blouse.

"Well, except for all that commotion last night, I slept pretty well."

"What commotion?" Erin asked nonchalantly.

Claire raised her eyebrows. "Cut it out, Erin."

"Cut what out?"

"I appreciate your attempts to shield me from certain unpleasant events but I'm not a bear. Loud noises and commotion tend to wake me up." Claire walked over to her nightstand, picked up her hair dryer and plugged it in. Still not knowing how much her friend actually knew, Erin decided to remain aloof.

"Why don't you tell me what you're talking about?"

"I'm talking about Sarah Allen," she said, flipping on the hair dryer for a few seconds and then turning it off. Erin wasn't quite sure if the gesture was a subtle way of saying she didn't want to talk about it.

"I thought you were asleep."

"My eyes were closed," Claire said.

Erin walked over to her friend, took the hair dryer from her, set it down on the dresser and said, "I remember when we were at Penn State, and you were annoyed at me for some reason and didn't want to talk . . . you used to turn the stereo on. The technique's the same. The only thing that's different is your choice of appliance."

Claire turned to her friend. "Did I really do that?"

"All the time," Erin answered.

"I don't remember," Claire said with a playful frown.

"I think you do." Claire made her way over to the recliner and sat down. Erin could see her eyes were just a little puffy. She reached down into one of the large pockets and pulled a tissue out. "Do you want to talk about it?"

Claire crumpled the tissue up in a closed fist. "Yes, I think I would."

"Okay."

"I heard the nurses talking this morning about Sarah losing the baby," Claire said.

"Sarah? It sounds like you know her?"

"We met the day before yesterday. Misery loves company, I guess. She had just finished her last test and we talked for a long time about the surgery."

"I'm surprised," Erin said.

"Why?"

"Because you barely know her."

"This is kind of an unusual place," Claire explained. "When everybody's in the same boat, it's easy to make friends. This is her third pregnancy. She has a six-year-old and a two-year-old who are both fine."

"It was just bad luck," Erin assured her. "It doesn't mean the same thing is going to happen to you."

"I'm starting to feel like bad luck is my middle name."

"C'mon, Claire," Erin said, her voice and expression up-beat. "Everything's going to work out fine. You've used up all your bad luck."

"Did you ever stop to consider that maybe I want this baby too much?"

"I'm not sure that's possible."

"It's all I think about. I feel like I've done something wrong and the baby's paying for it. I just want him to be healthy." Claire pulled another tissue from her pocket and dried a couple of tears resting on her cheekbone. "So many women get pregnant that don't even want a baby. It just doesn't seem fair."

Erin walked over to the recliner and sat down on the arm-rest. "I'm not sure this is an issue of fairness. Just try and stay hopeful. Do that for me . . . okay?"

Claire forced a smile. "Sure."

"When's Alex going to be here?"

"He called a few minutes before you came. I expect him any time," Claire said.

"Great, I'm going down to the administrative offices to check on my interview schedule. Is there anything I can get you?"

"No, nothing," Claire said.

Erin stood up, leaned over and kissed her friend and then started across the room.

"It means so much to me that you're here, I just wanted you to know." Erin looked back at Claire and smiled. "How's the story going, by the way?"

"I haven't really gotten too much yet," Erin explained. "But you know me. I'll wear them down with my boundless charms, and if that doesn't work I'll just have to show them my nasty side."

Claire gave her the thumbs-up. "You haven't changed a bit either."

"Why tamper with perfection?" Erin said in a pseudoso-phisticated voice.

"Please," Claire begged, feigning a grand yawn. "I'll have to call for my nausea medicine."

Erin faked a belly laugh, told Claire she'd be back in the morning and left the room.

Sarah Allen's door was open and Erin glanced in as she walked by. Lying on her back and wide-eyed, Sarah stared at the ceiling with hollow eyes. The temptation to go in and speak with her was strong but Erin resisted and walked straight down the hall.

Waiting for the elevator, Erin gazed down and smiled at a pregnant woman in a wheelchair. The woman, Maria Fernandez, had a rosy face and cherubic smile. A young nurses' aide in a white uniform stood behind the wheelchair next to a large cart filled with several fresh flower arrangements and the woman's personal items.

"Are you going back to Mexico City?" the aide asked Maria.

"No, we're going to stay with relatives until it's time for the baby to be born."

Erin couldn't help but overhear the woman's answer. Normally she didn't barge into other people's conversations, but her curiosity as a reporter and concern for her friend prevailed over her usual sense of good manners.

"My name's Erin Wells. My friend Claire Weaver's in room two-eleven. She's scheduled to have fetal surgery in the next couple of weeks."

The woman drew her right hand out from under a thin plaid blanket that covered her legs, slowly reached up and shook Erin's hand.

"It's nice to meet you. I hope your friend does well. I just had surgery last week."

"How was it? You look great for someone who just had an operation."

"It wasn't so bad," she said with a mild Spanish accent. "My baby's okay now. That's all that's important."

Erin tried to resist the urge to ask but couldn't. "You didn't have any problems?"

"No, but I didn't think that I would. Dr. Gallagher is so wonderful and the hospital's just great."

"That's what we've heard," Erin told her as she was reminded of their dinner date.

"I wish I could tell my friend something that would make her feel as confident as you are," Erin said.

Maria's eyes widened with a touch of excitement. "Tell her many women from my country have come to the institute in the last few years."

"Have you ever spoken with any of them?" Erin asked.

"No, but we all went to the same clinic."

"That's quite a coincidence," Erin said.

"Not really. The institute runs it and made all the arrangements for us to come to the United States. We were told by the staff that all of the women who had fetal surgery came through it fine." She paused for a moment and looked back when the elevator doors opened. "Tell her that," Maria suggested. "I'm sure it will make her feel better."

"That's . . . that's terrific," Erin said with a flash of a smile. "When are you having your baby?"

"In about three months."

The nurses' aide pushed Maria's wheelchair forward and then came back for the cart. The elevator was almost filled and Erin told them that she'd wait for the next one.

It was easy to understand why Maria was so confident. The knowledge that so many other women from Mexico City had undergone fetal surgery without a problem surely must have put her mind at ease. Erin stood with her back against the elevator door for a moment thinking about what Maria had said. *All the women who had come to the institute from the clinic in Mexico City had done well.* It seemed impossible. Nobody could question that fetal surgery had made enormous strides in the last several years, but from a scientific standpoint it was still in its infancy. All of the centers across the country were still reporting a significant number of failures.

When the elevator returned, Erin was still deep in thought. She stepped toward the back, entertaining the notion that perhaps the clinic in Mexico City was being less than truthful with the women it was referring to the institute. But if that were the case, why would the institute tolerate such an obvious breech of medical ethics? Erin could feel the muscles in the back of her neck start to spasm. Moments later a dull ache radiated its way up along her skull.

Half in a fog, Erin hesitated for a moment when the elevator doors rumbled open. A moment or two later, she stepped forward and entered the lobby.

The lobby was empty. A stocky security guard in a tight shirt tapped the brim of his cap and then watched her for a few moments. His manner unnerved her, but she cautioned herself against falling prey to an overactive imagination. But, in spite of her best efforts, her level of anxiety continued to heighten at the thought of the ever-expanding list of unexplained occurrences and coincidences.

Erin took a deep breath when she reached the street. She could see a cab in the distance. Desperate for answers, Erin could only offer a silent heartfelt prayer that Claire's surgery would go as smoothly as Maria Fernandez's had.

PART
Two

Chapter 11

As chief of security at the Fetal Insti-
tute, Frank Grafton was generally polite, efficient and responsive. He had just completed making out the week's
schedule, his last job of the day, when his pager went off. He
looked down at the digital display and groaned. Stopping at
the information desk in the center of the lobby, he picked up
the phone and called the operator.

"It's Grafton."

"We have a message from your office."

"Go ahead."

"There's a video surveillance tape they'd like you to review
before you leave this evening."

Grafton groaned louder this time, twisted the phone against
his ear and looked straight toward the ceiling.

"Are you sure they said tonight?" he asked against hope.

"They were quite insistent, Mr. Grafton."

"Fine," he mumbled and thanked the operator. "The sooner
I get this done, the sooner I can get out of here."

The central security office was a short walk from the main
lobby. After entering through the main door, he walked past a

fax machine, phone and computer sitting on a large desk. An interior door led to a second room that contained the hospital-wide monitoring equipment. A dozen color monitors stacked six on six sat recessed in a custom-made wall unit directly above a sophisticated control console. The room was brightly lit by a double row of track lighting. Grafton wheeled over a chair and sat down.

Four years ago, the institute had consulted one of the more experienced and pricey security firms on the East Coast to update the surveillance system. The result was a highly sophisticated system that monitored all key areas of the institute. By convention, it was the responsibility of the less senior security personnel to review the surveillance tapes on a daily basis. Once the review was completed, and assuming there were no irregularities noted, the tapes were filed away for twelve months and then discarded.

Grafton glanced down at the desktop and noticed a small plastic video box with his name taped to the outside. Twisting in his chair, he flipped on the monitor and slid the tape into one of four VCRs. It took only a few seconds for the machine to automatically reach the indexed area and indicate the time and location of the segment: SECOND FLOOR—CAMERA 4, TEN THIRTY-FIVE P.M., OCTOBER 5.

The first image was frozen and showed nothing more than the dimly lit hallway of zone four, which was the south end of the second floor. Grafton stretched his muscular legs under the desk, yawned and then hit the play button. For the first thirty seconds or so, the image remained unchanged. He was becoming impatient when the image of a woman appeared outside of room 213. She had her back to the entrance and after taking a quick glance in the room, looked up and down the hall. An instant later, she entered the room. Grafton leaned in to get a better view of the monitor and then flipped on the digital time display. Forty-five seconds later, the woman emerged from the room holding a plastic object in her hand. A few seconds later, she disappeared into room 211. Grafton studied the video for another minute or two and then hit the pause button.

Scratching his head, he quickly hit the rewind command and watched the entire segment again, this time freezing each frame for a few seconds. When the woman's face was facing the camera, he zoomed in and again froze the picture. The image was clear and he had no difficulty whatsoever identifying Erin Wells.

He shifted his weight back in the chair and rocked back and forth. His interest now piqued, he reached forward and again set the tape in motion, and then stopped it just as Erin emerged from the room. He set the computer to digitally enhance the area of her right hand to have a closer look at the object. The resolution was more than satisfactory, making the identification of the IV bag reasonably simple. He rewound the tape to ten minutes after ten, hit the play button and immediately saw all the commotion going on outside of room 213 as the staff scurried around trying to move the patient out of the room.

"Oh, shit," he said out loud. He whirled his chair around, booted up the computer and pulled up the hospital census for October 5. As soon as he tapped in room 213, Sarah's name came up. An instant later he had the phone in his hand and was tapping in a number.

"Yes."

"This is Grafton. I think we may have a problem."

"I'm listening," came the answer.

"Erin Wells may have been present the night Sarah Allen went into labor. I've just reviewed one of our surveillance tapes that shows her coming out of Mrs. Allen's room the night she had her miscarriage."

"Maybe she was just visiting."

"I don't think so. The room was empty. They had just transferred Mrs. Allen to the ICU." Grafton spun around in his chair and picked up the tape. "There's something else."

"I'm still listening."

"We have zoom capability on the surveillance camera. It appears as if there's something in her hand."

"Can you tell what it was?"

"I can't be completely sure, but it may be an empty IV bag," Grafton reported, tossing the tape back on the counter.

"We've never had a problem like this before, Mr. Grafton. We pay you a fortune of money because you assured us of your matchless skill and professionalism."

Grafton was measured in his response. "I'm just keeping you aware of what's going on. I never suggested I was uncomfortable dealing with the problem. If those are your wishes, by tomorrow at this time you will—"

"I'm not a person prone to impulsive behavior. This whole thing may be just a coincidence. For the time being just keep an eye on Ms. Wells and stay in very close touch with me."

"And what about Mrs. Weaver?"

"She's still just a patient. There are options available to us if her relationship with Ms. Wells becomes a problem."

"And what about Erin Wells? Do you want me to confine my activities strictly to surveillance?"

"I'm not sure I understand your question."

"It's quite simple. If you feel Ms. Wells is a problem, well . . . there are measures that can be taken to—"

"Mr. Grafton, I'm not interested in taking extreme measures at this time. Do I make myself clear?"

He clenched his fist. "Crystal."

"Good. Call me tomorrow."

Grafton had a look of total disgust on his face when he hung up the phone. Things were certainly different in the corps. If you identified a problem, you dealt with it definitively before the problem did the same to you.

"Civilians," he mumbled under his breath. "What a bunch of amateurs."

He slid the tape back into the recorder and cued it to the same sequence he had just reviewed and then stopped it. Tapping the frozen image of Erin Wells a couple of times, he whispered, "From now on, you and I are going to be spending a lot of time together."

Chapter 12

Noah and Erin had spent a pleasant evening in Fort Lauderdale strolling up and down the streets of the Las Olas section. Similar to South Beach, the area boasted an eclectic selection of art galleries, unique gift stores, outdoor cafés and a wide choice of restaurants. It was a mild evening. A full moon with a broad halo of light filled the evening sky. They had eaten a pleasant meal at an outdoor restaurant discussing a wide range of topics. Erin had decided before Noah picked her up not to mention anything related to the institute or her ongoing concerns for Claire.

"I enjoyed the evening," she told Noah as they started back toward Miami. She was wearing a white shift and leather thongs. She looked at his hand on the gear shift, and without giving it a second thought reached over and covered it with hers. He seemed comfortable with the arrangement, casting her a modest smile.

"Las Olas is a nice place," he said.

"Those art galleries were magnificent. I wish I had more time . . . and money to look through them."

"Maybe before you go back to Washington we'll have a chance to get back up here."

"That would be great," she answered, gently stroking the back of his hand.

The ride back to her hotel went by too quicky. She knew he was ready but would surely lack the nerve to broach the topic of romance. As she was giving serious consideration to inviting him into the hotel for a drink and helping nature to take its course, the monotonous tone of his beeper filled the car. Noah checked the number, opened the glove compartment and reached for his cell phone.

"This is Dr. Gallagher," he said as soon as the nurse picked up. "I see," he said and then began asking a series of questions about one of his post-op patients. When Erin saw his eyes focus on the digital clock, her plans for an amorous evening evaporated like a puff of smoke. "I'll be there in about thirty minutes," he told the nurse. "Make sure there's a central line setup in her room. Have the radiologist come in. I'm going to need her."

Noah slowly replaced the phone in the glove compartment. Erin had no way of knowing, but his dreams of a passionate evening had just gone up in the same puff of smoke as hers did.

"You have to go in?" she asked.

"Yeah. I'm afraid so."

"How long are you going to be?"

Noah cleared his throat and then stole a glance at Erin. "Several hours, I'm afraid."

Noah pulled up to the entrance of the hotel. Before the attendant could open Erin's door, he put his arm around her shoulder, waited for her to turn toward him and then kissed her until the loud snap of the door being pulled open ended the moment.

"I'll speak to you tomorrow," he said.

"Thanks for a great evening."

Erin stepped out, waved and waited on the curb until his car was out of sight.

Chapter 13

When Erin walked through the doors of the Avis car rental agency, she was pleased to see there was no line. Tired of being at the mercy of one fickle Miami cab company after another, she was more than relieved when the young lady with a pert smile completed the paperwork and handed her the keys to her rental.

Erin left the office and walked quickly under a royal-blue canopy, checking each car until she arrived at space 122, a white Firebird convertible. As soon as she was behind the wheel, she flipped the switch to lower the top, tilted her head back and watched as it dropped smoothly into the storage bay.

Since arriving in Miami, she had been toying with the idea of taking a ride down to South Beach, the flamboyant Art Deco district that she had heard so much about. It was a beautiful day and the urge to seize the moment and go was too much for her to resist.

The traffic was light on Ocean Drive as Erin proceeded south. A group of stagnant gray clouds hung like a painting, helping to deflect the sun's midday rays. Driving with one hand, she gazed over at the large leafy willows dipping down to partially veil the baroque homes that were set well back from the street.

She looked over at her purse sitting on the passenger's seat and then reached for her cell phone to call her editor in Washington.

Herb Porfino answered on the second ring.

"Herb, it's Erin."

"I recognize the voice," came the droll response. "Where the hell have you been? Are you working or taking a vacation?"

"You're a funny man, Herb," she said after a quick sigh. "I thought I'd call you between my facial and golf lesson."

"Terrific. It's nice to know where our money's going. If you don't mind me asking, how's the story progressing?"

"I'm not sure."

"Really. Who should I ask in that case?"

"C'mon, Herb. I'm serious. This place is weird. Nobody wants to talk, and when they do, it's in riddles. The physician in charge has everyone on a short leash. I don't think any of them make a move until they get their marching orders from him." Erin turned the wheel slightly as the road doglegged to the right. She was just about to elaborate on Dr. Archer when a blue Explorer driven by a man wearing a white baseball cap cut sharply into her lane without warning. She slammed on the brakes and jerked the car to the right, avoiding a collision by no more than a few feet. "You asshole," she yelled with a clenched fist as the car sped off as if nothing had happened.

"Are you talking to me?" Herb asked.

Erin shook her fist at the careless driver again.

"Of course not. Some lunatic just about ran me off the road."

Erin heard him clear his throat. "Listen, Erin. You're supposed to be doing a feel-good story about a prestigious hospital that's on the cutting edge of fetal surgery. In case you've forgotten, they're the flagship institution in the country. You're not Rod Serling and this isn't *The Twilight Zone*. Just write the damn story, please."

Erin rolled her eyes. "You're a sweet man, Herb."

"Never mind the compliments. I'd like to see the rough draft by the end of the month."

"And you shall have it."

"Good. By the way, I just finished reading the final copy of your last piece."

"And?"

"Not bad, not bad at all. I think your job is safe for now . . . but it's not going to be if you don't check in more often."

Erin slowed as the same Explorer that had whipped by her a minute or so earlier changed lanes in front of her. "Don't you trust me?" she asked. "Have I ever let you down?"

"It has nothing to do with that," came the response. "It's just that I get lonely and would feel better if I could hear the sound of your sweet voice from time to time."

"I see," she remarked, turning her head to the side. "By the way, do you have any connections at a medical lab?"

"I beg your pardon?"

"It's a simple question, Herb. Do you know anybody, preferably with a little discretion, who works at a medical lab somewhere in the DC area? I want to send something up for analysis."

Silence ensued as Erin braced herself for a series of probing questions. A cagey man, Herb probably wouldn't respond to her inquiry without at least some explanation. He was a mother hen, highly ethical, and rarely put his stamp of approval on anything out of the ordinary without a compelling reason.

"Okay, Erin. Let's have it. What are you getting into down there?"

"I'm not sure," she began slowly. "I've come across a couple of strange things since I started working on the story. I'm not exactly—"

"Strange things? What kind of strange things?" he asked in an exasperated tone. "I'm warning you, Erin. Don't do anything that's going to embarrass us."

Erin filled her lungs with the biggest breath she could hold.

She was well aware of Herb's disdain for shabby investigative reporting. Even in its most ethical and fair form, he didn't see the *AMA News*'s mission to do investigative pieces. But she knew the situation wasn't hopeless. On occasion Herb had caved in and allowed a reporter to file a well-researched story that cast a disparaging light on a particular aspect of the medical profession.

"I'm not sure everything is as pristine as it appears down here. It's that simple."

Erin could hear Herb making that strange clicking sound with his tongue that he always did when he was deep in thought.

"I don't suppose you want to tell me what you think you know?" he asked.

"Would you be crestfallen if I said no?"

"I don't think so," he confessed. "It's kind of what I expected."

"What about that medical lab?" she asked, reaching forward to lower the volume of the radio.

"Erin, I'm the editor in chief of a major medical publication. I've held that position for sixteen years. I think I've met enough people over the years that I might be able to find a medical lab willing to help us. What exactly do you want to have analyzed?"

"It's an empty IV bag."

"A what?"

"An empty IV bag. I want to know if there are any medications or other chemicals in the bag."

"Where did you acquire this item? Or shouldn't I ask?"

"You'd love Florida, Herb. You should come here on your next vacation. You could do wonders with your golf game down here."

Herb groaned. Erin knew he had a soft spot in his heart for her, and if anybody could push him to his limit and get away with it, it was her. Three years ago he had suffered a mild heart attack. He was hospitalized for five days at George Washington University Hospital, and Erin didn't miss a single evening's visiting hours. The gesture was genuine, and although he never said anything, Erin knew he appreciated her concern more than he'd ever be able to express.

"How are you sending it?" he asked.

"I'll FedEx it tomorrow."

"Okay."

"I love you, Herb . . . like a father, of course," she added before he could say anything.

"Call me, Erin. Don't get in over your head down there." There was a silence. "Do you hear me, Erin?"

"I hear you," she assured him.

Erin said a quick good-bye, put the phone back in her purse and continued south on Ocean Drive until she reached South Beach. Dozens of in-line skaters scantily clad in colorful bathing suits and helmets zipped along effortlessly. Gazing to the right, she noticed a number of eclectic boutiques and ethnic restaurants.

Directly ahead, a large green sign directed traffic toward a public parking facility. She turned left and eased the Firebird up to the automatic ticket dispenser, grabbed the ticket and easily found a parking space on the second level. As soon as the car was locked, she headed down the ramp toward the exit. She barely noticed as the blue Explorer slowly passed by and then pulled in three lanes away.

Frank Grafton, wearing a yellow golf jacket, emerged from the car and watched Erin leave the garage and start across Ocean Drive. Grafton made his way down the ramp, stopped in front of Erin's car and took a quick look around. Stepping between the Firebird and a white Tahoe parked next to it, he reached into his pocket and pulled out a small black electronic device that was about the size of a deck of cards. After a final look around, he dropped to the ground, rolled over on his back and quickly attached the magnetic beacon to the frame of Erin's car. A moment later he was back on his feet and jogging down the ramp.

By the time Grafton exited the garage, Erin had started down Ocean Drive, taking in the novel ambiance of South

Beach. Stopping frequently to window-shop and ogle the locals, she thought she had never seen such a ragtag, outrageously dressed group of people. Stopping in front of one of the small boutiques, she considered going in, thought about her dwindling bank balance and decided to resist the temptation.

She pushed her sunglasses down from the top of her head and set them gently on the bridge of her nose. Looking overhead, she noted there wasn't a cloud in the sky now. A glistening silver ultralight with bulky pontoons droned overhead. The craft couldn't have been more than a thousand feet off the ground when it started into a gentle bank toward the ocean.

When the ultralight was nearly out of view, she glanced across the street and noticed a man in a yellow golf jacket with his arms folded in front of him. His eyes seemed transfixed on her, and even though he was at a distance, Erin couldn't help but notice the strange smile on his face. When he didn't look away, Erin became nervous and turned away. She was immediately reminded of her junior year in college when she had been stalked by a graduate student for several months. Campus security eventually took care of the problem, but the experience left her leery of strange men who stared. Walking away, she tried to warn herself not to fall victim to an overactive imagination.

She stopped in front of an outdoor café with large round tables, high-backed wicker chairs and alabaster umbrellas. It was almost two o'clock, and most of the tables seemed to be occupied by tourists with scads of shopping bags at their feet.

She found a table easily enough. A young lady with a pleasant smile wearing a mauve golf shirt with the restaurant logo embroidered over the pocket took her order for an iced tea. The sidewalk was bustling with people. Erin smiled when a woman with a bright green sundress pushing a twin stroller passed by.

Considering herself a reasonable person, not prone to exaggeration or connecting the wrong dots, she couldn't for the life of her explain her uneasy feeling about the institute and her constant concern for Claire's safety. Even though Claire was doing much better and had experienced no further contractions or bleeding, Erin realized she still risked losing the baby. Noah finally allowed her out of bed but insisted she remain hospitalized until the day of surgery.

When she finished her drink, she paid the waitress and started back across the street. Joining the other window-shoppers, she again strode slowly down Ocean Drive. After about forty-five minutes, she spotted the parking garage, checked her watch and decided to head back to the institute for her afternoon interview.

As she drove down the ramp, she was lost in thought about Claire. She handed the gaunt attendant with long sandy-blond hair and a blotchy complexion a ten-dollar bill. While she waited for the change, she thought about the man in the yellow jacket. She still had an uncomfortable feeling and wished she had gotten a better look at his face. Erin shook her head, looked up and saw the young man looking down at her impatiently with her change in his hand.

"Whatever's bothering you, lady, I hope you figure it out."

Erin cast an acid look in his direction and reached for the money. The traffic was heavy, making her progress annoyingly slow. She stretched her neck to see beyond the stacks of cars in front of her. In the opposite direction, about six cars behind, Frank Grafton checked the electronic receiver. His smile was one of deep self-satisfaction. When he made the final adjustments, the signal was excellent.

One thing was for certain—wherever Erin Wells went, he'd know exactly where to find her.

Chapter 14

Almost immediately after John Freeman's death, Carl Chandler was appointed acting director of the lab. In a memo to all the department chiefs, Marc Archer announced that a national search had already been initiated to recruit a permanent director, but until such time as one was named, Dr. Chandler would assume the position.

When Erin arrived for her appointment with Chandler, the laboratory was operating at full throttle. A dozen technicians with clipboards tucked tightly under their arms scrambled up and down the long aisles of the lab checking scientific instruments and monitoring the status of various experiments in progress.

A man from across the room dressed in a three-quarter-length white lab coat approached Erin with an extended hand.

"You must be Ms. Wells," he said, shaking her hand vigorously. "I'm Dr. Chandler. We're all very excited about your story. Would you like the nickel tour before we get started with the interview?"

Erin smiled cautiously. She was a little taken aback by his animated and upbeat mood coming on the heels of John Freeman's death. To say the least, his temperament was in sharp contrast to Freeman's aloof and starchy nature.

"Of course," she said. "I'd love to see it."

Chandler pointed down the main aisle and then escorted Erin around the entire lab. His hair was cropped in military style, resting squarely above sparse eyebrows. His narrow chest merged awkwardly into a looping paunch. Being scholastically average and from an affluent family, he never had to struggle for too much. His father was overbearing and had always set goals for Chandler that exceeded his grasp. More of a company man than a leader, he was a polished expert at avoiding controversy.

Stopping at each station, Chandler explained the intricate scientific instruments and how they related to the research. His enthusiasm was palpable and Erin found the twenty-minute tour quite interesting.

When they finished he invited her into his office. A walnut desk was positioned caddy-corner against the far wall with two plain upholstered chairs facing it. His desk was quite orderly. A neatly aligned stack of files sat next to empty In and Out baskets. The only items decorating the walls were his diplomas and certificates of membership to various scientific societies. A small but robust potted plant sat in the corner opposite the desk.

"That was quite an impressive tour," Erin told him as she sat down and waited for him to walk around to the other side of the desk. His perfectly pressed white lab coat was buttoned all the way to the top.

"John Freeman is responsible for all of this," he said. "It was his vision that made it possible."

Erin opened her purse, removed her small tape recorder and placed it on the desk.

"Do you mind if I record the interview?"

"Uh . . . I'm not sure . . ."

"My note-taking skills aren't the greatest and I don't want to miss anything you say."

Chandler blushed. "Of course. I understand. Feel free to use the recorder."

"Did you work very closely with Dr. Freeman?" Erin asked.

"I'd say we were colleagues. Nobody was very close to John Freeman either inside or outside this lab. He lived alone and to the best of my knowledge had no family. He was a brilliant man. I learned an awful lot from him."

"Are you interested in becoming the permanent director of the lab?"

"Well," he began, trying to hide a coy smile. "I've thrown my hat into the ring. I'm sure my credentials are competitive but this is a unique position. It will be highly sought after. I'm sure Dr. Archer will have his choice of dozens of highly qualified applicants."

Erin listened carefully and was quite happy that Chandler spoke freely. He was certainly the exception at the institute. Maybe she'd finally get a revealing interview.

"Can you tell me something about the research you're doing?"

"Of course. Actually, John and I were interested in the same thing."

"Tocolytic agents?"

"That's correct. He must have mentioned that to you." Chandler reached forward, picked up a pencil and then lightly tapped the desktop with the eraser end.

"He did. What's the present status of your work?"

Chandler turned in his chair, crossed his legs and then unbuttoned the top two buttons of his coat. "We're working with several agents but John was particularly interested in one. It's been the major focus of his . . . I mean our research for the last several years."

"That's fascinating. Has it received FDA approval yet?"

"He submitted the results of the basic research and animal trials to the FDA about three years ago. They were pretty impressed. Within a year, he had permission to start clinical trials."

"You mean on real patients."

"Yes. The FDA makes you jump through more hoops than a three-ring circus."

"What's the name of the drug?" Erin asked.

"Tocalazine is the generic name. If and when it's approved, John wanted to call it Labrostat. It's an incredible drug."

"Really? What's so special about it?"

"It doesn't seem to have any effect on pregnant women who experience premature labor. It won't stop their labor. It only has an effect on women who have undergone fetal surgery."

"I don't understand. How's that possible?"

"We're still working on that but we think it has something to do with surgically opening the uterus. We're guessing that making an incision in the womb must release some chemical in the bloodstream that triggers the Tocalazine. But in the absence of an operation on the uterus, the drug doesn't work for beans."

"Which means what in practical terms?" she asked.

"Only that its commercial value would be severely limited."

"Why's that?"

"Because on a national . . . even an international level, the market would be very small if the drug's only application was for use in fetal surgery."

"I see," Erin said, trying to gather all of this in. "It was my understanding that patients are participating in a variety of clinical experiments," she mentioned.

"That's true. Those are clinical studies under the supervision of Leigh Sierra. You'll probably want to talk to her to get a better understanding of the specifics. I'm really not that familiar with them."

"Is that Dr. Sierra?"

"Yes. She's a Ph.D. She's been with the institute for several years. I believe she was in the private sector before joining us. She's a bit of a highbrow but very well liked and respected. She does an excellent job organizing and monitoring the experiments that directly involve the patients."

"She sounds interesting," Erin said. "I look forward to talking with her. Do you work closely with her?" Erin asked as she leaned forward to check the tape recorder.

"Actually, Dr. Archer prefers to keep the two divisions of research separate. He's made it quite clear on more than one occasion that he believes the results of our work might be biased if information between basic and clinical research were shared."

"What do you think?" Erin asked.

"I'm not sure, but it drove Dr. Freeman crazy." Chandler stopped for a moment and looked around. "And that's only half the story."

Erin leaned in. "What's the other half?"

"John Freeman had no idea about the finances of the lab."

"What do you mean?"

"Well," he began in a voice just above a whisper. "It's fairly customary for the director of research to be actively involved in formulating the lab's budget and to assist in fundraising activities."

"And you're saying Dr. Freeman wasn't?"

"Totally in the dark," Chandler said in a musical voice. "Archer wouldn't tell him a thing."

"Did that lead to a problem?" Erin inquired, thinking more about how this might tie in to her own suspicions than the story she was supposed to be writing.

"For a while, but they eventually had a heart-to-heart about it all. Marc Archer's always a gentleman, but I think he made it clear to Dr. Freeman that the financial matters of the research lab were Neotech's problem and not his."

"What did Dr. Freeman do?"

"He lowered his profile after that. But he always seemed to be biding his time until the day he could pull the rug out from under Archer's feet."

"Boy, this is starting to sound more like a movie script than a research lab."

Chandler laughed. "You may be right. A lot of this stuff is pretty common in a research setting."

"Stuff? What kind of stuff?"

"Oh, petty jealousy and one-upmanship . . . that kind of thing."

"I guess we see the same type of thing in the publishing business," Erin mentioned. She was having trouble believing all that Carl Chandler was telling her. There was no question that from her brief meeting with John Freeman, he acted like a man who was carrying around an enormous burden. In order not to raise Chandler's suspicion and risk losing him as an un-witting fountain of information, Erin restricted the rest of her questions to fairly mundane topics.

"You've certainly been very helpful," she told Chandler as she reached forward, picked up her tape recorder and turned it off.

"I'm more than happy to help. When do you think the ar-ticle will be out?"

"I'm not quite sure. I haven't even started writing it yet," she said. "You've been very kind and generous with your time."

"Well, if you have any more questions, give me a call or just come on over to the lab."

Erin replaced the tape recorder in her purse and thanked Chandler again.

As she left the lab and walked outside, she found herself wondering what mysterious facts John Freeman took to the grave with him about the research lab at the Fetal Institute. And more importantly, what he had intended to do with the information if he had lived.

Chapter 15

Noah Gallagher was pleased with the progress of Mary Evans's surgery. The blood loss had been minimal, her vital signs had remained rock steady and there had been no hint of premature labor. The CCAM, which was attached to the baby's right lung, was quite large, but Noah felt confident that he'd be able to safely remove it. Two preoperative ultrasounds had confirmed that the baby's left lung was completely normal.

It was late afternoon and Erin had come directly over to the operating rooms as soon as her interview with Carl Chandler was over. Before they entered the operating suite, Noah spent a considerable amount of time reviewing the hospital's guidelines governing her presence during surgery.

Erin maintained a polite and cooperative attitude. She had asked several questions but was astute enough to know when to remain silent and out of the way. Noah was a little conflicted by Erin's presence, but after some thought decided she didn't constitute a breach of his policy of always keeping his professional and personal life separate.

"Let me have the fetal ultrasound unit," he told his scrub

nurse, Bobbi. As soon as he had the small device in hand, Noah ran it over the thickened wall of Mary's uterus until he identified the exact location of the placenta. "It's absolutely mandatory that we avoid damaging the placenta when we open the uterus," he told the medical students, who all nodded simultaneously as if they were part of a synchronized dance team. "What would happen if we accidentally cut the arteries and veins from the fetus to the mother?" he asked the group.

"We could try to repair them," one of the bolder ones offered.

"I'm afraid that wouldn't be possible. The operation, and the pregnancy, would be over."

Noah looked up for a moment. "Erin, stand next to the anesthesiologist so you can have a better look at this. We're just about to open the uterus." Erin nodded and moved to a place on the other side of the anesthesiologist. Noah selected an area well removed from the placenta. Using a large syringe, he carefully inserted a long needle into the uterus. With a steady, backward pressure, he aspirated about a quart of amniotic fluid, placed it in a sterile basin and passed it to Bobbi.

"I think we're ready to open the uterus now." Without being asked, Bobbi passed him a special stapling device that was designed specifically to open the thick uterine wall without losing too much blood. Noah took a long look at the operative field, let out a slow breath and then, with extreme care, fired three successive applications of the device in the front wall of Mary's womb. "The uterus is open," he said in a slightly louder voice to alert the anesthesiologist. "Have you started the nitroglycerine yet?"

"About five minutes ago, Noah," came a confident voice from the other side of the anesthesia screen. "She should be ready. I can't get the uterus any more relaxed than it is."

Noah slowly reached into the uterus. Exploring gently, he soon found the tiny fetus's left arm. With a light but steady retraction, Noah rotated the unborn infant toward him.

"Let me have the oxygen-monitoring system," he said with a measured urgency.

"It's all ready," answered Bobbi as she handed him a small plastic monitoring band, which he immediately wrapped around the baby's palm.

"Are you getting a reading," he asked Tracy McCardle, the nurse anesthetist.

"Give it a sec to calibrate."

"Let me know as soon as you have something."

"You'll be the first to know."

While Noah waited for the oxygen monitor to register, he reached back on the table and removed a small radiotelemetry transmitter, which is placed under the infant's skin to measure the heartbeat and temperature. It took him only about five minutes to implant it. Looking back up at the monitors, he was pleased to see that all the fetal tracings were working.

"It's show time," he announced, glancing up for a moment to note the time on the clock.

It took Noah about thirty minutes to open the baby's chest and expose the large CCAM. Attempting to remove the mass itself would be dangerous, so Noah removed the entire lower lobe of the right lung that it was attached to, still leaving the baby with two other perfectly normal lobes. Before declaring the operation a success, he studied the operative field with great care, again reviewing in precise detail every step he'd just carried out. Finally, he was satisfied.

"I think we're ready to return the baby to the uterus and close," he said. "Any questions?"

"What about the amniotic fluid we removed in the beginning?" one of the medical students asked.

"As soon as the uterus is closed we'll replace it."

"How's Mom doing?" Noah asked Tracy as he sewed the deep currant uterine muscles with a running stitch, taking every precaution not to disturb any of the engorged and tortuous blood vessels that crisscrossed over its surface.

"I've never seen one go smoother," Tracy assured him.

"No signs of labor?"

"Not a single contraction."

"That's good news," he said with a sigh of relief.

Once the uterus was closed, it took Noah only about an-other thirty minutes to close Mary's abdomen. She remained rock stable, and as soon as the dressing was on, she was taken straight to the recovery room. Noah dictated the oper-ative note and told Erin he would meet her in the lounge after they both changed back into their street clothes. Noah was pleased. The operation had gone quite well and Erin's pres-ence had not disrupted a single detail of the procedure. The shock value of her direct personality still left him a little flus-tered, but after two dates and several phone calls, he was starting to adjust.

"Did you find that interesting?" he asked Erin as soon as she walked through the door to the lounge.

She was beaming. "That may have been the most exciting thing I've ever watched. Your technique was wonderful."

Noah's complexion became the color of a cherry tomato. "Are you on your way to visit Claire?" he asked.

"I am. Is that where you're headed too?" They left the lounge and headed for the elevators.

"No, I have to go to the ICU, but I'll probably stop in to see her a little later."

"I went down to South Beach today. It's quite a place. I re-ally enjoyed it."

"You went alone?"

Erin's eyes widened over a smile that the Cheshire Cat would have admired. Noah wanted to kick himself for asking and would have given anything to retract the question.

"Yes, I did. Were you concerned for my safety or afraid I had a date with another man?"

Noah's chin dropped for a moment before he realized it and closed his mouth. In a way he was thankful that her gen-tle jousting had kind of let him off the hook for an inappro-priate question.

"It was just a harmless question," he told her in his most formal doctor voice. "It's certainly none of my business."

The doors opened. Erin took a step forward and held down the open button on the control panel.

"Are you going to be working late?" she inquired.

"Do you mean tonight?"

"Yes, I mean tonight."

"Actually, things are very busy," he said.

"Do you want to ignore that fact and have some dinner with me later?" she asked.

Noah rolled his eyes. "If you would have given me another minute or two, I probably would have asked."

"I'm sorry," she said. "I guess I didn't see any compelling reason to stand on ceremony."

Noah tapped his toes nervously and then placed his hands on his hips. She was even more attractive than he remembered. He had never met a woman with such an assortment of facial expressions.

"I'll meet you in the lobby at eight. And no reading my mind this time . . . especially about sex."

"I only did that the first time we went out," she reminded him.

"Okay. I'll see you at eight . . . in the lobby." She giggled to herself as Noah walked away.

The door to Claire's room was open and she walked in without knocking. The radio was playing an old Frank Sinatra ballad. Erin smiled when she saw Claire and Alex slow dancing in the middle of the room. Her head was plastered sideways against his chest. His hands were gently interlocked around her waist.

"At least close the door if you two are going to carry on," Erin suggested.

"You're disturbing the mood," Alex whined without looking up. His eyes were closed tightly and the dreamy, puppy-dog expression on his face was pitiful. For the first time in the last few days, he was able to put aside the overwhelming pressure he was feeling about the potential loss of his job.

The song ended and Claire stopped dancing. She kissed her husband on the cheek and then gave him a long hug.

"Love is in the air," Erin sang softly.

"Dr. Archer was in this afternoon. He spent about an hour going over things with us," Alex mentioned.

"He's a wonderful man," Claire immediately piped in as she made her way over to the chair. "I really feel a lot better about everything. He has such a terrific bedside manner. He's the first one who's really been able to boost my confidence."

"Thanks a lot," Erin complained with her hands on her hips.

"I didn't mean—"

"I was just kidding. But that's great about Dr. Archer," Erin told her friend. "So you must be feeling great."

"This is the best I've felt in weeks," she said, slowly lowering herself into the chair with Alex's help. "I haven't had a single contraction or any spotting. The medicine is really working. The baby must love it too because he only wakes up long enough to give me a couple of good kicks."

Erin smiled at Claire and then placed a hand on her shoulder. Her ebullient attitude was a far cry from the despondent and disillusioned one she was expecting. Whatever Dr. Archer had told her must have done the trick.

"It's really great to see you so upbeat," Erin said.

"Dr. Archer said we may be ready to do the surgery within a week or two."

"That's terrific, Claire. I can't begin to tell you how happy I am for you." Erin looked across the room at Alex. He was grinning from ear to ear, obviously sharing in his wife's excitement. "What do you think about all this, Dad?"

"Are you kidding? I feel great. For the first time it really seems like it's going to happen."

Erin gave Alex the thumbs-up. She was trying her best to share in their excitement but she was a little surprised at their total disregard for the potential risks of the operation. Having the surgery was only the first step. She had discussed the long list of possible complications with Noah, and when all the facts were in it still seemed like a fifty-fifty shot at best. Erin could only wonder if Archer had painted a rosier picture than he should have. It was a little reminiscent of what she thought the clinic in Mexico City was probably doing. Irrespective of what he had said, Erin realized this was hardly the time to rain on their parade.

"Are you going to be able to stay for the surgery?" Claire asked Erin.

"Are you kidding? I wouldn't miss it for the world. I have plenty of work to do on the story. My editor isn't expecting me back in Washington until the end of the month."

Claire stood up and hugged her friend.

"I was hoping you'd say that. I feel so much more comfortable with you around." Claire pushed a few strands of hair off her forehead and held both of Erin's hands. "By the time I'm ready to have the surgery, you'll know this place backward and forward."

"I'm only a nurse, Claire, and this is pretty high-tech stuff that wasn't exactly around when I was still practicing. You're giving me a lot more credit than I deserve."

"No, she's not," Alex said. "We're counting on you to keep an eye on things."

Erin shook her head. "Okay, guys. You're starting to embarrass me."

"I'll be on a trip for the next three days," Alex said. "I left my itinerary with Claire in case you need me. I'm going to run back to the hotel and get a shower." He walked over to Claire and kissed her. "I'll be back in an hour or so."

"Erin said good-bye to Alex and sat down on the end of the bed. "You're a lucky woman, Claire. Alex is one in a million."

"He's been great," she said with a genuine smile. "I don't think I could have handled any of this without him."

For the next hour or so Erin and Claire talked about everything under the sun. Erin was overwhelmed to see how grounded Claire had become in just two days. Having totally lost track of the time, Erin eventually looked over at a small digital clock on the nightstand next to Claire's bed.

"I have to get going," she said as she stood up and grabbed her purse.

Claire frowned. "Where are you off to?"

"I'm going to get some dinner," she said quite casually.

"Some dinner?"

"That's right."

"I see," Claire said. "Who are you getting some dinner with?"

Erin put her hands on her hips. "I don't recall mentioning that I was going with anyone."

"And I don't recall you mentioning that you weren't."

Erin now folded her arms in front of herself. She knew Claire was playing a mind game with her.

"Why don't you just ask me?"

"Ask you what?" Claire questioned, as if she had no idea what her friend was talking about.

"You're hopeless," Erin said as she walked toward the door.

"Don't let Dr. Gallagher keep you out too late. I think he may have surgery in the morning."

Erin stopped dead in her tracks, waited a few seconds and then turned around.

"I don't remember saying anything—"

"Have you slept with him yet?" Claire asked with a wide-eyed look of anticipation.

"Good night, Claire. I'll see you tomorrow."

"Just tell me if he was a good lover or not."

"What?"

"Well, is it true what they say?"

"I don't know. What do they say?" Erin asked cautiously.

"That if you're good in the operating room, you're even better in the bedroom."

Erin emptied her lungs of a deep breath. She knew if they took the teasing out of their relationship it would be like stripping the *Mona Lisa* of her smile.

Erin took the few steps back to Claire and whispered, "I

could tell you some great things, but it might put you into labor. I'll see you tomorrow."

"I'm willing to take the risk."

"I'm not," Erin said without hesitation.

"I'll be pouting all night and won't be able to sleep."

"Then ask the nurse for a pill," Erin said, laughing as she walked out the door.

Chapter 16

Noah was already in the lobby when Erin stepped off the elevator. He had dispensed with the white coat and was wearing black cuffed dress slacks, a powder-blue dress shirt and burgundy penny loafers.

"Are you ready?" Erin asked as she approached him, wondering why he was dressed as if he were going to a fraternity rush.

"Let's go."

They made the short walk to his car and within a few minutes were heading north toward Fort Lauderdale. Erin looked back at the Miami skyline as they went over the newly constructed flyover. Their conversation had been continuous and fairly light. There were a million things on Erin's mind about the institute, but she decided there would be no business talk unless Noah broached the topic.

"Where are we going?" she asked.

"Well, it's a bit of a drive but there's a restaurant in Fort Lauderdale that I love. It's in Port Everglades on the water."

"Sounds great."

Twenty minutes later, Noah pulled into the valet parking at

Burt and Jack's. Erin got out of the car and gazed across the calm water. A large cargo ship, brightly lit by multiple spot-lights, was tied up on the opposite shore. An enormous crane swung smoothly over her deck. Several men, working in groups, toiled to unload dozens of massive wooden crates.

Erin loved the smell of the salt air and took a moment to take in a few deep breaths. It was a clear, balmy evening with no wind to speak of. A crescent moon hung high over the port.

The entrance to the restaurant was canopied and framed with lush plants in large pots. A stocky man in a black tuxedo with a full head of bushy gray hair greeted them as soon as they walked in.

"Dr. Gallagher, it's nice to see you again."

"Thank you," Noah answered as he shook the maitre d's hand. "Do you have a table on the water?"

"Of course, Doctor," he said as he picked up two large menus and escorted them to a small table with an excellent view. As soon as they were seated, a young woman in black pants and a white dress shirt took their drink order.

"This is a beautiful place," Erin said as she looked around at the vaulted ceilings, beautifully framed oil paintings on the walls and the regal oak tables and chairs.

"I try to get up here at least once a month," he told her. "How's the story going?" he asked as he opened the menu.

"I've uncovered some interesting things," she said.

"Really? What types of things?"

Erin tilted her head to the side. "We're in a beautiful restaurant and you're done with work for the day. Are you sure you want to talk about the institute?"

"Sure. I'm kind of interested in what you've found out. Maybe I can help you with some of the background material."

Erin raised her eyebrows and remained silent as the wait-ress placed a Long Island iced tea in front of her and a vodka martini in front of Noah.

"You have to understand that I'm not an investigative re-porter, but it seems like there are some strange things going on."

Noah took a sip of his drink and then placed the glass down.

"What kind of strange things?" he inquired as he picked up the toothpick with the olive on it and then dropped it back in the drink.

"Are you sure you want to hear this?"

He rubbed his five-o'clock stubble and laughed. "Yes, I already told you. I want to hear."

"I spoke with Carl Chandler."

"Carl's a good man. What did he have to say."

"He gave me a lot of basic information. He also mentioned Freeman and Archer didn't get along too well."

Noah shrugged. "I think I mentioned that to you too."

"It seems Freeman had an interest in the financial framework of the lab but was purposely left out of the loop. He didn't have any idea how much money was coming in or where it was going."

"I'm not sure it was Freeman's job to worry about the financial end of things," Noah said as he took another swallow of his drink. "It's been my experience that most researchers don't want to be bothered with such mundane matters as the day-to-day management of the lab. As long as they're getting the scientific equipment and staff they need, they're usually pretty happy."

Erin shook her head. "I don't think it's quite that simple," she said with a slight hesitancy. "I think Freeman discovered something that he wasn't supposed to or . . ."

"Or . . . what?"

Erin picked up the soft linen napkin from her lap, refolded it, and then replaced it. "I'm not sure. I don't think Chandler's exactly sure either. But he did say something about Freeman biding his time until the right day came."

"What's that supposed to mean?"

"I don't know," Erin said, raising her voice slightly. Noah took a quick look around. "I'm sorry. I'll lower my voice." She sat quietly for a few moments and then took the first swallow of her drink. Her best instincts told her that she had already gone too far.

"Are you still there?" he asked, waving his hand at her.

"I was just looking out over the water. That boat is beautiful," she said, pointing to a sixty-five-foot brightly lit yacht with about a dozen people enjoying cocktails on the stern. Noah turned and watched as the yacht gently nestled its way into the restaurant's private mooring.

"You were talking about John Freeman. . . ."

"You know," Erin whispered as she reached across the table and took his hands in hers. "Let's not talk about the institute any more this evening. We're in a beautiful restaurant and we're both supposed to be off. So, let's just enjoy it. I shouldn't have brought up anything about work." Erin felt Noah's gentle grip on her hands. She could see from his eyes that he understood.

"Okay," he agreed. "But if there are things bothering you that you want to talk about later, just let me know."

"It's a deal."

Just at that moment, a bald-headed waiter with a ruddy complexion arrived at the table and began displaying the evening's entrees on a silver platter. Noah selected the Maine lobster and Erin decided on the petit filet. Their meals were cooked to perfection and they spent the next two hours talking about their most profound regrets and the things they wanted most out of life. Noah's sincerity was evident and Erin grew more intrigued by him with each passing minute. Much to her delight, not another word was uttered about the institute.

The ride back to her hotel went by quickly. Erin decided to leave her car at the institute and take a cab over in the morning. From the time they left the restaurant their conversation never slowed for a moment. When they arrived, Noah escorted Erin to the lobby, kissed her briefly and told her he couldn't remember the last time he had so enjoyed an evening. She thanked him and kissed him again and watched as he walked across the lobby and out the revolving doors.

Noah handed the parking attendant his ticket and moved toward the curb under a broad canopy as the young man dashed off to retrieve his car. A minute or two later, Noah noticed the distinctive headlights of his car approaching. He handed the attendant two dollars and headed out of the parking lot. His mind filled with thoughts of the evening and how much he enjoyed the time he spent with Erin. He glanced down at the phone, began to reach for it and then stopped. *Calling her so soon might be a little pushy. What am I going to say? I'll look like a jerk.* Noah tapped the top of the steering wheel and then moved left as a large truck in front of him moved too slowly for his liking. He looked down at his phone again, trying to decide whether to call her or not. After a few moments of battling with himself, his pragmatic side prevailed and he decided against appearing like a lovesick puppy dog.

Erin was still in a dreamy and distracted state of mind when she ambled through the lobby. Just before she reached the elevators, she remembered she had picked up a message earlier on her voice mail that there was a package for her at the front desk. She changed directions, walked past several lavish shops and approached a young woman behind the registration desk with very short chestnut hair.

"My name is Erin Wells. I understand you have a package for me."

"Your room number, please," she asked with an easily recognizable French accent.

"Ten twenty-one."

The woman turned around, sorted through a large box containing several packages and returned with a large manila envelope with Erin's name on it. There was no return address but it had been sent via the mail. She was a little surprised because she assumed whatever was waiting for her had been sent by her office in Washington. Erin accepted the envelope from the woman and thanked her. It was rather thick and well secured with several strips of cellophane tape. On her way to the elevator, she flipped the envelope over a couple of times, again noting there was no return address. There was nobody else on the elevator and the ride to the tenth floor took only a few seconds.

Once in her room, Erin sat on the side of her bed and immediately opened the envelope. There were well over a hundred pages of information bound by a plastic spiral ring in a notebook. Erin thumbed through the document quickly. It was obvious that the material was scientific in nature. In addition to many handwritten notes, there were pages of calculations, graphs and computer printouts. But only after a much closer look did she realize that she was looking at the raw data of the animal studies done on Tocalazine, the drug Carl Chandler had told her about and the one Dr. Freeman was working on.

More than a little confused, Erin stopped for a moment and closed the notebook. She picked up the envelope and looked inside to see if she had missed an accompanying letter of explanation. There was nothing, but she did notice a Miami postmark. She drummed her finger across the binding, wondering who could have sent this to her . . . and why it was sent anonymously. Dr. Freeman had been quite specific that the research at the institute was strictly confidential.

Still deep in thought, Erin placed the document on her night table and went into the bathroom. She turned on the shower, adjusted the water to a suitable temperature and then slowly undressed. A moment later, she was in the shower enjoying the warm pulsating jets of water but still grappling with the enigma of who had sent her the report. She'd need expert help with respect to understanding the data, and if anyone could help her make the right connection, it was Herb. After about ten minutes, she turned off the shower, stepped out and toweled off. She reached up, removed the terry-cloth robe provided by the hotel and put it on.

Returning to her room, she picked up the report, walked over to a club chair on the opposite side of the room and sat down. Reaching up, she turned on a long gooseneck lamp with a silver base. Before she began reading it, Erin again wondered who the unidentified individual was who had sent it to her. Many of the people who worked at the institute were aware she was writing a story. She certainly wouldn't be the first reporter on assignment to be blessed with an anonymous guardian angel. She briefly thought about the people she'd met at the institute but nobody struck her as a likely silent collaborator. Erin placed the report on her lap and stretched her arms high over her head. A lazy yawn started to build but she swallowed it before it blossomed.

With the same intensity that she prepared for her nursing boards, Erin began on page one and decided to sit right there until she had carefully studied every last page of the document.

Chapter 17

In spite of reading through it three times, Erin hadn't gotten very far with the report on Tocalazine. She had already phoned Herb, who promised to start looking around for someone who could assist her with the intricacies of the data.

Her interview with Carl Chandler had left her with dozens of unanswered questions too. Pondering his open-ended invitation to visit the lab, she decided to take a chance and see if he'd speak with her again. If he were as loquacious today, she reasoned, it shouldn't be too difficult to extract more information about Freeman's work without raising his suspicion.

When Erin stepped out of the cab, she glanced over at the research facility, stopped and studied it for a moment. It was an overcast day and the tops of the trees were dead calm. She crossed the breezeway, entered the building through a revolving glass door and went straight to the lab. She was wearing a Burberry plaid skirt, a white stretch shirt and carrying a small leather attaché.

She looked around and almost immediately spotted Chandler in his office. The door was open and there was a woman sitting across from him. When Chandler looked up and noticed her, she smiled and waved a polite hello. He waved back, stood up and came out to greet her.

"Ms. Wells, I didn't expect to see you so soon."

Erin shook his hand and took one step closer.

"I spent quite a bit of time last night reviewing every word you said, and while things were still fresh in my mind I was hoping to ask you a few more questions."

"I see."

She looked over his shoulder into his office. "But if this is a bad time, I'll be happy to come back later."

"Nonsense," he said, reaching for her hand and holding it between his palms. "I'm meeting with an interior decorator." Erin looked back at the middle-aged woman, noting she had enough makeup on to accommodate an entire Broadway production.

"An interior decorator. That sounds great."

"The institute approved a few improvements for my office, so I figured what the heck. I'm not going to look a gift horse in the mouth, as they say. But as soon as I'm done, I'll be happy to talk with you." He looked down at his watch, mumbled something to himself and then said in a musical voice, "I should just be another few minutes." He looked around and then rubbed the back of his neck. "We really don't have a comfortable place for you to wait but—"

"Don't worry about it. I'll be fine right here."

"Nonsense. Wait a minute," he insisted, looking around. "I have an idea. Why don't you wait in Dr. Freeman's office? The door's open. I'll join you in a few minutes." He smiled and pointed to the office. Erin wasn't quite sure, but she suspected he was a bachelor, and somewhere at the bottom of his gracious behavior might lie a romantic agenda.

"Thank you, Dr. Chandler. I appreciate your willingness to help me with the story. I'll be sure to mention your cooperative spirit to Dr. Archer." Erin smiled and shook his hand again. "I'll just review my notes for a few minutes and organize my thoughts."

Erin crossed the lab, entered Dr. Freeman's office and sat down in the same chair she had the day she met Freeman. Through the large bay window she could see Chandler sitting across his desk from the woman. Erin looked around Freeman's office carefully. Stacks of letters and reports cluttered his desk, leading Erin to believe that nobody had organized his personal effects or work in progress. Two cans of orange juice sat directly in the middle of his blotter.

"Thanks for being so patient," Chandler said as he entered the room. Erin was daydreaming and didn't realize he had come in until he began speaking. "You must be getting a lot of information together for your story by now," he mentioned.

"The secret of writing a good story is accurate research and plenty of background. It's a heck of a lot easier to edit it later than be scurrying around looking for material when the deadline is bearing down on you like a runaway locomotive."

"That makes sense," he said, leaning back in his chair. Erin viewed him as a harmless and silly man, not a pompous one.

"From what you've told me, Dr. Freeman sounded like a very organized man."

"There's no question about it," he agreed. "You kind of have to be in this business. But there's more to this job than just being a good scientist."

"What else does it take?"

"Many things. You have to be a diplomat, manage people well and be sensitive to the corporate side of things. Just because you're the director of a research lab doesn't mean you can operate in a vacuum." The phone rang. Chandler looked down but ignored it. "I think Dr. Freeman spent too much time collecting information."

"Really?"

"Oh, yes. Especially after he and Dr. Archer had words. He documented everything."

"Why do you think he did that?" she asked without looking up, trying to make the question sound as nothing more than routine.

He shrugged and then grinned. "Maybe for a rainy day."

"A rainy day?"

Chandler cleared his throat and then picked up the phone. He dialed a four-digit exchange and asked the person who answered if the last call had been for him. He nodded a couple of times and then hung up. Erin was a little perplexed and couldn't figure out if he was trying to get her off the track.

"Have I told you about my plans for the future research of the lab?" he asked with a serious expression. "I've had a lot of ideas over the years for improving this place, but Dr. Freeman was not a man who embraced change. Things will be different now."

Erin looked at her watch. "I'd love to hear about them."

Chandler rocked back in Dr. Freeman's chair as if he were more than comfortable in his office. For the next fifteen minutes he waxed on regarding his grandiose plans to change the lab. As hard as she tried, Erin was unable to get him back on track.

"I have a very interesting plan for expanding the staff," he began. "It would involve—"

"That sounds intriguing," she interrupted. "But that's a story in itself that we'll need an appropriate amount of time to discuss . . . and I have another interview in a few minutes, so maybe we can set up a time in the near future."

"Sure, that sounds fine. Uh . . . maybe over dinner some night?"

If there were another shoe, it had just fallen. Erin knew she was in a tough spot. If he knew she'd been out with Noah, it would be silly to concoct some story about being married or in a serious relationship with someone else. "Why don't you give me your home number?" she asked without making eye contact with him.

"Okay. If I'm not there just leave a message for me on my voice mail. I also have a beeper. I'll write that down also," he said as he tore a piece of paper off of a small pad and held it out to her.

Erin reached for the paper, folded it a couple of times and put it in her purse. "Thanks again for everything. I'll be in touch."

"I'll look forward to it."

Chandler held the back of Erin's arm as he escorted her to the exit. She counted the steps. Not knowing when she might need him again, Erin said a pleasant good-bye and headed back to the main hospital.

Chapter 18

Erin was grateful that the weekend had passed uneventfully. She had used the time to visit Claire, put the finishing touches on an old assignment and do some sight-seeing in Coral Gables. Noah had spent most of the weekend at the hospital but had managed to break away late Saturday night to meet her for a drink at her hotel.

Exasperated from driving around the Jackson Memorial Hospital complex for the better part of half an hour, Erin finally spotted a visitors parking lot that wasn't full, turned in and parked her car. Making her way toward the main hospital, she stopped in front of a large relief map of the campus that was displayed in a glass case. She quickly located the school of pharmacy, took a few moments to get her bearings and then headed off to find the building. It was a short walk and ten minutes later she was standing in the lobby looking at a directory of the professors' offices. Dr. Thomas McGiver was in 616. The elevators were on the opposite side of the lobby and she was the only one aboard as it rose quickly to the sixth floor.

"My name is Erin Wells," she told Joyce Lerman,

McGiver's secretary of ten years, who regarded her without so much as a smile. "I have an appointment," she added after a few moments of silence.

Joyce rocked back in her beige manager's chair, peered into Dr. McGiver's office until she caught his attention. She then raised her hand and wiggled her fingers at him in a manner that Erin could only assume was some type of non-verbal system of communication the two of them had developed.

"Go right in," Joyce said. "He's expecting you."

Erin resisted the temptation to wiggle her fingers at Joyce deciding instead to nod politely and proceed directly into Dr. McGiver's office.

For the past eleven years Thomas McGiver had served with distinction as the director of research and chairman of pharmacology at the University of Miami School of Pharmacy. He was one of the few pharmacologists in the country who had earned a master's in molecular genetics in addition to a Ph.D. in pharmacology. He was a prototypical academic scholar and diplomat with more national committee appointments than any other professor in the School of Pharmacy. Just over six feet tall with a flat face, hunched shoulders and a barrel chest, Dr. McGiver was an average-looking man at best.

She smiled and extended her hand as he walked out from behind his desk to greet her.

"It was kind of you to see me on such short notice," she remarked, noticing the wrinkled collar on his white dress shirt and hideous dark-green tie.

"Dean Simpson is a good friend of mine. When he called yesterday and asked me to help you out, I was more than happy to be of assistance." McGiver pointed to a black leather chair and Erin sat down.

"I think my editor must know every leading medical academician in the country. When he told me he called the dean of the University of Miami Medical School my jaw almost dropped to the floor."

McGiver grinned and then rocked back in his leather chair.

His office was quite plain. The brown tile floor was in desperate need of replacement and the wood bookshelves bowed badly in the middle from the weight of the many tomes. The tarnished brass lighting fixture above his desk was almost an anachronism.

"How can I help you, Ms. Wells?"

"Please call me Erin," she said as she pulled a large file out of her attaché. "I'm doing a story on medical research and I'm trying to understand how you guys gather and interpret so much data." She smiled and placed the voluminous file containing all of John Freeman's computer printouts on his desk. McGiver leaned forward with a guarded expression and slowly picked up the folder. He pressed his lips together and looked down through his angular wire-frame bifocals. After about three minutes of thumbing through the papers, he looked up with a rather bewildered expression.

"Where was this data generated . . . if you don't mind me asking?"

"Oh," she said as casually as she could. "It's from the Fetal Institute."

"I suspected that," he said immediately. "Wouldn't it be more appropriate to request one of the researchers at the Fetal Institute to go over this with you?" He peered cautiously over the top of his glasses. "I . . . I assume you were given this material to review."

"Of course," Erin said. The image of a bolt of lightning crashing through the ceiling and striking her dead where she sat flashed in her mind. "Actually, if Dr. Freeman hadn't died, I would have gone over the material with him."

"I heard about John's death only a few days ago. I only knew him casually but he was an outstanding scientist. He was a brilliant medical researcher. We served on a couple of national committees together." McGiver looked down and re-examined the first several pages. "These appear to be data generated from animal experiments on Tocalazine. They're part of an FDA study."

"I was working quite closely with him on my story. He offered to explain his experiments with Tocalazine to me, but before we could meet, he died." Erin placed her clasped hands on the desk and sat forward in her chair. From McGiver's re-action, Erin was led to believe that he was genuinely shocked by his death. "Everybody who worked with him took his death very hard. I was uncomfortable asking any of his col-leagues to go over his research with me so soon after his death." Erin paused for a moment and then added, "I'm sure you can understand."

McGiver coughed loudly and then cleared his throat. "Okay, Ms. Wells. If you'll give me a few days to look this over, I'm sure I'll be able to make enough sense of it to help you understand his research."

"That would be wonderful. I can't tell you how helpful that would be."

"What a shame," McGiver said, his eyes unfocused.

"I beg your pardon."

"Dr. Freeman's death . . . what was it, a heart attack?"

Erin said, "I don't know if the cause of death was deter-mined but I think that's what everyone assumes."

"You are aware, Ms. Wells, that a report based on the in-formation in this material has already been submitted to the FDA, under the Freedom of Information Act you're entitled to see a copy."

"Yes, I know." Erin could see that McGiver was still a lit-tle taken aback by the thought of Freeman's death, and since he had already agreed to look at the research results, she stood up and extended her hand. "I won't take up any more of your time. It was nice meeting you, Dr. McGiver," she said as she shook his hand. "I truly appreciate your willingness to help me with my story."

McGiver stepped out from behind his desk and escorted Erin past his secretary's desk to the corridor.

"I had dinner with Dr. Freeman about six months ago. I just can't believe it. He looked so healthy."

"I only knew him for a short period of time but he seemed like a wonderful man."

"No question about it," McGiver agreed. "By the way, have you run into Noah Gallagher over at the institute?"

Erin was caught in midbreath. "Why, yes, I have. He's been quite helpful."

"Please give him my regards. We went to med school together. He was quite a character in those days."

"Really? I'll have to ask him about that," she said, wondering when she'd be able to tease him with McGiver's little tidbit. "I'll give your office a call in a few days. Maybe we can sit down and talk again after you've had the chance to look the data over."

"That sounds fine."

Erin walked down the short hall to the elevator and rode down alone to the first floor. Her meeting with McGiver couldn't have gone better. She would call Herb as soon as possible. He would know the fastest way of getting a copy of Freeman's report from the FDA.

Erin sensed there was something buried deep in the Tocalazine research that was bothering Freeman greatly. As she made her way across the lobby and toward the front door, her mind was filled with anticipation regarding what Dr. McGiver would uncover.

Chapter 19

When Erin walked through the main entrance of the Southside Hospital, she was still questioning her decision to go to the Department of Medical Records to review John Freeman's emergency-room record. In spite of her best efforts, she couldn't shake the nagging suspicion that his death was something more than a simple act of God. If a clue existed to his real cause of death, it would be in his medical chart.

Erin spotted the information desk as soon as she entered the lobby. An elderly woman with an upturned nose, too many face-lifts and bleached red hair smiled as she approached. Her name tag read Evelyn Wolfe.

"Can you tell me where the Department of Medical Records is located?" Erin asked.

"Are you a physician on staff?"

"No, I'm a nurse."

Evelyn looked down, studying the directory and hospital map in front of her.

"You're in luck. Medical Records is on this floor. Just walk past the elevators and then turn to your right. Keep going," she continued in a thick New York accent. "It's a very long hall. Medical Records is the last office on the right."

"Thank you," Erin said as the woman slid her glasses forward until they came to rest of the tip of her nose.

Erin marched past the elevators and turned to her right. The corridor was quite wide and teeming with hospital personnel and visitors heading in both directions. Financial contributors were recognized for their generosity by a series of ornate brass plaques displayed on both walls.

As soon as Erin reached Medical Records she opened the door and approached a middle-aged woman wearing a frilly sea-foam-green blouse.

"Excuse me," Erin said. "I'd like to get some information."

"How can I help you?" the woman asked.

"Several days ago my brother was brought to the emergency room. He had suffered a major heart attack."

"I'm sorry to hear that," the woman said.

"The staff in the E.R. was great but he . . . he didn't make it. In fact, he died that very afternoon," Erin explained in a cracked voice as she looked straight down. "I was in Philadelphia when it happened."

"I'm so sorry," the woman told Erin again.

"Thank you for your concern. I'm a registered nurse. My brother had the same family doctor for fifteen years. When I told him about John's death, he asked me a million questions. I . . . I just didn't have any answers."

"I see. How can we help you?"

"I was hoping that it would be possible for me to have a look at his chart."

The woman paused for a few seconds. Her expression was distinctly cautious. "I'm terribly sorry but I can't release any medical records without written authorization from the patient . . . or in this case, his next of kin. I'm very sorry," she said again as she clasped her hands in front of her.

Erin watched the woman carefully as she spoke, and from her eyes she felt there might be a chance of changing her mind. "I understand," Erin said in a voice just above a whisper, and then started to walk away. Just before she reached the door, she stopped, turned around and renewed her plea. "My brother wasn't married and our parents died several years ago. Would that make me the next of kin?"

The woman behind the counter sighed and then smiled. "I guess it would. Did your brother's family doctor request a copy of the records?"

"Actually, I told him I would bring a copy home with me. But I'm sure if I call him, he'll be able to contact your office. He really wanted . . . No, wait a minute."

"What is it?"

"I just remembered. He's on vacation. He said he'd be gone for two weeks . . . but I guess it can wait until then."

The woman looked at Erin, reached back on her desk for a small notepad and then picked up a pen.

"What was your brother's name?"

"Oh, thank you. His name was John Freeman."

"I'll need the exact date of his death."

"It was October fourth."

The woman tore the piece of paper off the pad, folded it once and said, "I'll be right back."

"Thank you again," Erin replied, and then stood in front of the desk waiting for her to return. With her usual level of impatience building, she picked up a pencil and started tapping the desktop.

The woman was extremely cordial and compassionate and Erin's conscience was starting to gnaw at her a little for deceiving her. She took a quick peek at the woman's desk. There was a delicate porcelain sculpture of a young mother holding her newborn baby and an eight-by-ten framed photograph of three children on a wooden fence.

"Here's the chart," the woman said as she approached Erin. "I made a copy for you. There really isn't too much. Just an E.R. record."

"That's a start," Erin said as she reached out and accepted the papers.

"Can I ask you to sign this authorization before you

leave?" the woman asked just as Erin was about to mount a hasty retreat.

"Of course. Where do I sign?"

The woman pointed to the bottom of the page. Erin reached for the pen in her hand. She knew she was looking at her and the last thing she wanted to do was appear indecisive and arouse her suspicion. Without giving it another thought, she signed Erin Carney and handed the pen back.

"I hope these documents give you the closure you're looking for. If your family doctor has any questions, please ask him to call me. My name is Helen Deal."

Erin folded the papers and placed them in her purse. She thanked Helen again and left the office. As she passed Evelyn Wolfe, the woman who had helped her when she first arrived, Erin waved and thanked her again. She moved through the lobby quickly, arrived at the exit and waited for an elderly couple to negotiate the revolving glass doors. After a few moments, she followed them out and then headed for the parking lot.

"Excuse me," said a stocky man dressed in a purple Los Angeles Lakers T-shirt and baggy chinos as he approached the information desk. He smiled, looked down at Evelyn's name tag and continued, "I was supposed to meet my sister here but I was delayed in traffic and I'm afraid I may have missed her. I wonder if you might have seen her?" Frank Grafton's manner and voice were quite charming. He had watched Erin cross the lobby five minutes earlier and had no difficulty in giving Evelyn a precise description of what she was wearing.

"Oh," she said with a lengthy sigh. "I think you may have just missed her."

Grafton pressed his lips together in mock despair.

"I was afraid of that. We were supposed to visit an old friend together . . . her name's Cynthia. She was admitted with a gallbladder attack."

Evelyn looked somber and then rolled her eyes up. "I had my gallbladder out eighteen years ago. I could tell you stories that would make your hair stand on end."

"My goodness," he said, shaking his head. "Cynthia's going to have surgery tomorrow." He then paused for a moment, scratched his head and said, "It just occurred to me that she was recently married and I can't for the life of me think of her new last name." Grafton reached into his pocket, pulled out some papers and began to unfold them.

"There must be some mistake," Evelyn informed him.

"Mistake?" he asked.

"Yes. Your sister went to the medical records department. Not to one of the patient floors."

"Are you sure?" he asked with a perplexed look.

"Oh, absolutely. I gave her directions myself."

Grafton said, "Well, I guess I'm a little confused. Maybe the best thing to do is just go call her. I left my phone in the car."

"You're welcome to use our phone if you'd like."

"That won't be necessary," he said. "Thank you very much for your help."

Evelyn acknowledged his courteous comment and watched as he left the hospital. He took his time crossing the parking lot, deep in thought and forced to admit he hadn't given Erin Wells enough credit. *Never underestimate the enemy.* It was an old worn-out admonition, but what it lacked in creativity it made up for in wisdom.

Grafton found his Explorer, opened the door and climbed in. There weren't too many reasons Erin Wells would have gone to the medical records department at Southside, he reasoned. Backing out slowly, he felt an obligation to make a phone call, but after further reflection decided to step up his surveillance for another day or two before reporting what he suspected.

●   ●   ●

The ride from Southside Hospital back to the Hotel Inter-Continental took Erin only fifteen minutes, but in her impatience to review the chart it seemed more like an hour. As soon as she valet parked the Firebird, she went directly to her room. After removing the copy of John Freeman's medical record from her purse, she sat down at a small antique desk in the far corner of her room.

The chart was only five pages. The main face sheet contained basic patient information such as initial vital signs and symptoms and was really of no help. The remainder of the pages contained lab results, records from the respiratory therapist and the nurse's notes. From her experience as an RN, Erin knew the most accurate and detailed description of what occurred could usually be found in the nursing notes.

The last page was a dictated death summary from the attending E.R. physician, Raymond Kincaid. It seemed fairly comprehensive compared to others she had seen, and Erin began reading it carefully. She noted from the time of the dictation that he must have done it at the end of his shift.

From what she could tell, John Freeman had arrived with barely a heartbeat and no blood pressure. He received several rounds of the standard medications routinely used to restore cardiac function and correct the high acid content in his blood. After a reasonable attempt, Dr. Kincaid decided to cease any further efforts at resuscitation.

Erin shook her head a couple of times and then turned to the nursing notes. They were quite complete and legible, but much to her chagrin, there was no mention of blood and urine tests. Erin knew that when dealing with an unexpected cardiac arrest in a relatively young person, it was a matter of routine to send off a battery of tests for a toxicology report, which would generally detect any drugs, legal or otherwise, in the patient's bloodstream and urine.

The room was a little warm. Erin walked over to the thermostat and tapped the tiny plastic lever down to about seventy degrees. She glanced over at her phone. When she saw there were no messages, she turned her attention back to the medical record.

Erin flipped back to the main E.R. cover sheet. Each hospital had their own specific format, but in general the information was more or less the same. Studying the sheet slowly from top to bottom, her attention was caught by a small box in the lower left-hand corner with the heading "Tests Ordered." Assuming this referred to X rays, Erin was just about to shift her focus when she noticed the last entry in the column was "Tox. Screen."

"That's it," she said aloud.

She quickly returned to the last page of the nursing notes where a computer printout of the blood-test results was fastened. She skimmed down through the many sets of arterial blood gases, electrolytes and other basic studies looking for the toxicology report. But when she reached the end of the reports, she found nothing. Redoubling her efforts, she began from the top and reviewed the entire section again. There wasn't a single report from the lab regarding any drugs or other substances found in Freeman's specimens. She looked up, tapped her lower lip a few times and then dropped the record on the desk.

She felt the room getting cooler and listened as the air conditioner droned softly. Reaching into the top drawer of the desk, she pulled out the Greater Miami phone book and looked up the number for Southside.

The operator picked up the call on the third ring. "Southside Hospital. How may I direct your call, please?"

"Medical Records," Erin answered in a cracked voice as her anxiety mounted. A brief pause and two rings later, a woman answered the phone.

"This is Mrs. Deal."

"This is Erin . . . Carney calling. I was just in your office about an hour ago."

"Of course," she answered. "Have you had a chance to look at your brother's records?"

"Actually I have," Erin told her as she picked up the papers and turned to the lab section again. "I was wondering if you could tell me if the chart is complete?" Erin was well aware that many of the toxicology screens for some of the less commonly used drugs could take several days to run, and perhaps the results hadn't made it back to the chart as yet.

"The chart should be complete, Ms. Carney. What area were you particularly interested in?"

"The toxicology report. I see from the chart that a screen was drawn but I can't seem to locate any of the results."

"Well, let's see. Your brother's death was a week ago. The longest turnaround time I've seen is forty-eight hours. Even allowing time for filing and placing the report on the chart, it should be there."

"I . . . I don't know what to say," Erin said softly.

"Let me check one thing, but I have to get to my computer. Can you hold for a moment?"

"Of course."

Erin reached into her purse and pulled out a roll of cherry LifeSavers. She had acquired the habit in nursing school and it was indeed a rare time when she didn't have at least one roll close at hand. For her last birthday, her editor gave her twelve packs of the candy and a gift certificate to the dentist of her choice.

"I just checked the computer, Ms. Carney. Our records show the chart is complete. I would suspect that the tubes of blood were never sent off."

Erin squeezed the phone a little harder to her ear. "I'm not sure I understand what you mean."

"It's quite a common practice in the E.R. to draw all kinds of blood tests and then never send them off."

"Why would that be?"

"When the nurses are caring for a very sick patient they routinely draw every color tube they can think of and just wait for the physician to tell them which tests to send to the lab. When the smoke clears they discard the tubes they didn't use."

"I see," Erin said slowly as she moved next to the desk.

"Here it is . . . a Dr. Kincaid ordered a tox screen. He wrote it on the chart himself. I can tell by the handwriting."

"In that case, you might want to contact Dr. Kincaid and see if he remembers ordering the tests. If he does, then I guess we can contact the lab and see if they actually ran them."

"That's an excellent suggestion. I think I'll give the E.R. a call and see if I can speak with him. Thanks again for all of your help."

Erin slowly replaced the receiver and sat back down in front of the desk. She liked Helen Deal and hoped her cooperative and trusting nature wouldn't come back to haunt her. Hopefully, Erin's unorthodox inquiries wouldn't come to the attention of any of her supervisors. She again dialed the hospital and asked to be connected to the emergency department.

"Emergency, Frank Myers," a man with a husky voice answered.

"My name is Erin Carney. Dr. Kincaid recently took care of my brother. I was hoping to have a word with him the next time he's scheduled to work. Can you possibly tell me when that will be?"

"I'm sorry, Ms. Carney. We have a policy against releasing information about the doctors' schedules, but since he's working today and standing about five feet from me I'll see if he can come to the phone."

Erin was elated with her good fortune. She listened to the background music for about thirty seconds before he picked up the call.

"This is Dr. Kincaid. How can I help you?"

"Thank you so much for taking my call, Doctor. My name is Erin Carney. As I mentioned to the gentleman who answered the phone, you recently cared for my brother. His name was Dr. John Freeman. He was the director of research at the Fetal Institute."

There was a brief silence before Kincaid answered. "Yes, Ms. Carney. It was a tragic case. I'm very sorry for your loss. Sometimes when a . . . a man such as your brother comes in with a massive heart attack, we're able to do something. But in his case . . . well, I'm afraid we just couldn't . . ."

"I'm sure you did everything possible," she said. "I'm a registered nurse and earlier today I picked up a copy of my brother's medical record for our family physician. I noticed something that concerned me a little and I was hoping you might be able to shed some light on it."

Erin closed her eyes and crossed her fingers. She knew this was a long shot and was already a little surprised that Dr. Kincaid had discussed even the most general details of one of his patients with someone who, for all intents and purposes, was an unidentified stranger.

"I'd be happy to if I can," he said without a hint of hesitation.

"I noticed that you ordered a tox screen but I couldn't find any of the results on the chart. Do you know if the tubes were ever sent off to the lab?"

"Absolutely. In a case like your brother's it would have been malpractice not to. In fact, I remember looking at some of the results in the E.R. later that same day."

Erin sat forward in her chair, unable to believe what she had just heard. "Were there any abnormalities?"

"As I recall, there were none. But I only saw the most preliminary of the results and they were the handwritten ones. But by now all of the results should be either in the computer or on the chart."

"I see," she said slowly.

"If you don't mind me asking, Ms. Carney, is there a particular reason you have an interest in toxicology results? Was your brother on any medications? We never were able to get a good medical history."

"No, it's just that he was in such good health. I guess I'm just trying to understand what happened."

"You said you were a nurse?"

"Yes, that's right."

"Well, to be perfectly frank, I don't understand it either.

We are seeing more and more men coming in with bad heart attacks but your brother was different."

"Really?" Erin asked while she pulled out her small notebook and pen. "In what way?"

"It was mostly in his response to the medications I gave him and his cardiac rhythm. We just couldn't get his heart going no matter what we did. That's not usually the case. We even put a temporary pacemaker in."

"I got the same impression from reading his chart," Erin told Kincaid as she started to jot down some notes. She jammed the phone between her shoulder and ear and flipped the notepad to the next page. "I worked in a cardiac care unit for two years."

"Are you sure your brother never had any heart problems?"

"I'm quite sure he didn't."

"It's certainly puzzling," Kincaid said. "I'm very sorry that we couldn't do more, Ms. Carney."

"As I said before, I'm sure you did everything possible."

"Is there anything else I can help you with?"

"No, not at this time. If something comes up, is it all right if I call you again?"

"Absolutely."

After saying good-bye, Erin walked across the room and sat down on the end of the bed. She closed her eyes for a moment and thought about John Freeman's death. From his voice, Kincaid sounded like a fairly senior emergency room attending who had probably supervised hundreds of code blues in his career. She found it interesting that he viewed Freeman's death as unusual. What concerned her more, however, was the fact that the full results of the tox screen were not part of Freeman's chart. Kincaid confirmed he had ordered the tests and actually seen some of the results. That had to mean they were at least sent to the lab. The question at hand was whether the more sophisticated tests for poisons and other drugs were ever run at all. Southside had an enormous lab and Erin reasoned that they probably handled all their own toxicology.

Erin fell backward, her head landing on one of the three down pillows. She wondered if there was a way to get into Southside's lab's computer system and access the results of John Freeman's toxicology report. She was tired and the more she tried to organize her thoughts, the more drowsy she became, and within a few minutes she had fallen into a restless sleep.

Chapter 20

Standing in the lobby in front of the in-
stitute's main elevators, Erin watched as the red digital display over the door went from two to three and then froze
there. Her impatience getting the best of her, she took a step
forward and tapped the large black call button several times
in rapid succession. It was almost seven p.m. and she was
anxious to spend some time with Claire.

Erin's thoughts turned to her conversation with Dr. Kincaid, causing her to wonder if she would ever be able to uncover the results of Dr. Freeman's toxicology tests. The
elevator door finally opened and Erin stepped in. She was
alone in the car as it rose to the second floor. She smiled for
a moment when she thought about the short afternoon nap she
had stolen, something she hadn't done in years. The door
opened silently, and she stepped out and started down the corridor.

Not wanting to disturb Claire if she was sleeping, Erin
pushed the door open slowly. As she suspected, Claire was fast
asleep. A woman dressed in white pants, a pink top and a small
nursing cap stood at the side of the bed with her back to Erin.

"What the hell are you doing?" Erin demanded.

The nurse attending to Claire's IV stopped immediately and turned around. Her expression was startled but at the same time mindful.

"I beg your pardon?" she asked in a guarded tone.

Erin renewed her question in a lower voice as she looked down at Claire, who remained asleep. "I asked what you were doing."

"And who might you be?" the nurse inquired.

"My name is Erin Wells. I'm a registered nurse and Ms. Weaver's best friend." Erin looked carefully at the woman for another few seconds. She had a syringe in her right hand and was in the process of reaching for the injection port on the IV tubing. She was less than five feet tall, and Erin was quite certain she wasn't the same nurse she'd seen in Sarah Allen's room.

"My name is Consuela Diaz. I'm the nurse caring for your friend this evening."

With her eyes bolted to Consuela's, Erin took a few steps forward. "You still haven't answered my question."

Consuela was an experienced nurse who had handled as many difficult situations as anyone with RN after their name. She had been a staff nurse at the institute for seven years. A single mother with two kids and a mortgage payment that kept her up at night, her record at the institute was spotless. She was an attractive woman, with haunting black eyes, an athletic figure and a petite mouth.

"I'm attending to the IV," she said calmly, as if she were dealing with an unpredictable patient.

"The charge nurse informed me that all IV medications are added in the pharmacy," Erin pointed out.

"Yes, that's quite true."

"Then if that's the case, what are you putting in the IV?"

Consuela capped the needle and placed the syringe in her pocket. "Perhaps we should call the charge nurse, Ms. Wells. I don't think I like the tone of your voice. As a nurse, I'm sure you understand that the medications this patient is receiving are none of your business."

"Why don't you simply answer my question?"

Consuela reached into her pocket and removed the syringe and a small bottle. "It's saline, Ms. Wells. I'm merely irrigating the IV. I'm not adding a medication." Consuela took a few steps forward, opened her hand and extended it. "You're welcome to examine it if you like."

"How do I . . . know what's really in the syringe?" Erin asked in desperation, starting to feel a little bit foolish.

Before Consuela had the opportunity to respond, Claire opened her eyes and sat up. "How long have you been here for?" she asked Erin.

Erin smiled and walked toward her bed. "I just got here a few moments ago."

Claire looked over at Consuela's perturbed expression.

"Ms. Wells has some concerns about what I might be adding to your IV," Consuela said.

Claire looked puzzled. "I don't understand, Erin."

"It's nothing. I was just being a mother hen." Erin turned to Consuela. "If I've said something to offend you, I apologize. We've all been under a lot of pressure and I'm very worried about my friend. I hope you'll overlook my overzealous concern."

Consuela remained straight-faced. "There's nothing to apologize for, Ms. Wells." Consuela turned her attention back to the IV, irrigated the line and then started for the door. The tension in the room was obvious to everyone. "The IV's working fine now," she said. "I'll come back later, after visiting hours."

Claire's expression remained confused even after Consuela had left the room.

"What's going on, Erin? What did you say to Consuela? She looked pretty upset. She's been my nurse several times. She's very caring and compassionate."

"I made a mistake, Claire. I acted impetuously. I'm sure

Consuela understands. Believe me, it's happened to all of us. She'll get over it. I promise."

Claire propped her pillow behind her and sat up a little higher. "Do you want to tell me what's going on here?"

"I just told you. There's nothing going on. I made a mistake. Let's just forget it. Okay?"

"Sure," she said as she reached for a glass of water on her nightstand. "How's the story coming?"

Erin put on the best smile she could. "I'm still gathering information. I haven't even started writing it yet."

Claire got out of bed, walked across the room and looked out the window. Standing with her forehead pressed against the window, she watched the headlights of the cars moving in a steady stream across Arthur Godfrey Road.

"How many more interviews do you have?" Claire asked.

"To tell you the truth, I'm not sure."

"What do you mean?"

"Well, I'm kind of doing them one at a time and using each interview to decide who to speak with next." Erin yawned, waved her hand as an apology and added, "It seems to be working out fairly well."

"Why shouldn't it? This is a great place," Claire said with confidence. "More people should know about it."

"And they will, but it's not as if I write for *People* magazine, Claire. Our circulation is almost exclusively professionals in the field. Outside of doctors and nurses, not too many people read the *AMA News*."

"Didn't you tell me one time that if you hit on something particularly interesting that sometimes one of the national magazines picks it up?"

"Yes, that has happened from time to time."

"And as along as we're on the topic of the institute, how's your relationship with my doctor going?" Claire asked, turning away from the window.

Erin was quite familiar with the devilish smile on Claire's face. Erin closed her eyes and shook her head. "Don't you have enough on your mind without worrying about my personal life?"

"Actually, I'm kind of getting bored around here," Claire confessed. "I'd love to hear some juicy gossip. Especially about your tawdry little love life."

Erin walked over to the nightstand next to Claire's bed and reached for some plump green grapes in a decorative wicker basket. She and Claire were quite close, but for some reason she felt reluctant to discuss the details of her relationship with Noah.

"It's going okay," she said in a casual tone.

Claire leaned her head forward and wiggled her finger at Erin as if she were calling a kindergartner over.

" 'Okay'? What's that supposed to mean?"

"Okay means . . . okay."

"Boy, this is like pulling teeth," Claire complained. "Since when have you been so aloof about things?"

"I told you. I don't want to burden you right now."

"Erin, I'm going to have fetal surgery. I'm not dying, for goodness sakes. Now c'mon, I want to hear what's going on. I hope this isn't about him being my doctor. Because if that's the case, believe me, I couldn't care less."

Erin eyed Claire from across the room. She loved her dearly and was starting to feel both uncomfortable and foolish trying to conceal things from her. "Okay, here it is. He's very special."

"What do you mean exactly?"

"He's just . . . so different from most of the guys out there. He's very in touch and incredibly intellectual . . . but . . ."

"But what?"

"Well, he's kind of a . . . how did he put it? Oh yeah . . . a dinosaur. His work at the institute comes before everything, and it seems like he's always struggling to keep the little boy in him from popping out." Erin turned and glanced up at the TV for a moment. She reached for the remote control and muted the volume.

"How does he feel about you?" Claire asked.

"I think he really likes me."

"Did he say that?"

"Not in so many words. It's just something I feel."

"You've covered a lot of ground in just a few days."

"It's more than just a time thing. When he calls me, he's so easy to talk to. When we're together . . . I don't know where the time goes." Erin set the remote control back on the dresser. "We've gotten to know each other very well in a short period of time."

"Is that so? Just how well are we talking here?" Claire asked with an affectionate smirk.

"I beg your pardon," Erin answered in an animated huff. "Are you asking me if we've slept together?"

Claire raised her hands straight over her head and then turned her palms up so they faced the ceiling. "That's exactly what I'm asking you. But from that silly look on your face and that longing in your voice, I think I already have my answer."

"Good, then I don't have to say anything."

"I'm looking for confirmation here."

"Forget it."

"You were never into casual sex, Erin. So I guess you must really like this guy."

"The fireworks and harp music are definitely there."

Erin checked the small digital clock on the dresser. She smothered a yawn before walking over to Claire and giving her a long bear hug. "I think your attitude about the surgery is great. This baby's going to do just fine," she told her as she patted her swollen tummy a few times.

"Thanks."

"Listen, I'm going to head back to the hotel. Will you be okay? I'll be back first think in the morning. When's Alex due back?"

"He's getting in late tonight. I'll be fine. I'll see you tomorrow." Erin walked back over to the dresser and picked up her purse. "I'm very happy for you," Claire said. "Nobody deserves happiness more than you do."

•   •   •

It was nearly ten p.m. when Erin finally made it back to her hotel room. As soon as she flipped the light on and threw her purse on the bed, she flipped on the TV. After one quick lap around the channels, she settled on an old Clark Gable movie. She was just about to plop down on the bed when she noticed the orange message light on her phone was flashing. She picked up the receiver and followed the prompts to access her voice mail. There was only one message.

"Erin, this is Herb. Give me a call when you get in. I'm at home. I have the laboratory results on that IV bag you sent up here."

Erin quickly exited the voice mail, reached for her purse and pulled out her calling card. She had long since committed Herb's phone number to memory and within a few moments his line was ringing.

"Herb, it's Erin. I just got in."

"Where have you been?" he asked in a sleepy voice.

"Out, Herb. I've been out. It's only ten p.m., for goodness sakes. Not everybody goes to bed right after dinner. In case you haven't noticed, there's a whole world out there."

Erin heard a major yawn and then there was a pause.

"I guess that whole world out there, as you put it, has just kind of passed me by. I'm just a poor country editor trying to squeeze out a small living for himself. My boring life has been one wife, one child and one job. It's not much but it's all I have."

Erin realized that she could trade sarcastic comments with Herb all night. It wasn't as if they hadn't done it a million times before, but she was a little anxious to hear about the laboratory findings.

"When did you get the results?" she asked.

"Late this afternoon."

"Why didn't you call me sooner?" she inquired impatiently.

"I don't know, Erin. Maybe it had something to do with trying to get this month's issue put together in time to go to press. I guess playing James Bond wasn't exactly number one on my priority list. Now do you want these results or not?"

"Sorry . . . and yes I'd like very much to hear what they found."

"Well, it wasn't too much. When I gave the IV bag to my friend, she wanted to know what type of patient it had come from."

"What did you tell her?" she asked as she moved the phone to her opposite ear. He wasn't moving very quickly but she didn't want to offend him by hurrying him to the point.

"I told her it was from an obstetric unit. Isn't that correct?"

"Absolutely, close enough—now what did they find?"

"She said the contents of the IV bag were pretty standard. A dilute saline solution, some potassium and the usual vitamins they add."

"That sounds pretty routine," Erin said in a discouraged tone. "Was there anything else?"

"Uh . . . yeah. There was something called pit . . . pitress . . . Oh hell, I can't pronounce it. Let me get the report. I'll be—"

"Pitressin?" she asked with a sharp intensity in her tone as she changed the receiver to her opposite ear. "Did they say there was Pitressin in the IV?"

"Yeah, that was it. She told me it was a very commonly used drug on an obstetric floor. Have you ever heard of it?"

"Have I? You bet your life."

Erin could feel an annoying tug of anxiety at the top of her stomach as she tried to figure out why Pitressin, the most common drug used to induce labor, should be in a patient's IV where the main goal of therapy was to prevent labor at all costs.

"Erin? Are you still there?"

"Yes, Herb. I'm here."

"You're not saying anything. That's not like you."

"It's nothing. Do you think you could fax me a copy of the report right now? I have a fax machine in my room." She looked down at the machine and then gave him the number.

"I don't see why not. I'll do it as soon as we hang up. Is there something going on down there I should know about?"

In spite of her dry mouth, Erin swallowed hard. "To be honest, I'm not sure. I'll call you in a few days . . . oh, and by the way, thanks for setting me up over at the University of Miami. I think they may be able to help me."

"Don't mention it. I'm not sure I like the sound of your voice, Erin. Listen . . . do you want me to come down there?"

Erin smiled. "Not yet, Herb. I promise if things start to heat up I'll give you a call." After a few minutes of failing to change her mind, Herb begrudgingly agreed and assured her he'd give her a call tomorrow.

Erin slowly set the receiver down then picked it up immediately and paged Noah. She sat down on the side of the bed and stared across the room at a very boring commercial oil painting of a fruit bowl. Erin had been a nurse long enough to know that mistakes happen. Wrong medications and dosages are given to patients with an alarming and disturbing frequency. The Pitressin in the IV bag could have simply been a mistake, but what about the nurse she saw adding something to the IV. Was that a *mistake* too?

Erin reached in her purse, pulled out a small spiral notepad and started jotting down some notes to jog her memory. She stopped for a moment, thinking about how enlightening it might be to review Sarah Allen's chart.

Within five minutes of paging Noah on his digital beeper, her phone rang.

"Hi, Erin," Noah began. "How was your—"

"Where are you?" she interrupted.

"Uh . . . I'm on my way to the institute. One of my patients has developed some postoperative bleeding. Why?"

"I have to talk to you."

"Okay, but I may be working pretty late. I'll give you a call first thing in the morning and we can—"

"No, not tomorrow, tonight, Noah. It's important."

"Are you okay?" he asked after a few moments of silence.

"I'm okay," she assured him.

"I'm pretty sure I won't have to operate, so why don't you meet me in my office in about an hour?"

"Can you just come get me in Claire's room. I'd rather wait there for you."

"No problem. I'll be there as soon as I'm done."

As soon as she hung up, Erin grabbed her purse off the bed, picked up the fax Herb had sent her and then bolted out of the room.

Chapter 21

Grafton's Explorer was in a space toward the back of the Hotel Inter-Continental's parking lot. The engine was idling quietly. On the front seat next to him was a crumpled paper bag with wrappers from his Big Mac and fries stuffed down inside. The car was cold enough to hang meat—the way he liked it. Grafton was dressed in black Dockers and a blue work shirt with the top two buttons open.

He removed the headphones, placed them on the seat and flipped open the glove compartment. He removed his cell phone, tapped in a number and waited for the answer he knew would come before the second ring.

"It's Grafton. The monitoring device is working perfectly. She just got off the phone with her editor. I'm afraid she knows there was Pitressin in the IV bag."

"Are you sure?" came the guarded but calm response.

"I'm sure."

"Anything else?"

"I've been tracking her movements pretty carefully. She's been a pretty busy lady," Grafton said.

"Yes, I'm well aware of all that."

"How would you like me to proceed?" he asked.

"It's time to turn up the heat a little. Go ahead with that we discussed yesterday but nothing more. Are my instructions clear?"

"Yes, but I would also recommend we consider terminating Claire Weaver's reason for being at the institute. If she should disappear, so would Ms. Wells. I think it's—"

"I don't pay you to think, Mr. Grafton. I pay you to carry out my instructions. If it's of any comfort to you, the matter of terminating Claire Weaver's pregnancy sooner than later is under consideration."

"I didn't mean to—"

"I'm sure you didn't. Good evening, Mr. Grafton."

The line went dead. Grafton lowered the phone and stared at it for a moment before tossing it back in the glove compartment. He looked up just in time to see Erin handing one of the attendants her claim ticket. He reached over, picked up his baseball cap and fitted it squarely on his head. He tapped the steering wheel with his fingertips, watching for Erin's car to be brought around. "Turning up the heat," he said softly. "Perhaps my recollection of yesterday's conversation isn't as vivid as I thought it was."

Waiting for her convertible, Erin looked out over Biscayne Bay. A group of bright spotlights illuminated the first twenty or thirty feet of the bay. The water was calm. She glanced at a plump pelican sitting peacefully atop a wood piling that protruded a few feet above the surface.

Erin thought about it for a moment and then decided not to put the Firebird's top down. She pulled out of the parking lot and headed east across the causeway. The traffic was sparse. A canal, bordered by a broad grassy shoulder and a series of widely spaced olive trees, paralleled the street. Erin lowered the window about halfway and set the radio to a mellow jazz station.

She was just starting to daydream about Noah when the lights of a rapidly approaching car appeared in her rearview mirror. She gazed back and glared when she realized the car was a little too close for her liking. The lights were higher than a standard sedan and she assumed it was a sport utility vehicle. It was a four-lane road and Erin wondered why the car didn't simply pass her on the left.

After a few moments, the car abruptly pulled out and slowly accelerated until it was directly next to her. She glanced over at the driver but she couldn't make out his face, only that he was wearing a cap.

It was in the next few seconds that Erin realized something was wrong. Instead of speeding up and passing her, the car suddenly swerved to the right, instantly slamming into the front of hers. The powerful impact forced the back tires of the Firebird to skid out with a deafening screech. Erin screamed and instinctively jerked the wheel to the left as she felt her car flying off the road toward the olive trees. As soon as she hit the wet shoulder, the back end of the car skidded out farther, sending it sailing through the first group of trees and directly toward the canal. Erin reared her shoulders back and slammed on the brakes. The rear of the car bucked hard, which started the small convertible spinning toward the canal.

Grafton slowed his car and pushed the brim of his baseball cap up. He watched with an emotionless expression as the image of Erin's car in his rearview mirror skidded out of control with no hope of recovery. He would have preferred to stop and admire his work, and revel in what he presumed to be the last few moments of Erin Wells's life, but he resisted the temptation. Instead he gently squeezed the accelerator, reached over and picked up his cell phone.

Erin screamed again, closed her eyes and pushed her locked arms against the steering wheel in a bracing maneuver. A moment later, the passenger side of the car smashed into a small tree. With her eyes still tightly shut, she prayed the impact would be enough to prevent her from going into the canal. She sensed the car slowing and she opened her eyes. It was dark and her vision was obscured by a dense framework of dangling branches, but just when she thought she might be out of trouble, the front end of the Firebird took a fierce dip over the embankment, and like a roller coaster starting down the first drop, plummeted straight down.

The impact of the front end of the car against the water sent her head flying forward against the steering wheel. The impact must have been oblique and did not trigger the air bag. She was conscious but stunned and didn't even notice the steady stream of blood running down her forehead. Still dazed, she felt the car slowly drop, as if it were passing through a fluffy white cluster of clouds. There was a tranquil rushing sound in the background that reminded her of rolling waves breaking against a sandy beach at night.

By the time the water hit Erin's face, the Firebird was totally submerged in ten feet of water. The sudden shock immediately roused her from her twilight state. She knew immediately where she was and exactly what had happened. Murky water continued to rush in through the partially opened window. In spite of her desperate situation, Erin remembered from a safety course she had once taken that when enough water had entered the car the pressures would equalize and she would have a chance of opening the door.

Water continued to fill the car. Terrified and gasping for air, she reached over and pulled up the lock. Only a few inches of space below the convertible top now remained unflooded. Erin pushed her face against the top and turned it to the side. Heaving one last long breath, she yanked as hard as she was able on the handle and banged her shoulder over and over again against the door. She could feel it start to move as the cold water crept up against her gaping mouth.

She was still hitting the door when she heard a strange noise behind her. It almost sounded like the many times she had stood beside her mother as she shredded old sheets into rags. Water filled her mouth and, soon, the desperate need for oxygen began to disappear, her mind could no longer focus and a sense of complete relaxation began to consume her.

Her shoulder had just bounced off the door for the last time when she felt a hard tug on her shirt collar. The last thing she remembered was two powerful hands grabbing hold tightly under her arms and pulling her upward.

"Give her mouth to mouth," the young woman in a white tank top and denim shorts yelled at the man who had just pulled Erin from the canal. Josh Oshea was twenty-five years old, in perfect shape and a rookie social studies teacher at Beach High. He was well over six feet tall and an even two hundred pounds.

"She's not breathing," he told his girlfriend as he leaned over Erin, fitted his mouth over hers and then gave her three quick breaths. "Go call 911 right now." He reached down and placed his fingers on the side of Erin's neck. Her carotid pulse was strong and he immediately gave her three more controlled breaths. Just as he removed his mouth and readied himself to start chest compressions, Erin coughed violently and then tossed her head from side to side, spitting out a mouthful of water. Josh could see her chest moving and watched as she opened her eyes.

His girlfriend came running back clutching a cellular phone in her hand. "The ambulance is on the way."

"I think she's going to be okay," Josh said, looking down at Erin. "She's breathing on her own. Can you hear me, miss?"

Erin waved her hand at him, continuing to cough but less violently. "Sit me up. Please help me up," she asked in a hoarse voice with her eyes now wide open.

Josh reached forward and gently cradled her neck under his palm. With a gradual effort, he slowly helped her to a sitting position. There was just enough light from the streetlamps for him to see she was pink and breathing fairly well on her own.

"What happened?" he asked.

She heaved a deep breath and then cleared her throat, and then coughed several times before saying, "I . . . I don't know. I think I was forced off the road."

"I saw your car go into the canal. We were headed in the opposite direction," Josh said.

Erin was now breathing steadily through her mouth but her chest ached with each breath she took. The wind picked up for a few moments, chilling her entire body.

"I don't know how I'm going to get back to my hotel."

Josh smiled. "I wouldn't worry about that right now. There's an ambulance on the way. I think they'll want to take you to the hospital to get checked out. I'm sorry about your car. I had to cut a hole in the top to get you out."

"Under the circumstances, I forgive you. Anyway, it's a rental," she said.

The wail of a siren filled the night. Erin looked up just as a police cruiser and an ambulance arrived. Leaning forward, she pulled her knees in for support. A young paramedic with blond surfer hair approached carrying a large orange box of medical supplies. His partner, an older man with a stout physique, thinning hair and muscular arms, trailed a few steps behind.

"What happened?" the younger paramedic asked, placing an oxygen mask on her face. Erin was soon breathing normally and the realization that she was alive was starting to sink in.

"I'm not quite sure. One moment I was on my way to see a friend and the next I was underwater. If it weren't for the young man standing next to you I'd be a statistic by now."

The paramedic looked over at Josh, who had his arm around his girlfriend.

"We're going to take you over to the Ryder Trauma Center at the University of Miami just to make sure everything's okay." He turned for a moment. "The police are going to want to talk to you," he told Josh.

"If I give you the number, would you page Dr. Noah Gallagher and ask him to meet me there?" Erin asked. "He's a physician on staff at the Fetal Institute." Her voice was much clearer now and she coughed only rarely.

"As soon as we're rolling, I'll be happy to have him paged."

The two paramedics gently lifted Erin onto the stretcher and then strapped her in. They were moving quickly and were about halfway to the ambulance before she remembered that she hadn't thanked the young man who had risked his life to save hers. Raising her head for a moment and taking an extra moment or two to focus, she saw Josh out of the corner of her eye. He was standing several feet away talking to a police officer who was taking notes on a small pad. She waved and then caught his eye. He smiled, winked at her once and then gave her the thumbs-up.

Once they had her hoisted into the ambulance, they locked the stretcher into place and slammed the rear doors shut. As the ambulance bumped along Alton Road, Erin felt her eyes start to flood with tears.

Chapter 22

"If it makes you feel any better, it could have been a lot worse," Noah offered in a vain attempt to console Erin. "The emergency room doctor could have recommended an overnight admission for observation." Erin sat in the front seat of Noah's car looking straight ahead with her arms folded in front of her, thinking back about the events of the evening.

By the time she had reached the Ryder Trauma Center, she was having no difficulty breathing and the immediate shock of her near-drowning experience was starting to subside. When she arrived, there were a number of seriously injured patients being cared for, but the attention and treatment she received were prompt and professional. Erin's clothes were still sopping when she arrived. A sympathetic orderly liberated a pair of oversized surgical scrubs from the operating room and gave them to her to wear home.

"I could have been killed," she insisted for the third time. "And the only reason they didn't make me stay overnight is because you're a doctor and threw your weight around."

"I didn't throw anything around. I spoke to the E.R. physician and he thought it was perfectly safe to discharge you."

"I wonder why the idiot who ran me off the road didn't even stop?"

"How do you know that?" Noah asked.

"The officer who interviewed me at the hospital told me."

"Maybe the driver didn't know," he hypothesized.

Erin's face was dour. "He didn't simply cut me off, Noah. He slammed into my car and kept right on going. There's no way he didn't know I was in trouble. How could he just take off like that?"

"I'm sure he didn't intentionally drive you off the road, Erin. He must have just panicked." Erin looked over at Noah. Until he made the comment, she hadn't given serious thought to whether the collision was, in truth, just an accident. Noah stole a quick peek in her direction and then added, "Anyway, you can't worry about that now. The police will sort it all out," he assured her and then reached over and put his hand on hers.

"Thanks for coming to get me. I guess I should have mentioned that sooner."

"I'm just glad you're okay. I called the car rental agency for you. They're going to bring you another car tomorrow."

"Maybe I should request a submarine," she pouted.

Noah laughed. "At least you haven't lost your sense of humor. By the way, what was it that you wanted to talk to me about that was so urgent?"

Erin closed her eyes and let her head fall back against the headrest. When she had charged out of her hotel room three hours earlier, she fully intended to brief Noah on everything she had discovered about the institute. She knew now that it was an impetuous decision that might lead to a rift in their relationship. Her intuition told her she was on to something, but the pieces of the puzzle were scattered and separated by large gaps. She trusted Noah but he hadn't been overly receptive to listening to her about possible problems at the institute. Sharing information with him prematurely might backfire on her. It simply wasn't the right time.

"It was nothing, Noah. I overreacted to something that Claire told me about one of the nurses. I'm just so worried about her."

"Is everything okay now?" he asked.

"Yeah, I spoke to Claire and we straightened everything out."

Noah turned back toward Erin with a bewildered look. "When did you speak with her?"

"Right after I spoke with you. Just before I left for the institute," she answered without making sure the fabrication held water.

"I don't understand. If the problem was taken care of, why did you leave for the institute?"

Erin's throat felt as if someone had just snugged a noose around it. In the next instant, a warm flush, the same one she always felt when she was caught in a lie, eased down her face and neck.

"Uh . . . because I wanted to see you, of course."

"I could have come over to your hotel after I was done."

"I . . . I had cabin fever," she explained. "I wanted to get out."

Noah shook his head. The befuddled expression remained. "You're a disturbed woman, Erin."

She squeezed his hand. "You disturb me."

"That's great," was all he could manage.

Erin closed her eyes again and the next thing she knew Noah was tapping her shoulder. She looked up just as the hotel valet opened the door. Noah stepped out of the car and accepted a parking ticket from a second valet.

"Shall we leave it up front for you, sir?" he asked.

"That won't be necessary," Erin told the young man from the other side of the car. "He won't be leaving until the morning."

Noah looked at the attendant and shrugged his shoulders. "You heard the lady," he said.

Noah walked around to the other side of the car and put his arm around her. She responded by letting her head fall on his shoulder. They walked slowly through the lobby, straight to the elevator and went upstairs to her room.

"I wonder if the police will find that jerk who ran me off the road," Erin said to Noah as she kicked off her shoes. Noah opened the mini-bar and poured them each a glass of wine.

"It might be tough," he said. "They really don't have much to go on. How are you feeling?"

"I'm starting to feel a little scared again. The only thing I can remember is that cold, filthy water creeping up my neck." Erin's body shuddered from a sudden chill that flashed down her spine. She took the wine from Noah's outstretched hand and climbed on the bed. Using two pillows for support she sat up against the headboard. The wine was dry and she savored the first few sips. "I'll never be able to fall asleep," she complained.

"Why don't you finish your wine and close your eyes?"

She frowned at the suggestion. "I have to take a shower," she announced.

"But . . . what?"

"I'll be out in a few minutes, Noah. Don't panic. Romance is the farthest thing from my mind right now."

"I didn't mean to imply I would expect—"

Erin was off the bed and on her way to the bathroom while Noah was still searching for something appropriate to say. As he listened to the drone of the shower, he wondered what made her so uninhibited. Five minutes later she emerged from the bathroom dressed in the hotel's white terry-cloth robe with her hair wrapped in a towel.

"I feel much better," she said, climbing back on the bed. She grabbed one of the pillows, laid down on her stomach with her feet on the headboard and stared at Noah, who hadn't moved from the chair. Erin let her head fall on the pillow as they talked about the evening's events again. Noah successfully changed the topic to some of the dumber things he'd done in college, hoping Erin would become sleepy listening to his boring stories. Within a few minutes her eyes were closed and she was breathing deeply.

Noah tiptoed to the closet, reached up to the top shelf and removed a folded blanket. When he gently laid it across her, he could smell the fresh coconut fragrance of her shampoo. After a few moments of looking down at her, he turned out the lights, found his way back to the club chair and let his head fall back against the soft headrest.

Eight years of surgical residency had trained him to sleep anywhere, and after a few minutes, he too was fast asleep. His last thoughts were of Erin.

Chapter 23

"Am I on time?" Erin asked as she poked her head into the treatment room. Claire was lying on the examination table with a half-folded white sheet draped across her abdomen. An IV bag containing normal saline dripped slowly into her vein.

As part of the routine tests before a fetal procedure, Noah had requested an amniocentesis. Claire had already been sedated, leaving her eyes glassy. Alex stood beside her with an anguished expression.

"We're just about ready to get started, Ms. Wells," Dr. Halliday, the attending obstetrician, said as he put on his sterile gown and gloves. Robert Halliday was a compulsive physician who measured every detail of his patients' condition with precision. Harvard trained and a consummate gentleman, Halliday was a sensitive and reassuring doctor. "Claire insisted you be here. We're glad to have you."

"I'm happy to be here," she said.

It had been almost twenty-four hours since her car plunged into the canal. Erin was struggling to put the harrowing event behind her but she was experiencing horrific flashbacks of the dank blackness of the canal as the water slowly engulfed her. She considered calling Herb to talk about what happened but decided it might open a regrettable can of worms. As perceptive as he was, there was no question that he'd pick up on her suspicions that the accident may not have been a product of pure chance. The mother hen in him would emerge, resulting in a one-way ticket back to DC for Erin.

"She's kind of out of it," Alex said, his face a little gray.

"Are you sure you want to stay for this?" Halliday asked him.

"I promised Claire."

"Well, okay, but if you feel faint, let us know," Halliday whispered.

"You can count on it," Alex assured him as he pulled one of the small metal chairs a little closer.

Halliday nodded at the nurse, who injected another two cc's of Valium into the IV. Halliday watched as Claire slowly closed her eyes. Reaching over, he picked up a needle and syringe that contained the local anesthetic and took a step closer to the table.

"You'll feel a little mosquito bite, Claire. After that you shouldn't feel a thing." He looked over the top of the sterile drapes but Claire was too heavily sedated to respond. In the next moment he inserted the small needle just under her skin and raised a weal about the size of a quarter.

"What will you be testing for?" Erin asked Halliday.

"There are a number of things. The technology has advanced dramatically over the past several years. We're now able to do DNA analysis and test for such diseases as sickle-cell anemia, cystic fibrosis and many others." Halliday replaced the small needle and syringe on the sterile table and reached for a larger syringe with a much longer needle. Applying counterpressure to the abdomen and using an ultrasound transducer for guidance, he gently inserted the needle through Claire's abdomen into the amniotic fluid and applied steady back pressure on the plunger. The result was an immediate flash of pale yellow fluid into the syringe. Halliday removed the syringe and then passed off the specimen to the nurse. Holding the needle in place, he attached a second syringe and again aspirated enough fluid to fill the entire barrel.

"What else do you test for?" Erin asked.

"Well, there are certain markers that if present in abnormally high quantities can signal the presence of a number of birth defects."

"What type of markers?" she asked.

"Oh, there are several, but alpha-fetoprotein is probably the most important."

"I don't recall that one . . . but it's been a long time since I did my obstetric rotation," she confessed. "What does alpha-fetoprotein test for?"

"Neural tube defects," Halliday began. "Which would be malformations of the brain and spinal cord. Some of the diseases can be devastating. It's a very helpful test, especially when it comes to genetic counseling."

"I see," Erin muttered, a little disappointed in her lack of knowledge and feeling that modern nursing was starting to pass her by.

"That ought to do it," Halliday announced as he removed the needle and reached for a Band-Aid. "We'll have to be very careful over the next several hours."

"Why's that?" Alex asked, now sitting down with most of the color still drained from his face.

"Because one of the risks of amniocentesis is premature labor. It's a very small risk but we still need to keep a careful eye on your wife."

"I see," Alex said, dropping his chin to his chest.

"You're looking pretty peaked," Erin told him. "We may need to keep a closer eye on you than Claire."

"Very funny, Erin."

"Now you know how we feel back in the cabin when you guys at the controls are bouncing us all over the sky like Ping-Pong balls."

Alex tried to look up. "I'm not sure it's the same thing."

The nurse finished placing a second Band-Aid on Claire's

abdomen and pulled the gray pin-striped hospital gown down below her waist. An orderly dressed in blue scrubs helped Claire off the table and onto the cart.

"When can we expect the results, Doctor?" Erin asked as the orderly started to gently wheel Claire out of the room.

Dr. Halliday finished putting his white coat on, grabbed Claire's chart off the counter and tucked it under his arm.

"It should just take a day."

"You're not expecting any problems?" Claire asked in a bit of a slur.

"Your pregnancy is progressing fine. I don't anticipate that there will be any complications."

Dr. Halliday led the group out of the treatment room. As soon as the nurse was finished filling several smaller tubes with Claire's amniotic fluid and placing them in the outgoing lab box, she turned off the light and closed the door behind her.

With his feet crossed and propped up on the control panel, Frank Grafton continued to watch the main surveillance monitor even after Claire was wheeled out of the treatment room. He had watched the entire procedure, and to his untrained eye, he assumed it had gone off without a hitch. As soon as he pulled the videotape out, he swung his feet off the console, flipped the monitor off and left the security office.

Five minutes later, he was standing outside the treatment room. He glanced down at his watch, confirming he had another twenty-five minutes until the next lab pickup. Having checked the schedule and armed with the knowledge that the next patient scheduled for an amniocentesis was not for another hour, he was quite comfortable slipping into the treatment room. The room was not monitored routinely by the surveillance system. If one of the security agents had a reason to monitor the room, which was highly unlikely, they would have to specifically activate the camera.

After quietly closing the door behind him, Grafton walked directly to the lab pickup box and removed the sample tubes containing Claire Weaver's amniotic fluid. Each tube was color coded, and as soon as the blue-topped tube was in his hand, he placed it in his pocket. Reaching into his opposite pocket, he then removed a tube of amniotic fluid in an identical blue-topped tube, which he then placed with Claire's other specimens in the lab pickup box.

His purpose completed, he opened the door and stepped out into the hallway. He looked down and checked his pager. There were no stored messages. Things were quiet. Making his way slowly down the hall, he stopped for a moment and smirked. He could only imagine the expression on Claire Weaver's face when she was informed of the results of her amniocentesis.

Chapter 24

"I wish I could be of more help," Thomas McGiver told Erin.

"I'm not quite sure I understand," Erin said as she walked out of Claire's room, pressing her cell phone more tightly between her ear and shoulder.

"I've reviewed the data sheets you left with me and I'm having a hard time making heads or tails of them," he explained.

Erin paused for a moment and then asked, "Is it because your lab is different from the institute's?"

"Absolutely not. We all employ similar scientific methodology and research techniques. It's practically a universal language, Ms. Wells."

Erin stopped a few feet in front of the elevators. "Can you offer a guess as to why Dr. Freeman's work is so difficult to interpret?"

"It's hard to say. Some of what you gave me makes sense. The data is accurate and organized. But some of the experimental results don't seem to jibe."

"In what way?" she asked.

"A substantial part of the experimental results you asked me to look at involved the teratogenic effects of Tocalazine. Now if—"

"Excuse me, Dr. McGiver, but you just lost me. What do you mean by terra . . ."

"Teratogenic. It refers to the ability of a chemical, or in this case, a drug, to cause birth defects. It's a very important part of the basic studies that are FDA-required on all medications before they're approved for use."

"You mean like the birth defects caused by thalidomide?"

"That's exactly what I mean," he said.

"I'm not sure I understand what you're saying. Are you suggesting—"

"Ms. Wells, let me offer a suggestion. I'd like to take a much closer look at Dr. Freeman's work."

"I'm not sure I understand."

"A more intensive review of the research product would place me in a better position to discuss the matter with you."

From the tone of his voice and his resolute expression, Erin quickly realized this was not the time to press the point. McGiver was in no way obligated to help her, and the last thing she wanted was to lose his cooperation and willingness to remain involved.

"I know how busy you are. I won't take up any more of your time," she said. "You have my phone number at the hotel. I'll look forward to hearing from you."

Erin started back toward Claire's room. Stopping for a moment at a bright silver water fountain, she leaned over, took a slow drink and looked at the distorted nature of her reflection.

The question that plagued Erin was a simple one. With more time and effort, would Thomas McGiver be able to make heads or tails of Dr. Freeman's work?

Chapter 25

"Claire's amniocentesis went fine," Erin told Noah. She dropped the last ice cube in his scotch, walked across the room and handed him the drink. Noah was seated in a white club chair with his tie loosened down to the second button of his powder-blue dress shirt.

"I heard," he said.

"So soon?"

"Erin, she's my patient, for goodness sakes. I spoke to Halliday this afternoon. He said the results should be out tomorrow." Noah jiggled the ice around the rim of the glass for a few seconds and then took the first sip. Erin watched him for a moment. He looked tired. She knew he had been in the operating room all day, and noticed just a hint of puffiness under his eyes. She was hoping her black leather pants and beaded bustier would bring a little life back to him.

"Apart from you, Halliday's the first normal person I've met at the institute," she said, sitting down in front of him on the floor and crossing her legs in a Buddha position.

"Thanks a lot. It's a real comfort to know that you regard

one of the most prestigious hospitals in the country as nothing more than a 'Ripley's Believe It or Not.' "

"Don't misunderstand me. I think the hospital's okay."

"Really. You could have fooled me."

"It's the people running it I wonder about."

Noah smothered a short laugh and took a second sip of the Dewar's before setting his glass down on the small circular table next to him. "Are all reporters like you?"

"What do you mean?"

"So suspicious about everything." Noah picked up his drink and held it in front of him as if he were about to propose a toast. "Sometimes a cigar is just a cigar."

"Well, in this case, I think if you take the wrapper and binder off the cigar you might find some pretty interesting things."

"For example?"

Erin had already had two glasses of Chablis and was afraid the wine was talking. The issue of sharing some of her concerns with Noah had been on her mind constantly since the night of the accident. They were seeing each other quite a bit and were growing more and more comfortable with each passing day.

"My perspective may be clouded by my concern for Claire but I find it hard to dismiss certain facts."

Noah pursed his lips. "For instance?"

Erin stood up, walked over to the refrigerator and took out the bottle of Chablis. She poured about half a glass and then walked back over to Noah and sat down.

"Are you sure you want to hear this?"

"Absolutely."

"Will you try to be objective and not get up on your high horse because it concerns the institute?" she asked.

"I promise."

"Some of the things I may have already mentioned to you," she began with a hint of hesitation, still concerned he might not take her seriously. "Remember I told you I accidentally went into Sarah Allen's room and interrupted a nurse adding a medication to her IV?"

"Yes, I remember."

"Well, it turns out there were traces of Pitressiin in the IV bag."

"How do you know that?"

"I had the bag analyzed."

"You what?" he asked incredulously.

"I took the bag out of her room and sent it up to a lab in Washington to be analyzed."

Noah's changing expression stopped somewhere between appalled and dumbfounded. He crossed his arms in front of him and rolled his tongue along the inside of his mouth. Erin wanted to say something but decided to wait.

"I . . . I guess I don't understand. Why would you do that?".

"I don't know. I guess it was because I was told that the nurse I saw attending to Sarah Allen's IV didn't exist."

"Who told you that?" he asked.

"The charge nurse on duty that night."

"Did you say the lab found Pitressin?"

Erin nodded. "That's what I said."

"But that doesn't make any sense."

"My feelings exactly," she said with a slight head tilt.

"Maybe the lab was wrong," he suggested.

"I guess that's possible. But let's just suppose they weren't. Why would there be Pitressin in her IV? As I recall from nursing school, Pitressin acts to initiate labor, not stop it."

"It doesn't make any sense," he admitted, tilting his head back and looking at the ceiling.

"And what about John Freeman?" she asked.

Noah lowered his eyes and looked directly at Erin. "What about him?"

"There was something funny about his research. And his unexpected death is a little hard to swallow as well."

"Why?"

She forced a coy smile. "Because I went to Southside Hospital and reviewed his emergency room chart."

Noah sat forward in his chair and took a final swig of his drink. "Are you saying you got a copy of his medical record?"

"I did."

"That's illegal, Erin."

"That's not the issue," she told him flatly.

"Okay then, what was so funny about his research? Everything that's come out of the lab has been scrupulously monitored by the FDA. I can't believe—"

"I brought his research to Dr. McGiver at the University of Miami. He said he was having trouble interpreting the results."

"Thomas McGiver?" Noah asked.

"Do you know him?" she asked, already knowing the answer to the question.

"Yes, we went to med school together. How did you get Freeman's research?"

"Let's just say it was given to me."

"Is that the truth, Erin?"

She looked around the room. "No comment," was her answer.

"Great. Listen, Erin, I'm a physician, not a reporter. I deal with science. That doesn't leave much room for coincidence or speculation. I don't know why the lab in DC thought there was Pitressin in the IV. All I know is that our pharmacy is run by very conscientious and meticulous people."

"I'm sure the institute's lab is second to none." She paused for a moment and gave a second thought to the wisdom of beginning this conversation. "What about research on Tocalazine?"

He shrugged. "I don't know that much about it. I'm not involved in basic research so I can't really comment on John Freeman's research."

"Something's wrong, Noah. I can feel it."

Noah looked down at her for a moment and then moved off the chair and sat down next to her. She looked straight down into her wineglass and didn't respond when he put his am around her shoulder.

"You're letting your concerns about Claire cloud your thinking. When you see she's fine, all these things you're concerned about will all turn out to have a logical explanation."

"My friend's life depends on the institute. People and things aren't always as pristine as they appear. I'm not sure of a lot of things but I can tell you this. I'm going to keep my eyes and ears open. If in the end my suspicions turn out to be nothing, then I'll be the first to admit it."

Noah pulled his legs in and hooked his knees with his clasped hands. "I can't tell you how to do your job. But I think you'll find as you accumulate more information, you'll be convinced that there's absolutely nothing out of the ordinary going on at the institute. By the way, you haven't said much about the accident."

"What's there to say? I'm still terrified to go within a hundred yards of water. And," she said, standing up and walking across the room, "I'm not sure I'd call it an accident."

Noah nodded. "Of course it was an accident, Erin. Things like that happen. The guy just got scared and ran."

"Maybe," she said, her thoughts again flashing to the blurred vision of the man with the baseball cap who was driving the car. Erin realized she hadn't persuaded Noah of anything. Sharing any more information with him at this point would be useless. The moment for damage control had arrived.

"I hope you're right," she said about the possibility of her accident being exactly that.

"I'm sure I am."

"Will you keep this conversation totally confidential?" she asked.

"I will."

"Is that a promise?"

"Scout's honor," he said.

She wasn't very surprised by his overall skepticism about her observations concerning the institute, but she was disappointed. She did believe his promise to keep their conversation confidential, but in her heart she knew the topic of the institute would come up again.

"I'm tired," she finally whispered.

"It's getting late. I better get going."

"Why don't you stay. We could sleep in, order room service and pretend we're on vacation." Noah was already moving toward the door when Erin's proposition registered. He turned around, but before he could come up with a clever response, she continued, "Don't look so enthusiastic," she teased. "I'm not that grotesque . . . am I?"

"No . . . of course not. I wasn't even thinking . . . I was—"

"It's not like you haven't stayed over before," she reminded him.

"As I recall, I slept in a chair," he said with a frown.

"What did you expect under the circumstances?" she asked.

"I didn't expect anything, of course. . . . What kind of guy do you—"

"I was driven off the road and almost killed. It's a little hard to get in a romantic mood after a midnight swim in an alligator-infested canal." Erin watched Noah wrinkle his brow and then shove his hands in his pockets. Trying not to embarrass him any further, she forced away an affectionate grin. *How could a man with such a commanding presence at work become so squeamish and clumsy every time the topic of sex came up?*

"That's totally understandable," he said, more as a doctor than a man being seduced. "I'm sure I would have felt the same way." He shoved his hands deeper into his pockets and looked straight past her.

She renewed her question. "Do you want to say over or not?"

"Uh . . . you mentioned room service—do you think they have Belgian waffles?"

Erin took a few steps toward him and then clasped her hands around the back of his neck. "If they're not on the menu now, I'll make sure they are by the morning. that's the kind of girl I am."

Noah smiled and then kissed her on the cheek. He walked over to the door and flipped the main lights off. Five minutes later they were in bed.

Chapter 26

The next morning found Claire Weaver just finishing her breakfast. She was about to take a peak at her newest book on baby names when Drs. Gallagher and Archer came through the door. From their somber expressions, she knew instantly something was wrong. She placed the book on her nightstand and propped herself up a little higher against the headboard.

"Good Morning, Claire," Archer began. "I hope you slept well."

"I slept very well, thank you. The nurses were kind enough to skip the four a.m. vital signs."

Noah smiled. "That's against protocol. I'll have to speak to them about that."

"Why don't you gentlemen have a seat," Claire suggested. "You look like you have something on your minds."

Noah walked to the other side of the room, grabbed two chairs and brought them back to Claire's bedside. Archer, who was wearing a double-breasted black sport coat, salmon-colored button-down shirt and gray cuffed dress slacks, thanked Noah and took a seat.

"We have the results of your amniocentesis," Archer said.

"I must be a pretty important patient to rate two doctors to report one simple test."

"For the most part it was normal," Noah interjected as he crossed his legs.

Claire could feel the same terror mounting as the day she was told about her baby's CCAM.

"What part wasn't so good?" she finally managed.

"I'm afraid the alpha-fetoprotein was very elevated," Archer told her as he flipped open her chart to the laboratory section. Claire watched him as he studied the chart and then listened as he cleared his throat. "That could mean we have a serious problem."

"What kind of problem?" Claire asked directly, wishing that Alex was standing beside her and not at thirty-one thousand feet in the air somewhere over New Mexico.

"Yeah, what kind of problem?" Erin echoed as she walked into the room.

Archer looked over at Claire with eyes that were asking for some guidance. "I'd like Erin to stay," she told him.

"Well, Ms. Wells, as I was just telling Claire, the AFP is extremely high."

"What does that mean?" Claire asked.

"Well, it can mean several things," Archer answered in a calm tone. "Our greatest concern is that there is something very wrong with the baby's neurologic system."

Claire turned away and gazed out the window. Erin walked over to the far side of the bed and sat down next to her.

"What can we do about it?" Erin asked, reaching over and taking Claire's hand.

"We'd like to do some further tests," Noah said.

Erin dropped her head for a few moments and then looked up. "She's already been through so much," she reminded them softly.

"The additional tests may help to define the problem," Archer said.

"What does that mean?" Claire asked in a monotone. It seemed to Erin that her jitters had now given way to despair.

Archer closed the chart and sat back in his chair. "If we determine the baby has additional birth defects besides the CCAM . . . well, you probably would not be a candidate for fetal surgery."

"What?" Erin demanded above Claire's sobbing. "I don't understand. What does one thing have to do with the other?"

Archer explained, "If the fetus has a condition that is not compatible with life, then to expend the enormous resources necessary to remove a CCAM probably isn't justifiable."

"Well, excuse me for saying it but that sounds a little cold-hearted," Erin insisted, reaching over and picking up a small packet of tissues from Claire's nightstand. She plucked one out and handed it to her friend.

"I think these conversations may be little premature," Archer offered as he fiddled with his perfectly tied Windsor knot. "We need to see the results of some further tests and then present the entire picture to the committee."

"What committee?" Claire asked.

"Once a month several key members of the institute meet to discuss each of our patients. Medical and ethical problems like this come up all the time, and I can assure you we are very careful not to make any rash decisions."

Claire crumpled the tissues in her hand. "What do you think about all this, Dr. Gallagher?"

"It's too early to say, Claire. We just got the results of the tests a few minutes ago. Actually, I'm very surprised. Usually we have some hint that there might be a problem before we get the results of the AFP."

Noah stood up and walked over to the bed. Erin had her arm around Claire's shoulder.

"I don't know what to do," she cried. "I wish Alex was here."

Noah put a hand on Claire's shoulder as well. "We should all try to remain calm until we're able to sort all of this out.

Right now we're dealing with one abnormal lab test. We need more information before making any recommendations."

Archer stood up, buttoned his sport coat and said, "I agree completely with Dr. Gallagher. We'll talk again in a few days. Now if there's anything you need in the meantime, please call me."

Archer turned and left the room. Erin looked up at Noah and signaled him outside with severe eyes and a quick head turn.

"I'm going to talk to Noah for a moment, Claire. I'll be right back."

Claire didn't complain about not being included or being left alone for a few minutes. She simply nodded and then reached for another tissue. The room felt warm to her and her eyes were heavy and swollen from crying. Her mind bounced from one thought to the next. Her initial terror had now given way to an overwhelming feeling of doom and despair. She had never felt sorry for herself but she was on the verge of making an exception.

"All I want is a healthy baby," she said, looking straight up. "Is that really asking too much?"

"Of course not," Erin assured her. "This isn't over yet. I promise you."

Erin stood up. Noah took a couple of steps back and then headed for the door. Erin made sure to close the door as they stepped out into the hallway.

"What the hell's going on, Noah?"

"You were there. Her AFP is off the wall."

"Why didn't you tell me?"

"I beg your pardon."

"I asked why didn't you inform me about the problem."

Noah's eyes narrowed. "Claire Weaver's my patient, Erin. Not you. It would be unethical for me to discuss her hospital course with you. You're a nurse, for crissakes."

"Spare me the selective medical ethics. If you know me well enough to share my bed, you know me well enough to keep me posted about my best friend."

Noah shook his head. "I'm not sure I agree with that. One thing has nothing to do with the other. Just because we've been intimate doesn't entitle you to medical information about one of my patients."

Erin took a step closer and locked eyes with him. "She's not just one of your patients. She's the closest thing to a sister I have." Erin was forced to stop for a moment, feeling the annoying pressure in her throat. "I . . . I love her."

Noah took a deep breath and placed his hands on his hips. "Erin, let's get the rest of the tests. Maybe there's been a mistake."

"Why would you think that?"

"I'm not sure. I was just surprised to see the AFP so high. Usually we have some inkling when there's a problem with the baby's brain or spinal cord."

"But that's not always the case."

"No, not always, but . . ."

"What is it? What's bugging you about this?"

"Nothing, it's just that after a while you rely on your instinct. Maybe that's a mistake. But as time goes by you develop a sixth sense about pregnancies. It's almost like you can tell right from the beginning which are the really bad babies." Noah pushed his hand through his hair and then rubbed the back of his neck.

"I assume from the way you said that you didn't feel that way about Claire's pregnancy."

"No, I didn't."

"Were there any other abnormalities in her tests?" Erin asked.

"No, everything else was right on the money." Noah stopped for a moment. "We might want to repeat the amnio in a few days."

"What for?" she asked.

"Because an elevated AFP could call for very drastic measures."

"I hope you don't mean termination of the pregnancy," Erin said as she crossed her arms in front of her.

"I'm afraid that's exactly what I was referring to."

Erin waited in silence as a tall orderly in a short white coat pushing a cart of supplies and humming an old Beatles' ballad approached. He smiled as he walked by.

"There's no way in hell Claire will ever have an abortion," Erin told him plainly.

"She might not have to, but if faced with the decision, I'm sure she and Alex will make an informed choice. All we can do is make the situation as clear as possible and present the options."

Erin let out a long breath. "Do me a favor?"

Noah's face was wary. "I guess that depends. What is it?"

"Don't schedule another amniocentesis until you've spoken with me."

"Erin, I'm not going to do anything—"

Erin held up her hand as if she were stopping traffic.

"Just do me this one favor. I'm not asking you to breach any canon of medical ethics, for goodness sakes. Just speak to me first."

Noah sighed. "I'll think about it. Do you want me to go back inside with you?"

"No, I'm sure she's too upset right now to talk about this any further. Alex is due back around dinnertime. Can you stop back then?"

"Of course."

"Call me later," she said as he started to turn.

Erin watched as Noah walked away. There was something unusual in his professional demeanor with Claire. He had lost his usual confident and optimistic tone. It was almost as if he were totally baffled by the results of the amniocentesis. Maybe Archer's presence made him uneasy. But whatever the reason, Noah wasn't himself and Erin wasn't sure why. She closed her eyes for a moment, cleared her mind and started back for Claire's room knowing full well it was going to be a tough visit.

Chapter 27

Nobody would ever miss Claudia Harris—a fact Frank Grafton pondered as he stood over her lifeless body. She was facedown with her frail arms twisted under her torso like a contortionist.

She lived alone in a one-bedroom garden apartment. In the spring of 1994, three weeks after her sixteenth birthday, she withdrew the entire twelve hundred dollars from her Minneapolis savings account, and with nothing more than a backpack, boarded a bus for Atlanta. She eventually made her way to Miami, remained a loner and made her living by any means necessary. She hadn't spoken to her parents in four years.

It had been a simple enough matter to plan her death. Her apartment complex was devoid of a security system, which made getting in a piece of cake.

Once she was asleep, he slid into her room and administered a deep muscular injection of succinylcholine. The drug, which is fast acting and a favorite choice amongst anesthesiologists for stopping spontaneous breathing, worked with predictable efficiency. The dose he chose would have been fatal to someone three times Claudia's weight. As he expected, she awakened immediately when he plunged the needle into her thigh. But she wasn't particularly strong and with his weight on top of her and gagging her mouth, it was all over in under a minute.

Grafton looked down at her limp body. Her lips were already a dark blue. She was dressed in a long pink nightshirt. There were no marks on her face or neck. Her head was tilted to the side on a big fluffy pillow as if she were in a deep sleep. Her hair was black with bangs to the middle of her forehead.

Pulling the covers up around her shoulders, he realized that he'd never been fond of her. She lacked the military precision that was essential in their chosen field. Claudia had helped him satisfactorily on several occasions, but her debacle the night she was discovered by Erin Wells adding Pitressin to Sarah Allen's IV was an unforgivable error. He had trained her better than that. Her stupid mistake made him look like a fool to the people he answered to.

Grafton left the apartment through the front door after checking the hall. It took him only another minute or two to reach his car and pull out of the parking lot. When he was a few miles away and heading across the Julia Tuttle Causeway, he reached for his cell phone and punched in a number.

"Hello."

"This is Grafton. We're all done here. There were no problems."

"I expected nothing less," came the reply. "Are you sure Ms. Harris understood?"

"We had a very long heart-to-heart. She understands the seriousness of the situation and what she needs to do."

"When will she be leaving town?"

"I told her if she wasn't gone in three days she wouldn't require any travel arrangements." Grafton had a difficult time keeping a straight face as he continued the lie. Asking someone who could put him in prison for a very long time to leave town was not exactly his first choice in dealing with the problem. His approach was a much more permanent solution.

"How can we be sure she'll comply?"

"She has a daughter in foster care," he said. "She understands what I'm capable of. I think I can guarantee you won't be hearing from her ever again. What about Erin Wells?"

"What about her?"

"She, on the other hand, is not going to go away."

"You surprise me sometimes, Mr. Grafton. We've just gone to extraordinary lengths to make sure Claire Weaver never has fetal surgery at our hospital. She'll be leaving soon enough . . . and I assure you, Erin Wells won't be far behind."

"I hope you're right," Grafton responded. "I would have handled it differently."

"Really? I thought we did try it your way, but Ms. Wells is still very much with us."

Grafton felt the long muscles of his neck lock. Having his failures pointed out to him was not something he would generally tolerate. "Not every war is won with the first battle," he said.

"You sound very much like a man who has acquired a taste for blood. As I've told you before, I was foolish enough to go along with your first misguided plan to eliminate Erin Wells. Our responses will be proportional from this point on."

"I'm not sure—"

"Just keep an eye on her. The last thing we need is to bring attention to the institute. When Mrs. Weaver comes to terms with the fact that her baby will be a neurologic monster, she'll opt for an abortion. When that happens, Ms. Wells will quickly finish up the research for her article and be on her way."

"I hope you're right."

"By the way, was it a problem getting the amniotic fluid?"

"No, it was a piece of cake," Grafton answered. "The computer kicked out three patients who have had recent amniocentesis with elevated alpha-fetoprotein levels. It was a simple enough matter to make the switch."

"It's a shame. I'm sure Claire Weaver would have had a perfectly lovely child. I'll speak with you tomorrow, Mr. Grafton. Try to remain calm. My solutions generally work."

Grafton was a little put off by the comment, assuming reference was again being made to his failed attempt to drown Erin. He accelerated down the entrance ramp to I-95, reached into his glove compartment for a pack of cigarettes and then pushed in the lighter. Killing Claudia Harris was certainly a lot easier than coming up with some half-assed extortion scheme. There was no regret in his heart about handling it the way he did.

Grafton glanced at the digital clock and then pushed the speedometer up to seventy, hoping to get home in time to catch Leno. As he took the first drag, he thought about recent events at the institute and wondered just how far Erin Wells would take all this. He then thought about Claire Weaver for a moment and smirked. *You better take the bait and go for the abortion, Mrs. Weaver, or you can kiss your little college pal good-bye.*

Chapter 28

Leigh Sierra entered the institute's administrative conference room wearing a lightweight gray wool jacket and matching black drawstring pants.

"You must be Erin Wells," she said, extending her hand. "I've looked forward to meeting you. Dr. Archer told me to give you my full cooperation."

Erin stood up and shook Leigh's hand, wondering when she would start an interview without her subject mentioning to her that Dr. Archer requested their unconditional cooperation.

"Everyody's been very helpful. I can't tell you how impressed I am with your hospital." Erin sat back down at an oval mahogany conference table with a deep finish and waited a moment while Leigh took her seat. The wall directly across from Erin contained finely crafted floor-to-ceiling wood bookcases packed tightly with a variety of medical texts and journals.

"Where do we begin?" Leigh asked.

"My understanding is that you are in charge of the clinical research program here at the institute."

"That's correct," Leigh said, placing her purse on the seat next to her.

After asking if it would be okay, Erin turned on her small recorder.

"Tell me something about your background and what sparked your interest to take a position at the Fetal Institute." Erin returned Leigh's smile and took a careful look at her face, estimating her age to be about forty. Her large hazel eyes, high cheekbones and smooth complexion made her an attractive woman. Leigh's outfit was perfectly tailored and Erin noticed immediately that her taste in jewelry was both impeccable and expensive. She was not wearing either an engagement ring or a wedding band, but her white gold earrings and diamond flower necklace were dazzling.

"I grew up right here in Florida," she began. "Just outside of Orlando. I have a master's in hospital administration and a Ph.D. in biochemistry from the University of Alabama. I came to the institute two years ago after directing the clinical research program at Interspec Pharmaceuticals."

"What made you leave that job . . . if you don't mind me asking?"

"Not at all," Leigh assured her. "It was a boring and lackluster position in a male-dominated company. I was grossly underpaid, and after the twenty-fifth executive claimed he slept with me at the company retreat . . . well, I figured it was time to move on."

Erin laughed. "I appreciate your candor but I probably won't use that in my story."

"It might jazz it up. Fetal surgery is not the most exciting stuff to some people," she pointed out with a broad grin.

Erin liked her already. Her infectious personality was complemented by her ability to meet someone and instantly make them feel like they've known each other for years.

"What's the most important thing about doing clinical research?" Erin asked.

"Honesty," she said. "We're working with actual patients every day. It's much different from what goes on in the basic research arena. We're not running rats through a maze or looking for minute molecular changes in some experimental drug."

"What are you working on now?"

"We've got a number of projects going on. We're looking at everything from psychological stress on the mothers after fetal surgery to postoperative infections." Leigh stopped for a moment, reached over and pulled a small black leather notebook from her purse. She flipped to the middle of the book and ran her finger down the page. "In all we have twelve clinical research studies in progress."

Erin looked up. "How in the world do you manage to coordinate all that and still know what's going on with each study?"

"Well, in the first place, I have a lot of help. And we have an extremely sophisticated computer system. You'd be surprised how much data you can accumulate and still keep track of."

"Are you doing any drug trials?"

"Oh yes, several. It's a very important part of what we do."

"I interviewed John Freeman and he mentioned a drug called tocolytic agent."

She nodded. "It's one of our most important experiments."

"Can you tell me anything about it?" Erin asked, a little surprised that Leigh was being so candid.

"It's a drug with a lot of potential. It has the ability to stop labor more reliably than any other drug out there."

"Really? How soon will it be available to the public?"

"Not for quite some time, I'm afraid. The FDA is a tough group. The process can take years."

Erin adjusted the volume on the recorder and turned it more in Leigh's direction. An elderly volunteer in a pink pinstripe uniform pushed a cart containing several dozen books slowly across the floor until she reached the bookcase and began reshelving them.

"I thought the drug was still undergoing laboratory analysis," Erin inquired.

"That's true; but the FDA signed off on the preliminary work and approved it for Phase I clinical trials. At the present time we're the only center allowed to use it."

Erin was surprised. "Why is that?" she asked.

"Because the drug was developed here at the institute," Leigh explained. "It's not the product of some big pharmaceutical conglomerate."

"So is the drug the answer to all the problems connected to fetal surgery."

"No, I'm afraid not." Leigh paused for a moment or two and then added, "You seem surprised."

"No, it's just that Dr. Freeman was so positive about the drug."

"And with good reason. It has an intriguing potential, but the answer to all of our problems . . . hardly."

"I see. Are there any major problems with the drug?"

Leigh looked bewildered. "Such as?"

"I don't know." Erin's plan was to remain aloof but she was quite interested to find out if Leigh had an inkling about the drug's lack of commercial potential.

"A lot of the data isn't in as yet," Leigh explained. "And as I'm sure you know, our research protocols are double-blinded, so neither the patient nor the researcher knows which patient receives the drug and which one does not. Follow-up studies haven't even started as yet."

"Yes, Dr. Archer mentioned something about that to me."

"Dr. Archer?" Leigh asked.

"Uh-huh."

"I'm a little surprised," Leigh mentioned. "Dr. Archer makes it a practice to stay out of the nuts and bolts of the day-to-day work we do."

Erim stroked her chin as if she were thinking about something. "Maybe you're right. It may have been Dr. Freeman. I've spoken to so many people it gets hard to remember who said what."

"Well, if you spoke with them at the same time, I'm sure

you'd remember," Leigh said. "The temperature would have been a little chilly."

"I'm not sure what you mean. They were both very nice to me."

"Individually they were fine but there was no love lost between them. Some felt that Freeman was terribly jealous of Archer."

Erin pushed her chair out a little and extended her legs and crossed them at the ankles. She placed her legal pad and pen on the table hoping the gesture would put Leigh at even more ease than she already was.

"We have the same thing where I work," Erin said. "I guess these things are pretty universal."

"I suppose you're right."

"I wanted to ask you what you know about the preliminary research on Tocalazine that was done in the lab."

"Not too much really. We kind of keep the two areas of research separate, but I do know the FDA was very impressed with the efficacy and safety of the drug and approved it with very few questions for Phase I clinical trials."

"But you don't have any idea of how the drug's doing?"

Leigh smiled and then looked around the library. The volunteer had finished reshelving the books and had left. There was no one else in the room except the two of them.

"Are you asking me if I've hedged a little and looked at the results?"

Erin nodded. "My curiosity would be killing me by now."

"Off the record?"

"Absolutely."

"Well, we've enrolled a fair number of patients in the study and it seems as if Tocalazine is the best thing out there for stopping labor."

Erin could feel her pulse start to quicken. She felt the burst of adrenaline but was not about to change the pace of the interview. There was one more piece of information she had to have.

"What do you think of the commercial value of a drug like this could be?" she inquired.

Leigh paused for a moment in thought. "Probably not too much. Neotech's not too interested in that industry."

"Neotech's your parent company as I recall."

"That's right. They're much more interested in acquiring specialty hospitals than promoting pharmaceuticals."

"I remember now. Someone else was telling me about Neotech. What else can you tell me about Tocalazine?"

"It's pretty expensive and we're not sure its effect is as potent in the absence of fetal surgery."

"I'd like to ask you something else."

"Sure," Leigh responded.

"What's it like working with these women? They must be on an emotional roller coaster."

"It's very exciting. As a group, I'd say they experience giant mood swings with each new piece of information they receive about their pregnancy."

"I'd like to get back to that in a moment, but I wanted to ask you if they are mostly local women or are they coming from farther away?"

"That's been one of the most interesting parts of this job," she said without hesitation. "We see patients from all over the world. It's been a real education. They seem to be a common group separated only by their native languages. As I alluded to a moment ago, their reactions are very similar."

"Do you see a lot of patients from Mexico?" Erin asked without looking up from her notebook.

"I would say we see a fair number of patients from the Latin American countries."

"Do you have any hospitals or clinics down there?"

Leigh thought for a moment. "I'm fairly sure we have a small clinic in Mexico City where preliminary evaluations are done for potential transfer to the institute. But you have to remember that I have no role in patient selection. The first time I see them is when they're admitted to the institute. We have to handle it that way to keep the research free of bias."

"Are they included in the research studies or just those patients from the U.S.?"

Leigh cocked her head. "That's a strange question."

"If you'd prefer not to answer that's—"

"No, that's okay. All of our patients are urged to participate. Some women decline, but the vast majority participate." Leigh stood up and walked over to the water cooler. Her short curly blond hair made her look more like one of the medical students than a senior-level research scientist. She plucked a small paper cup from the dispenser, filled it with cold water and then took a couple of sips before dropping it in the wastebasket. "Excuse me," Leigh said. "Would you like some water?"

"No, thank you. You seem to really like your job."

"It's incredible. Working with these women has been so personally fulfilling that I . . . I just can't articulate it."

For the next thirty minutes or so, Erin continued to ask a broad range of questions. Leigh's answers were all direct and quite responsive. She liked Leigh's down-to-earth nature, enthusiasm and effervescent personality. Her sincerity about her work was the most refreshing thing Erin had observed since arriving at the institute.

"I want to thank you for agreeing to speak with me," Erin told her, flipping off the tape recorder. "It's been a very interesting interview. Do you think we may be able to talk again?"

"On one condition," she said.

"Let's hear it."

"You have to answer one simple question."

Erin gazed up, pushed her chair back a foot or so and smiled. "Go for it."

"How did you get Noah to ask you out?"

"Excuse me."

"C'mon. This is woman to woman now."

"I'm not sure—"

"It's just that you've succeeded where dozens have failed. I'm a single mom with her eyes open."

Erin fumbled with her recorder. She wasn't offended by

Leigh's question; to the contrary, she was a little flattered that she felt comfortable enough to ask about Noah.

"I guess there aren't too many secrets around here," Erin eventually said.

"In this place? Forget it. We make Peyton Place look like a weekend Bible retreat." Both women laughed at the same moment.

"It just kind of happened," Erin admitted with a shrug.

"Well, I wish you luck. Most of us in the trenches think he's wasting his time here." Leigh looked around and then whispered, "We think he should be an emergency room doctor on television."

"I'll mention that to him," Erin teased.

"Oh my God, you wouldn't," she said, wide-eyed. "I'd die of embarrassment at the next staff meeting."

"I'm just kidding. Your secret's safe with me."

Erin and Leigh continued the small talk for a few minutes and then left the conference room. Walking down the hall they talked about the possibility of getting together for a drink to compare notes on life as a modern woman hanging on to a high-powered job in a traditionally male-dominated industry.

They said a short good-bye at the elevator. Riding up to the second floor to visit Claire, Erin thought it would be nice to have a friend like Leigh Sierra in Washington.

Chapter 29

The toxicology lab at Southside Hospital is located on the fourth floor. A large facility with state-of-the-art equipment, the lab served as a resource center for several of the smaller hospitals in the greater Miami area when they had a difficult toxicology problem.

Dressed in a short lavender jacket and a matching skirt with side slits, Erin approached the information desk. The lab technician was hunched over a fax machine and didn't notice Erin had walked in. She was stocky with very short brown hair, plain in appearance and with poorly applied makeup. Erin guessed she was about thirty years old. Her name tag read Amanda Vincent. Erin was just about to say something when the young lady looked over and noticed her. She smiled at Erin and asked if she could be of assistance.

"My name is Erin Carney. I recently visited the medical records department and picked up a copy of my brother's medical chart. He was a patient about a week ago in the emergency room. He had a massive heart attack. The E.R. staff was great, but he . . . he didn't make it."

"I'm sorry to hear that," Amanda said, looking up from the paper immediately. "How can I help you?"

Erin reached into her purse, removed John Freeman's E.R. sheet and lab reports and then placed them on the counter in front of Amanda.

"It seems that a rather complete tox screen was drawn on my brother but the results were never reported."

Amanda picked up the records for a closer look. Her hands were as stubby as the rest of her.

"Are you sure we got the blood? Sometimes the people in the E.R. draw several tubes but—"

"I'm aware they don't always send the tubes up," Erin interrupted. "But they did in this case."

"How do you know?"

"I called the E.R. attending and he assured me that he had sent them."

Amanda studied the records for a second time. "This may take me a while to track down. This is a big lab and we report to many hospitals. Anything's possible . . . including that I won't be able to find them."

"I don't understand," Erin said, trying to maintain a cooperative and calm appearance.

"Well, I guess it's like anyplace else. Specimens get misplaced, misread, misfiled and every other mis you can think of."

"Do you think you might be able to give it a shot for me? It's very important that I get the results of the tox studies."

Amanda nodded her head methodically. "I can try but I'm not sure I'll be able to locate them. The best thing for you to do is leave this with me and give me a call back. It's going to take me a while and we're swamped at the moment."

"That sounds great," Erin told her, reaching out to shake her hand. Erin's own experience working in a big hospital had been that missing lab reports could usually be tracked down if the right person was looking. Erin couldn't be sure, but Amanda struck her as someone who knew what she was doing. "When should I give you a call?"

"Give me a few days," Amanda said as she looked up.

"I really appreciate your help. In fact, I'm going to give you my phone number just in case you come up with something before I call you. Would that be okay with you?"

"Absolutely."

As Erin rode the elevator down to the lobby, she felt her trip had not been a waste of time. She had no idea what the tox screen would show but she was damn sure that Amanda Vincent was going to try to find out what happened to Dr. John Freeman's blood tests.

Driving back to the institute from South-side, Erin couldn't get her mind off of John Freeman's death. Whether Amanda would locate the results of his tox screen was a complete mystery. It suddenly struck her that she hadn't called Herb in a couple of days. She was going to need his help, and irritating him by not calling was a very dumb move.

Erin pulled into the parking lot and went directly to the lobby and then upstairs to Claire's room. When she came through the door Clair was sitting by herself staring out the window. She was wearing a pink terry-cloth bathrobe with a matching sash tied in the middle. She had a mug in her hand.

"How's it going?" Erin asked, walking across the room and tossing her purse on Claire's bed. "It's hot as hell in here, for goodness sakes. What are you trying to do, make this place into a sauna?" She reached the other side, leaned over and kissed Claire on the cheek and immediately felt the warm tears against her lips.

"You can make it cooler if you'd like," Claire said in a monotone. "The thermostat's over there behind the door."

Erin pulled up a chair and sat alongside her friend. "I spoke with Noah again last night about your amnio results. He thinks it may be worth repeating. I think he's baffled by the results."

Claire turned toward Erin. "Are you saying there's a chance my baby's not some neurologic disaster?"

"Well, I guess that's what he's going to try and find out by repeating the amniocentesis."

Claire grimaced a little and then gently covered her lower abdomen with the palms of her hands. Erin noticed it at once and pulled her chair in a little closer.

"Are you having contractions?" Erin asked.

"Just a twinge every now and then. I'm fine. It's nothing. Dr. Halliday told me to expect them from time to time."

"Is there anything I can say to cheer you up?" Erin asked as she gently locked arms with Claire.

Claire smiled. "I'll be okay. Alex and I talked for a long time this morning. He's behind me one hundred percent. Whatever I want to do is okay with him. I got a message that Noah would be in later today." Claire's facial expression was now less strained. "He's such a nice man."

"I know. He really cares about you."

Claire massaged the bridge of her nose for a few moments and then stood up. "Will you excuse me for a few minutes. I want to take a shower and wash my hair. I'll be right out. But I don't want you to leave. Okay?"

"Leave? Are you kidding? I'll be right here when you get out watching Lassie reruns."

Claire giggled for an instant, walked slowly to the bathroom and closed the door behind her. A moment later Erin could hear the steady drone of the shower. She reached for the phone, dialed a long-distance number and waited for an answer.

"Herb Porfino."

"Herb, it's Erin."

"Where have you been? Did you lose my phone number or something?"

Erin clenched her fist. "Shit," she muttered under her breath.

"What?"

"I'm sorry, Herb. I've been so damn busy that—"

"Gimme a break, Erin. You're not the first reporter to go

out on assignment. You're supposed to call in. I thought we talked about this."

"We did . . . we did."

"So to what do I owe the honor of this call?" he asked.

"I need some help," Erin told him and then moved the phone about an inch from her ear. She didn't know how he'd react but decided to expect the worst.

Erin heard a soft moan. "I should have figured that's why you were calling. Okay, Erin, how much is it going to cost me?" His tone was definitely calm and maybe a bit theatrical.

"Not a dime. I just need you to put one of the interns on a fact-finding mission."

"Sure, Erin. They're all just sitting around here doing nothing waiting for you to call in with a list of errands for them to do."

"Be nice to me, Herb. It's been a rough few days."

"Okay. What do you need?" he asked.

"The Fetal Institute is owned by a company called Neotech. I'd like to find out as much about them as possible."

"For instance?" Herb asked.

"Everything from their corporate history, board of directors, holdings . . . and then right down to their most current financials."

"Wait a minute, let me write this down," came the response. "You said the name was Neotech?"

"Yeah. And one other thing, please."

"Shoot," he said.

"The FDA recently approved a drug for clinical trials at the institute. It's called Tocalazine." She waited in silence and then added, "Maybe you should write the name down, Herb."

"Just gimme a second, Erin. You're going pretty fast."

Erin gazed up at the ceiling and counted silently up to five. "I want to see everything the FDA has on the drug."

"I'm a little rusty on my health care law so I'm not too sure how much of that is public information," Herb pointed out.

"A lot of it should be available under the Freedom of Information Act," she said, still listening to the shower in the background.

"Okay, Erin. I'll put somebody on this right away."

"Thanks, Herb. You're one in a million."

"Never mind the lube job . . . just remember, there better be a story at the end of all this."

"I don't think you'll be disappointed," she said. "I'll call you soon." Erin hung up the phone and grinned. *I must have caught him coming off the best round of golf of his life. The man's a teddy bear.*

By the time Erin browsed through the morning paper, Claire had finished her shower and was out of the bathroom. "What time is Alex due back?" she asked.

"In a few hours."

"Maybe I'll come back and we can all hang out like the old days," Erin said.

"Hang out? Sure, Erin."

"It's a date then. I'd ask Noah but I think he's still wrestling with mixing business and pleasure."

Claire walked over to the window and gazed out in silence. "They're wrong about my baby. They've made a mistake. There's nothing wrong with his brain. I know I'd feel it if there were. They screwed up the test just like Noah said. Just wait and see."

Erin walked over and put her arm around Claire. "That's not exactly what Noah said, but I'm glad to hear you with some gumption in your voice. Do you know why?"

"No."

"Because I feel the exact same way myself. My god kid's going to be a Rhodes scholar."

Claire hugged Erin and for the next hour they talked about everything under the sun except Claire's pregnancy. Erin couldn't believe how upbeat she'd become. Denial was probably at the root of it all, but amateur psychology aside, whatever was making Claire feel better was a blessing as far as Erin was concerned.

"I have another interview," Erin told her. "I'll try to come back later but I may not see you until tomorrow."

"I'll be here."

Erin decided to take the stairwell instead of riding the elevator. She stopped at the small coffee shop just off the lobby and ordered a Diet Coke with an extra slice of lemon. She sat alone at the counter wondering if she would really turn up anything concrete about the institute . . . and if she did, how in the world would she tell Claire that her baby was in jeopardy.

Chapter 30

The first thing Erin noticed when she walked into her hotel room was the blinking orange message light on the phone. Afer dropping her purse on the bed, she went directly to the phone to retrieve the message. After a tedious series of prompts, she listened as Herb asked her to give him a call as soon as she got in. There was an unusual intensity in his voice and the entire message struck her as a little curious, seeing as how she'd just spoken to him a few hours ago.

Herb picked up on the second ring.

"Herb, it's Erin. I just walked in and got your message. What's up?"

"I had an idea after we hung up and wanted to bounce it off you."

"Okay," she said, pulling up one of the chairs and sitting down. "Just give me a sec." She popped off her shoes and then swung her feet up on the bed. "That's better. Let's hear what's on your mind."

"Before I do that, I need you to tell me everything that's going on down there."

"I'm not sure I have enough to do that yet," she explained.

"It wasn't a request, Erin. This is your editor in chief speaking now, not your Dutch uncle."

Erin had spent enough time with Herb to know when he was being serious. This was unquestionably one of those times, and for the next five minutes she related every detail of what she had discovered, including her theories since arriving. Herb didn't utter a single word until she was finished.

"What do you think?" she asked, crossing her fingers and closing her eyes.

"To be honest, Erin, it may be a little thin."

"I can live with thin for the present."

"I'm not sure I can." There was silence for a few moments. "Okay, let's go with it a while longer. Do you know Sam Forbes?"

"No, should I?"

"He's handled some delicate investigations for me over the years. He's very professional, very complete and very discreet."

Erin's jaw dropped like it was made of lead.

"Are you saying this man's a private eye, Herb?"

"The best. He'll do more in a week than most of my gophers could do in a year. I think it's worth the investment to send him down there."

"I, uh . . . I don't know. I've only worked with a PI on one other occasion."

"And?"

"It worked out fine." Erin pulled her feet off the bed, stood up and walked toward the desk. She suddenly stopped and shook her head. "Wait a minute, Herb. This isn't your subtle way of sending a bodyguard down here, is it? Because if that's what all this is about . . . I'd rather—"

"Relax, that has nothing to do with it. But I will tell you he's a seventh-degree black belt in Go-ju."

"What the hell's Go-ju?"

"A very aggressive form of martial arts."

"Great, Herb. That's just who I need down here, some Jackie Chan type who—"

"Hardly, Erin. Sam has a bachelor's in business, a master's in criminology and a law degree from Columbia. He's been an investigator for a long time and only gets involved with unusual and lucrative assignments. He's not your run-of-the-mill PI snapping pictures of a guy nibbling on his secretary's neck in some dark restaurant. If anybody can help you, it's Sam Forbes."

"I'll take him," she said without stopping to take a breath.

"I've already spoken to him. He'll contact you as soon as he arrives in Miami."

"Sounds great."

"One piece of advice, Erin. Be square with this guy. Don't keep anything from him."

"Okay."

"Did you understand what I just said, Erin?"

"I hear you loud and clear, boss."

"Keep me advised, please. And Sam suggested you use your cell phone whenever possible. They're harder to monitor."

"Monitor? C'mon, Herb, I hope this guy doesn't turn out to be some—"

"Don't prejudge the guy, Erin. He can really help you. And if he makes a suggestion, I would give serious thought to taking his advice."

Following a lengthy sigh, Erin thanked Herb for his support and hung up the phone. She looked toward the bathroom and started dreaming about a long hot bath before heading back to the institute. Two minutes later, she was out of her clothes and in the white terry-cloth robe the hotel provided. The faucet was wide open. Sitting on the side of the tub testing the water with her open hand, she wondered if she'd ever really be able to get to the bottom of all this.

Chapter 31

Frank Grafton sat calmly in his car. He removed the earpiece that had just enabled him to listen to Erin's conversation with her boss. He grinned and then tossed the earpiece on the passenger seat next to him. Frank had become well connected in Miami. One hundred dollars to the right bellman was all it took to get him into Erin's room and insert the monitoring device into her phone.

"This guy, Forbes, sounds okay," he said aloud. His competitive juices flowing, Grafton reached for his cell phone and punched in a number.

"The *AMA News* is sending some high-priced private eye down here," he said.

"Is that so? When's he arriving?"

"That I don't know. But I suspect I'll have the information before he gets here. What do you want to do about all this?" Grafton asked as he reached over and picked up an empty Styrofoam cup.

"Nothing."

"Nothing? Are you sure?"

"That's correct. Just keep an eye on things. Don't get too

overzealous. We have the advantage. Are you able to intercept Ms. Wells's cellular calls?"

"I'm still working on that."

"That's fine. In the meantime, let's just sit tight and see what happens. There will be plenty of time to act later."

"Whatever you say," he said calmly. "You do recall she has Dr. Freeman's medical records from Southside. She went over there again."

"Are you sure the arrangements you made at Southside won't come back to haunt us?"

"Not a chance. They're totally secure."

"Like Claudia Harris?"

He made a tight fist and ignored the comment. "I just wish I knew why Ms. Wells went over there again."

"Do your job and find out," came the response, and then silence followed the disconnect.

Grafton shut his phone off and placed it in the center console. He leaned over the steering wheel, annoyed but in control. In order to step up his surveillance he decided to take a week's vacation from the institute.

Grafton's grip on the Styrofoam cup steadily tightened until it snapped under the pressure. Grafton knew he could never be simply a follower. He had ideas of his own. Ideas he had no intention of sharing with the people he was taking orders from. He had already decided to kill Erin Wells. The only unknown was when. But this fellow Forbes might be a different story. A classy publication like the *AMA News* could afford to hire someone with some expertise and training. Maybe even someone who was his intellectual equal instead of the usual collection of neophytes and dolts he was forced to deal with. Hopefully Mr. Forbes would stick his nose into enough wrong places to convince the right person that he was expendable.

Grafton tossed the shattered cup on the seat next to him. His thoughts intensified. His mind, as it frequently did in these situations, worked in several directions at the same time. The thrill of the hunt heightened with each breath as he meticulously laid out various scenarios he might employ to assassinate Sam Forbes.

Chapter 32

Sam Forbes stopped to fill his lungs with the fresh ozone that always seemed to follow a South Florida downpour. He looked up for a moment, noting the small cluster of amorphous rain clouds as they drifted slowly to the east and out over the ocean. The cab line in front of the Delta terminal was short, and as soon as a young mother with two children clinging to her legs managed to get them into a cab, Sam moved to the head of the line.

The ride to the downtown Hyatt took only about twenty minutes, and after a quick check-in, Sam headed directly up to his room. He traveled today, as he always did, with a Coach tan leather carry-on and a light suit bag. Sitting down at the desk, he reached into his bag and pulled out his cell phone. As a matter of habit, he always used his cellular when he was on a job. Removing a small leather notebook from the inside pocket of his blue blazer, he quickly located Erin's portable number and dialed it.

"Ms. Wells?"

"Yes."

"This is Sam Forbes. I'm in Miami. I was hoping we could get together this afternoon."

Erin had just finished interviewing the director of nursing at the institute and was about to head back to her hotel. It had been a long morning.

"I'm . . . I'm a little surprised to hear from you," she said. "I didn't know you were arriving today. Did you leave a message at my hotel?"

"No. I prefer to keep my travel plans confidential. And if I need to contact you, I'll call you on your cellular. When we meet, I'll give you my number."

"I'm on my way back to my hotel now. We could meet at the coffee shop just off the lobby. Do you need directions to—"

"It's a beautiful day now that the rain has passed. Why don't we meet outside?" he suggested.

"I beg your pardon?"

"There's a nice place in Hollywood called T.Y. Park," he told her as he tucked his notebook back in his pocket. "To tell you the truth, I could use the fresh air. It should take you about thirty minutes to get there. Just take I-95 to Sheridan Street and go west for about a mile. You can't miss it. I'll meet you at picnic area number six in forty-five minutes."

"Mr. Forbes, this sounds more like espionage than routine background investigation."

"You'll love the park. Forty-five minutes then?"

"I'll be there," she told him.

Sam Forbes's estimate was precise. It took Erin exactly thirty minutes to reach the entrance to T.Y. Park. She entered and slowly drove past an empty guard booth and then followed the signs to area six. It occurred to her that she had no idea what the man looked like. Hopefully, Herb had given Forbes a description of her and he'd be able to pick her out. As she slowly made her way toward area six, she wondered how a PI living in Washington, DC, knew so much about a park in Hollywood. The park itself was sprawling, with a large lake in the southwest corner. A small path bordered by a large chain-link fence encircled the entire park and was crowded with joggers, dog walkers and in-line skaters.

Erin had no trouble locating area six. She slowly turned off the main access road and pulled into the first parking space. There were only three other cars in the lot. She looked around for a moment before grabbing her purse off the passenger seat and leaving the car.

Under a large wooden shelter with a pitched roof there were two picnic tables and a large brick grill. Just outside the shelter, a steel swing set and a volleyball net stood next to each other.

Erin slowly made her way across a small field dotted with sparse burnt-out grass until she reached the shelter. A man, about thirty yards away, wearing a white golf shirt and jeans, left the jogging path and started toward the shelter. His step resembled synchronized marching more than a normal gait. At first, Erin assumed he had just been out for a walk, but as he closed the distance her instinct told her she was about to meet Sam Forbes.

The man, whose head was completely bald, smiled as he entered the shelter. Erin wasted no time in sizing him up. Better than average looking, he had a bull neck, ample shoulders and hard, deep-set eyes. She guessed he was just under six feet tall and his thick, muscular forearms and large hands made him look more like a longshoreman than a private investigator.

"Ms. Wells?"

"Yes."

"I'm Sam Forbes. Thank you for meeting with me. Herb was anxious that we get together as soon as I arrived in Miami."

Sam pointed to one of the picnic tables and they both sat down.

"How come all the cloak-and-dagger stuff?" Erin asked as she extended her legs and crossed her ankles in front of her.

"Just a habit," he said. "I've always worked this way."

"Herb said you're more than just a private investigator."

He smiled. "Herb has always been generous with his praise."

"It was kind of you to drop everything and come down to Florida. Do you do a lot of bodyguarding?"

Sam's expression never changed. He leaned back against the table and looked straight ahead. "Herb was concerned about you. I said I'd help."

"I don't need a baby-sitter," she told him directly. "I need information."

He nodded a few times. "Are the two mutually exclusive?"

Erin stood up and walked a few paces toward the large brick grill and removed her sunglasses. Sam struck her as a deliberate man with considerable poise who was not prone to shooting from the hip.

"I think there's something strange going on at the Fetal Institute," she informed him. "How much has Herb told you?"

"Just the basics. He suggested I get a detailed account from you."

"I got the feeling from Herb he thought I was crazy, that my imagination was out of control," she said.

"That's not the impression he gave me."

"Really? That's the first bit of encouraging news I've had today." She walked to the edge of the concrete floor and then turned. "Do you think you'll be able to listen to me objectively and at least give me the benefit of the doubt?"

Sam rubbed his dome and then stood up. He walked across the shelter until he was a few feet from Erin. "I have a very special practice, Erin. Over the years, I've seen some very intelligent people conspire to do things that struck me as unbelievable. I wouldn't be here if I thought you were part of the lunatic fringe. Now why don't we sit down and you can tell me the whole story."

Erin could be as skeptical as the next person, but she felt Sam was being genuine. For the next half hour she briefed him on every detail of the strange and unexplained events surrounding Claire Weaver's hospitalization. Erin watched

Sam's face carefully during the entire time without detecting an expression of skepticism or disbelief.

"That's certainly a strange course of events, which naturally raises the question if they are just some enormous coincidence or if there's a common link." ·

"Assuming there was a single explanation for all this, what could it possibly be?" she asked him.

He shook his head. "That's hard to say. But it's been my experience that there's a wide variation in the scenarios, but money or power are usually woven into the fabric somewhere."

"Where do we go from here?" she asked.

"I think we need to find out more about Neotech and John Freeman's death. Obviously his research is a factor in this whole thing." Sam looked up and smiled. "We have a lot of work to do."

Erin reached out and shook his hand. For a black belt in martial arts, he had a gentle grip. She noticed the gold Florentine wedding band on his left hand, which put an end to any thoughts she had of fixing him up with Leigh Sierra.

"How old are you?" she asked him without giving the personal nature of the question much thought.

"I was forty last month."

"Kids?" she asked, thinking he looked every bit his age.

"Two. They're both in junior high."

"How long have you been married?"

"Seventeen years this month."

"What does your wife think about the way you make your living?" she asked.

He shrugged his shoulders and then chuckled. "It never came up."

Sam escorted Erin back to her car and then walked around the back and took a quick look at her taillights. Erin had rented another Firebird and insisted upon a convertible. When he walked back around she looked at him quizzically.

"What were you doing?"

"Looking at the back of your car."

"Yes," she said, becoming more comfortable with him. "I realize that. But why?"

"Oh, I just wanted to see if any of your taillights were punched out."

"And the reason for that would be?"

"It's an old PI trick used mostly by rank amateurs. It makes it easier for them to follow you at night."

Erin's pulse accelerated as she marched right by him and around to the back of her car. Her taillights were fine.

"Are you trying to scare me? Because if you are, it's working."

Sam pushed his hands down in his pockets and stood there with a sheepish expression. "Not at all. I've always been a mother hen."

Sam pulled out a piece of paper with his cellular phone number and handed it to Erin. "Call me tonight when it's convenient for you. I want to think things over for a couple of hours, make some phone calls and then talk to you again in more specific terms about how I plan to proceed."

Erin anchored her eyes to his, wondering what she was getting herself into.

"Where's your car?" she asked, looking around and noting that the three cars present when she arrived had all left.

"It's in Washington," he said.

"I didn't see any hotels in the area so I have to assume you're not walking back to your hotel."

"That would be a correct assumption."

"May I offer you a ride?"

"I prefer cabs."

Erin looked around. "I don't see any."

"There should be one here in about five minutes," Sam assured her, looking down at his watch.

Erin wiggled her index finger in his direction. "You're a strange man, Sam Forbes."

"You're starting to sound like my wife."

"I'll call you later," she told him.

Erin made the trip back to her hotel in forty minutes,

spending most of that time in light traffic and thinking about the man Herb had sent to Miami to help her. He was obviously thoughtful, with a deductive mind and a penchant for attention to detail. If nothing else, his presence had a calming effect.

Her last thought as she handed the parking valet her key was to wonder just how good this guy really was and how much he'd be able to find out.

Chapter 33

Claire Weaver was pacing up and down in her room when Erin came through the door. Alex, who had just returned from a two-day trip to the Pacific Northwest, sat silently in a chair with a blank expression on his face watching his wife.

"What's going on?" Erin asked. "You guys look like you're waiting for the results of your final exams to be posted."

"We're waiting for Drs. Gallagher and Archer. They called earlier today and arranged a meeting for this afternoon," Alex answered. Claire never broke stride and acknowledged Erin's presence with a cursory wave. Erin walked over to Claire and gently took her by the forearm.

"Why don't you have a seat? You're making the baby seasick and wearing out the floor."

Claire stopped, grinned for a moment and then pulled the chair out from under the desk and took a seat.

"The committee met yesterday," she told Erin.

Erin was a little surprised because Noah, who had shared her bed last night, had not mentioned anything. She was sure he was aware of the committee's decision, and his failure to tell her could only mean one thing.

"How do you know the committee met?" Erin asked.

"Because that's the message we got from Dr. Archer's office," Alex said with an impatient voice.

"Did they say anything else?" Erin asked Claire.

"No, only that he and Dr. Gallagher would be here this afternoon to go over everything with us in detail. Where could they be? They should have been here by now," Claire said, throwing her hands up in the air. She was dressed in new maternity jeans and an oversized Georgia Tech sweatshirt. Her hair was done and her makeup was on.

"Do you want me to give Noah a call?" she asked.

"That won't be necessary," came a voice from the doorway as Noah walked in. "Dr. Archer will be here in a minute. How are you feeling, Claire? Any contractions today?"

"No, none at all," she promised, holding the bottom of her belly in her cupped hands.

"That's great," he said and walked over to check the IV. "It looks like the medications are really doing the trick," he told her.

"How am I doing?" she asked Noah for reassurance.

"You're doing fine," he said as he reached down and gave her hand a gentle squeeze.

Alex stood up and tucked his fingers into the back pockets of his khaki Dockers. "Do you know when Dr. Archer will be here?" he asked.

Noah checked his watch. "It should be any time now. How was your trip?"

"Uneventful," Alex answered.

"I guess if you're an airline pilot, that's what you want," Noah offered.

"No question about it," Alex agreed. Both men smiled politely.

"I see we're all here," Marc Archer announced as he entered the room. He was dressed to perfection in a charcoal-gray suit, a white shirt and a green-and-white striped Ivy

League tie. He stood just inside the doorway and waited for Claire to take a seat on the side of the bed. "As you know, our ethics committee met last night and considered Claire's situation. Now, if you recall, I mentioned to you that the institute has a strict policy against operating on fetuses with profound associated problems to their primary surgical disease. In this—"

"Shouldn't that be up to the parents . . . or at least shouldn't we have a vote?" Claire asked in desperation. Erin watched the moist redness come to her eyes and could almost feel the same terror she knew Claire was struggling with.

Archer swallowed and then adjusted the knot of his tie. "We always try to include the parents, Claire, but there are certain issues that are not discretionary. We have to live with the rules."

"Rules?" Erin jumped in. "This is about a baby's life and the parents' right to demand that everything possible be done. Rules? This isn't a parliamentary proceeding we're talking about, for goodness sakes."

Archer nodded his head in what Erin felt was nothing more than an act of pacification.

"Are you telling us that the committee has decided not to offer our baby the procedure?" Claire asked in a voice just above a whisper.

Archer looked straight past Claire to Alex. His face was blank.

"I'm very sorry. The decision was unanimous."

Alex sat down beside his wife. Claire immediately dropped her head onto his shoulder and began sobbing. Alex sat in silence for a few moments and then asked, "Is it possible that one of the other fetal surgery centers in the country might feel differently?"

"Yes, but I highly doubt it. When it comes to matters of ethics we try to stay on the same page. But you're of course welcome to investigate the possibility."

Erin let out a deep breath wondering why Archer always had to speak in metaphors.

"So what are our options at this point?" Alex inquired as he gently massaged the back of Claire's neck.

"I would say there are two. Claire can return home, carry the pregnancy to term and deliver as planned. Conventional means can then be used by the pediatric surgeons on staff at your regional children's hospital to deal with the CCAM. Any other congenital malformations can be evaluated at the same time."

Noah never looked at Archer when he spoke. His eyes never moved from the floor in front of him. Erin watched as Alex struggled to ask appropriate questions, knowing the woman he so desperately loved was teetering on the edge of emotional collapse.

"And our second option?" Alex asked.

"That would be to terminate the pregnancy," Archer answered softly.

"What if the results of the amniocentesis were wrong?" Erin inquired. "Maybe we should repeat the test. None of the other tests showed anything abnormal. Am I right?" she asked, turning her palms up and holding her hands out in front of her. Erin looked directly at Noah. She could sense from his eyes he felt helpless. This was Marc Archer's show.

"The chances of the amniocentesis being inaccurate are minuscule. It's a very specific test. If you do decide to take the pregnancy to term, I'm not sure it's worth the risk to the baby to repeat the exam."

"Is there any hope you can give us, Dr. Archer?" Claire asked as she looked up at him.

"I wish I could but I'm afraid the situation is beyond our control."

"I guess there's nothing else to say, then," Claire uttered.

A deep silence descended upon the room. Erin walked over to the window and looked out over Biscayne Bay. The sky was bright blue and the bay was alive with recreational crafts of all descriptions. After a few moments Archer excused himself. Noah stayed on and answered a few more of the Weavers' questions. Erin was only half listening. She couldn't believe what she had just witnessed. She looked over at Noah, caught his eye and motioned him out in the hall.

"Claire, I want to talk to Noah for a few moments. Maybe it's better if we go outside."

Alex looked up with a mindful expression. "Do you want me to come?" he asked.

"Maybe it would be better if you stay here with Claire," Erin told him.

Erin walked across the room and joined Noah in the hall. At Noah's behest, they walked down the hall to a family conference room, which had nothing more in it than a black leather couch, two matching chairs and a small wooden coffee table with a phone on it.

"What do you think we should do?" Erin asked as they sat down on the couch. Her tone was concerned, not confrontational.

"I agree with Archer. There's no role for major fetal surgery if there's an associated life-threatening congenital problem."

"Okay, I'm beginning to understand that . . . but supposing there is no other problem?"

"What do you mean?"

"Just what I said."

"C'mon, Erin, you're a nurse. Claire's alpha-fetoprotein wasn't just mildly elevated. It was sky-high. There has to be something wrong with the baby's brain, spinal cord or both."

"I would agree. If the test was accurate."

"You keep coming back to that. Why wouldn't it be?"

"I . . . I'm not sure."

Noah looked directly at her. "Are you talking with your heart, Erin? I know how much you care about Claire, but—"

"Repeat the amnio . . . and don't tell anybody you're doing it."

Noah was frustrated. "Why?"

"Because it's Claire's only chance and I'm asking you to give it to her."

Noah stood up and walked around the room and then pushed his long fingers through his hair.

"This is highly irregular, Erin. I could get in trouble."

"Why? I don't understand. You're Claire's doctor. You can order any test you want. Repeating a test in medicine is hardly an act of heresy. This is about Archer, isn't it? Why does he have to approve everything anybody wants to do around this place? I've never seen any other hospital run like this. Is this guy a hospital director or a dictator?"

Noah sat back down and shook his head. Erin knew there was something about Claire's medical course that was bothering him as much as it was bothering her. But his respect for Archer was quite obvious, and it didn't come as a total surprise to her that Noah would want to tread lightly.

"Okay," he finally said as he stood up. "If it's what Claire and Alex want, we'll repeat the amino. I'll ask Jessica Bartels to stay over and run the a-fetoprotein . . . and keep her mouth shut about it."

Erin jumped up and hugged him around he neck. "You won't regret the decision," she promised.

"I already do," he complained. "Listen, Erin. There's no reason the Weavers need to know anything more than we're just simply repeating the test to be one hundred percent positive."

"You got it. When can we do it?"

"We'll try for Monday. That will give me a chance to speak with Jessica."

"Great."

Erin and Noah returned to Claire's room and met with nothing but genuine excitement about the decision to repeat the amniocentesis. As soon as they left the room, Noah made plans to meet Erin for dinner after his evening teaching conference with the residents.

Erin pulled out of the parking lot and made the quick left onto Alton Road. Thinking about what happened, she felt even closer to Noah. There were many things that were unclear, but she was suspicious that he had more than one reason for agreeing to proceed with a second amniocentesis. It went beyond their relationship and his genuine concern for Claire and Alex. Erin could only wonder if her suspicions were starting to get his attention.

Chapter 34

Sam Forbes's phone call to Herb Porfino was brief, and by the time his cab reached the Aventura Mall, he had already informed the editor in chief of the *AMA News* that he felt there was enough merit in Erin's suspicions to warrant further investigation. The elderly cab driver pulled the taxi up to the valet parking and dropped Sam off.

Once inside, Sam checked the large three-dimensional display of the mall, located the Cheesecake Factory and headed off to meet Erin. Sam lived by rules and rarely accepted an assignment based solely on one interview. He had learned early on in his career when he practiced international law in Washington that introspection, planning and avoidance of impetuous behavior served him well in his professional life. Successful and respected, Sam might still be practicing law today were it not for the deadly boring nature of the work.

After strolling by Bloomingdale's and a number of national chain clothing stores, he finally reached the restaurant. A young woman with a broad smile greeted him and directed him over to the bar. The marble floors were immaculate. As he walked past a large freezer displaying dozens of different cheesecakes he slowed for a moment. Estimating the number of calories in each piece helped him resist the temptation. Sam turned into the bar and spotted Erin sitting at a small table. She was dressed in jeans and a white tube top.

"How long have you been waiting?" he asked, having a good look around at the half dozen or so other people in the bar.

"Just a few minutes. I hope you don't mind, I ordered a drink," she answered, lifting her glass a few inches off the table.

Sam looked down. "No, not at all. It looks good. What is it?"

"It's a ginger ale, Sam. Would you like one?"

He took a second look at the glass. "No, thanks."

"Where do we stand? Have you been able to find anything out about Neotech?"

"Actually, I have. I spoke with Herb and picked his brain about what he'd uncovered and then spoke with several contacts I have in corporate health care."

"And?"

"Neotech's a private corporation run by a guy named Carter St. John. It has a small board of directors and I believe his wife is also on the board. Most of what I found out was routine, but the one interesting thing is that there's been a hush-hush deal going on."

"What kind of deal?" Erin asked.

"Healthspan's hot to buy them. The number I heard was in excess of one point two billion dollars. The deal's been percolating along for a few years. The information I have is that it's in the final stages and should be done within the next month of two. Evidently most of the analysts and experts who follow these complicated acquisitions think Healthspan's way overpaying."

"Why do you think Healthspan's so anxious to acquire Neotech?"

"I don't have the specifics, but Neotech's an extremely well run, financially solid corporation with a very rosy future," he said as he folded a cocktail napkin in half. "It would be a smart move to bring them on board."

"Do you think we can get any more information?"

"Well, depending on how tight the security system is on Neotech's computer network, we may be able to dig around a little. Sometimes you can get into a company's internal memos file."

"Is that legal?" Erin asked.

Sam ignored the question and just smiled at the naive nature of her inquiry. "The fact that they're a health care corporation gives us a little bit of an advantage because they're forced to operate under federal guidelines and scrutiny. If there have been any problems, there should be a paper trail."

Sam took a quick look around and watched a middle-aged couple seated at the end of the bar engaged in quiet conversation. Three elderly women seated at a booth a few feet away were in the process of paying their check, while a man wearing a collarless white shirt sat at another booth watching ESPN on a TV mounted over the bar.

"What can I do?" Erin inquired.

"At the moment, not too much. It's going to take me a few days to get all of this rolling."

Erin crossed her arms in front of her, reminding Sam of his daughter when she was pouting.

"I thought we'd be working together," she reminded him.

"We are. But if there is something going on at the institute, the last thing we need is to raise their suspicions."

"But . . . I—"

"Right now, I don't want you to lose your access to the hospital. I'm not going to do anything without discussing it with you . . . and whatever I find out, you'll be the first to know."

"You mean right after Herb,"" she said with a touch of sarcasm in her voice.

"Well, technically, we both work for him."

"I know," she lamented with a genuine affection. "I get up every morning and ask myself why."

He laughed. "I've worked for a lot of people over the years, Erin. Herb can be a little difficult at times but will generally listen to reason. And you never have to worry about him blindsiding you. If he's angry he'll use a frontal assault."

For the next twenty minutes Sam explained in more specific terms his plan to gather as much information about Neotech as possible. Erin struck him as attentive and unlikely to hinder the investigation by ill-advised tactics. Her questions were thoughtful and she seemed to process information very quickly. Her attractiveness had not gone unnoticed, but Sam was a homebody and never ventured beyond his own bedroom.

They got up together and Sam paid the bill. As they walked out he cast a second glance at the man watching the sports channel. They crossed the mall quickly and Sam waited with Erin until the valet pulled her Firebird around.

"I suppose it's a waste of time to offer you a lift," she said as she handed the attendant two dollars and got into her car.

"I think I'll hang out here for a while. I saw a martial arts dojo just down the street. I may go see if I can work out with them."

Erin looked up at him through her open window.

"I thought you came down here to work."

"Karate makes me think more clearly, which has a positive impact on my work."

"You're serious," she said slowly.

"I am."

"Shopping has the same effect on me."

Sam smiled and watched her pull away. Turning toward the other side of the parking lot and using his hand to shade his eyes from the sun, he carefully scanned the area. It didn't take him long to spot a man jogging across the parking lot. When he reached an Explorer, he quickly opened the door and got in. Sam immediately recognized him as the man from the bar with the collarless white shirt and blue trim sleeves.

Seven years earlier, Sam had coauthored a book for the Atlanta Police Department on advanced surveillance techniques and was now regarded as an authority. Spotting a wooden bench a few feet away, Sam decided to walk over. Almost before he could sit down, the blue Explorer pulled out, went down one of the feeder lanes and fell into line three cars behind Erin. Putting his immediate plans for a workout on the back burner, Sam flagged down a cab and hopped in. The driver was a husky young woman from the Dominican Republic with a robust voice. When Sam asked her to follow the Explorer, she slapped her thigh, let out an enormous belly laugh and slammed down on the accelerator.

"Where do you think they're going?" she asked.

"I don't have the foggiest idea," he answered.

"Do you do this type of thing a lot?"

"More than I'd care to admit," he confessed.

"Are you a cop?" she asked, sneaking one quick look after another in the rearview mirror.

"No. I work for the government," he explained, pointing ahead to Grafton's car so she wouldn't lose it in her enthusiasm to cross-examine him.

"Enough said. I won't ask you any more questions."

"The less you know, the better off you are," he told her in the most serious voice he could conjure.

She struck a low monotone whistle for about three seconds and then said, "I got ya." She then dropped down a little in the seat, leaving just enough room to peer over the top of the wheel.

Sam wasn't concerned about the man in the Explorer becoming suspicious he was being followed. Obviously a novice, he thought to himself. If the man was sharp, he would have made damn sure he knew where Sam was when he left the mall.

The traffic was light. When Erin pulled into the parking lot of the Fetal Institute, Grafton was about four cars behind her. Sam remained in the cab and watched as Erin parked her car and then marched straight across the parking lot and into the main entrance.

The Explorer moved to about fifty feet from the front door,

parked and stood there with the engine idling. Sam was close enough to see the driver talking on his cellular phone. He was gesticulating as he turned his head from side to side. After another minute or two, the man dropped the phone on the seat next to him, jammed the car into gear and pulled away.

Sam paid the cab driver, taking great pains to praise her driving skill. She insisted he call her directly on her cell phone if he needed a discreet and practiced driver to help him again. Placing her card in his pocket and assuring her that he would call, Sam got out of the cab and walked the short distance to the institute.

Chapter 35

It was just after five p.m. when Mike Fitzpatrick, from patient transportation, helped Claire out of the wheelchair and onto the examination table. She was only a little nervous earlier that morning, but as the day progressed her level of apprehension mounted. Alex had done his level best to calm her but his efforts were mostly in vain. As she struggled to find a comfortable position on the examination table, she suddenly regretted her decision to decline a mild intravenous sedative.

Noah was already in the room and attending to the ultrasound unit. He was dressed in fresh green scrubs under a knee-length white coat. Erin and Alex were already in the room.

"Here you go, Doc. Safe and sound. Just like I promised," Mike said.

Noah looked up and gave him the thumbs-up. "Thanks. I appreciate it."

Edith Carswell, one of the more experienced ultrasound technicians in the hospital, stood behind Noah. A team player and always professional, it wouldn't have occurred to her to inquire why an elective amniocentesis was being done so late in the day.

Alex closed the door, took a seat at the head of the table and immediately found Claire's hand. Gently drawing her hospital gown up above her convex abdomen, Noah applied an antiseptic iodine solution to her lower abdomen. It was cold, forcing Claire to jump a little and then shift her weight.

As soon as the sterile towels were in place, Edith stepped up with the ultrasound transducer and gently applied it to Claire's abdomen. Claire watched as the image of the baby appeared on the monitor. She had undergone a dozen ultrasounds but she never lost the thrill of seeing her unborn baby's image on the monitor.

"I thought Dr. Halliday would be doing the amniocentesis," Claire mentioned.

"We both do quite a few of them," Noah explained. "If you'd prefer, I can—"

"Don't be silly," Claire told him in anticipation of his offer. She looked around and then lowered her voice. "Actually, I'm glad you're the one doing it." He nodded and then turned to hide his boyish grin.

"There's a great pocket of fluid," Edith said, pointing to the screen.

Noah nodded, aligned the needle on Claire's abdomen with the screen and gently inserted it. Drawing back on the syringe as he steadily advanced, there was a sudden flash of clear amber fluid into the syringe. When he had drawn off about twenty cc's, he stopped, removed the needle and transferred the fluid into a plastic specimen container.

"That ought to do it," he told Claire. "Did you have any discomfort?"

"Not a lick," she answered.

Noah removed the sterile drapes, placed a Band-Aid over the puncture site and motioned to Mike, who immediately helped Claire back into the wheelchair.

Five minutes later, Claire was back in her room sitting by the window looking out over the bay. Her heart had stopped hammering as soon as Noah announced he had the fluid and everything on the ultrasound looked great.

Claire watched as two sleek sailboats with towering masts passed effortlessly by each other as if it had been rehearsed dozens of times. The sapphire-blue water was dead calm. Alex was by the bed speaking to flight operations at the airport. She looked down, whispering words of encouragement to the baby and gently rubbing her abdomen as if it were a magic lamp. With the amniocentesis finished, the only thing that disturbed her total state of relief was dread of waiting for the results.

Noah made sure the cap on the specimen tube was tight before dropping it into the waist pocket of his white coat. He told Erin he would meet her in Claire's room as soon as he could and left immediately for the lab, which was located on the third floor. He had already spoken to the technician, Jessica Bartels, and promised to drop the specimen off by six o'clock.

When Noah entered the lab, Jessica was sitting at one of the small lab benches stooped over a microscope. When he cleared his throat loud enough to start the New York City Marathon, her head popped up.

"Can you run the AFP tonight, Jessica?"

"Sure."

"The parents are very anxious. Will you page me?" he asked.

"Of course. Now get out of here and let me do this," she said, giving him a light push. "It may come as a great shock to you that some of us actually have a life outside the hospital."

"New boyfriend?"

"Yeah, I was getting tired sitting by the phone waiting for a certain fetal surgeon to call."

Noah faked a grimace. "That cut deep, Jessica."

"Good, the deeper the better. I'll call you as soon as I have the results."

Noah walked slowly back to the elevator still wondering if he had done the right thing. If the results were identical to the first amniocentesis, it was likely Archer would never be the wiser. But if the findings were different, Noah wold be faced with the sticky political challenge of explaining his actions to Archer.

The doors rolled open and Noah stepped out of the elevator and walked directly to the surgeons' locker room. A long wooden bench faced a bank of olive-drab steel lockers. Noah peeled off his scrubs and sat down on the bench. The events of the day were still pressing on his mind and he knew Erin would be waiting for him. Not really knowing what else to do for the moment, he decided to wait for the results of the amniocentesis before giving Claire Weaver's problem any further thought.

It took him only about five minutes to get dressed. A little more relaxed now, he looked forward to joining Erin and spending the evening with her.

Chapter 36

It had been a long day for both of them and Noah and Erin agreed to eat at a small outdoor café just around the corner from the Jackie Gleason Theater for the Performing Arts. The tables were placed fairly close together but only about half were filled. Noah ordered chicken marsala while Erin opted for a gourmet Cobb salad. Their conversation was light and Erin made a point not to talk about anything related to the institute. They ate slowly, and when they finished their main courses stayed on for a little while longer to enjoy the balmy tropical evening and a cappuccino.

Just as Noah handed the waiter his American Express card he felt his pager vibrating on his right hip. He recognized the institute's laboratory number and wasted no time pulling out his phone.

"It's the lab," he told Erin while he tapped in the number. She smiled and crossed her fingers on both hands. "Hi, Jessica. Thanks for calling so soon." He placed his wallet on the table and covered it with his palm.

"The AFP's normal," Jessica said. "Not even a hint of an elevation."

"Are you sure?" he asked, more out of amazement than a suspicion that what she was reporting was an error.

"I ran it twice. There's no question about it. I assure you, it's normal."

Noah moved the phone to his opposite ear. Erin stood next to him with an anxious expression.

"It's normal," he whispered to Erin, covering the mouthpiece. She leaned over, hugged his neck and kissed him on the cheek.

"Uh . . . Jessica, do you know if we have any patients in the hospital with elevated AFPs?"

"Two that I know of, but there may be a couple more. Why? Do you think there was a specimen mix-up?"

"The thought crossed my mind," he answered. "What do you think?"

"It's possible," Jessica admitted after a moment or two of thought. "It might be interesting to go back and cross-reference Mrs. Weaver's against the other positives in the hospital. There's such a broad range in the AFP values, it shouldn't be too hard to figure out. Do you want me to give it a try?"

Noah looked over at Erin, taking note of the intense curiosity and impatience in her eyes.

"What's she saying?" she asked, and then renewed the question almost immediately when he didn't answer.

He held his hand up and waved her off, trying to concentrate on what Jessica was saying above her badgering.

"I think that's a good idea," he finally said. "Can we keep it unofficial?"

"Why?" came her response.

"It would be easier that way."

Jessica sighed. "Are you trying to get me canned?"

"I wouldn't dream of it. What do you say?"

"I'm not keeping score but I think I'm way ahead on the favor spreadsheet."

"How will I ever be able to repay you?"

"I'll think of something," she assured him. "I'll page you in a day or two."

"Thanks."

Noah pushed the end button on his phone and looked over at Erin, whose head was bobbing up and down in anticipation.

"Well?" she asked.

"I told you. The test was normal. It's great news for the Weavers. The lab screwed up, I guess. When do you want to tell them?"

"That's it? The lab screwed up?"

"Yes, Erin. That's it," he told her directly. "It's a big lab. They make mistakes from time to time."

Noah had decided before he got off the phone with Jessica that he was going to downplay the lab error with Erin. Her misgivings about the institute hadn't come up for a while, but he sensed they were ever present on her mind and he had no interest in fanning the flames of her suspicions.

"A lab error? That's the best you can do?"

Noah put his credit card back in his wallet. She was starting on one of her rolls and his only interest at the moment was to defuse the situation.

"I'm the woman's doctor, Erin. Nothing more. I'm not an investigative reporter. A month doesn't go by when I'm not faced with one hospital error or another. It's a reality. Thank God that ninety-nine percent of them never result in an injury to a patient." His voice was calm, his explanation reasonable. Noah forced a smile and pointed in the direction of his car. He again raised the question, "When do you want to give the Weavers the good news?"

"As soon as possible."

Noah looked down at his watch. "Would you like to stop off on the way back to your hotel?"

"That would be great," she answered.

•   •   •

The doctors' parking lot was half empty
when Noah and Erin pulled in. The drive from Miami Beach
had taken only about fifteen minutes. Erin's excitement
about telling Claire and Alex had peaked when the elevator
doors opened on the second floor. When they entered the
room, Alex and Claire were both on the bed watching TV. It
took every particle of self-control Erin cold muster to remain
silent while Noah gave the Weavers the good news.

At the sound of the news Alex was visibly dumbstruck,
and after a few moments of trying to speak, he began to cry.
Claire was also speechless. When they both regained their
composure, Noah answered a litany of questions, mostly
from Alex, about the pregnancy and what they could expect.
Noah assured them he'd speak with Dr. Archer as soon as
possible, but was confident that Claire's surgery would be
back on the schedule.

"I don't know how to thank you," Claire told Noah.

"Just have a healthy baby," he answered.

Alex, dressed in his airline uniform, stood up, walked
over to Noah and shook his hand. He glanced over at Erin,
smiled broadly and winked. "We're very excited," he said.
"This is the best news Claire and I could have hoped for."

Erin walked over and hugged Claire. "I told you it was
going to work out," she said. Claire could only nod. Her eyes
were still a moist red. Erin held Claire's hand as Noah answered several more of their questions.

"Maybe we should leave you guys alone," Noah suggested. "You probably have a lot to talk over."

"I think that's a good idea," Erin said. "I'll be back tomorrow," she promised, giving Claire a long hug and saying
good night to Alex.

The lobby was still brightly lit when Erin
and Noah stepped off the elevator and headed for the exit.

"Are you staying over?" she asked him, tucking her hand
under his arm. It had become a little cooler and many of the

stars that were visible earlier were now obscured by scattered stacks of thin clouds.

He smiled. "I just happen to have my overnight in the car."

"This is turning out to be one great evening."

During the short ride to the hotel, Erin was as animated as Noah had seen her. And, at least for the moment, any concerns she had about the institute were far overshadowed by her sheer joy for Claire and Alex.

Chapter 37

Erin and Noah awakened early and were out of the hotel by seven-thirty. When they arrived at the institute, he invited her to join him in the medical staff dining room for breakfast.

The dining room, located just off the lobby, was not particularly large. The carpet was plush emerald green and the walls were covered with fine wood paneling. There were eight widely spaced tables large enough for about five people each. A long self-service counter containing a wide variety of both hot and cold foods occupied the entire far wall.

They went through the line quickly, with Noah selecting the same thing he did every morning, fresh orange juice, cold cereal and raisins. Erin opted for low-fat peach yogurt and a croissant. As they came through the end of the line, Noah looked up and saw Marc Archer sitting with a tall gentleman in a dark blue suit. Archer caught his eye and waved him over. Noah smiled, tapped Erin on the shoulder and pointed in the direction of Archer's table.

"Won't you join us?" Archer suggested as Noah and Erin

approached the table. "This is Carter St. John. He's the CEO of Neotech. I'm not sure you two have met."

"Actually, I don't think so," Noah said, placing his tray down and then extending his hand to shake St. John's.

"Carter, this is Dr. Noah Gallagher and Erin Wells," Archer said. "Ms. Wells is a reporter for the *AMA News*. She's in the process of writing a story about the institute."

Erin smiled, placed her tray next to Noah's and shook St. John's hand.

"It's a pleasure to meet you both," St. John said, pushing his tray over a little bit to give Erin a little more room. She couldn't help but notice his thick hair, which was the color of coal, his professional manicure and raspy voice. He was an attractive man with a well-polished manner and commanding appearance. His gold Rolex was quite similar to Archer's.

"How's the story going, Ms. Wells?" St. John inquired.

"Please call me Erin. The story's going very well. You have a lot to be proud of around here."

"That's kind of you to say," he acknowledged, lifting his coffee cup and taking a short sip. Erin took a second look at his monogrammed white shirt and his perfectly tailored navy-blue pinstripe suit, which she guessed must have had a price tag of over two thousand dollars.

"How many hospitals does Neotech own?" Erin asked, picking up her croissant, taking the first bite from the corner and then almost choking when Noah kicked her under the table. She looked over at him with charged eyes that assured him she knew what she was doing.

"Thirty-nine altogether. And they're all specialty hospitals. We like to feel the concept is unique in today's health care industry."

"That's certainly impressive," she said. "Do you have any other holdings?"

"We dabble a little here and there, Erin, but we're committed to the hospital industry," St. John answered.

Archer cast a scornful glance at Erin and then said,

"Noah's our chief of surgery and doing a hell of a job. We're lucky to have him."

"I've heard nothing but good things about you, Dr. Gallagher," St. John stated like a politician.

"Actually, I feel fortunate to have the opportunity to work at the institute," Noah responded. Archer then patted him on the back a couple of times in an apparent gesture of approbation for his answer.

"I've had a pretty good look around the last couple of days," St. John said. "I think the institute is becoming the flagship hospital in our system."

"There's some rumors out there that Healthspan would love to buy Neotech. Any truth to that?" Erin asked.

St. John's expression never changed. "It's hardly a rumor. We've been in negotiations with them for well over two years. We've tried to keep things as confidential as possible, but in the present atmosphere, well . . . that's hardly possible."

"Do you think the merger will go through?" Erin asked.

"Well, I'm not at liberty to say, but, off the record, we're very close."

"In that case, I'll offer my congratulations in advance. Have you always been in the health care industry?" Erin asked.

"In one form or another. I got a master's from the University of Pennsylvania in health care administration twenty years ago and have served the industry ever since."

Noah looked over at Erin with eyes that begged her to lighten up, but it was also clear from her willful face that she would press on. St. John looked down at his watch and then at Archer.

"Well, we have a meeting in about five minutes," Archer said, pointing at an antique-style clock hanging on the far wall.

St. John removed the paper napkin from his lap and placed it on his tray. "I've enjoyed talking with both of you," he said to Noah and Erin. "If you need any further information about

Neotech for your story, Erin . . . just give my secretary a call. I'd be happy to help you."

"Thank you," Erin told him, realizing she had just been blown off by a master. The two gentlemen stood up.

"Noah, may I have a word with you for just a moment?" Archer asked.

"Of course."

"I'll just be a moment, Carter," Archer said.

St. John reached for his small attaché. "I'll just make a quick stop in the washroom while you gentlemen are talking."

"I saw the results of Claire Weaver's second amnio," Archer said.

"I was going to call you this morning about it."

"Your methods are a little unorthodox. I was surprised."

"It was a last-minute decision, Marc. The Weavers really wanted to repeat the test, the technicians were here and I had the time."

"Well, it seems quite fortunate that you had the sense to disregard my recommendation about repeating the amnio. I obviously feel quite foolish in light of the second results." It was rare that Archer didn't look directly at Noah when he spoke. "I guess when I made the decision to stay out of clinical medicine I should have done just that."

"It was a shot in the dark, Marc. If the Weavers hadn't been so damn insistent, I probably never would have done it either."

Archer took a deep breath and then cleared his throat. "Thanks, I appreciate your forbearance. This obviously changes everything. Claire Weaver is again a candidate for surgery. As soon as you're ready, put her back on the OR schedule."

"Thanks, Marc."

"I should be the one thanking you . . . but in the future, try to keep me in the loop."

"You can count on it," Noah said with a sense of overwhelming relief and watched as Archer left the dining room to meet St. John. He shook his head and then returned to the table.

"What was that all about?" Erin asked.

"Archer knew about the amnio."

"How?"

"I don't know. He was so damn nice about the whole thing I never asked."

"What about the surgery?"

"He told me to schedule it whenever I thought it was appropriate," he told her. "And I hope this puts to rest any concerns that you might have about the institute," he added.

More excited about the good news than the comment that followed, Erin clapped her hands loudly.

"Let's go upstairs and tell them what Archer said," she insisted.

Noah agreed, and as soon as they had set their trays into a large receptacle, they were on their way.

Chapter 38

Erin had just finished a humdrum interview with the institute's public relations coordinator when she decided to pick up the messages on her voice mail. She was immediately thrilled when she discovered Dr. Thomas McGiver from the University of Miami had called. Ignoring her other messages, she quickly tapped in his number.

A woman with a British accent answered the phone. "Pharmacology Department."

"Dr. McGiver, please. This is Erin Wells returning his call," she told the woman.

"Oh, yes, Ms. Wells. Please hold. He's expecting your call."

A moment later she heard a man's voice. "This is Dr. McGiver."

"Hello, it's Erin Wells. Thank you for calling me back."

"I have some information on the data you gave me," he informed her.

"That's great. Should I make an appointment or can we talk on the phone?"

"The phone is fine," he said without hesitation. "You have

to understand that the material you gave us is raw data. We don't have at our disposal the methods that were used to interpret the information."

"I'm not sure I understand," Erin said.

"We have the results," he tried to explain again, "but we don't know how the institute arrived at their conclusions."

"Will you be able to figure it out?" Erin asked, looking at the secretary who had now returned to her computer station.

"In time, probably. But for the moment we're a little confused."

"I don't understand," Erin said.

"The methods of scientific research and interpretation of data are fairly standard," he explained. "One scientist should be able to evaluate a fellow researcher's work, analyze the data and understand the process that was used to arrive at the experiment's conclusions."

"I'm getting the impression that you are unable to do that in Dr. Freeman's case."

"That's correct." There was a distinct pause as Erin waited for Dr. McGiver to elaborate. The tone of his voice was hesitant and Erin was struggling to decide whether he was just simply confused or perhaps embarrassed that he was unable to interpret John Freeman's work. "If you don't mind, I would like to look at this work further. Perhaps the problem is that we just haven't had sufficient time to study the problem."

"I understand totally, Dr. McGiver. I've heard wonderful things about your department and I'm sure you'll be able to work the problem out."

"We'll give it our best shot."

Erin thanked Dr. McGiver and hung up the phone. The woman in the long skirt looked over the top of her half-moon glasses at Erin and then walked away. After thanking the secretary for the use of the phone and feeling like she needed a little more privacy, Erin decided to step outside to use her portable to fill Sam in about her conversation with Dr. McGiver.

She took a short walk around to the side of the campus

where a small park had been constructed. Two emerald-green park benches sat in the middle of a nicely landscaped green space. She removed her cell phone, set her purse down beside her on the bench and dialed Sam's number.

"Yes," came the response after two rings.

"It's Erin."

"Where are you?" he asked.

"I'm sitting outside the institute."

"Are you on your portable or a land phone?"

A little taken aback by his question, she answered, "Sam, I just told you I was outside. There aren't too many regular phones out here."

"You could be on a pay phone," he reminded her.

"I'm on my cellular. What the hell's the difference anyway?"

"Nothing, I was just asking."

Erin didn't know Sam that well as yet, but if she had learned anything from her conversations with him, it was that he didn't ask innocuous or inconsequential questions.

"I just spoke with Dr. McGiver at the university."

"And?"

"He hasn't been able to interpret Dr. Freeman's research yet."

"Why?"

"I'm not sure, but he sounded almost as if he thought Dr. Freeman's data was bogus."

"Did he say that?" Sam asked in a cautious tone.

"Not in so many words." Erin reached up and pulled on her collar a few times trying to force some cool air in. It was a muggy day and the shade of the olive trees was welcome.

"I have a contact at the FDA who may be able to help," Sam said. "I'll give her a call later and see what she can send me."

"That's great," Erin said. "By the way, as long as I have you on the phone, have you found out anything new on Neotech?"

"Not a whole lot, but I've done quite a bit of digging. The

whole thing would be a lot easier if it were a publicly owned company."

"What have you found out?" she asked.

"I've been in touch with several Florida state agencies, including the Department of State. I've also checked several credit agencies, the Bureau of Better Business and the Internet."

"It sounds like you've been busy," she told him.

"I spoke with a friend who's a health care attorney here in Miami. I had a long conversation with him about an hour ago. He said he'd snoop around a little bit and get back to me."

"So tell me what you have."

"Neotech's star is on the rise," he began. "They're showing strong financial growth every quarter. As I think I told you, the board of directors is a small but talented group of individuals, but the CEO, Carter St. John, seems to call all the shots. They acquire hospitals very slowly and with great care. There's not a loser in the group, which is an amazing accomplishment when you consider all the HMOs and hospital acquisition companies that are going belly-up every day in this country. They're a prime target for a buyout. I guess that's why Healthspan wants to buy them."

Impressed with the amount of information Sam had gathered, Erin listened carefully. She flipped open her purse and squeezed off two cherry LifeSavers and popped them in her mouth. "I met Carter St. John this morning," she mentioned.

"He's quite well known in the industry. He's the ultimate smoothy . . . probably would have made a great commodities trader. He's also an accomplished corporate raider. I understand that he's snubbed out a lot of promising careers over the years."

"Sounds like a great guy to work for . . . kind of makes me appreciate Herb."

Sam chuckled. "I remember St. John from when I practiced law. A few of his business practices were felt to be fairly cutthroat by other major players in the field, but he never had any trouble with the feds. One thing's for sure. He runs the show at Neotech. It's hardly a democracy."

Erin rolled the rapidly dissolving LifeSavers around in her mouth. She leaned her head back against the top of the bench and crossed her ankles in front of her.

"Do you know if Neotech has any foreign holdings?"

"None that comes up on routine screening, but I wouldn't completely dismiss the possibility. Actually, I planned on doing some further digging on that."

"Why?"

"The attorney I spoke to suggested it. He's heard some rumors. By the way, I also contacted the Agency for Health Care Administration in Tallahassee. I thought I'd check on licenses, patient complaints, filings of certificates of need and anything else I could get my hands on that's public information."

"And?"

"I haven't found out too much but I may have to make a trip up to Tallahassee."

The low battery alert on Erin's cell phone beeped three times in succession. She snarled at herself for forgetting to charge it up the night before and then tried tapping it a few times. "My phone's dying, Sam. I'll call you back later."

Erin turned her phone off and looked straight up between the delicate branches. Bright blue patches of sky peeked out between the layers of dull cirrus clouds. A male nurse wearing a white collarless shirt marched along quickly pushing an empty wheelchair toward the side entrance of the institute.

Erin closed her eyes, feeling the warmth of the sun on her face. She thought about Sam, concluding that he was both inventive and industrious . . . but more importantly, he cared. Erin opened her eyes and sat forward. After another few moments, she stood up and headed back for the institute.

Frank Grafton had every sophisticated piece of electronic surveillance apparatus at his disposal. Cloning

Erin's cell phone, monitoring her calls and recording them was a minor challenge. Wearing a gray T-shirt, white basketball shorts and running shoes, he sat about fifty yards from Erin wearing a small set of silver headphones. To anyone walking by, he appeared to be a jogger with a Walkman taking a break from his workout.

Grafton popped the headphones off and tucked them into a large fanny pack he wore high on his hip. He had several new developments to brief his employer on and wondered if the seriousness of the situation would be appreciated and a proportionate response set into motion. Erin Wells was two things at this point, a threat and expendable. Grafton had looked into Sam's background and had come up with very little. He viewed him as a minor entry who could be dealt with as swiftly and discreetly as Ms. Wells.

Grafton pulled the green and orange University of Miami baseball cap down in his forehead. Committed to a daily program of physical fitness, he started out in a medium jog toward Alton Road. There would be time enough after his workout and shower to make his daily phone call.

Chapter 39

Recently constructed, and without much re-
gard for economy, the outdoor patio attached to the institute's
main cafeteria was a frequent destination of hospital employ-
ees on break. Large tropical potted plants bordered the
smooth wooden deck. A half dozen circular white tables with
large floral umbrellas were spaced around the deck.

Erin ordered an iced tea, and after adding lemon and arti-
ficial sweetener walked out on the deck. The last empty table
was the nearest to the sliding glass door that accessed the
deck. Erin set her iced tea down on the table, pulled out the
chair and took a seat. A wisp of a cool breeze was just sufficient to take the heat out of the air.

"Can I join you?" came a voice from behind her.

Before Erin could turn, Leigh Sierra walked past her and
took the chair directly opposite to Erin's. Her conservative
blue business suit was covered with a white lab coat.

"Be my guest," Erin said. "It will be nice to have someone
to talk to."

"I know the feeling," she said, placing her fruit salad down
on the table. "How's the story progressing?"

"No complaints."

"I can't wait to get out of here Friday," she said, looking around, giving Erin the impression she didn't want anyone to hear her.

"How come?"

"I'm going away for the weekend." Leigh raised her eyebrows and nodded.

"Is there a man at the bottom of this somewhere?"

"I wish," she said with a frown as she harpooned a piece of pineapple.

"Where are you going?" Erin asked.

"To the Bahamas with a few friends. We go about three times a year and always have a great time. The place is a haven for eligible men. We're staying on Paradise Island." Leigh looked up with a devilish expression. "Are you interested?"

Erin grinned. "It sounds great but I think I'll pass."

Leigh popped another piece of fruit in her mouth and waved her plastic fork at Erin. "You can bring Noah if you want. We won't drool too much."

"Pass again. Uh . . . can I ask you a question?"

"Shoot."

"Would it be possible for me to have a look at the files of the patients who have participated in your studies?"

Leigh thought for a moment and then said, "I'm not sure. There may be some patient confidentiality issues involved. How come you're asking? Were you thinking of interviewing some of them?"

"Yes. I really think that will add something to the story."

"Okay, let me check with Dr. Archer. If he says it's okay . . . have a go at it. But it's a long shot, Erin. I can't imagine he'll go for it, but if he does, I'll call you."

Erin turned in her seat and then leaned forward. The breeze had picked up a little, blowing calmly across the back of her neck.

"Okay," Erin said with a forced smile, knowing that Archer

would never approve the request. "You're probably right. He's got a lot of other things on his mind at the moment."

Leigh looked at her quizzically. "Like what?"

Erin gazed around and then leaned back. "The merger with Healthspan."

"Oh, everybody knows about that," she said, waving her hand. "All the bigwigs have been stewing about it for the last few years."

"What do you think about it?"

"I couldn't care less. As long as my job and paycheck are unaffected, I have no interest in corporate chess."

Erin and Leigh talked another ten minutes about a number of innocuous topics. Erin broke out laughing several times, finding Leigh's fatalistic attitude about men and her professional life both witty and amusing.

Leigh looked down at her watch. "If you change your mind about this weekend, let me know. It will be an experience you won't forget."

"So was the Asian flu."

"I'm not sure I can go along with that analogy," Leigh teased.

The two women got up together, walked back inside and headed off in different directions. Erin enjoyed the few minutes with Leigh and under different circumstances might have taken her up on her offer to go to the Bahamas.

Chapter 40

Amanda Vincent was regarded as the most experienced technician in Southside's toxicology laboratory. Rarely discouraged and never slipshod, she was the obvious choice for the soon-to-be announced assistant director position. Having recently celebrated her thirty-second birthday, she was ready for the promotion.

Amanda had been behind her computer for over an hour, working through lunch, trying to locate the results of John Freeman's toxicology assays. She was no stranger to long computer searches for misplaced labs, having seen just about every glitch that could result in a lab report either disappearing or winding up on the wrong patient's chart.

In John Freeman's case the trail ended after the specimens had been delivered to the tox lab. The first thing she had done was check the main log book, which recorded every blood and urine sample dropped off at the lab. On the date John Freeman was taken to the Southside Emergency Room, his toxicology studies were logged in at exactly 11:35 P.M..

Having exhausted every trick she knew to locate a missing lab report, Amanda sat in front of her computer tapping the desktop with her pen. She knew the results were in the system somewhere, even though the computer insisted they weren't. Amanda briefly considered asking the techs who worked the morning John Freeman died, but dismissed the thought almost as quickly when she considered the number of tests run each day and the amount of time elapsed since Freeman died.

She inched forward in her chair and then tapped in the code that brought up all the patients admitted to Southside the same day as Dr. Freeman. She studied each of the names, hoping that one of them might be a close match with Freeman's, but none were.

Amanda covered an unintentional yawn with her hand and then decided to have another look at Freeman's basic admission information. She looked for a moment and then noted he was admitted as a "John Doe" when he first arrived, which was actually more the rule than the exception when any patient was admitted in full cardiac arrest and the normal admission process had to be bypassed. "That's interesting," she said, more to herself than anyone around her, and then stood up. "I'm going down to Medical Records," she hollered to her coworkers as she headed for the door. "I'll be right back."

When she walked through the doors of the medical records department, Amanda was happy to see things were relatively quiet. She looked around at the many secretaries seated in small cubicles with their heads frozen in front of their computer screens. After a few moments, she caught Caren Patrick's eye, an assistant supervisor whom Amanda had known for years.

"Do you have a sec?" she asked Caren as she approached her desk.

"Sure. What can I do for you?"

"Can you check the number of John Does admitted on October fourth?"

Caren was about ten years older than Amanda, quite thin with high cheekbones and a flat nose. She was conscientious, diplomatic and well liked in the department.

"Sure. It'll just take a minute." Amanda waited as Caren advanced through a number of screens until she hit the one she wanted.

"Here it is . . . huh? That's interesting."

"What?" Amanda asked.

"Actually we had two John Does that day."

"Bingo," Amanda said. "That's what I was hoping for. One's name was John Freeman. Can you give me the name of the other?"

"Sure, it was Michael Stevenson."

"Great. Do you have his medical record number?"

"It's 210454-2. Does that help you?"

"I'm not sure," Amanda answered. "Do you think somebody could pull the chart for me?"

"I'll do it myself."

Caren popped up and walked down a narrow passageway that led to the chart room. A minute or two later, Caren returned with the chart and handed it to Amanda.

"Thanks a lot. I'm just going to have a quick look at it. You can have it right back."

"Take your time," Caren told her, sitting back down at her desk and starting to shuffle through a stack of about twenty charts.

Amanda walked over to an empty desk. She flipped open the chart and read the admission note. Mr. Stevenson was a psychiatric patient who arrived at the emergency room in a catatonic state. From the record, he arrived with all his medications and other personal items in a small gym bag. Amanda flipped to the lab section of his chart. A broad, self-satisfied smile covered her face when she found several lab slips with the handwritten results of an extensive toxicology evaluation. The name at the top of the slips read only "John Doe." Scanning the reports, her attention was caught by an extremely high and probably fatal level of digitalis in Stevenson's bloodstream.

"He wasn't even on dig," she mumbled to herself as she rechecked the list of medications he had brought to the emergency room. "Bingo," she said again when she compared Mr. Stevenson's medical record number with the one on the lab slips. They were completely different.

She reached into her pocket and pulled out a piece of paper with Dr. Freeeman's medical record number written on it. She unfolded the paper and laid it down next to the toxicology slips. The numbers matched. Amanda renewed her smile and would have patted herself on the back if she were able. Picking up the chart, she stood up and went straight back to Caren's desk.

"I found an error with one of the charts. You had two John Does come in on the same day. One of them was a Dr. John Freeman, the other was a Mr. Stevenson." She handed the chart to Caren, who flipped it open and browsed through it briefly.

"What's the error?" Caren inquired, still leafing through the chart.

"You have Freeman's lab results on Stevenson's chart. I matched up the medical record numbers." Amanda waited for a moment as Caren turned to the lab section of the chart. "I'm not sure it makes much of a difference now, but this guy Freeman's digitalis level was pretty high. He probably died of dig toxicity."

Caren continued nodding even after Amanda completed her explanation. She pushed her delicate wire-rimmed glasses a little higher up on the bridge of her nose. "You're absolutely correct. I'll notify the attending physician."

"Thanks for the help," Amanda said.

"I think I should be the one thanking you," Caren answered as Amanda headed for the door.

Caren walked over to one of the cubicles. Justin Merryweather, one of the rank and file in the department, had been a medical records clerk for just over six months and dreaded coming to work each morning. His performance evaluations had been marginal at best and he was holding on to his job by the thinnest of hairs.

"Justin, the lab reports on this chart were placed in error,"

Caren said, handing him the chart. "Would you please pull a Dr. John Freeman's chart and place the toxicology results on his chart?" she asked politely, handing him a copy of Freeman's medical record number to make the already menial request even easier. "We'll also need the standard letter to go out to the attending physician advising him of the late filing. Would you take care of it as soon as possible, please?"

"Sure. I'll be happy to," he said without ever looking up.

Caren smiled, left the chart on his desk and walked away. When she was well out of sight, Merryweather peeked out from behind a large stack of charts. He picked up Stevenson's and immediately shoved it to the bottom of the mound. He looked over at Caren and grinned.

"Sure, Caren," he said sarcastically under his breath. "I'll take care of this right away. That's just what I need . . . fall behind in my assigned work and give you something else to bitch at me about."

He grumbled again and then pulled the top chart off the pile, opened it with a groan and returned to work at his usual sluggish pace.

Erin had finished her last interview by three p.m., and after a brief visit with Claire decided to head back to her hotel. Finishing up a long, hot shower, she barely heard her cell phone ringing. She grabbed a large, plush bath towel, wrapped it around herself and went racing out of the bathroom still trying to tuck the towel in place. She reached the phone when it rung for the fifth time.

"Hello," she said quickly, a little out of breath.

"Is this Erin Carney?"

"Erin who?"

"Erin Carney," Amanda repeated.

"Yes, it is," Erin answered just as she was about to inform the caller they had the wrong number. Thank God she had used her real first name when she visited Southside.

"This is Amanda calling from the toxicology lab at South-side."

Erin tucked the towel underneath her a little tighter and sat down on the bed. She bunched her wet hair and tossed it over her shoulder. "You have to excuse me, I just stepped out of the shower."

"Would it be better if I called back?" Amanda asked.

"No. I've been waiting for your call. You must have some news for me."

"Actually, I do. I finally found your brother's lab reports. They were filed in somebody else's chart."

"Boy, how often does that happen?"

"It's more common than you might think. But usually it's not a problem because every patient's lab is supposed to be in the computer."

"But you told me his wasn't," Erin said.

"That's right. And that's why I had such a hard time finding the results. For some reason they were never entered into the computer. The only thing I found was the handwritten copies that go to the emergency room."

"Were there any abnormalities?"

"Only one. Your brother's digitalis level was extremely high. If it wasn't a fatal dose, it was pretty close."

"Digitalis, the heart medication?"

"Yes," Amanda answered.

"I wasn't even aware he was taking dig."

"Well, he must have been. I hope this helps you. The Department of Medical Records has already rectified the mistake."

"Will they notify the medical examiner's office?" Erin inquired.

"Uh . . . that I'm not sure of. You should probably check directly with the administration."

"I will," Erin said. "May I ask you a question?"

"Certainly," Amanda answered.

"You mentioned that the lab results were never entered

into the computer. Is it possible that they were entered and then deleted?"

"I guess so . . . but there would be no reason for anybody to do that."

"I see. I can't thank you enough for your help."

"You're quite welcome. If there's anything else, just call me."

Erin held the phone for a few moments and then slowly hung it up. She stood up, walked back to the bathroom and grabbed a second towel and began drying her hair briskly. Everyone at the institute had told her that John Freeman was in excellent health. But they also said he was a very private man, which could mean that he kept the state of his health confidential. It was quite possible he had a significant cardiac problem, took digitalis and was still able to lead a relatively normal life.

Erin zipped open her makeup case and then looked into the mirror. *Freeman was a highly educated scientist. If he were on digitalis, how could he have allowed his levels to become so dangerously high?*

Closing the makeup case, Erin slipped on the heavy white terry-cloth robe and walked back to the phone. Her fingers had a fine tremor as she dialed Sam's phone number. Sam answered on the first ring and listened carefully as Erin relayed the circumstances of John Freeman's death.

"It's certainly suspicious, Erin. But you realize it could all be on the up-and-up. Maybe he was on digitalis and just simply overdosed by mistake."

"What will happen next?"

"I guess the hospital will report their mistake to the medical examiner," he said. "It's then up to them if they want to do an autopsy."

Erin moved the phone to her opposite ear and walked the few steps to the thermostat. "I wish I knew what was in John Freeman's head the day he died," she said, tapping the small control to the right. "I know he knew something."

"What makes you so sure?"

Erin hesitated in the knowledge that she didn't have a logical answer to his question. "I . . . I just know," she finally managed, imagining Sam listening with his perplexed expression, nodding in agreement out of politeness.

"Insinct's a valuable tool," he said. "As long as you don't rely on it too heavily and never totally dismiss it. It's the perfect balance you're looking for."

They talked for another few minutes before ending the call. Erin gazed out the window at Biscayne Bay and caught herself biting her fingernails—something she hadn't done since high school. She couldn't get Dr. Freeman off her mind. She recalled his strange comment about never underestimating the power of the media. *Power of the media . . .* those were his exact words. Erin stared down at her phone for a moment and then dialed Washington, DC, information and requested the number for the FDA, for which she was promptly given the 800 number.

Erin went through several recorded prompts before deciding to hit the O key and speak with a live representative. To her delight, a man with a calm tone to his voice answered and identified himself.

"I have an unusual problem," Erin sated. "I am Dr. John Freeman's senior research assistant here in Miami. Dr. Freeman was actively involved in FDA research and recently died unexpectedly. Going though his calendar I noted he had an appointment at the FDA next week. Unfortunately, there's no mention of the individual he was supposed to meet with."

"How can I help you?" came the robotic response.

"I would like to call the person with whom Dr. Freeman was supposed to meet to explain the circumstances of why he was unable to keep his meeting at the FDA."

"Unless you have a name, it would be impossible for me to connect you to the appropriate division."

"I see. Uh . . . perhaps if you reviewed the various divisions of the FDA for me, I might be able to figure out where he was headed." There was a distinct pause before the operator began reeling off the various divisions. When he reached the Office of Compliance, Erin stopped him. "I think that may be it," she told him. "Could you please connect me? Thank you," she said.

It took the operator about a minute to come back on the line. "I have the Office of Compliance on the line."

"Can I help you?" a woman with a friendly voice asked.

"I hope so," Erin said, and then took a few minutes to identify herself and carefully review the same details of Dr. Freeman's death that she had just told the operator.

"You said your associate's name was Dr. Freeman?" the woman asked.

"Yes, that's correct."

"Is that Dr. John Freeman?"

"Yes, it is," she said, a little dumbfounded that her long shot had actually paid off.

"I have it right here. He was scheduled to meet with our director, Paul Hunsinger, on the twenty-second. Mr. Hunsinger is out of town but I'll be happy to relay your message to him."

"Thank you. I assume Mr. Hunsinger was aware of why Dr. Freeman was so anxious to see him."

"I scheduled the appointment, but I don't believe they actually spoke. . . . Is there anything you'd like me to add to the message?"

"No, just that Dr. Freeman died unexpectedly."

"I should be hearing from Mr. Hunsinger later today. I'll tell him you called, and please accept our condolences. If you don't mind me asking, will someone else from the Fetal Institute be contacting us?"

"I would be surprised," Erin said. "Thank you, again."

By the time Erin replaced the phone, she was already deep in thought. It was possible that Freeman's meeting in Washington was nothing more than routine, but if that were the case why would it be with the Office of Compliance? Erin had to concede that her phone call to the FDA only strengthened her suspicions that Freeman harbored real concerns about the research center.

Erin again thought about his strange comment about the press. A few seconds later, an ample smile covered her face. The mysterious identity of the person who had sent the detailed description of the Tocalazine animal studies to her hotel didn't seem to be so mysterious anymore.

Chapter 41

Frank Grafton walked across the parking lot of the Dadeland Mall. The morning was overcast and damp. When he reached Area C, he turned down the third aisle and proceeded at a quick pace until he spotted a red Lexus coupe. He tapped on the passenger window, waited for the click of the lock release and then got in. The fan on the air-conditioning was set at its maximum and his first move was to close the vent directly in front of him.

"Where do we stand?" the driver asked.

"Erin Wells went over to Southside Hospital the other day."

"Really? Do you know where?"

"She went to the toxicology lab," he said, reaching forward to make sure the vent was closed.

"Do you have any idea why?"

"I assume she was trying to find out what happened to Dr. Freeman."

"Ms. Wells is becoming quite a thorn in our side."

"There's a simple solution to the—"

"Please, Mr. Grafton. I've already been foolish enough to

go along with one of your misguided plans to deal with her. I assume she won't be able to find out anything."

Grafton gazed out his window, turned completely around and then looked out the back of the Lexus. "There's no record of Freeman's blood tests in the computer. They don't exist. They've been deleted. She can't find out a thing."

"You're sure?"

"As I've told you, the individual at Southside who took care of this for me is totally reliable. I have no concerns."

"I'm glad to hear that. What about Mr. Forbes?"

"A minor entry," Grafton answered. "From what I can tell he's spinning his wheels accumulating facts that are basically public information. But I can't guarantee you he won't accidentally stumble into some sensitive areas."

"Mr. Forbes's future is a matter of indifference to me. Do whatever you think is necessary. Just make sure nobody will ever be able to connect him back to you or the institute."

Grafton nodded. "Consider it done. I have another matter of concern. Claire Weaver's surgery is coming up."

"I know that, Mr. Grafton. What's your concern?"

"We're having enough trouble with Erin Wells at the moment. I'm sure she'll become even more difficult and suspicious when Mrs. Weaver's surgery ends in an abortion. Perhaps we can create a way to delay the procedure for a while."

"You continue to surprise me. I'm starting to think you've fallen victim to the Peter Principle. You have obviously risen to your level of incompetence."

Grafton remained stone-faced at the insult, but made a fist until his hand blanched. He would have slit his own wrists before reacting outwardly to what he felt was a lame attempt to test his patience.

"Sometimes you have to give people what they want," the driver said.

"I'm not sure I understand your point," Grafton confessed.

"Well, what everyone seems to want is a successful surgery for Claire Weaver. That would certainly please Ms.

Wells, make all her doubts go away, and, most importantly, get her off our backs."

Grafton looked up with a muddled expression. "But the only way to ensure that would be to give Claire Weaver—"

"That's correct. She will receive Tocalazine, have a smooth operation, suffer no postoperative labor and be discharged from the hospital with the expectation of delivering a normal healthy baby. The Weavers go away happy . . . and so does Erin Wells. Whatever happens in the future . . . happens. We'll worry about it three months from now."

"It's perfect," he said softly.

"I appreciate the accolade. I'll expect to hear from you tomorrow."

Grafton shook his head and got out of the car. He watched as the sleek Lexus disappeared toward the exit. He still had his doubts and was convinced his methods, while not as delicate as some, had the advantage of being foolproof. The people he was taking orders from better hope their techniques were as reliable, because if they weren't, the price they'd pay would be extremely high.

Chapter 42

Marc Archer had invited Susan St. John and Erin to use his office for their meeting. Erin assumed this was just more of Archer's nauseating kowtowing and truckling to the CEO that she had witnessed when introduced to him at breakfast.

It was late in the afternoon and Erin arrived about five minutes late. Dr. Archer's secretary greeted her politely and immediately ushered her into the office. Dr. Archer was sitting behind his desk with a plastic smile that would have made any politician envious. Across from him sat Susan St. John. As soon as she entered the room, Archer stood up and escorted Erin to where Susan was sitting.

"This is Susan St. John," he said to Erin, who extended her hand. Susan was absolutely exquisite looking. Her classic facial features and smooth complexion perfectly complemented her jet-black hair, which was pulled straight back. The blended color tones of her eye makeup had been applied flawlessly. The gold watch on her left wrist was adorned with alternating emeralds and diamonds. The matching necklace was even more elegant. "Well, I'll leave you two ladies alone to talk . . . unless of course you'd be more comfortable if I stayed," he said to Susan quite deferentially.

"That won't be necessary," she answered without a smile. "Erin and I will be just fine." Susan pointed to the chair across from hers and waited for Erin to sit down.

"It was kind of you to meet with me," Erin said.

"It's a delight. If the publicity will be beneficial to the institute, then it is my pleasure to help."

"It's my understanding that you direct the fund-raising efforts."

"That's correct."

"Do you have any other responsibilities at Neotech?"

"I sit on the board of directors," she answered. "But my main interest lies in fund-raising."

"How long have you been involved with that endeavor?"

"In one capacity or another, since we acquired the institute. I've been the official director for the past three years."

"Do you sponsor special events or rely on pure donations?"

"We've never found it necessary to enter the arena of special events. Most people find them dreadfully boring," Susan explained. "We've always favored planned giving and bequests."

"I see. Where is the money directed?"

"A number of areas, which mostly depends on the donor's preference. The largest portion goes toward research."

"How do you handle donor recognition?"

"We have gold plaques and naming opportunities, but a large proportion of our supporters prefer to remain anonymous."

Erin continued to take notes, opting before she ever entered the room not to use her tape recorder. She found Susan rather subdued, which surprised her a little because it had been her experience that most people who develop an interest in fund-raising are very passionate and animated about their causes.

"Do you receive many donations from outside the U.S.?"

"Some. We have a lot of grateful patients and families from Latin America and the Far East."

Erin was finding the interview forced. Susan's facial expression never changed. She had asked several questions and had received nothing more than cursory answers. Erin looked directly at Susan again, noting her hollow, emotionless eyes.

"Would you say the contributions from outside the U.S. surpass the domestic?"

"I'm not sure. But under Florida law our financial statements are available for review by anyone. I'm sure you can find the answer there."

Susan raised her wrist, openly checked her watch and then smiled gratuitously. The two women spoke for another fifteen minutes or so. Susan's answers were responsive but still devoid of any real emotion or substance. Her frustration mounting, Erin thanked her and concluded the interview. Susan St. John said nothing further and left the room without offering Erin another interview.

Chapter 43

Noah's office was smaller and more modestly decorated than Erin had expected. A plain oak desk with a hutch and an L-shaped return stood as a unit against the far wall. A small bookcase filled to capacity with medical texts occupied a corner, while two simple upholstered club chairs faced the desk.

The decision to share her concerns about the institute with Noah had come only after a considerable amount of deliberation. She had considered bouncing her dilemma off of Sam Forbes but decided against it, mainly because she was afraid he'd tell her what she already knew . . . what did she have to gain by confiding in Noah? "I know how you feel about the institute, Noah, but you can't let some misguided feelings of loyalty blind you to the truth."

"We've been over all this, Erin. I was hoping you'd realize how silly you're being and just write the story the way your editor suggested."

"At least extend me the courtesy of listening to what I have to say. Is that really asking so much?"

Noah stretched his neck like a crane and looked like someone who had just been told his three-week Hawaiian vacation had been canceled.

"Are we going back to this conspiracy thing again?" he asked in a monotone.

Erin walked back across his small office and sat down in one of the chairs that faced his desk.

"I'd rather not label it as anything right now," she told him. "I just want you to listen to me."

"But I've already—"

"Five minutes, Noah. That's all I'm asking. If you listen to what I have to say and still think I'm crazy then I'll never mention another word about any of this again."

Noah was sitting behind his desk with his hands interlocked behind his neck. Erin could see from his soft eyes that he was teetering on capitulation.

"Okay, Erin," he said finally, breaking the silence. "I'm going to listen to everything you have to say, but when you're done, you have to keep an open mind about my thoughts. Do we have a deal?"

"We do."

"Go for it."

"Let's start with John Freeman."

"Okay."

"I went to Southside Hospital's toxicology lab," she began slowly, ever mindful of monitoring Noah's expressions. "They had quite a bit of difficulty locating the results of his tox screen. But when they finally did, it showed he had overdosed on digitalis."

"I beg your pardon?" Noah said, moving forward in his chair.

"He had a fatal level of digitalis in his bloodstream the day he died."

"I wasn't even aware he was on the drug," Noah said, frowning. "He never mentioned it to—"

"What makes you think he was?" she asked directly.

"On digitalis? Because you just said he had a toxic level on board."

"Maybe somebody gave it to him."

Noah dropped his head and pressed his lips together. "So of the two possibilities, one being he was on the drug and accidentally took too much and the other that he was mysteriously poisoned, you're gong with the latter?"

Erin smiled. "I'm just presenting you with the facts."

"In that case, what else do you have?" Noah stood up, walked across the room to a small refrigerator and pulled out a bottle of iced tea. "Would you like something to drink?"

"No, thank you," she said, turning to look at him and noticing a long shelf cluttered with novelty medical art that ran around the entire office.

"I'm still listening, Erin."

"Dr. Freeman's research."

Noah walked back past his oak bookcases and sat down in the chair across from Erin. "What about his research?"

"It was flawed. The report he sent to the FDA was garbage." Erin knew she was exaggerating, but she was growing frustrated with Noah's skepticism.

"What's that supposed to mean?"

"Dr. McGiver at the University of Miami reviewed his results for days and couldn't make heads or tails of them. He compared them with the report Dr. Freeman filed with the FDA and couldn't see how he could have reached the results he did."

"And he's willing to go on the record about that?"

"On the record? I don't know. We didn't get that far. What does that have to do with anything?"

Noah shook his head. "I still don't get it, Erin. How does all this tie in?"

"I'm not sure," she confessed with a sudden loss of enthusiasm in her voice. "But there's more."

"Go ahead."

"Sarah Allen. I think we've already discussed it. There was Pitressin in her IV bag, and there was a woman whom nobody can identify fiddling with her IV thirty minutes before she went into labor."

Noah again stretched his neck and rubbed the back of it for a few seconds. He looked tired and Erin was starting to feel that maybe her timing was off a little.

"I suppose the next thing you're going to tell me is that somebody intentionally ran you into the canal." Erin looked over at Noah with an extremely serious expression. He stopped, crossed his legs and shook his head in abject disbelief. "I wasn't serious, Erin."

"Well, maybe you should be."

"Oh, c'mon, for crissakes."

Erin leaned back and let her head fall lightly against the top of the chair.

"I think that somehow there's money at the bottom of all this and I don't think Neotech is completely innocent."

"Do you have any proof?" he asked.

"No, but I will. I'm not going to let anything happen to Claire. You can count on that."

"What's that supposed to mean? You happen to be talking to her doctor."

"I'm sure your heart's in the right place but you don't know everything that's going on around here."

"And you obviously do," he said sarcastically.

"I'm not going to turn my back on the obvious. I didn't arrive in Miami with any suspicions or preconceived notions about the institute."

"This is unbelievable, Erin. All you have is a series of unrelated coincidences. That's it. Your imagination has gone crazy."

"Really? In that case you won't mind getting me a list of all the patients, and their addresses, who have been operated on in the last few years. You have access to the hospital's information systems. It should be easy enough for you to do."

Noah's eyes were like saucers, his eyebrows pulled down toward the center of his forehead. "I can't do that, Erin. It's a violation of patient confidentiality. You're a nurse, for God's sake. You know what I'm talking about."

"Make an exception," she pleaded. "I just want to call

some of the mothers and see how they're doing. I won't di-
vulge a thing. I'll tell them I'm calling as part of a research
follow-up from an independent organization."

"I . . . I just don't know."

"Please, Noah. I need this information."

Noah stood up and walked toward the door. "I'll have to
think about it. You're asking me to do something that's totally
unprofessional."

Erin got up, walked slowly across the room and joined
Noah at the door. She felt thoroughly defeated. He hadn't
even considered the possibility that anything she said might
have validity. Noah stood with his hands buried deep in the
pockets of his white coat, staring up at the ceiling. She knew
he was more upset than angry. She kissed him on the cheek,
opened the door and walked down the long hallway to the elevators. It was still early and a visit with Claire just might
cheer her up a little.

"You look like you just lost your best
friend, for goodness sakes," Claire told Erin as soon as she
walked through the door. "What's going on?"

Erin hadn't expected her present mood to be so transpar-
ent. She was disappointed by her conversation with Noah,
but she'd known before she ever entered his office that there
was a chance he wouldn't see things her way. Worse than
anything, she had used the special nature of their relationship
to ask him to do something he considered professionally
wrong.

"Erin? Are you there? What's with the glum face?"

"It's nothing," she told Claire. "I'm having a little trouble
coordinating all my interviews—that's all."

Claire nodded with a skeptical expression. She walked
across the room, picked up a glass of orange juice from her
nightstand and took two or three swallows. "I've seen the
'I'm having professional problems' face. That's definitely not

it." She took a few steps closer and pretended to study Erin's face with a marked intensity. "No, I'd say that's more like the 'I'm having trouble with my boyfriend' face."

"My love life is fine, thank you. How are you feeling?"

"Okay, if you want to keep things inside until you bust—well, who am I to rain on your parade? I'm feeling fine, thank you."

Erin walked over to the dresser and admired a decorative gift basket containing exotic foods. After perusing the contents, she decided to stick with a conventional diet.

"Do you have a definite date for the surgery yet?" Erin asked.

"Not yet. Noah promised to check his calendar and get back with us by tomorrow. It can't be soon enough for me. I'm still floating from the news about the alpha-fetoprotein."

"No one can blame you for that."

Claire finished the juice, set the glass back down on the nightstand and slowly sat down on the side of her bed. "It's funny," she said. "In all the excitement I never asked Noah why the results of the two tests were so different."

"It's really not that uncommon," Erin explained. "I remember seeing it all the time when I was a nurse in Atlanta. More often than not a specimen gets mislabeled. Noah's already reported the problem to the pathologist."

Claire looked surprised. "Why the pathologist?"

"Because they're in charge of all matters related to the lab. According to Noah, there have been several patients in the last few weeks with elevated alpha-fetoprotein levels. His best guess is that your first sample got confused with one of theirs."

Claire shook her head. "I never thought I'd be happy to find out I'd been the victim of a hospital screwup."

"How about taking a little stroll outside?" Erin asked as if the idea was a revelation. "You could use the fresh air and lord knows it wouldn't hurt me any."

Claire placed her palms on her swollen abdomen. "I don't know, Erin. Let's ask the baby."

"Oh, c'mon," she prodded. "I'll even take you in a wheelchair. It'll be fun."

Claire's eyebrows were drawn down in thought. She moved her head as close to her tummy as she was able, cocked her head and pretended to listen. She nodded a few times and then smiled. "You know, now that I think about it, it sounds like a great idea to me too. Let's go."

For the next hour Erin pushed Claire around the institute's grounds. The temperature was exactly seventy degrees and the late afternoon dusk, with the sun hanging over Biscayne Bay, was a beautiful sight. Alex was due back at about six, so at exactly five of, they returned to Claire's room. Wanting to allow Claire and Alex some time alone, Erin made her excuses and promised to return in the morning.

Noah was walking through the lobby when he spotted Erin just on the other side of the large glass revolving door. He quickly changed direction and joined her as she walked slowly across the circular driveway on her way to the parking lot. As it was prone to do, the weather had changed abruptly, heralding a rapidly approaching rain shower and a dreary evening.

"No more interviews today?" he asked, taking her arm.

"I'm afraid I'm about interviewed out," she confessed, getting up on her tiptoes to give him a quick peck on the cheek.

"Come across anything interesting?"

"Is that supposed to be funny?" she asked with a twist of her head.

He smiled. "Take it easy on me, Erin," he said. "Here, I have something for you."

Erin gazed to her right just as Noah passed her an envelope sealed and reinforced with several broad strips of cellophane tape.

"What's this?" she inquired as she put a hand on the envelope.

"It's what you asked for."

"The patient list?" For a moment, she held the envelope between the two of them as if a tug-of-war was about to begin.

"You look surprised. Is there something else you've asked me for recently?"

"No . . . it's just that I . . . I thought you had decided against giving me the list. What changed your mind?"

"More faith and less practicality. It's something I need to work on," he said with a shrug and then pushed the envelope in her hand.

Erin asked, "Is this going to create a problem for you with Archer?"

"It's one in a million anyone will ever notice I ran off a list, and if they do, it probably wouldn't raise a suspicion. I've been involved in the care of all these women in one way or another." He looked at Erin, feeling as if it were a defining moment in their relationship. Not totally understanding why he had caved in to her request for the list, Noah was a little surprised that he didn't feel the regret he anticipated. Still feeling Erin was a victim of her own overzealous imagination, he had to admit there was a certain passion in her convictions. Dismissing professional practicalities and falling back on faith and their relationship, this was something he wanted to do for Erin.

Erin looked at the envelope and then back at Noah. "Don't think this means that I'm going to sleep with you."

"A little late for that, Erin," he whispered with a blush.

"Oh, yeah. I forgot."

"Thanks."

"What are you doing now?"

"I have a conference with the residents," he said.

"Dinner later?"

"I'll meet you in the lobby of your hotel at eight."

Noah watched as Erin quickly reached her car, jumped in

and pulled away. She waved, pinning her cellular phone between her shoulder and cheek. Noah turned and headed back into the institute, confident that Erin would be discreet with the list.

Chapter 44

After a dozen tedious phone calls to various state agencies, Sam concluded that reviewing Neotech's requisite documentation with respect to bed requests, certificates of need, code violations and patient complaints would be best accomplished with a one-day trip to the Agency for Health Care Administration in Tallahassee.

Jet service from Miami to Tallahassee was quite limited, but the thought of taking a turboprop commuter to better suit his schedule took a distant second to Sam's preference for jet transportation.

Refusing a second offer of coffee from a perky flight attendant, Sam reclined his chair, closed his eyes and listened as the captain announced in a smooth southern drawl that they would be on the ground in thirty minutes.

Also headed to Tallahassee, but on a flight that departed from West Palm Beach twenty minutes before Sam's, sat Frank Grafton. Dressed in a tweed sport coat and black dress slacks, he sat comfortably in an aisle seat sipping on the last of his orange juice.

By the time Sam's flight touched down in Tallahassee,

Grafton had already walked across the expansive lobby of the single terminal and made his way to the far end, where a man in a late-model Dodge pickup waited.

"Just drive," Grafton told Nick Dawson as he climbed into the cab. A small-time hood who worked as a roofer in the absence of any action, Nick had first met Grafton in the military, and Grafton had enlisted his services on several occasions over the years. Loyal to a fault, Nick was efficient and reliable as long as the task wasn't too demanding.

"Where are we going?" Nick asked.

"To the Greyhound station," Grafton told him, pulling his shoulder harness across his chest and buckling it.

"I don't know where that is."

"I do. Follow this road to the exit and turn left. At the second light turn right until you hit I-5."

"Okay," Nick said.

"Where did you get the truck?"

"In Destin," he answered. "Out of a strip mall."

"And the plates?"

"Already changed. Just like you told me."

"How long ago?"

"This morning. Just like you told me," he said again with added accentuation.

The ride to the bus terminal took only about fifteen minutes. They rode in silence. Nick got out and left the engine running, leaving the odor of his bargain aftershave hanging in the cab like a patch of fog. Grafton walked around to the other side, handed Nick an envelope and climbed in behind the wheel.

"There's no need to count it, Nick. It's all there."

"I never doubted it for a second, Gunny."

Grafton raised his eyebrows and turned his head in one motion. "Drop the military crap," he said and then rolled up his window and drove away.

Nick snapped his shoulders back, saluted briskly and then gave Grafton the finger. He slit the envelope open and pulled out a stack of new one-hundred-dollar bills. Grafton was right. There was no need to count them. All twenty-five were there. Tucking the bills back in, he folded the envelope and shoved it deep into the front pocket of his washed-out jeans. A moment later he was heading for the terminal to check the schedule back to Mobile.

After three hours of poring over every document the Agency for Health Care Administration could locate on Neotech, Sam leaned back in a small wooden chair, gathered his papers in a neat pile and slid them into a large envelope. He had reviewed every patient complaint, request for remodeling, certificate of need and possible Cobra violation. Tomorrow he would forward the documents along to one of his colleagues who specialized in health care law, but from what Sam could deduce on his own, Neotech was squeaky clean and perhaps even exemplary.

Sam stood up and walked over to one of the administrative assistants who had helped him. The young man, dressed in a button-down white shirt and plain navy-blue tie looked up from his computer screen.

"Should I call for a cab or can I just grab one out front?" Sam asked him.

"I'd just head outside. You shouldn't have a problem."

"Thanks for all the help."

"Any time," he said.

As soon as he walked outside, he noticed it hadn't warmed up very much. Sam pulled his white Polo sweatshirt down below his waist and walked down a broad path to the sidewalk. The traffic on Mahan Street was busy, leading Sam to assume the young man was right and that flagging down a cab wouldn't be a problem.

Grafton had parked at a meter on the same side of the street as the agency about two hundred feet away. He recognized Sam as soon as he exited the front door and sat up in his seat as the intensity of the hunt began to heighten. He reached above the visor and pulled down a pair of black wraparound sunglasses and slipped them on.

The engine idled quietly. Grafton tapped the steering wheel as his eyes darted between watching Sam and checking his side-view mirror for approaching cabs.

A long line of parked cars stood between Grafton and his prey. Finally the small image of a white minivan with an illuminated Taxi sign on its roof appeared in the mirror. Sam must have caught sight of it at the same instant and advanced off the curb with a raised hand.

Grafton gave the visor of his black baseball cap a sharp tug. On either side of his forehead he could feel the pounding throb of his pulse. A new drizzle of sweat loosened the perch of his sunglasses. With the image of the approaching cab growing larger in the pickup's mirror, Grafton slammed the accelerator, darted out and raced past a series of parked cars.

Waving to get the cab driver's attention, Sam took a few more steps forward. The cab lagged several car lengths behind Grafton, who had already bolted his eyes on Sam, hoping his attention would remain focused on the cab. In a matter of seconds, there was nothing between him and Sam. Grafton tightened his grip in anticipation of jerking the wheel to the right. Another two seconds and he yanked the wheel over. The tires screeched as the back of the truck swerved into an S and veered directly for Sam, whose eyes were already on Grafton.

With a speed Grafton had never seen, Sam lowered his body, started forward and launched himself like a catapulted navy fighter and was instantly airborne. Grafton watched, stunned, as Sam's shoulders sailed over the front right side of the hood.

The Dodge sped forward for another twenty feet before Grafton realized he'd missed. With panic now in the equation, he yanked the wheel back to the left, but before he could pull the truck back into its lane, the front end crashed over the curb and up on the sidewalk. Two coeds, jogging in Florida State T-shirts, dove out of the way as the truck swerved back to the left, causing the cab to rock like a carnival ride.

Without losing his grip on the wheel, Grafton was thrown hard against the door. Before he could recover, the truck jumped off the curb and was back on the street. Its back end still wobbling, Grafton was finally able to focus ahead and make the final correction to regain control. As soon as he reached the corner, he turned left and disappeared.

The smell of burning rubber was still in the air when Sam was helped to his feet by a young man in a white sweat suit. Brushing himself off, he looked down the street in a calculated and calm stare. From hundreds of hours of full-contact sparring, he knew he wasn't hurt. He recognized the man driving the Dodge as the same one who had followed Erin out of the Cheesecake Factory at the Aventura Mall.

"Are you all right, buddy?" a second man in khaki carpenter pants and a tan golf shirt asked.

"I think so," Sam answered, scanning the area for his envelope. A young lady handed him the envelope. He thanked her with a smile and then thanked the man in the white sweat suit who had helped him up.

"I called the cops," another man told him, pointing to his cell phone. "We've got too many drunk drivers in this town."

"I guess it's a problem everywhere," Sam offered without the slightest suspicion that the man behind the wheel of the truck was intoxicated.

A cruiser, with its lights flashing, pulled up. After spending the better part of a half hour with a police officer who couldn't have been out of the academy for more than a year, Sam hailed a cab and headed back to the airport.

Frank Grafton left the Dodge pickup in the visitors' parking lot of the Tallahassee Community Hospital, walked to the last row and got into the black Ford Taurus that Nick Dawson had rented. He checked his watch. Even if it took him three hours to reach Pensacola, he'd still be in plenty of time to catch his flight back to Miami. Failure to accomplish his mission never entered his mind when he left for Tallahassee, but his ego hadn't grown to such a degree that a contingency plan was not in place.

Grafton hadn't gone more than a couple of miles when his cell phone rang.

"Yes," he answered.

"Do you recognize my voice?" Ronald Thurston inquired. His shift at Southside's patient accounts department was just about over when he had decided to call Grafton in spite of the strict instructions never to do so again.

"I recognize your voice but I can't say I'm very happy to hear it. I thought we covered this ground about contacting me."

"I think you'll want to hear what I have to say. John Freeman's toxicology results have reappeared in the computer."

Grafton had experienced enough disappointment for one day, making Thurston's revelation the last thing he wanted to hear. "How's that possible?" he asked. "Do I need to remind you of the guarantees you made me?"

"I kept my promise," Thurston insisted.

"Really? Then why are the results back in the computer?"

"I deleted them permanently. The only way they could be back in the system is if someone reentered them."

"What are you trying to say?" Grafton asked, squeezing the steering wheel tightly until his fingers were drained of blood.

"I'm saying that nobody knows the Southside computer system better than I do . . . so I went down to Medical Records and pulled Freeman's chart. The handwritten results from the E.R. are back on his chart. Somebody must have been making inquiries, otherwise nobody would think to check if the results were in the computer. They'd just assume they were."

"You have created a difficult problem for me. You were paid an enormous amount of money based on assurances you made."

"I . . . like I told you—"

"I'm not interested in listening to any of your feeble excuses. I'm only interested in results. I recommend you resign

your position at the hospital and take up residence in another
state as soon as possible."

"You can't be serious," Thurston said.

"As serious as a heart attack . . . if you know what I mean."
Grafton disconnected the call and tossed his phone down on
the seat next to him. He knew exactly who had been making
inquiries at Southside Hospital. Erin Wells had gone too far.
It was his ass that was now on the line and he'd be damned if
he'd take any further orders from someone who lacked the
guts to make a hard decision.

Sam Forbes, hands clasped in his lap, watched
as a rangy young man in a smartly pressed U.S. Air uniform
began the check-in process for his flight back to Miami. He
estimated there were about two dozen people in line. Raising
his hands and then rubbing his lower lip, he remained in deep
thought about the institute. There was no question in his mind
that Erin Wells was antagonizing some powerful people.

After the line dwindled a little, Sam stood up and fell in
behind an elderly couple arguing about who should be responsible for their carry-on luggage. Their prattle became distant as Sam focused on the events of the day. His anger was,
as always, in check, but that in no way changed his resolve.
Amidst an extremely confusing situation, one truth remained:
*Someday, he would confront the man who drove the Dodge
pickup and tried to kill him.*

Chapter 45

It was the end of a long day and the last place Erin wanted to be was stuck in traffic. She had spent most of the afternoon with Claire. All of her tests had been normal, leaving Claire even more excited and confident about her upcoming surgery.

Erin leaned out the window of her Firebird and looked between the long lines of stalled traffic. About a half mile ahead, on the left, she could see several emergency vehicles with their red and blue lights spinning in synchrony. With a deep frown on her face, she brought her head back in just as her cell phone rang. She recognized the man's voice at once. "How was your trip to Tallahassee?"

"Interesting," Sam answered.

"Did you come up with anything?" she asked, lowering the volume of the radio.

"Not really. It looks like Neotech, at least on the surface, is pretty clean."

"It doesn't surprise me. If anything's going on, I doubt it's going to jump out at us." Erin crawled forward a few yards as the traffic started to move a little. "I have some good news for you."

"I wouldn't be opposed to getting some of that," he said.

"I got the list of patients."

"I'm impressed. How did you pull that off? Or shouldn't I ask?"

"Noah gave it to me."

"I see," he said, feeling a little guilty about his decision not to share the details with Erin about his trip to Tallahassee. "One other thing," he added as an aside. "Have the hotel change your room."

"I beg your pardon," she said, sounding more than a bit confused.

"Ask the hotel to change your room."

"Why?"

"Just to change your pattern."

"Pattern? What are you talking about?" she asked in an exasperated tone.

"I'm a mother hen . . . humor me."

Erin put both hands on the wheel, looked in the rearview mirror and swallowed hard.

"Are you trying to scare the hell out of me?"

"Not intentionally," he assured her.

"That's an answer?" she asked with raised eyebrows.

"For now, it's the best I can do. By the way, is there anything new on Freeman or his research on Tocalazine?"

Erin shook her head. "No, not since I spoke with Dr. McGiver. I guess he's still working on it. He said he'd call me if he turned up anything."

"It would be nice if we could get back into Dr. Freeman's office," Sam mentioned.

"That's an interesting notion," she said with too much enthusiasm for Sam's liking.

"Forget it, Erin. You'll only get yourself in trouble."

"I'll call you later," she promised.

"Remember what I said—" he began, but the line was already dead.

Erin had already replaced the phone in her purse. The car was cooling off nicely and she set the fan all the way down. Her level of frustration was growing as the date of Claire's surgery rapidly approached. She was reminded of her childhood when she sat stuck over a complicated jigsaw puzzle with her father, who had taught her to align the outer pieces first . . . *the ones with the straight edges,* he used to say. His words echoed in her head as she visualized hundreds of multicolored pieces of a tricky puzzle of the Sistine Chapel laid out on the family's dining room table.

Erin gazed out the window as she finally passed the accident. A small two-seater convertible had obviously struck the guardrail and spun out. The driver, who appeared uninjured, was out of the car and talking to the police. The impact had resulted in extensive front-end damage and caused the car to come to rest facing in the oncoming direction. As soon as she went by the collision site, the pace of the traffic promptly returned to normal. Hitting the accelerator, she changed lanes and moved along at a speed that would have tested the indulgence of the Florida Highway Patrol.

Her thoughts returned to her conversation with Sam, especially his comment about Dr. Freeman's office. She slowed the car, exited the causeway at the first opportunity and headed back to the hospital. Once in the parking lot, it took her only another few minutes to reach the main lobby. To her relief, she spotted Noah's car when she crossed the lot. He was in the lobby five minutes after she paged him.

"What's up?" he asked. "I wasn't expecting to see you until later. What's the favor you need?"

"I need to get into the library."

"Did you call security?"

"Yeah, but they said if I wasn't a doctor or nurse, they couldn't let me in. May I borrow your key?"

"I'll do better than that," he said. "I'll go with you."

"I'm going up to Claire's room first. I'd like to spend some time with her. I probably won't go to the library for another half hour or so."

He looked at his watch and then reached into the waist pocket of his white coat and pulled out his key ring. It took him a few moments to slide his passkey off of the double ring. "I have to meet the residents in about fifteen minutes for evening rounds. Just let yourself into the library. I'm sure security won't mind."

"Thanks," she told him, reaching for the key. "I'll see you later."

"Same place and time?" he asked with a modest smile.

"You bet."

Consumed with excitement and not thinking to call Sam for his opinion before venturing forth, Erin quickly made her way out of the hospital. With Noah's passkey gripped tightly in her hand, she walked down the path leading to the research center. She was wearing black cargo pants and a cardigan but could still feel a chill beginning at the base of her neck and running down her arms. Moving at a headlong pace, the possibility that the research area was monitored by surveillance cameras never entered her mind.

Once inside the building, she followed the dimly lit hallway that approached the lab. Even in the poor light she could appreciate the immaculate walls and sharply polished tile floors. The building was cool with the smell of an ammonia chemical in the air, making Erin wonder if the janitorial service might be about. Craning her neck, she checked the hall in both directions and saw nothing. She took the last few steps slowly and stopped in front of Dr. Freeman's lab. There was more than enough light to slide the key in, and with one turn the lock tumbled and the door opened.

Walking quickly down the main aisle, Erin turned at the last work center and then past a large bank of monitors with flashing digital dispslays that she assumed were some form of timed calibration. She forced herself to disregard the painful tightening in the pit of her stomach.

The door to Dr. Freeman's office was slightly ajar. She took the last few steps cautiously and with a light push watched as it swept open silently. Placing her purse on one of the chairs that faced his desk, Erin looked around for a few seconds, feeling the first nag of remorse about being in Freeman's office.

Stepping slowly around the desk, she stopped next to the first set of drawers. Moving his chair over just slightly, she opened the top drawer, peered in, but saw nothing more than a few pens, two small writing pads and some small syringes still in their plastic wrappers. Toward the back of the drawer she noticed two Snickers bars. Quietly sliding the drawer closed, she noticed a distinct tremor in her fingertips.

After looking through the remaining three drawers and scanning the top of the desk, Erin turned and walked over to the file cabinet. The small white refrigerator had not been disconnected. In an otherwise silent office, the hum was quite conspicuous. She cracked opened the door and the light came on. Apart from a dozen or so neatly aligned cans of orange juice, two Cokes and a large bar of chocolate with the paper torn off of one end, there was nothing. "A chocolate fanatic," she said to herself. "If I were on this guy's diet, I'd weigh three hundred pounds."

Freeman's bookcase looked about the same as the first couple of times she had studied it. The lab remained quiet. Her intensity and sense of purpose combined to partially quell her nervousness. She turned to the large metal file cabinet and slid open each drawer, taking sufficient time to glance at each file. After finishing, she glanced down at her watch and figured she'd been in the office about twenty minutes.

Feeling a little more comfortable and perhaps too brazen, Erin sat down behind Freeman's desk. She leaned forward, closed her eyes and focused on her interview with him.

Why was he so nervous? She'd never seen anybody that jumpy and clammy during an interview. It just didn't seem in character for a veteran research scientist.

Reaching in her purse, Erin pulled a cherry LifeSaver off of a new roll. She looked at it for a second and then popped it in her mouth. A minor vice, she thought. A simple and relatively safe indulgence that had always served her well as a hedge against the jitters.

In the next instant, Erin's eyes snapped open and she sat bolt upright. Her pulse hammered and a drizzle of sweat layered on her neck. In one quick motion, she spun the chair to her right and pulled open the top drawer of the desk again. "Syringes and chocolate," she mumbled as she covered her mouth. Erin jumped up and went over to the refrigerator and yanked it open. There was the juice, but there were no diet sodas, just Coke. No other drinks or food . . . just the chocolate. She whirled in place with a new intensity.

"Where is it? It's got to be here."

Erin ran her hand over the top of the file cabinet and felt nothing. The cabinets were high and an unlikely place to find what she was after. Her eye was caught by the desk drawers again. Sliding the top one open and reaching all the way in the back behind two small notebooks, she felt a small leather pouch with a zipper that felt almost identical to the makeup bag she carried in her purse.

Sliding it out slowly, she held it in her left hand and then slid the zipper open. A smile of relief came to her face as she looked down at the small bottle of insulin. She tucked the small bag inside her purse, took one final look around and wasted no time in leaving John Freeman's office.

"Chocolate fanatic nothing," she said in a huff, storming out the side entrance to the research building, oblivious to the light sprinkle of rain. "The man was a diabetic."

Armed with new information about Dr. Freeman, Erin couldn't wait to get to her car and call Sam. It was about two hundred feet to the parking lot if one followed the back path behind the research building. It was poorly lit and there was a light rain that was starting to mount. Erin pulled her cardigan up around her neck, looked up at the sky and figured it would take her half the amount of time to reach her car if she took the path. The small amount of light coming from a crescent moon was screened by thick rolling thunderclouds. The ground, slippery from the rain, made it difficult to walk quickly. The air was heavy and smelled of freshly cut grass.

Erin was about ten feet from the end of the building when a man in dark pants, a button-down work shirt with the institute's emblem on the pocket and a baseball cap turned the corner. In the poor light, she couldn't quite make out his face but assumed he was from maintenance. Erin looked straight down and then picked up her stride a little. In another few steps she'd be past him, onto the parking lot and to her car. Their distance closed. It was raining harder and the wind picked up. Erin's eyes remained fixed on the ground. She felt his presence but his footsteps made no sound as he approached.

The pain from his crushing grip was like no other she had ever felt. In the next instant she felt her feet leave the ground. Twisting in midair like a palm leaf in a hurricane, she was whirled against the building. A large hand, which smelled of fresh soap, was over her mouth muffling any attempt to scream. She had to struggle to breathe. He turned his shoulders slightly and then used his knee to pin her against the building. His eyes were hollow and lusterless, but hardly those of a madman.

She whirled her hips and pushed against him but accomplished nothing. She continued to gasp for air but his hands never moved as he seemed to wait for her to capitulate to the situation.

"I'm not going to harm you. Stand still, don't scream and I'll remove my hand. If you try to run, I'll break your pelvis into tiny pieces before you get two steps. Do we understand each other?" Her mind was spinning, trying to recall everything she'd ever read about a hypothetical attack. Should she fight? Should she submit? "Do you understand?" he repeated. She nodded slowly under the power of his hand. "Good," he said slowly, lowering his hand.

"What do you want?" she demanded. "Take my purse. My money and keys are in there."

Grafton looked down at the ground where her purse had

fallen and shrugged. "I already have a car," he said nonchalantly. "Anyway, it's not even yours."

"Then take my money."

"Actually, I'm flush at the moment."

Erin was still breathing quickly and feeling light-headed
from hyperventilation. His eyes hadn't changed. This was
business and she knew it.

She renewed her question. "What do you want?"

"Answers."

"To what?"

"Well, for starters, what were you doing in Dr. Freeman's
office?"

"Who are you?"

"I'm the chief of security around here," he said calmly.
"I'm not real tolerant of uninvited guests wandering into our
research facility after hours."

"I had permission."

"Sure you did. I was watching you on the surveillance
monitor, you know. Do you really think you can just stroll in
and out of my facility whenever you feel like it?"

"Your facility?"

Grafton's expression changed. "Never mind that. What
were you looking for?"

"Look. There's been a misunderstanding. My name's Erin
Wells. I'm a reporter doing a story—"

"I know who you are."

"Then let me go, for crissakes."

"As soon as you tell me what you were up to."

"I just told you. I was working on a story."

"Really," he said, reaching into his pocket and pulling out
a thick, curved knife with a heavily serrated blade. "Then
you'll have no objection to escorting me to the police department. My car is right over there."

"Why don't you just call from here?" she asked, staring at
the knife. "I'll be happy to speak with the police as soon as
they get here."

"Let's do it my way," he suggested, raising the tip of the

knife to the base of her neck. "Start walking." Grafton backed off two steps and used his knife to point in the direction of the parking lot. He reached forward and again gripped her arm just above the elbow. Erin was too terrified to give much thought to his unorthodox methods of doing his job, but her instinct was enough to convince her not to go anywhere near his car.

"I would really prefer it if you would call the police from here," she told him, figuring that she had about thirty yards to try an escape.

"Shut up, lady," he said, yanking her forward. "You broke into our facility and were illegally trespassing. You don't get a vote."

When they were just a few feet from the end of the building she caught sight of a figure turning the corner. In one motion the man's foot came up like a piston and Grafton's knife went flying. Pushing Erin to the side and spinning around, Grafton faced the man and threw a wild overhead right. The man easily measured him, sidestepped the punch and then vectored him away by catching his arm above the elbow and spinning him around like a figure skater. When the man turned and the light caught his face, Erin realized it was Sam.

Chapter 46

When Grafton whirled back around, Sam launched a short elbow, catching him squarely in the face, shattering his delicate nasal bones and sending a stream of blood flying in all directions. Grafton, powerful and not without training, again turned back into the combat. Always willing to give up something to get something, he came in behind a left hook. Sam ducked the punch, grabbed Grafton's wrist and rolled it over into an arm bar. With the right side of Grafton's chest now exposed, Sam turned into him and caught him with a quick right hand just under his armpit. The force of the blow took out three ribs, sending splinters of bone like shrapnel into his lung.

Writhing from pain, Grafton hit the ground like a collapsed building. Air escaping from his punctured lung gathered quickly in his chest cavity, causing an immediate and total collapse of his lung. The blow was devastating, decisive, and left Grafton gasping for each breath. As Sam was well aware, a fight with a trained technician rarely lasted more than thirty seconds.

"C'mon," Sam said to Erin, stepping around Grafton. "We have to get out of here."

"Wait . . . what about him?" she asked, paralyzed in place.

"Just leave him. Let's go."

"We . . . we can't just leave him here."

"He was going to kill you, Erin. Now let's get out of here."

Sam took a few steps forward and grabbed Erin's hand. Just as he did, Sam saw a flash of reflected light sail past Erin's thigh. Still breathless, Grafton was now on his back with the knife clenched in his hand. As he started his second lunge, Sam made the catch, wrenched Grafton's wrist until his hand and forearm were almost perpendicular, and then with a powerful jerk rotated them outward. Grafton screamed in pain as the knife fell to the ground. Sam twisted harder until he felt Grafton's wrist shatter from the torque. In the same motion, he rotated his hips ninety degrees, flexed his knee and got off a side kick that caught Grafton square in the forehead. His head snapped backward, leaving him unconscious.

Sam reached down and scooped up her purse. "C'mon, Erin. Let's go," he said, extending his hand.

"Aren't you going to call somebody?"

"I don't think so," he said.

"What about that guy?"

"He's on his own. Now let's go."

They walked quickly across the parking lot in silence. He took out his keys and helped her in on the passenger side. Erin sat motionless as Sam slowly pulled out of the parking lot. Her head was turned to the side, staring out the window. After a few moments, she looked back at Sam, amazed that he hadn't even broken a sweat. He felt her eyes on him.

"It's over, Erin."

"Until they send someone else," she said in a monotone.

"They won't."

"Easy for you to say with all that kung fu stuff you were doing."

"That has nothing to do with it."

"Is he the one who killed Dr. Freeman and drove me off the road?"

Sam drove carefully, taking care not to exceed the speed limit. "I wouldn't be surprised. He's been following you for days."

"Thanks for sharing that with me," Erin said, watching the hypnotic effect of the lights of the oncoming cars. "Maybe it's time to go to the police," she said.

"And tell them what? That I beat the hell out of the institute's chief of security when he was trying to detain you for illegally snooping around in their research lab."

"Well . . . I'm sure—"

"It's all on their videotape, Erin. You can count on it."

"I know he killed Freeman," she said as Sam exited the causeway and headed north.

"That's a great theory. Got any proof?" Sam gazed into the rearview mirror.

"That guy who attacked me. I didn't even know—"

"His name's Grafton," Sam said. "He's an ex-Marine."

Her voice was still collected, almost as if she had taken a tranquilizer. Sam had seen many people after a frightening experience, and had seen many of them act like Erin . . . as if they were in a near zombie state.

"Dr. Freeman was a diabetic. I should have figured it out sooner," she said. "That first time I spoke to him he was all clammy and kept drinking juice. His sugar must have been real low from taking too much insulin. I took care of dozens of people in insulin shock when I was a nurse." She pushed the button on the center console and lowered her window a few inches. "His office was loaded with chocolate. I should have put two and two together when I first interviewed him." She stopped for a moment and then added, "Grafton knew he was a diabetic."

"How does that add up to murder?" Sam asked.

"Dr. Freeman died of a digitalis overdose. I'm sure of that now. Grafton must have figured out some way to replace his insulin with digitalis."

"I don't get it," he said.

"Freeman assumed he was taking his normal morning shot of insulin but instead he injected himself with a fatal dose of digitalis. The symptoms can look just like a heart attack." Erin shook her head and gazed out the window again. She was exhausted. "Now what do we do?" she asked.

"I'm not sure. I'm still waiting for some information. Just sit tight for a little while longer. We don't have enough to go to the authorities yet. Is Noah staying over tonight?"

Her chin dropped. She finally seemed a little more animated. "I beg your pardon?"

"I'm supposed to keep an eye on you. It's my job to know everything . . . anyway, Herb insisted."

Erin made a fist and shook it at Sam. "Herb's my editor. The job of my father's already taken."

"I'll mention that to him. Listen, I'm going to drop off my car and take a cab back to the institute so that I can pick up yours." He waited for a few moments before pointing to her purse. "I'll need the keys, Erin."

She opened her purse, fumbled around for a few seconds and then pulled out the keys.

"Here," she said.

"I'll valet it so you'll have it in the morning. Now, what about Noah?"

"I'm sure he'll stay over," she said as if she were being treated as a child. "But he's not a tenth-degree black belt."

"Seventh."

"What?"

"I'm a seventh-degree black belt."

"Sorry."

"Uh . . . I wouldn't share any of this with Noah right now," Sam advised.

"Fine," she said. "Why did you have to beat Grafton up so badly?"

Sam turned and without a moment's hesitation he explained, "Because I respected him."

"I don't understand."

"You're not supposed to. You're not a martial artist. Just go straight to your room and wait for Noah. Are you going to be okay?"

She managed a quick smile. "For the last twenty minutes I've been trying to figure out how to thank you. If you weren't there . . . I, I don't know what—"

"But I was there. So don't think about it."

"Sure," she said in that sarcastic tone he was already familiar with. "I'll probably never give it another thought."

The car slowed. Erin looked up to see the lights of the Inter-Continental. A young man with a baby's complexion and freckles covering his arms opened the door for her. She stepped out and kept watching until Sam was out of sight. She was still daydreaming when a loud horn startled her.

"I thought I was going to meet you inside," Noah said as he stepped out of his car.

"I . . . I just came out for some air."

"Are you ready?" he asked.

"Ready?"

"Yeah. I thought we were driving up to Fort Lauderdale for dinner."

Erin sighed. "I'm a little tired, Noah. Would you mind if we just stay here and eat at the hotel?"

"Of course not. I'm kind of tired myself. Did you find what you were looking for in the library?"

"What?"

"The library. Did you find what you were looking for?"

"Oh, yes," she replied, reaching into her purse and returning his passkey. "I found exactly what I was looking for."

Chapter 47

The public library in Hollywood shares a finely landscaped campus with the Broward Community College. Set back from Pines Boulevard by about two hundred feet, the two-story structure of international architecture attracts not only a large number of undergraduate students but an eclectic group of local residents as well.

Sam's instructions to Erin were quite specific. He told her to meet him in the small room adjacent to the periodical files. As soon as she passed the main desk, Erin spotted Sam seated at a small wooden table.

"How long have you been waiting?" she asked, pulling out one of the heavy chairs and taking a seat directly across from him.

"About five minutes. Did you have any trouble finding the place?"

"No, your directions were perfect." Erin zipped open her attaché and pulled out a stack of papers separated into several piles by silver paper clips. "These patient lists are interesting. I think I may have come up with something." Sam's expression remained neutral as he watched her organize the piles. "I spent quite some time on this today."

Erin laid out the documents and fiddled with them for a few moments. "The FDA's list includes all the women who have participated in the Phase I trials of Tocalazine. It was an easy enough matter to cross-reference them against Noah's list." Erin turned the piles toward Sam and showed him the lists. His reading glasses sat perched on the tip of his nose but he still had to back up another few inches to get the focal length just right. He ran his index finger methodically down each of the lists.

"This seems pretty straightforward," he finally said.

"That's what I thought at first," she said with an increased intensity in her voice. "But if you count up the total number of patients the institute enrolled in the study since 1996, it comes out to ninety. But when I checked Noah's list, which includes all the patients who had fetal surgery in the same period of time, the number is one hundred and sixty-three. That's seventy-three patients that are unaccounted for."

Sam sat back in his chair and shrugged. "They're not necessarily unaccounted for, maybe they just didn't participate in the study. It's quite possible when given the choice they decided not to—"

"No way," she interrupted with a fast shake of her head.

"What makes you so sure?"

"Because I interviewed Leigh Sierra."

"You'll have to refresh my memory," he said slowly.

"She's the director of clinical research. She told me that compliance in the studies was near one hundred percent, and Noah told me the same thing. Each patient was counseled and had to sign a consent. The FDA's very specific about strict compliance with the protocol."

"Are you sure?"

"I checked my notes," she assured him, pulling the two stacks of papers back toward her.

"So what's so special about the seventy-three that didn't participate?"

She leaned forward and put her hands on the table. "That, my friend, is the sixty-four-thousand-dollar question. I've already cross-referenced age, diagnosis and prior pregnancies."

"And?"

She shook her head. "There's no common thread that I can see so far."

"So far?"

Erin frowned at the doubt in his voice. "There's something here, Sam. There were one hundred and sixty-three fetal procedures done at the institute since the animal studies were approved and permission granted to initiate Phase I trials. Only ninety women were enrolled in the study. What happened to the other seventy-three?" She watched as Sam pushed his chair back and crossed his leg over his knee. Much to her chagrin his expression remained guarded.

"Why don't you ask Leigh Sierra?" he asked.

"I thought of that. I was just about to call her office when I decided against it."

"How come?"

"I'm not sure. I guess I was afraid I'd have to answer a bunch of questions and . . ."

"And what?" he asked.

"I really like Leigh. We kind of hit it off and I don't want her to think I'm taking advantage of the fact."

Sam slowly wrinkled his brow. "That doesn't sound like a reporter talking."

"If I'm still at a dead end by tonight, I'll give her a call," she said. "There's something else that's still bothering me." Sam looked at her without saying anything. "Sarah Allen."

"The woman with the strange nurse in her room?"

"Yeah. Her IV bag was the one I asked Herb to have analyzed . . . the one the lab in Washington discovered Pitressin in."

"I remember."

"I still don't have a logical explanation why there was

Pitressin in her IV. I can't buy it was a routine pharmacy mistake. It's just too coincidental."

"What do you mean?" he asked.

"Well, of all the drugs they could have accidentally put in her IV, what's the likelihood it would be Pitressin?" She stopped for a moment and rubbed the back of her neck. "The odds against such a thing would have to approach infinity."

"What do you plan to do about it?"

"I think the answer may be in the medical records department. I'm going to review her chart and probably pull a bunch of the others as long as I'm there."

"What are you going to compare?"

She took a deep breath. "I'll just have to figure that out when I get started. There's a lot of information in those charts."

"It sounds like a long shot."

Erin sneered. "Don't rain on my parade, Sam. I'll call Herb on you."

Sam feigned a frightened face. "Anything but that," he joked. "Can I have a look at these?" he asked, pointing at the stacks of papers.

Erin nodded and passed the papers to Sam. The table was quite large, and apart from Erin and Sam, nobody else was seated there. Taking a moment to organize the papers, Sam began laying them out until the entire tabletop was covered. "That's better," he pronounced, as if he had just figured out the problem.

"What's better?" Erin asked with a trace of cynicism.

"The organization is better," he told her, and then turned his attention to the list of patients from Noah's office. Each page was made up of about six names and included both a demographic profile and basic medical information regarding diagnosis, date of the surgical procedure, postoperative complications and the expected date of the baby's delivery. "Okay," he announced confidently. "Read me the names of the ninety patients from the FDA list."

"You mean the ones who participated in the study?"

"That's exactly what I mean." Erin picked up the FDA list and slowly began reading from it. As she did so, Sam followed along on Noah's list and carefully drew a line through each patient she mentioned. When he was done, he spread the papers out a little farther on the table.

"I've already done all this," she said. "There's no common element."

Sam didn't respond in words, only with a sheepish smile that annoyed Erin. He stood up, moved the chairs to one side and began walking up and down in front of the papers.

"I agree with you," he finally announced. "There's no common factor linking their diseases, dates of surgery or complications."

"I told you that fifteen minutes ago," she said in a self-satisfied voice. "Now why don't we try—"

"The demographics are interesting," he mentioned.

"I beg your pardon."

"The demographics. I said they're interesting."

Erin stood up, stood shoulder to shoulder with him and studied the lists. "What do you mean?"

"Well, from what I can tell, all the women who didn't participate in the study are from either Mexico or some other Latin country. The ninety women on the FDA list are all from the United States." He sat down and stroked his chin. "That seems more than just a little coincidental, don't you think?"

Erin leaned forward, placed her palms on the table and then tapped her fingers. She was mortified and could only pray her face was not as red as she feared. *How could I have overlooked such an obvious thing?* Placing her hands on her hips she walked up and down in front of the documents in much the same manner as Sam had. Happy he wasn't gloating, Erin continued to steal a glance in his direction every few seconds.

"You're right," she said. "Now what the hell do we do?"

Sam stood up, gathered all the papers together and placed them in a large manila envelope. He smiled and pointed toward the door. "I don't know about you," he said casually, "but I'm on my way to Mexico."

"Wait a minute," she said, chasing after him. "When?"

Sam waited for her to catch up and then said, "There's no time like the present."

Chapter 48

The Ryder Trauma Center, located on the campus of the Jackson Memorial Hospital, is a state-of-the-art facility. Recently opened to accommodate the rising number of trauma victims in Dade County, the center serves a vital role.

Mike Casteneda, chief resident on the Red Trauma Service, stood in the intensive care unit at the foot of Frank Grafton's bed with his intern, Jason Hurlow, at his side. The ventilator, connected firmly to Grafton's recently created tracheotomy, droned with precision as it delivered one vital breath after another. A large plastic tube, which had been inserted into Grafton's chest cavity to re-expand his lung, was connected to a suction device that hooked over the end of Grafton's bed.

"Where do we stand with this guy?" Mike asked his intern, reaching for Grafton's clipboard where it was lying on a small table at the foot of the bed. Mike had been in the operating room for the last eight hours and wanted to be brought up to speed on his patients as quickly as possible.

"His head CT's unchanged," Jason began, shuffling

through a stack of three-by-five cards that he carried on each patient. "He still has a small subdural hematoma."

"What did the neurosurgeons say?"

"They just want to watch it," Jason informed him. "They think it's too small to operate on now, but they want another CT in twelve hours."

"Make sure you order it. They'll probably forget."

"Got ya."

"And his chest?" Mike asked.

"His lung's re-expanded but I had to go up on the suction. He's got at least five broken ribs but no flail chest." Jason hesitated for a moment and then added, "He's also got a bunch of facial bone fractures. The oral surgeons want to take him to the OR as soon as we give them the okay."

"Not till neurosug says it's okay." Mike approached an X-ray view box and looked at Grafton's chest film. "What the hell happened to this guy?" Mike asked.

"Nobody seems to know," Jason explained with a shrug. "He was brought in by the paramedics. Someone said he's the director of security over at the Fetal Institute. We're guessing he got jumped and beaten up by some prowlers."

"Are there any other injuries?" Mike asked.

Jason took another quick glance at his card. "No, that's it."

"Fine," Mike said, stepping back and waving his intern on to the next patient. "From the look of things, it doesn't look like Mr. Grafton will be going anywhere for the next few weeks."

Chapter 49

Alex and Claire were seated on her bed gig-
gling with an empty pizza box between them when Erin
walked through the door. Claire was dressed in a pink Disney
nightshirt with her legs stretched out beneath her swollen
belly. Alex had his shoes off and his tie loosened. His first officer's cap lay propped against the pizza box.

"What are you guys doing?" Erin asked, wondering why
they both seemed to be in such a jubilant mood.

Claire looked down at the pizza box and then at Alex. "We
just finished a romantic dinner for two."

Alex laughed. "It's not much. We'll do better when I make
Captain."

Claire caught Erin staring at the box. "Alex ate most of it.

"I'm sure he did. Does the hospital nutritionist know what
you're eating?"

"What's the difference?" Claire asked with a shrug. "The
baby's doing great. Forty-eight hours from now he'll be all
fixed and I'll probably still be in the recovery room." Claire
leaned back against the headboard and stretched her legs out
across the soft cream-colored blanket.

"You're in a good mood," Erin said.

"I wish I could just close my eyes, open them an instant later and it would be all over."

Erin smiled, trying to share in her friend's optimism but, unfortunately, she could not. Owing to the events of the past several days, her fear for Claire and the baby had only intensified.

"Can I borrow your husband for a few minutes?" Erin asked.

Claire looked over at Alex with a perplexed look on her face. "Are you two planning something?" she asked.

"Don't look at me," Alex said, holding both hands straight up in the air.

"Erin?"

"Sorry, it's a secret. But I only need him for about ten minutes."

"Take him if you must," Claire said, waving her arms in the air like an empress. "I've grown weary of him anyway."

Erin and Alex walked down the hall to the family lounge. Erin was pleased to see the room was empty. She pointed to one of the couches, and after Alex had taken a seat she sat down across from him.

"What's up?"

"What I have to tell you is very difficult but you have to listen to me."

"Sure. What's going on?"

Erin sat forward and took an extra moment to gather her thoughts. "I want you to take Claire to another hospital. I've already made some calls and there are two other centers interested in—"

"What? . . . Another hospital? Slow down, Erin, and tell me what you're talking about. Why in the world would I want to move Claire two days before her surgery?"

"I just think it would be safer if she were at a different hospital." Erin sat back, completely filling her lungs with a deep breath, and held it for a few moments before allowing it to escape. "There are certain things—"

"Wait a minute. You used the word safer," Alex said with a clear emphasis on the word. "Maybe you should tell me what you meant by that."

Erin paused. From the expression on Alex's face she wanted to be careful how she phrased things. "In order to write my story, I've had to do a lot of research on the institute. I've come across some things that concern me."

"For instance?"

"For instance," she repeated, looking straight up, almost as if she were expecting some kind of divine guidance. "Well, for one thing, people have been very hush-hush about how things run around here."

"It's a hospital. Maybe they have a policy to—"

"And I think there may be some problems with the medications they're using."

Alex stood up, ran his fingers through his hair and then walked to the other side of the room. Erin watched nervously as he stared out the window.

"You're a reporter, Erin. This is a hospital. You can't blame them for being a little cautious about what they say."

"They've been more than a little cautious," she said.

"You mentioned something about medications?"

"I'm not sure their choices are correct," she said.

"Did you discuss it with Noah?"

"I did," she answered in a discouraged tone.

"And what were his feelings on the subject?"

"He felt there was a logical explanation," she said barely above a whisper.

The perplexed look returned to Alex's face as he interlocked his fingers and placed his hands atop his head. "With all due respect to your training as a nurse, I would have to defer to Noah's opinion. He's a physician."

Her frustration was only made worse by her realization that Alex's response was perfectly logical. "There are other things, Alex," she finally managed.

"I'm listening."

"I think this hospital has become involved in questionable research activities."

"What kind of activities?" he asked. "And is that something that would have a direct impact on Claire's care?"

Much to her chagrin, Alex had again responded in a manner that made it practically impossible to offer a convincing argument. "I'm not quite sure. All I can tell you is that there appear to be some problems."

"I'll repeat my question. Does Noah know about this?"

She billowed a breath of disappointment. "Yes . . . and before you ask, I can tell you that he doesn't share my concerns." Erin stood up and joined Alex next to the window. "Listen, Alex, there's such a thing as faith . . . and that's what I'm asking for now. I don't have all the facts. All I know is that every instinct I have tells me to get Claire out of this place."

Alex turned to face her. "Erin, you know how Claire and I feel about you, but I'm a pilot, and while I agree there's a role for instinct, I don't make critical decisions using that alone. There's nothing in what you've told me that would make me want to change hospitals."

"Maybe Claire will feel differently," she announced as she headed for the door.

Alex took three quick steps and blocked her exit. "Wait a minute, Erin. I hope you're not planning to go back in there and upset Claire with all of this?"

"It's her baby. She should have a vote."

"Let's just talk about this for another minute or two." He pointed to the couch. Erin frowned but sat back down. She was tempted to decline his request, but after a moment of thought she dismissed the notion. "Claire's mood and outlook have never been better. If you tell her the things you just told me, all you'll accomplish is to capsize every hope she has. Even if she decides to stay, she'll be terrified."

"I understand that . . . believe me, but I feel very strongly about this, Alex. I guess upsetting Claire is a chance I'll just have to take if it means saving her and the baby."

"No, it's not," he insisted, moving toward the door. "I've tried to reason with you. Now I'm begging you. Please think this over for another day before talking to Claire. If you still feel this way tomorrow night . . . we'll go to her together and let her decide." Alex wiped his forehead with the back of his hand. The desperation in his face was obvious. "That will also give me another day to think things over. What do you say?"

"I'm not sure," she said slowly.

"One day isn't going to change anything, Erin. What harm is there in waiting until tomorrow night, for God's sake?" Alex shoved his hands in his pockets and looked past her with a vacant stare. "This couldn't have come at a worse time, Erin."

"I'm sorry, Alex. But it's not like I planned it this way."

Alex focused directly on her. "I've just been informed by the airline that as of January first, they will no longer be requiring my services."

"What . . . what happened?" she asked, wondering if he had gotten himself into some aviation disciplinary issues. She could tell by the immediate change in his expression that she hadn't disguised her concerns very well.

"Nothing happened," he said. "It's a general layoff. Claire and I are going to have real financial problems next year."

"You'll get something else," she said with total confidence. It crossed her mind to offer financial help if necessary, but then dismissed the notion without much further thought for fear of bruising his ego. "You'll get a great job," she assured him again, trying her best to give his spirits a much-needed boost.

She watched as he nodded his head and then swallowed.

"I certainly hope so for the baby's sake."

"Does Claire know?" Erin inquired.

"No. And I'd kind of like to keep it that way." His tone was polite and clearly not antagonistic. "Let's not talk about it. Okay? What about my suggestion to wait another day before talking to Claire?"

Erin placed her hands on her knees and looked straight

down at the floor. Trying to be objective, she gave serious consideration to his request. With the bombshell he just laid on her, she certainly didn't want to add to his stress. Maybe she owed it to him, but more importantly, if she did wait, he might be much more open-minded when they spoke to Claire. "Okay," she finally said. "Just as long as I have your word that we'll speak to her tomorrow night if I say so."

"It's a promise." Alex walked over with a look of great relief on his face, extended his hand and helped Erin up. "Now when we go back in there, what are we going to tell Claire we were talking about?"

"I'm not sure," Erin answered. "How about plans for a baby shower?"

"Well, we can give it a shot," he declared with a laugh, putting his arm around her shoulder. As they left the lounge and headed down the hall, Erin tried to smile, but she couldn't imagine what would make her change her mind about speaking to Claire in the next twenty-four hours.

It was just after eight p.m. when Erin left the institute. She was relieved that Claire had not pressed too hard for information about what she and Alex had talked about. Just before she left Claire's room she paged Noah, but the operating room nurse told her that he was still scrubbed and was expected to be in the operating room for another two hours. She considered waiting for him, but when she recalled how inaccurate predictions are for how long operations could take, she decided to return to her hotel.

Most of the way back to the Inter-Continental Erin thought about her conversation with Alex. It hadn't gone as well as she'd hoped but at least his mind was still open and there didn't seem to be any hard feelings between them. By the time she crossed the hotel lobby and reached the elevators, she was comfortable that with some further thought on the subject there was a good chance that Alex would come around to her way of thinking.

Erin walked across the bedroom and into the bathroom. Stopping in front of the large Roman tub, she noticed a small pink container of bubble bath the hotel provided sitting on a small shelf. "Why not?" she said, leaning over and giving the hot water faucet three hard turns. She was just about to add the bubble bath and blend in the cold water when the phone rang.

She reached for the phone and picked it up just after the second ring.

"It's Sam. I'm glad I caught you in your room."

Erin smiled. "How's it going in Mexico City?"

"The climate's great but I'm having a little problem getting used to the food."

"I'm sorry to hear that," she said, having a pretty good idea of what he was talking about.

"I think I've come across some pretty interesting stuff."

"I'm all ears," she said, sitting down on the side of the tub and turning down the faucet to a trickle.

"We already know that there were about seventy-three women from Latin America who came to the institute through the clinic in Mexico City over the last two years."

"That's right."

"We also know that most of them live in Mexico."

"As I recall, that was the case," Erin said as she placed the small plastic bottle of bubble bath back on the shelf.

"I was able to locate sixty of them over the last three days."

"What do you mean, locate?"

"I've either spoken with them personally or conducted a phone interview," Sam answered. "I posed as a researcher at the institute doing routine follow-up."

Erin stood up, walked over to the sink and looked into the mirror. "Did they believe you?"

Sam chuckled. "They must have because not a single one refused to talk with me. Thank God my Spanish is still pretty good, although most of them spoke English." Erin's head bobbed lightly as she listened. "Are you sitting down?" he asked.

She looked back at the tub and said, "No."

"All of the women I spoke to gave birth without a problem."

"Sam, that doesn't make any sense. At least half of them should have suffered a spontaneous abortion from the fetal surgery."

"Listen to me, Erin. I'll repeat what I just said. Seventy-three women had fetal surgery at the institute. I've spoken to sixty of them and none of them aborted the pregnancy."

"That still doesn't make any sense. Your percentage is way too high. It's impossible—" Erin's grip on the phone tightened as she again glanced at her image in the mirror. "It's impossible . . . unless—"

"Unless what?" he asked.

"Unless they all got Tocalazine," she answered in a hush.

"That may seem more likely to you when you hear the rest of it."

"There's more?" she asked.

"Of the sixty women I was able to interview, forty-five of them reported a serious health problem with the child."

"Health problem? What type of problem?"

"There were several, but the two most common were neurologic birth defects and brain tumors . . . mostly in early infancy."

"What type of defects?" she asked.

"I'm not a doctor, but a few of the women referred to them as . . . wait a minute. Let me check my notes. Uh . . . here it is. Neural tube defects. More specifically spina bifida and anencephaly."

"My God," Erin whispered, and then sat down on the corner of the tub and closed her eyes. Sam had presented her with a lot of facts and she was struggling to process them logically.

"What are those diseases?" he asked.

"Spina bifida is a severe disease affecting the spinal cord. The children are usually wheelchair bound with an endless list of health problems. Anencephaly basically means to be born without a brain." Speechless for the moment, a chill gathered at the base of her neck and then shot straight down her spine. Her throat was so tight she couldn't even muster a dry swallow. Her next thought was of Claire. "How many of the children have died?" she asked in the same monotone.

"Sixteen," he answered. "Most of the others are still in treatment. I . . . I would expect we'll see more deaths in the next year or two. This is bad stuff, Erin."

Erin's chin dropped. She took three slow breaths. "Sam, listen to me. There are about fifteen women you still haven't spoken to. Maybe the same thing hasn't—"

"I'll try to track them down in the next day or two. But what's the chance that they'll be any different. This drug is great at preventing premature labor, but I'm afraid the price these women are paying is enormous. Do you have any idea why Noah didn't know any of this?"

Erin's thoughts were still with Claire and she had trouble focusing on Sam's question. "Uh . . . he told me he was too busy just keeping up with the surgery. Once the patients left the institute, they gave birth at their local hospitals. He had no way of knowing what happened to the babies after that." She paused for a moment. "He couldn't have possibly known," she said in a voice seeking Sam's reassurance.

"No, of course not," he assured her with a calmness she appreciated. "You've done an incredible thing here, Erin. I hope you know that. I'm sure Claire and Alex will never forget what you've done for them." He lingered for a few seconds before asking. "Which is Claire's surgery?"

"The day after tomorrow. I'm pretty sure it's the first case of the morning."

"You said something about speaking with Alex."

"I spoke with him earlier tonight," she said. "He wasn't real receptive but agreed to sleep on it. He said we could speak to Claire tomorrow night if I still felt strongly about things."

"By the way, there's one other thing. When I tried to con-

tact one of the women, I was told by her sister that she was in
Florida with her baby at the Broward Children's Hospital."

"You mean now?" she asked.

"Yes."

"What's wrong with the baby?"

"He's being treated for a very aggressive brain tumor."

Erin sighed and then asked. "How old is he?"

"Six months. I only mention it because I thought you
might want to speak with the mother. Her name is Amelia
Carillo. The baby's name is Miguel."

"That might not be a bad idea. I'll give it some thought
overnight and decide in the morning. I don't want to add to
the poor woman's misery."

"Think it over. I'll speak to you as soon as I get back to
Miami."

"Okay, I'll probably—"

"Oh, there's one last thing. What's going on with Sarah
Allen? Have you had a chance to go to Medical Records yet
to have a look at her chart?"

"No, not yet, but I did take a walk by there last night. It
seemed pretty deserted. I don't think it'll be a problem once I
get in there. I have all the medical record numbers from
Noah's list. I'm pretty sure I can figure out how to pull the
charts off the racks. It's a pretty big place and it's probably
never locked. If I work in the back, nobody should notice
me."

"I wish you luck. I hope you turn up something."

"Thanks," she told him before finishing up the conversation by making more specific arrangements to meet him when
he returned.

Her mind was already starting to preview the scene when
she confronted Alex with the information that Sam had just
given her. Sam's information was persuasive but she still
wondered if Alex would believe her. It was probably a moot
point because if his position didn't change, she would take her
case directly to Claire. The trust between them would su-
percede any doubts that she might have. The only question

that remained was when to confront Noah. He had been skeptical from the beginning, but he was a pragmatic man who embraced logical thought. There was no way he'd be able to refute the obvious.

Erin gazed into the mirror again. The lower margins of her eyes were puffy and her complexion looked more than a little pasty. She slowly turned the cold water faucet and watched for a few seconds as the water siphoned down the drain. She reached forward with cupped hands and splashed some cold water on her face. Her exhaustion was unrelieved by the chilly splash and she quickly decided to speak with Alex in the morning after a decent night's sleep. "I'll be sharper then," she said aloud. Her mind kept coming back to the same thought—*Thank God Sam had called tonight and not tomorrow night.*

Erin walked back into the bedroom and sat down in a soft club chair. Her eyes burned and closing them only seemed to make the stinging worse. She let her head fall back against the soft headrest. She thought about her conversation with Sam in detail, wondering how she could possibly figure out from the charts which patients received Tocalazine and which ones received the placebos included in the experiment. Her mind was now doing cartwheels and she felt as if she had just finished a whole pot of coffee.

In less than twenty minutes she was dressed and on her way back to the institute. It was a long shot but she had to get into the medical records department and have a look at those charts.

Chapter 50

It was just after ten p.m. when Erin pulled into the institute. The visitors' parking lot was well lit but Erin took a few extra seconds to select a space as close to the main entrance as possible.

Visiting hours had been over for an hour, and apart from the soft melody of an easy-listening instrumental, the lobby was quiet. Crossing the lobby quickly, Erin passed a small gift shop and then a circular granite information desk on her way to a long hallway that led to the administrative offices.

When she arrived at the medical records department, Erin peeked through the window before reaching for the door. As she had hoped, it was unlocked, probably to accommodate the less-organized physicians with unpredictable schedules. Erin pushed the door open slowly, took a quick look around and heaved a sigh of relief when she saw the room was empty. Walking directly to the back, she found a small table that was well concealed by a series of tall metal shelves housing hundreds of neatly filed patient charts.

Relative to other hospitals the Fetal Institute was fairly small, making the chore of locating charts less challenging.

With her list in hand, Erin began by checking Sarah Allen's medical record number. It then took her only a minute to locate the thick chart on the shelf. Stretching high to reach it, she pulled it down and set it on the table.

She then located two dozen charts of women who had come to the institute from Latin America—women whom Erin strongly suspected had been intentionally excluded from participating in the FDA study. Becoming more familiar with the filing system as she went along, Erin pulled the charts of an equal number of women who had taken part in the FDA study.

With the two stacks of medical records in front of her, she pulled up a small wooden chair and sat down. The first chart she reached for was Sarah Allen's. It was partitioned by color-coded tabs and it was an easy matter to locate the medication section. All the drugs Sarah had received were well documented except for one—the Pitressin.

"I didn't figure they'd include that one," she whispered, confirming her suspicions, and then tossed the chart back on the table.

Erin stared at the charts neatly stacked in front of her for a few moments before deciding to have a look at those patients who were on the FDA study. The first thing Erin confirmed was that they were all United States citizens. None had been referred from foreign countries. The drug given to prevent premature labor in each case was not listed by name, but instead was referred to as the "study drug." A four-digit code number was assigned to each drug, which could only be decoded by the research personnel—a routine safeguard to prevent the physicians, nurses and other health care providers from knowing which drug a particular patient received. But after going through each chart carefully, Erin was unable to identify anything out of the ordinary. She slouched in her chair, rubbed her eyes and then decided to move on to the other pile consisting of those charts belonging to the Latin patients.

As she had done with the first stack, Erin turned to the

drug section and reviewed each of the medications. Again, there was one section devoted to the study drug. Erin opened four of the charts to the identical page and spread them out next to each other.

Running her finger down each page, something suddenly struck her as quite strange. Her eyes darted from one chart back to another, stopping only for a few seconds to take note of the solution used to mix the drug for IV administration. *Dextrose in every case. Why in the world would they put the drugs in a sugar solution?* Erin recalled from nursing that saline, which is salt, is almost always used to mix drugs for IV administration.

As soon as her suspicions took form, the adrenaline rush hit her and sent a cold chill streaking down her spine. Sitting down slowly, she counted to ten hoping to collect herself. She could feel her palms moisten. Starting with the first chart, and again concentrating on those women who participated in the FDA study, Erin focused on the section pertaining to the study drug.

With one glaring exception, all of the medications had been mixed in saline. Sarah Allen's was the only exception— *her's was prepared in dextrose.* Erin closed the chart, staring with blank eyes at its cover. Caught somewhere between disbelief and outrage, she tried to organize her thoughts. It took her only a few seconds to realize she was on unfamiliar ground . . . but fortunately, the next step was obvious—she'd call Sam.

It took Erin about ten minutes to refile the charts. She moved the small wooden chair back to it original position, took a final look around and quickly made her way back to the entrance. Her pulse raced. Until this moment she hadn't given enough thought to the risk of being caught in Medical Records. Realizing now that she had no logical explanation for being there, she began to panic.

She listened at the door for a moment. Hearing nothing, she slowly pushed it open a few inches. She eased her face up to the crack and looked down the hall. There was nobody.

Two deep breaths, and her hand found the knob again. She gently slid the door open a few more inches and then peered down the opposite way. There wasn't a soul in sight. Without wasting another second, she stepped out into the hall, walked at a normal pace until reaching the lobby and then headed outside toward the parking lot.

Erin looked up. There was no moon and she noticed the temperature had dropped several degrees since she had arrived. By the time she reached her car, she was calmer. Looking up again for a moment, she thanked whoever had been watching over her. Fumbling with her keys, she finally found the one to the ignition, started the car and pulled out.

Driving slowly, Erin stretched for her purse on the seat next to her, quickly opened it and pulled out her cell phone. She turned on the overhead light and then reached into a zippered side pocket and pulled out a small piece of paper with Sam's phone number on it. With her eyes now darting back and forth between the phone and the piece of paper, Erin tapped in the number. To her delight she didn't have to wait long for an answer.

"Hello," came a sleepy voice.

"Sam, it's Erin. I've just finished going through Sarah Allen's chart and a bunch of others."

"What did you find?" he asked after a long sigh, his voice now more alert.

"I think the medical records have been forged, tampered with or both," she announced with total conviction. "I don't think a single woman from Mexico or any other Latin American country was ever included in the official FDA study. I bet the whole research study was a sham and they were all guinea pigs."

"Slow down, Erin," he cautioned. "What do you mean?"

"I'm pretty certain they all got Tocalazine. That would explain not only why there were no spontaneous abortions, but also why the birth-defect rate was so high." Erin pinned the phone between her shoulder and ear as she reached forward to lower the fan on the air conditioner. The traffic was light but she still caught herself glancing in the rearview mirror every few seconds.

"How can you be sure they all received Tocalazine?" he asked in a guarded tone. "You told me nobody except the research personnel knew which patient received which drug."

"That's true," she said, moving the phone to her opposite ear. "But what they do list is the solution used to mix the drug in to prepare it for IV administration."

There was a slight pause. "I'm sorry. I don't understand."

"All of the Latin women had their drug mixed in pure dextrose."

"So?"

"Sam, that's very unusual. Almost all drugs are mixed in a salt solution."

"I guess that's not something the average private eye would be expected to know."

"Sorry," she said. "But I have a feeling Tocalazine's the exception. Hopefully," she said, crossing her fingers as she spoke, "the answer's only twenty minutes from here sitting in my attaché case. I'll call you back as soon as I know."

Sam assured Erin he wasn't going anywhere and would wait for her call. Measurably calmer now, she tossed the phone back in her purse. Whatever other emotions she was feeling were far outweighed by her anger, which was squarely directed at whoever was at the bottom of this unholy conspiracy.

Exactly twenty-five minutes after she left the institute Erin inserted the card key into her hotel room lock. She tossed her purse on the bed and went straight over to the desk, opened her attaché and pulled out Dr. Freeman's report. She thumbed through the voluminous descriptions of the experiments but couldn't find a reference to the solution used to mix Tocalazine. She stopped for a moment, tapped the papers together to form a neat pile and cautioned herself to slow down.

Beginning more deliberately this time, Erin carefully studied the description and results of the experiments. Under the extensive section termed "Experimental Methods" she found what she was after. EACH MOUSE RECEIVED ONE MILLIGRAM PER KILOGRAM OF TOCALAZINE. DEXTROSE WAS USED TO PREPARE THE DRUG TO AVOID DEACTIVATION KNOWN TO BE CAUSED BY SALINE.

Erin closed her eyes for a few moments and then opened them to read the sentence again. Tocalazine had to be given in dextrose. She raised her hand slowly and pushed a few stubborn strands of hair off of her forehead.

It was true then—all the Latin women who came to the institute through the Mexico City clinic had received Tocalazine. There was nothing random about the experiment. It was fixed from the start. The revelation left her furious. The deception was unspeakable and beyond anything Erin could conceive of. She crossed the room, opened the mini-bar and poured herself a Diet Coke. After three slow sips, one fact was crystal clear. If she were to see this thing through, she'd have to maintain her cool.

Erin walked back to the desk, returned the report to her attaché and reached for the phone. Just before she lifted the receiver, she stopped. In processing all the information she had gathered over the last few hours, the obvious question had escaped her. *If all the Latin women received Tocalazine . . . then what drugs had the women in the official FDA study received?*

She picked up the phone to call Sam. "My God," she whispered after pondering the question for a few moments. "These people are monsters."

PART
Three

Chapter 51

"Are you sure about these figures?" Tom McGiver asked in a disbelieving tone as he rocked back in his chair.

Tony Winkler, his brightest and most innovative graduate student, stood to the side of McGiver's desk, towering over his professor. Prematurely bald with a chicken neck and dressed in a worn-out denim work shirt, Tony rarely gave a second thought to his appearance. It was just after eight a.m.

"I've worked on this thing nonstop for three days, Dr. McGiver. I've gone over the calculations a dozen times. I don't have much of a reputation, but whatever small one I do have, I'd stake on the facts in front of you."

McGiver shook his head and leafed through Tony's twenty pages of computations again. He pushed back in his chair a little farther and interlocked his fingers behind his head. McGiver's respect for Tony was hardly without foundation. He was just a few weeks away from defending his Ph.D. dissertation and McGiver never felt more confident that one of his students would come through it unscathed.

"Are you sure the Fetal Institute's animal model reached sufficient numbers? Maybe that's the problem."

Tony reached past his professor's shoulder and pointed to the bottom of the second page. "We ran the standard verification tests. There were more than enough mice subjected to Tocalazine to make the figures reliable. There's no question about it. They're statistically significant."

"Who helped you with the computations?"

"Donna Hassler."

"The one with two masters and a Ph.D in bio-statistics?"

"Yup."

"Wasn't she the one who helped us with the benzodiazepine studies?"

"That's her," Tony replied.

Without giving it a thought, McGiver placed his tongue on the roof of his mouth and let out a long slow whistle that he'd become famous for. "She's so damn smart I never know what the hell she's talking about. This is unbelievable."

"My feelings exactly."

"There's no question it's by far the best drug ever discovered for stopping premature labor, but if your conclusions are correct then Tocalazine, at least in the animal model, is the most teratogenic substance since Thalidomide. The birth-defect rate is more than fifty percent, for crissake. I've never seen anything like this."

"I don't think you could make a more dangerous drug if you tried," Tony added, crossing his lanky arms in front of him. "What are you going to do?"

McGiver tapped his chin a few times with his index finger and then let out a long slow breath. Several issues of professional ethics amongst other dicey problems popped into his head. He hadn't officially spoken to anyone at the institute but he was quite familiar with John Freeman's report to the FDA.

McGiver stood up and walked to the opposite side of his office. He stopped in front of a small automatic coffeemaker, grabbed a plain white mug and held it up in Tony's direction. "Would you like a cup?"

"Is it decaf?"

"Uh, no, I think it's regular," he said, looking at the pot and then twisting it a couple of times by its plastic handle.

"I'll pass."

McGiver poured himself a cup, added a splash of skim milk and returned to his desk.

"I guess I'm obligated to give someone a call over at the Fetal Institute. I wish John was still alive. I'm not real familiar with this fellow Chandler who replaced him."

"Maybe the reporter . . . uh, what's her name?"

"Erin Wells."

"Yeah. Maybe she can give you some more information that might help. She's the one who brought all of this to us."

McGiver looked at his student with dubious eyes. "It was just a thought," Tony pointed out.

"Maybe," McGiver said. "Why don't you leave all this with me," he suggested, pointing to the papers. "I want to have another look at them."

"No problem."

"Thanks for your help," he told Tony as the young man headed for the door. "And Tony?"

"Yes, sir."

"I'd like to ask you to keep this matter strictly confidential until I've had a chance to sort it all out."

"I was never here," he told him before leaving the office.

"Thanks."

McGiver picked up Tony's report, tapping the papers until they fell into a neat pile. Reaching forward, he snatched a large blue paper clip from a University of Miami cup on his desk and fastened the papers together. Placing the stack toward the middle of his desk, he sat back down and stared at the phone before finding Erin's phone number and dialing.

Rotating in his chair from side to side like an impatient child, McGiver listened to the drone of one unanswered ring after another. He slowly replaced the receiver and considered his options. Perhaps it was a mistake trying to contact Ms.

Wells, he thought, feeling a little relieved that she wasn't in her room to answer his call.

Picking up the phone again, he rested it on his shoulder for a few minutes before reaching for his Rolodex. It took him a minute or so of spinning through the phone numbers until he found the one he was after. He studied it for a minute or so and then flicked the card a couple of times with his index fin- ger before placing the call.

Chapter 52

Erin had been awake for almost thirty min-
utes, gazing out of her hotel window at the blazing morning
sun over the bay. She knew there were still many unanswered
questions, but enough facts were on the table to confirm her
fears that the institute was guilty of scientific dishonesty and
of violating basic human rights as pertains to scientific research. Alone, she might not be able to unwind the entire Gor-
dian knot, but with Sam's help, she felt confident she could.
The only thing that mattered now was convincing Claire to
leave the institute.

After a night's rest the decision to go to the Broward Children's Hospital was an easy one. Erin felt comfortable enough
talking to people to dismiss any thought of offending Mrs.
Carillo. After a long hot shower and getting dressed at a
leisurely pace, she grabbed her purse and left the room.

When the phone began ringing in her room, she was already in front of the elevators and well out of earshot.

The morning traffic on I-95 was rapidly thinning out, allowing Erin to move along quickly. Remaining in the center
lane, she scanned each sign, carefully looking for the Sheri-

dan Street exit. Once off the interstate, she made the short ride west until she reached the Broward Children's Hospital.

The double arched entrance of the five-story structure led to a magnificently decorated lobby. A hand-painted mural of a sandlot baseball game covered the entire back wall. The artist's use of bright colors and unique attention to detail caught Erin's eye, giving her reason to stop for a moment and admire the work.

The information desk was fashioned after a large lemonade stand. An elderly gentleman in a red vest with a full head of snow-white hair directed Erin to room 344. He informed her the majority of the third floor was dedicated to care of infants and children with cancer.

The elevator doors rumbled open and Erin stepped off. As was the case in the lobby, the decor had a baseball theme with cartoons, paintings and an eclectic group of 3-D wall hangings providing a pleasant and upbeat atmosphere.

Room 344 was almost directly across from the elevators. Erin crossed the hall, stopped at the open doorway and peered in. It was a private room with one crib against the far wall. A woman dressed in dark blue jeans and a light sweatshirt sat on a love seat reading the morning paper. Her hair was dark black and pulled straight back in a ponytail. She was thin, with a tapered waist, a swanlike neck and angular facial features.

"Excuse me," Erin said softly at the same time she tapped on the door. The woman smiled, motioned her forward, and then pointed at the baby and brought her index finger up to her lips. Erin returned the smile, nodded and entered the room.

"My name is Erin Wells. I wonder if I might talk with you for a few minutes?" Erin noticed a specially labeled IV bag hanging over the baby's crib, which she immediately recognized as chemotherapy.

"I'm sorry. I don't recognize you," the woman whispered.

Erin took a second look at the baby, who was outfitted in a

small blue hospital nighty. "Why don't we talk over there. I don't want to wake Miguel."

The woman put her paper down and walked with Erin to a place on the other side of the room.

"My name's Amelia Carillo. You already seem to know my baby's name. Do you work here?"

Erin took a breath. "No. Actually, I work for the *AMA News*. I'm presently doing a story on the Fetal Institute and hoped you might be willing to—"

"I don't think I'm at liberty to do that," Amelia said flatly with an expression of sudden apprehension.

"Your English is excellent. My understanding is you live in Mexico," Erin commented, trying to come up with a different approach.

"Thank you. I was raised in Texas."

"That explains it," Erin said with a grin. "I've been turned down for a lot of interviews and comments. Unless you're a politician, you chose a funny way of saying no."

"I'm not trying to be difficult," Amelia said with obvious sincerity. "My husband and I signed a confidentiality agreement before we came to the institute."

Erin took a step back before saying, "I beg your pardon? I don't think I understand."

"Let me explain. When we were first seen in the Mexico City clinic, it was made clear to us that if we agreed to undergo surgery at the institute, then all matters related to that hospitalization were to remain strictly confidential."

Erin smiled. "Why?"

Amelia slowly brought her shoulders up. "That I'm not sure of. And to tell you the truth, I never really thought about it. They were so nice about everything and we were so excited about being selected, it seemed like a small enough thing for them to ask." Amelia turned and looked over her shoulder at the baby. He was asleep on his tummy, breathing quietly and rhythmically.

"Maybe if they paid your medical expenses, they could make such a request but—"

"They did."

Erin cocked her head to the side. "What? Pay the medical costs?"

"Yes, plus a very generous amount for our travel expenses."

Erin wasn't an expert on international research protocols but the information struck her as a bit peculiar. She was intrigued by Amelia's comment and more than just a little interested in knowing just how generous the institute had been. She thought about pursuing the question but decided to wait.

"How's the baby doing?" she asked.

"Not well, I'm afraid," Amelia answered. "He's already had three operations, radiation therapy, and is now on chemotherapy."

Erin watched Amelia's eyes as they blinked a few times and then became watery. "I'm so sorry," she said, placing her hand on Amelia's shoulder.

"Listen . . . miss . . . I'm sorry . . . what was your name again?"

"Erin Wells, but please call me Erin."

"The Fetal Institute treated me wonderfully. Everybody connected with the hospital was great. I only have praise for them."

Erin nodded. "May I ask you a question?"

"I've already said more than I—"

"Did you participate in any of the research protocols?"

"I'm not sure I should—"

"Amelia, supposing I was to tell you that your answer could potentially help a lot of women whose babies are facing the exact same problem your son is."

Amelia's eyes became watchful. She placed her hands on her hips and studied Erin. "I'm not sure I understand what you're trying to say. Are you referring to Miguel's brain tumor?"

Erin waited a moment and then said, "Yes, I am," and then renewed her question. "Did you participate in any of the drug studies?"

Amelia took another look at her son and then gazed back at Erin. "Yes, I did."

"What were you told?"

"We were told the drugs were perfectly safe and all the women at the institute having fetal surgery received them." Amelia's expression suddenly became wary. "Is that not the case?"

"I wish I knew for sure. It's something I've been looking into." Erin doubted that her answer had been convincing. "Do you know any of the other women who were treated at the institute?"

"Not really. We were asked to avoid personal contact with the other patients, especially when we returned to Mexico."

"Did they insist?" Erin asked.

"No. It was a recommendation. They said it might compromise the validity of the research."

"I see."

"I'm an intelligent woman, Ms. Wells. Now please pull up a chair and tell me what you know about my baby."

Erin knew she had moved too quickly and was now in a quandary regarding how to proceed. She gazed away for a few moments to gather her thoughts but she could feel the intensity of Amelia's eyes following her. Erin extended her neck and looked up toward the ceiling. Her silence spoke volumes. Finally she pulled out a small chair from under a desk and waited for Amelia to sit down on the end of the love seat.

For the next thirty minutes, speaking quietly to avoid waking the baby, Erin discussed her concerns regarding the institute in great detail. With the information Erin imparted, Amelia now felt quite comfortable discussing her hospitalization. Erin was hardly an expert in such matters, but seventy-five thousand dollars for travel expenses seemed a tad generous to her.

The ride back to the Fetal Institute took about thirty minutes. Erin was drained. She had learned a great deal from her conversation with Amelia Carillo and now felt confident going to both Alex and Noah with the information. She checked her watch. It was almost eleven. Hopefully Alex would be there and she'd be able to get him alone for a few minutes. Alex had his faults and peccadillos, but his love for Claire was immeasurable and when he found out what was really going on, he'd have Claire signed out and on her way to another hospital within the hour.

Erin opened the door to Claire's room and was surprised to see the room was empty. With the last of her tests now completed, Erin assumed Claire would spend her last day before surgery just relaxing. A little perplexed, she hoisted her purse a little higher on her shoulder, left the room and walked down the corridor until she reached the nurses' station. The unit secretary, Peter O'Banyon, sat behind a large computer monitor trying to pull up the morning lab results. He was a lanky young man with curly hair and a pug nose. He was obviously totally preoccupied by what he was doing.

"Excuse me," Erin said. "I was looking for Mrs. Weaver. She doesn't seem to be in her room. Would you happen to know where I might find her?"

After several seconds, O'Banyon pulled his head out from behind the screen, pulled off his thick black spectacles and squinted at Erin. He appeared somewhat less than pleased with the interruption. "She's in surgery," he said and then disappeared back behind the screen again.

Erin shook her head. "Excuse me," she said in a louder voice. "There must be some mistake. Her surgery's not until tomorrow."

O'Banyon put both his hands on top of the monitor. "She's in surgery. Trust me. She left the floor about three hours ago."

The surge of panic hit Erin before the words were barely out of his mouth. She forced a nervous swallow and then looked up at a large clock hanging on the back wall of the nursing station. "I'd like to speak to the nurse in charge," she said in an even tone.

"Okay, I'll call her for you," O'Banyon said as he picked up the phone and dialed Kate Sensurian. Erin leaned against the long desk and waited for the charge nurse to appear.

"Can I help you?" Kate asked.

"Hi, my name is Erin Wells," she said, extending her hand. "I think there's been a mistake. Claire Weaver's surgery is scheduled for tomorrow but I've just been informed that she's down there now."

Kate was about thirty years old, very attractive and had recently been promoted to charge nurse. "That's correct, Ms. Wells. The date of surgery was changed last night."

"I . . . I don't understand. Why would they do that?" she asked in a frenzied voice.

"I believe her husband requested it."

"Alex? Are you sure?"

"That's what I was told in report." Kate hesitated for a moment and then said, "You said your name was Erin Wells?"

"Yes, that's right."

"I was with Claire this morning when they picked her up for surgery," Kate explained. "She was upset you weren't there. I distinctly remember Mr. Weaver assuring her that he'd phoned you and that you were aware that surgery had been moved up one day."

"That no-good double-crosser," Erin said softly, making a fist, thinking about her conversation with Alex the day before. *He knew I'd never change my mind about talking to Claire. He didn't believe a thing I told him.*

"I beg your pardon?" Kate said.

"Nothing, it's nothing," she assured Kate.

"Is there anything I can do, Ms. Wells?"

"No. I appreciate your help," Erin said, trying to appear as calm as possible. "I'll just go to the surgical waiting room. What time do you think they began?"

"Oh, I'd be guessing but I'd say about eight forty-five."

"Thank you."

Erin was fuming. It wasn't very hard to figure out that Alex had changed the surgery date to prevent her from sharing her fears about the institute with Claire. The rage welled in her like a monsoon. She had trusted Alex and he'd played her for a chump. His words were clear in her mind. Please think this over for another day before talking to Claire. If you still feel this way tomorrow night . . . we'll go to her together and let her decide. And then that pathetic look on his face. "How could I have been so dumb?" she mumbled.

Chapter 53

Erin had no intention of going to the family waiting area. Walking quickly past the radiology department, she pushed the large double doors open and headed straight for the operating room. Pausing for a moment to catch her breath and get her bearings, she decided to turn down the first hall, which led to the recovery room.

As soon as she arrived, Erin stopped in front of a square steel plate that activated the huge electric doors. There was little remaining of her dwindling patience as she pounded the plate several times with the side of her fist and watched as the doors swung open with a whoosh. There were five recovery bays for postoperative patients but only one was occupied. Erin immediately locked eyes on the patient's face. It wasn't Claire's.

"Excuse me," she said to a tall spindly nurse who was attending to the patient. "I was wondering if Claire Weaver's surgery is over yet?"

The nurse, who was charting on a wooden clipboard, peered over the top of her glasses and then set the clipboard down on a small table.

"Excuse me, miss, but this is the recovery room. Family members aren't permitted in this area." The nurse's tone was firm but not confrontational. Her Carribean accent matched her polished facial features. "We have an information desk in the family waiting room. I'm sure they'll be able—"

"I just need to know if Claire Weaver's surgery is over," Erin insisted. "I'm a registered nurse."

"Mrs. Weaver is still in the operating room. Now, I'm sure if you go out to the waiting room, someone will be able to give you more specific information regarding the status of her surgery."

Pleased with the news that Claire's surgery was still in progress, Erin thanked the nurse and immediately stepped back outside. According to the protocol she had read last night in her hotel room, the experimental drugs were always given toward the end of the operation. *There's still time.*

She took a couple of steps back and leaned against the wall. Two nurses, both chatting at the same time, came out of the locker room and headed for the entrance to the main operating room. Erin considered calling into the operating room and trying to speak with Noah but realized the chances of anyone putting the call through were next to zero. She looked across the hall and caught an image of herself in a window. Not being in scrubs and standing around in the hall was probably a bad move. It was just a matter of time before someone of authority asked her what she was doing there. Not in scrubs? she thought as a coy smile crept to her face. She took an extra moment, looked down the empty hall and marched directly toward the women's locker room.

The room was small and had recently been painted a dull shade of blue. There were two rows of narrow dark-green lockers divided by a wooden bench. Built-in shelves along the far wall were stocked to the top with scrubs. It took Erin about three minutes to get into a pair of scrubs, shoe covers and a mask. Once out in the main corridor, she walked casually to the main desk. She stopped for a moment and checked the digital board that listed each operating suite and the procedure that was in progress. Starting at the top, her eyes scanned downward until they reached OR #4: WEAVER, CLAIRE, REMOVAL OF CCAM.

With her mask snugly pinched on the bridge of her nose, Erin walked down the main corridor and stopped outside OR four. After reassuring herself she was doing the right thing, she pushed the door open and entered the room. Noah was standing on the right side of the table flanked by two residents in sterile gowns. The scrub nurse, a tall woman with stocky shoulders, was on the opposite side of the table. Noah's eyes were fixed on the wound. The room was cool and brightly lit. Erin took a couple of cautious steps toward the head of the bed. The nurse anesthetist was busy charting, and having no particular reason to be suspicious of Erin's presence, ignored her.

Matching stainless-steel IV poles flanked the head of the operating table. Craning her neck, Erin tried to read the labels on the medication bags. From her limited knowledge of pharmacology, neither appeared to be agents routinely used to prevent labor. An eerie feeling came over her as she realized there was nothing more she could really do. The operating room environment wasn't totally foreign to her, having spent at least a month of her nursing training assigned to a busy surgery service. But, if she didn't busy herself doing something, sooner or later her unnecessary presence would become obvious. Unfortunately, it was to be sooner.

Walking to the opposite side of the room, she pretended to be checking supplies in the cabinet. She listened as Noah discussed the operation with the residents. When he suddenly became silent, she slowly looked up—already knowing what she was going to see. His eyes were trained on her like a computer-guided smart bomb. He stepped back from the table, removed his sterile gown and snapped his gloves off. In one quick overhand motion he tossed them into a large circular bin.

"Thanks, everybody," he said. "Seth, close the skin with staples and put the usual dressing on. I'll be in the recovery room." The chief resident nodded and reached for the skin-stapling device in the scrub nurse's hand. Noah walked slowly over to Erin and placed his cupped hand under her elbow. "Are you out of your goddamn mind?" he whispered.

"Hardly," she whispered back.

"I know this is a dumb question, but I don't suppose you have administrative permission to be here?"

"Not that I recall."

Noah shook his head in disgust, flexed his head forward and massaged the back of his neck. "Let's go to the recovery room," he suggested in a tone that didn't call for a response.

"Did everything go okay?" she asked.

"Absolutely," he answered as they walked down the hall. "Now do you mind telling me what the hell you're doing here?"

"It's a long story."

"Try me."

"A lot has happened in the last twenty-four hours," she said with as much conviction as possible in response to his deliberate eyes. "We have a lot to talk about . . . and this time you better listen to me." She took a couple of steps beyond him, turned and blocked his entrance to the recovery room. "Why didn't you tell me Claire's surgery had been moved up a day?"

"Alex insisted. I had to honor his request." Noah pulled off his surgical cap and then tucked Claire's chart under his arm. "Let's go into recovery." The distress on Erin's face would have been plain to anyone over the age of twelve. She took a step to the side, the doors opened and they walked through the door. Noah pointed to a small desk in the corner flanked by two small wooden chairs.

They had only been talking for a few minutes when the electric doors catapulted open, allowing two orderlies pushing Claire's bed to enter the recovery room. The same recovery room nurse who objected to Erin's presence earlier began the routine procedures of monitoring her vital signs and checking her IV line. Before Noah could stop her, Erin was on her feet.

"Did she go into labor?" Erin asked, looking back at Noah as he pushed his chair under the desk and started toward her.

"No," he told her, flipping open the chart and writing his postoperative orders. Erin looked up and spotted a small medication bag hanging from the IV pole with a red sticker on it that she hadn't noticed in the operating room. From the bold serial number on it, it was obviously the experimental drug. Her agitation again mounted but her self-control prevailed.

"I see she's already gotten her study drug," Erin said in disgust.

"That's correct, Erin. It's part of the routine."

"And I suppose it's fifty-fifty that she got Tocalazine?"

Noah looked surprised. "That's a strange question. Why would you ask that?"

"I'd be happy to tell you but since you haven't believed anything I've told you about this place, it would probably be a grand waste of time," she declared, pronouncing each word as if it were the most important one in the sentence. She knew Noah could sense her anger, but didn't care.

"What's your problem, Erin?"

She lowered her mask and placed her hands squarely on her hips.

"My problem is this hospital and that drug you may have given to my best friend," she snapped, pointing to the empty IV bag.

Remaining silent, Noah stopped writing, closed the chart and glanced over at Claire. "What are you talking about?" he asked in a casual tone that Erin found more than just a little irritating.

"The institute better pray she didn't get Tocalazine," Erin said. Reaching into the back pocket of her scrub pants, she pulled out a small spiral pad and wrote down the serial number on the medication bag. "It's too bad you don't know the code numbers on the drugs, but believe me, the Weavers' attorney's going to find out."

"Find out what?" he asked.

"If Claire got any of that poison or not."

"Do you mean Tocalazine?" Noah asked. "Because if that's what you're so worked up about, I already checked the number."

Erin's eyebrows went up as her pupils dilated. "I beg your pardon?"

"I said, I've already checked the number. Claire was supposed to be in the Tocalazine group."

"What do you mean you checked the number?" Erin asked. "This is a double-blind experiment. Remember? You're not allowed to know what drug she got."

"That's not entirely true," he said calmly.

"Then why don't you explain it to me, Noah? Because I'm telling you right now, if Claire got any of that shit, there's going to be a lawsuit slapped against this place that's going to make the tobacco litigation look like a small-claims action." As she spoke, her index finger came closer and closer to him, stopping not two inches from his face. "And I'll see to it that it gets more national media attention than the damn summer Olympics."

Noah looked around and then gently moved Erin's finger away from his face.

"Claire didn't get any Tocalazine," he informed her.

Erin leaned forward to improve her hearing. "But you just said—"

"I said she was assigned to the Tocalazine group. I didn't say she got the drug."

"But I thought—"

"Well, you thought wrong." Noah looked away and Erin took a step back.

"Then what did she get?" Erin asked.

"Indomethacin, Brethine and Nitric," he said without hesitating. "All standard drugs. She hasn't had a single uterine contraction."

"I . . . I don't understand," Erin said. "What about the experimental drug?"

"It was normal saline."

"Saline?"

"That's correct. Maybe if you'd stop shooting from your hip and listen, you might understand." Erin was unsure of where all this was going but had the good sense to remain quiet and listen. "As the attending surgeon, it's my prerogative to remove any patient from the study if I think it's medically indicated." Noah nodded his head. "And that's precisely what I did.".

Erin bowed her head slowly. Her pulse had slowed to a normal rate.

"Why?" she asked.

"Did I take her off the study?"

"Yes."

"Because I received a very strange phone call this morning."

"When?" she asked, finding herself doing a slow dance-in-place as she always did when she was embarrassed.

"We had just put Claire to sleep. I was on my way to scrub when Tom McGiver from the University of Miami called. He said he had tried to reach you this morning but couldn't. He left a message on your hotel voice mail."

"I . . . I haven't checked my messages today," she muttered.

"From your actions of the last few minutes, I didn't think you had. Anyway, he gave Dr. Freeman's research results to one of his grad students. The guy worked on it for a long time and concluded that Tocalazine is highly teratogenic. When he reviewed the data from the animal studies, he found the birth-defect rate to be higher than any drug ever reported."

Erin closed her eyes. The breadth of her smile almost hurt. "I tried to tell you but—"

"Tom McGiver was probably the brightest guy in our med school class. I couldn't dismiss what he told me so I instructed the circulating nurse to pull Claire off the study."

Erin couldn't ever remember feeling such relief. "Thank you, Noah. I don't know what to say."

"Don't mention any of this to anyone. I'm still not sure what's going on around here. But rest assured you have my attention now. As soon as I'm done here, we're going to my office, locking the door and having a very long talk."

"I think you should know that I've been working with someone," Erin told him. "He's kind of the Rolls-Royce of private investigators. I think he's someone you're going to want to talk to." Her voice was calm, her expression tranquil.

"I'll look forward to it."

Erin heard a soft moan and looked over at Claire. The anesthetic agents were starting to wear off and her eyes were struggling to open. Erin gazed at her and then looked back at Noah.

"Go sit with her," he told her. "I'll go speak with Alex."

Most of the commotion at Claire's bedside had subsided. A nurse in white pants and a pink top stood by attending to the IV. Erin looked up at the monitor. The red and green digital display demonstrated normal vital signs and excellent oxygenation. Claire's face was angelic and peaceful. Erin moved in closer and reached down for her friend's hand. The moment she touched it and felt its warmth, Claire fully opened her eyes and gave Erin's hand a slight squeeze.

"Everything went great," Erin whispered in her ear.

"I knew it would," Claire replied in a raspy mumble. "I told you there was nothing to . . . to worry about."

"You were right," Erin said, watching her close her eyes and then drift back to sleep.

Erin looked up to see Alex standing across from her. Noah was at the foot of the bed. "I guess we need to talk," Alex said to her.

"Later," Erin answered. "There'll be plenty of time for that later."

Erin watched Alex. He swallowed hard and then in a jerky and uncertain motion moved his hand down to his wife's.

Erin beamed at Noah. For the first time in weeks the sword of Damocles wavering over her head was gone.

Without much regard to anything going on around her, Erin walked straight up to Noah, put her arms around him and hugged him like she'd never hugged a man before.

Chapter 54

Carl Chandler sat with his ankles crossed and his legs propped up on the corner of his desk. A large Styrofoam container of coffee with its cap half off sat a few inches from his feet. He was looking down, reviewing an extensive file on one of the lab's recent experiments when Erin knocked on his door. He looked up, and in one motion swung his feet off the desk and waved her in.

It was just after eight a.m., and apart from a few technicians who had arrived early to calibrate the instruments for the day's experiments, Erin and Chandler were alone. Dressed in a double-breasted black blazer and cuffed charcoal dress slacks, he stood up with that same sappy smile she remembered, and then pointed to the chair in front of his desk.

"I hoped I'd catch you here," Erin said as she sat down.

"I like to get here early. It's the only quiet hour of the day. In forty-five minutes this place will be a zoo. How's the story going?"

"Actually, I'm just about finished," she said.

He moved the container of coffee a little farther off to the side and sat upright in his new high-backed leather chair. "I

hope the information I gave you was helpful. Will I get to see
a copy of the article before it's published?"

"Of course," she assured him, wondering if he was trying
to figure out if he'd been included in the story. "Actually, I
used quite a bit of the details you were kind enough to pro-
vide. I hope I spelled your name correctly."

Chandler glowed as if he had just won the Nobel Prize.
Erin couldn't remember the last time she'd seen anybody
wear such pomposity on their sleeve. "I never imagined you
would actually include me in the story," he said unconvinc-
ingly.

"I wouldn't have it any other way. Do you think you could
help me finish it up?"'

He sat forward, placed his palms squarely on the desk and
said, "Of course. Whatever I can do."

"I need help with the technical aspects of some of the research that was done in the lab."

"Sure. What specifically are you referring to?"

Erin took out a small notepad from her purse and flipped
through several pages before stopping. "Here it is. The drug's
name is Tocalazine. When we first spoke, you mentioned it to
me," she said with a quick smile.

"Tocalazine?"

"Yes, I'm particularly interested in the animal studies that
were done on the drug prior to the FDA approving it for
human trials." She closed her pad and looked up just as the
last bit of color drained from his face.

"Uh . . . that's kind of an unusual request," he finally managed after clearing his throat for a second time.

"Really? Why's that?"

"Well, it's . . . it's just that the information's of such a technical nature. I don't understand why that would be important
for your story."

"Actually, I'm just following up on some information that
Dr. Freeman gave me."

Chandler rocked back in his chair. "John gave you information on Tocalazine? I'm . . . uh, a little surprised." There was a definite crack in his voice as he tried to speak.

"He gave me quite a bit of information to go over. He seemed very nervous about the drug. Do you have any idea why?"

Chandler shook his head. "No, I can't imagine why."

"Neither could I, so after he died, I submitted the work to the University of Miami to review, and do you know—"

"You did what?" he demanded, standing up and pushing his chair backward against the bookcase. His eyes were wide. A cluster of small, tortuous veins popped up on his chalky brow.

"I asked the Department of Pharmacology over at the university to go over the basic research on Tocalazine so I could better understand it. Is that a problem?"

"I . . . I'm not sure if—"

"Do you know Dr. Thomas McGiver?" she asked. The prominent veins on his forehead were now lightly dotted with beads of perspiration.

"Yes, I know him."

"Do you know what he told me?"

"I haven't the first clue." His words were muffled by his hand, which was now squarely over his mouth.

"He said the animal research on Tocalazine was faulty— that the results that were reported didn't reflect the actual experiments."

Chandler paced behind his chair and then walked over to the water cooler and poured himself a small cup. "I guess he's entitled to his opinion," he finally said. "There's a lot of petty envy and backbiting in this field. We're not without our share of professional jealousy. Perhaps Dr. McGiver should take a long hard look at his code of professional ethics." Chandler tossed the paper cup into the wastebasket and sat down. From the tone of his voice and more relaxed appearance, Erin felt as if his confidence was building. "If you don't mind me asking, what exactly did Dr. McGiver object to in our research?"

"Oh, I'm not sure he objected to anything. He just concluded that Tocalazine was an extremely dangerous drug that had a high potential for causing birth defects and should never have been approved for human trials."

"That's absurd. We took every precaution. There's no way those results were tampered with, and anyway—"

Erin's eyes flashed on him. She could feel the rhythmic hammering of the pulses in her neck. "Tampered? I never mentioned anything like that. I only said he disagreed with your results."

"But you implied—"

"I implied nothing, Dr. Chandler. What do you know of the clinical trials of Tocalazine?"

"I . . . I don't know anything. That's Leigh Sierra's department. We don't exchange information with the clinical research division. I'm sure Dr. Freeman told you that."

"As a matter of fact, he did. And it didn't make any sense to me. I've called a dozen prestigious research institutions around the country and do you know what they told me?"

"No," he said, letting out another slow breath and looking straight down. "But I'm sure you'll share that information with me."

"None of them have that policy anymore. It's anachronistic and anti-intellectual," she told him directly, wondering how far she could push him.

"I'm not sure I agree," he answered with a shrug.

"How many directorships across the country have you applied for in the last few years?" she asked him.

"I beg your pardon?"

"It's a simple question, Dr. Chandler. How many directorships have you applied for?"

"I don't see why that's any of your business," he said indignantly. "And I'm starting to grow tired of this conversation."

"Why won't you answer my question?"

"I'm a research scientist, Ms. Wells. It's not unusual for someone in my position to keep their eyes and options open." He suddenly looked at her with a resentful smirk. "I wonder what you would do if the *New York Times* came knocking at your door with a job?"

"I might take it. But I don't have half a dozen headhunters out there beating the bushes for me," she informed him. Erin had no way of knowing if this was true but her intuition told her it might be.

Chandler shook his head. "In our profession, retaining a headhunter is the most expeditious way of moving up. I'm not ashamed of letting a professional do my legwork for me."

"How many directorships have you been turned down for?"

Chandler's face was filled with disdain. "The number is unimportant," he said quite distinctly and in a louder voice. "I'm an extremely qualified individual with a strong fund of knowledge in basic research . . . and administrative skills as good as anyone's."

"Would you say you were as qualified to head up a research program as John Freeman?"

Chandler, caught up in his own ego, sneered. "Maybe more so."

"In that case, when's the official announcement?" she asked.

"What are you talking about? What official announcement?"

She smiled and looked at him as if he were a child trying to con his mother. "The official announcement that you are the new permanent director of the research facility, of course. That's what they promised you . . . isn't it?"

"Ms. Wells," he said slowly, "I have no idea what you're talking about."

"Really? Well, maybe if Dr. Freeman were still alive he could help us out."

Chandler's face turned to cherry red. He shook his head a few times, looked straight at Erin and then pounded his fist on the desk. "I had nothing to do with John Freeman's death. He was a colleague, for God's sake."

Erin remained calm in her response. "I never said you did. But you're hardly an innocent man."

"And what the hell is that supposed to mean?"

"You made sure the animal studies on Tocalazine would be granted FDA approval. That was the only way the human trials could get started."

"You're making an enormous mistake . . . and this is nothing more than a cheap journalistic trick to—"

Erin ignored his accusation. "You're a very ambitious man, but in the end you were just a corporate pawn," she said, shaking her head in disgust and then standing up. "Was the promise of John Freeman's job so tempting that you threw away every professional ethic you ever had?"

"You have no idea—"

"What did they tell you to soothe your conscience . . . that if the drug was really harmful to people, they wouldn't market it? How could you believe them, for God's sake? Were you really willing to take that chance?"

Chandler was silent, his palms flat on the desk with his eyes transfixed downward. "I never hurt John Freeman," he said in a voice just above a whisper. "I just assumed he died of natural causes."

Erin stood up. "You didn't pull the trigger, but you might as well have," she said, walking toward the door. "If I were you, I'd use the next twenty-four hours to speak with an attorney." Erin had seen beaten men in her time, and at the moment, Chandler clearly fit the profile. "You made one mistake," she said and waited until he looked up at her. "Whoever has you in their back pocket promised you they'd just fire Freeman, not kill him. Am I right?"

"I really don't think I should—"

"Did it ever occur to you that Freeman was a very bright man who was bound to figure out that the experiments had been tampered with, and that the results sent to the FDA were fraudulent? Did you really think Neotech would just let him walk out the door and take a new job somewhere else with what he knew?"

"I . . . I don't know."

"Consider our little conversation this morning your wake-up call. It's my advice to come clean with the FDA. If there is a way out of this mess for you, that's the only way."

Erin didn't wait for a response. Whatever small doubts she had about Carl Chandler when she walked into his office had been dispelled. She walked down the main corridor of the lab. A few more technicians had arrived and were checking and calibrating the instruments for the day's experiments.

She stopped, turned and looked back at Chandler. With a vacant expression, he slowly reached forward and picked up the phone.

Chapter 55

Erin entered Leigh Sierra's reception area just as she walked out of her office with a young couple. The woman was pregnant, carrying the baby higher on her tummy than most. She was wearing a plain white maternity dress tied loosely at the waist. Her eyes were bright, her expression beaming.

"Mr. and Mrs. Morales, I'd like you to meet my secretary, Andrea," Leigh said. "She'll make all the arrangements for your admission to the institute."

Luz Morales reached out and took Leigh's hand. "We can't thank you enough for all you've done for us, Dr. Sierra."

"Just have a healthy baby. That will be enough thanks for me. I hope your stay with us will be more pleasant than your trip up from Mexico City. Missing connections is never very pleasant."

"I'm sure it will be," Mrs. Morales said.

Erin waved and caught Leigh's eye just as she was getting ready to go back in her office.

"Hi, Leigh. You got a second?" Erin asked. "If it's a bad time, I can come back later."

"Not at all. I'll be with you in a minute."

Erin nodded and had a seat on a plum-colored leather couch. The essence of the expensive Corinthian leather was unmistakable. Leigh finished up and signaled Erin into her office. As Erin walked past the secretary's desk, Mrs. Morales smiled confidently at her.

"Have a seat," Leigh said, pointing to the chair in front of her desk. "How's the story going?"

"No complaints. How was your weekend in the Bahamas?"

Leigh rolled her eyes and grinned ear to ear. "You don't want to know. You really missed a great time. There were men everywhere."

"I don't know how you do it?"

"What do you mean?" Leigh asked.

"Oh, run this department and still have time for such a great social life."

"It's a simple fact—if you work hard, you have to play hard. No matter what anybody tells you, the best things in life cost a lot of money."

Erin laughed along with Leigh. "There's something I want to talk to you about. I'm not sure if it's important or not."

"What is it?" Leigh asked. "Is it something juicy about Noah, because if it is—"

"No, no. It's not about him. It's about Tocalazine."

Leigh frowned. "Tocalazine? How boring."

"Remember you told me Tocalazine was very effective at stopping labor but didn't work in normal pregnancies, only on women who had fetal surgery, and that its commercial potential was quite limited?"

"Sure, I remember."

"I've done a little research and . . . well, I think you may be wrong."

"What do you mean?"

"I've spoken with three nationally renowned pharmacologists who agree that the sales potential of the drug is immeasurable. All three agreed that if a drug works to prevent labor, its action is on the uterus. Fetal surgery has nothing to do with it. They said there's no way the body could tell the difference."

Leigh furrowed her brow just enough for Erin to notice. "That they're aware of, you mean," she responded, reaching forward and pouring herself a glass of water from a metal pitcher.

"Do you think they could be right?"

Leigh shrugged. "I don't know. Maybe we should hire these guys. But since we're the only lab working with Tocalazine, I guess they're offering an opinion about something they know little or nothing about." Leigh looked down at her desk and pretended to be looking over some reports. Her annoyed expression betrayed her rapidly diminishing patience. Without looking up and in an offhand manner she asked, "What difference does all this make, anyway?"

Erin crossed her arms in front of her. "The difference is that I don't think you wanted me to know that Tocalazine had enormous commercial potential."

"I beg your pardon?"

"You intentionally misled me," Erin said.

Leigh sat back in her chair and crossed her arms. Her guarded expression matched her defensive gesture. "I'm sorry you feel that way, Erin. But we're as interested as anyone in making money. If the drug shows commercial promise, believe me, we'll pursue it."

Erin smiled. "Who's *we*, Leigh? I thought you were an employee of Neotech?"

"I . . . I am." Leigh rolled her chair back a few feet and stood up. "What's your problem?" she snapped.

Erin stood up, leaned across the desk and locked eyes with Leigh. "I think there are a lot of bad things going on around here and I think you're up to your eyeballs in them."

Leigh pointed her finger directly at Erin. Her eyes widened with intensity. "You're out of your mind."

"Am I?"

Instead of escalating the confrontation, Leigh remembered

herself, slowly sat back down and placed her hands on the desk in a gesture of guarded forbearance. "Okay, Erin. I don't deserve any of this but I'll play along. What's on your mind?"

"Tocalazine's a dangerous drug and I'm pretty sure you knew it," Erin said, sitting back down. "The animal studies showed an incredibly high rate of birth defects and cancer. But you and your pals at Neotech chose to ignore that fact, faked the report to the FDA and deceived them into approving further tests on humans."

"Why in the world would we do that?" Leigh asked in a collected tone that Erin assumed took every drop of restraint she could muster.

"Because Tocalazine was the bait for the Healthspan buyout."

"The Healthspan buyout?"

"Sure, why else would they pay one point two billion dollars for Neotech? It's all about Tocalazine. That's the only reason they wanted to acquire Neotech. Without Tocalazine, you're just another mediocre hospital company."

Leigh closed her eyes and then rubbed the bridge of her nose slowly with her thumb and forefinger.

"I thought your degree was in nursing. When did you cross over into evaluating complex corporate acquisitions?"

Leigh opened her top drawer, pulled out a pack of cigarettes and took no time in lighting one up. Erin had no idea she smoked and was sure the practice was prohibited on hospital premises. After taking two long drags, she peered across the desk with an apprehensive expression.

"It's really not that complicated," Erin explained. "It must have been one hell of a job convincing Healthspan that Tocalazine was a safe drug. You must have snowed them the same way you did the FDA."

"And what makes you such a damn expert?" Leigh asked, rubbing the cigarette out in a decorative crystal candy dish.

"Because I've done my homework. Healthspan's an impeccable company. They wouldn't dream of acquiring a company if there was even a hint of improper conduct."

"For goodness sakes, Erin. Why would we proceed to human studies if we knew the drug was so dangerous?"

Erin watched as the last bit of smoke cloud drifted past her. The odor was offensive. "In a word, greed," she explained. "And your unconscionable willingness to gamble the lives of innocent women."

"That's a despicable accusation," Leigh yelled, clenching her fists.

Erin ignored the outburst. "You were hoping the animal studies were wrong and the drug wouldn't cause birth defects in humans. If your theory was right, and it was harmless, well . . . Tocalazine becomes one of the hottest drugs in the world and Neotech slash Healthspan's profits go through the roof." Erin leaned in and added in a very soft voice, "And nobody's the wiser about the phoney animal experiments . . . not Healthspan, not the FDA."

Leigh reached for her glass of water. She took two quick sips and then replaced the glass. Erin couldn't help but admire her outward composure under fire, but she would have loved to reach across the desk and feel Leigh's pulse. If she were any judge of human nature, she knew her heart must have been galloping.

"I have a question," Leigh stated. "Assuming your theory is correct, and I'm totally denying that it is, what would we have done if Tocalazine was harmful to humans?"

"In the first place," Erin began without a moment's indecision, "I think we both know the drug is harmful to humans. But to answer your question . . . keep it a secret."

"And how would we do that?"

"By only giving Tocalazine to the foreign patients and then not including them in the official FDA study. They were nothing more than guinea pigs to you."

"That's nonsense. All patients were enrolled in the official study." The inflection in her voice was nervous but at the same time obviously dismissive.

"You're lying, Leigh. The patients from Latin America were never enrolled in the study. If they had been the FDA would have known about the high rate of birth defects and tumors those poor babies suffered from."

Leigh tapped her fingers on the desk and then steepled them in front of herself. "You claim we knew Tocalazine was dangerous . . . that it caused birth defects and tumors."

"You're damn right," Erin said with conviction.

"Doesn't that kind of defeat your argument? I mean how could we market this drug if it was so dangerous?"

Erin was anxious to answer. "Now that you know Tocalazine is just as horrible in humans as it is in the mice, Neotech bails out of the project by providing a report to the FDA that Tocalazine was great at preventing labor in mice but not in humans. The issue of the birth defects and tumors never even comes up. By that point, the merger's a done deal and you have all those millions from Healthspan."

"Don't you think Healthspan would have waited to complete the purchase until they were sure about Tocalazine?" Leigh inquired.

"Not a chance," she told Leigh in no uncertain terms. "The human trials would have dragged on for years. That would have delayed the deal considerably and allowed other corporations to get wind of Neotech's value when Tocalazine hit the market. That's not exactly something Healthspan would want." Erin turned in her chair slightly and crossed her ankles. "Healthspan's making the right move by acquiring Neotech now."

Leigh again turned and reached for her water glass. A noticeable tremor in her hand made the water almost spill over the top. "It sounds like you've got this . . . this hallucination all tied up in a neat little package."

Erin answered, "As did you . . . except for one slight miscalculation. You didn't count on Dr. Freeman figuring out that you tampered with the results of the animal studies."

Leigh shook her head again and said, "This all makes for great theater, Erin, but nothing more."

Erin moved forward in her chair. "Dr. Freeman had purchased an airline ticket to go to Washington the week he died.

He had an appointment with the FDA. I think you knew that."
Erin paused for a moment, waited for Leigh to look directly
at her and added, "That's where Mr. Grafton came in."

"Who?"

"Frank Grafton. The director of security here at the institute. Your right-hand man and main enforcer."

"C'mon, Erin. I barely know the man."

"That's funny, because his cell phone statements show he
spoke with you at least once a day for the past several
months . . . until he was hospitalized, that is."

"Cell phone records? I thought those were confidential in
Florida."

Erin had no intention of responding to Leigh's observation
of her methods, but instead watched carefully as the trepida-
tion in her eyes intensified. It was clear to Erin that Leigh was
not acting as if she viewed the accusations as nonsense. To the
contrary, she was obviously absorbed in what Erin had to say.
If that weren't the case, Erin assumed she would have been
invited out of the office by now.

"Airline tickets, appointments with the FDA, criminals
working in our security department. Does this madness ever
end?"

"I don't know. You tell me." Erin stood up and moved behind her chair. "You knew Dr. Freeman was a diabetic."

"I beg your pardon?" Leigh said.

"I said you knew Dr. Freeman was a diabetic. You used
that little piece of information to stage that phoney heart attack. He died of digitalis toxicity, which was arranged by Mr.
Grafton."

Leigh let her head fall back against the top of her chair and
shook her head. "What's this now?" she asked.

"You should have told Grafton to go back to the lab for the
phoney insulin bottle."

"What phoney insulin bottle?" Leigh asked.

"The phoney insulin bottle he put in Freeman's leather
case. I guess he was too arrogant to assume anyone would figure out what he'd done." Erin walked back around the chair

and sat down. "I'm afraid he made a big mistake. The police have the bottle now."

Leigh turned her chair to the side, stretched her legs out and then crossed her ankles. She reached for her gold Cartier bracelet on her left wrist and began fiddling with it. "Even if any of this were true, I guess it would be Mr. Grafton's problem."

"Well, he's not exactly available for comment at the moment. He's still recovering in the hospital. But once the police confront him with the evidence, do you really think he's going to go down without taking you with him?"

"I guess that's something—"

"How about bribing Carl Chandler with the directorship of the research lab if he'd fake the animal studies for you?"

"Carl Chandler's career is of no interest to me."

"If my guess is right," Erin said, "he's already met with his attorney. He's well aware that once the data from the animal experiments and the FDA report is evaluated by experts, he'll be exposed." Erin paused for a moment and then added, "I suspect the legal advice he'll get is to come clean and cut his losses. And, just like Mr. Grafton, I don't think he'll think twice about implicating you to save his own skin."

Leigh sat silently for a moment or two, nervously drumming the desktop with her fingers. "If your theory's right and Chandler did tamper with the animal experiments, maybe he acted alone. Maybe he figured the fastest way to get Dr. Freeman's job was to make him look incompetent. Implicating me might be nothing more than an act of desperation on his part to spread the blame around."

Erin responded immediately, "I hardly think that's the case."

"Maybe, but I guess my theory's as good as yours."

"You're a clever woman, Leigh. There's no question about it. I'd like to believe that I'm a pretty good judge of people, but you really had me snowed." Erin reached forward, picked up the pack of cigarettes and tossed them at Leigh. She made no attempt to catch them and they landed on the credenza behind her. "You may need a lot more of those where you're going. I only hope that whatever jail you wind up in, you're there for a very long time."

"I hardly think that's going to happen. Everything you think you've uncovered has an alternative rational explanation. Remember. We're an extremely prestigious institution doing God's work."

"God's work?" Erin asked in utter disgust. "You can't be serious."

Leigh pulled her legs in, spun her chair around and stood up. "For the past twenty minutes I've listened to the drivel . . . now you're going to listen to me," Leigh insisted.

Erin turned her hands palms up and remained silent.

"Let's consider this—who are you? A young ambitious reporter desperately trying to write that blockbuster story that's going to send her career racing into the arena of high-profile investigative reporting." Leigh shook her head with an arcane smile. "I'm afraid you've wasted a lot of time for nothing. You don't have a shred of proof. Nobody's going to believe this lunacy. Now, if there's nothing further, I have a lot of work to do."

"Why did you do it, Leigh? Was the temptation of the money so overwhelming? What was Neotech going to do? Make you the new CEO when St. John moved up to join Healthspan's board? The offer must have been incredible if you were able to disregard every thread of moral and ethical fiber in your body."

"Just for the sake of conversation," Leigh responded, "some people would say that one point two billion dollars and major corporate power are things to be seriously coveted. But I guess that's something a bottom dweller such as yourself would never understand."

"There's not a decent bone in your body, Leigh."

"And there's another thing. There's a big difference between being a sharp businesswoman and breaking the law. I may have moved the line a little, but I never crossed it."

Erin's eyes flashed in disbelief before she could respond.

"Knowingly reporting fraudulent information to the FDA, bribing potential patients from foreign countries to participate in your study and failing to give them informed consent about drugs you knew were potentially dangerous?" Erin glared at Leigh. "You call that moving the line? Hell, you're so far over the line you can't even see it anymore."

Erin stood up, walked across the room and left the office. Leigh fell back in her chair. She reached into her top drawer and pulled out a small mirror she used for putting on her makeup. She held the mirror up to eye level and glanced at her image. Her hands were shaking and her complexion was ashen. Before she had time to think, Erin returned with Mr. and Mrs. Morales. The three of them stood shoulder to shoulder just beyond the entrance to the office.

When Leigh spotted the couple she had just counseled, she immediately reached for the phone.

"Who are you calling?" Erin inquired.

"Security, and then the police," came the response. "How dare you involve these poor people with your lunatic theories."

"That won't be necessary," Erin said.

"Good," Leigh said, replacing the phone. "I assume that means you'll be leaving my office?" Without waiting for an answer, she turned toward Mr. and Mrs. Morales. "I'm so sorry this happened, please have a seat and we'll—"

"No. It means the police have already been called."

Leigh looked up immediately and watched as Luz Morales slowly reached under her maternity dress, pulled out a pillow and blew out an enormous breath. "That was a tough delivery," she said.

At the same time, Mr. Morales reached into an inside pocket of his sports coat and pulled out a leather wallet. Holding it high, he allowed it to flip downward, displaying his gold FDA badge.

"Leigh," Erin began, "I'd like you to meet Sylvia Mendoza and John Fredericks. They're special agents attached to the FDA's Office of Criminal Justice. They have a tape they'd like you to listen to. It's only about fifteen minutes old and you're the key player on it."

Sylvia Mendoza stepped forward, pulled a small tape recorder out of her purse and held it straight out in front of Leigh.

"That . . . that won't be necessary," Leigh said flatly. "I . . . I want to speak with my attorney."

"The tape's quite interesting," Inspector Mendoza said. "It's not often I get offered a hundred thousand dollars to take part in a research study. It was kind of you to review all the specifics of what we were promised by your clinic in Mexico City if we agreed to take part. I especially liked the oath of silence."

Leigh collapsed in her chair, her chin fell flush against her chest. Just as the FDA special agents approached her desk, two husky Dade County police officers appeared at the door.

Fredericks advised Leigh of her rights at the same time Sylvia was handcuffing her. There was a conspicuous absence of tears, but as Leigh stared down at the shackles her expression of disbelief was like none Erin had ever seen. A hypnotic glaze shrouded her vacant eyes. There was no scene, no outburst of emotion or desperate attempts to explain herself. Only silence. As Leigh Sierra was escorted from her office by John Fredericks, she neither looked up nor said a word.

Alone in the office, Erin gazed over at the far wall and studied Leigh's formidable and impressive display of diplomas. Erin bowed her head in frank disgust. For some inexplicable reason, the anticipated sense of victory was completely absent.

Chapter 56

"Where are you off to?"

Recognizing Sam's voice, Erin turned around and was already smiling when she looked into his eyes. The lobby was crowded. In the next moment, the elevator doors behind her opened and a half dozen people quickly exited.

"I was on my way up to see Noah. Do you want to join me?" she asked.

"I'll pass. You guys probably need some alone time."

Erin crossed her arms and cocked her head to the side. An amused expression covered her face.

"Since when are you an expert on relationships?"

He just shrugged and then asked. "I guess things went okay with Leigh Sierra?"

"Couldn't have gone better. She's on her way to jail even as we speak."

He only nodded. "And Claire?"

"Doing great," Erin told him. "When are you heading back to Washington?"

He looked at his watch. "In about two hours."

"You know I'll never be able to thank you," she said, her voice cracking just a little.

"No need to try," he assured her.

Erin detected just a hint of childlike discomfort in his manner as if the moment was an awkward one for him and he was a tad flustered. She moved forward and wrapped him in the tightest bear-hug she could. He slowly raised his arms and patted her gently on the back a few times.

"When am I going to see you again?" she asked letting him go and turning to the side so he wouldn't notice her moist eyes.

"Well, if you're not on the road chasing after some story and Noah can find a hole in his schedule to come up to D.C., we can have dinner. I'd like you guys to meet my wife."

"We'd love that."

He looked at his watch again. "I better get going," he said.

Erin moved forward again, this time kissing Sam on the cheek and leaving a few warm tears on his face.

"Don't think we won't take you up on that dinner offer," she said in a raised voice as he walked away. "And you're buying."

Without stopping or turning around he said, "I wouldn't have it any other way."

Erin continued to watch as he walked out of the lobby. Even when he was out of sight she still stared outside. Finally, the rumbling of the elevator doors opening again snapped her mind back and she turned around. As soon as an elderly man using a walker managed his way off she got on.

Erin found Noah behind his desk with his nose in a medical journal. She stood in his doorway until he sensed her presence and looked up.

"How did it go?" he asked.

"It's over."

"What do you mean?"

"They arrested Leigh Sierra a few minutes ago," she said, walking across his office and taking a seat in front of his desk.

"The whole thing's unbelievable," he said, shaking his

head. Erin could sense he was relieved by the simple finality of the scandal, but she still detected a hint of embarrassment in his voice. "I don't know what to . . . I mean I still don't have the first clue what to say to you. I've tried—"

"Forget it."

"I should have been more involved the last few days," he stated, tossing the journal toward the center of his desk.

She shook her head. "We discussed all that. The FDA made it clear they wanted you to stay clear. It wasn't a medical issue."

"What about Marc Archer?" Noah asked.

"As of right now, it doesn't appear he was involved. He's a bit inflexible and autocratic but he's an ethical physician who always had the best interests of the institute at heart." Erin stood up, walked around the desk and softly rubbed Noah's shoulders.

"I'll give you an hour to stop that," he moaned as his head fell forward. "By the way, there was something I thought of after we talked. The Tocalazine study was double-blinded. Not even the researchers knew what patient was getting which drug. How did you get into the clinical research department's computer to get the codes?"

"I didn't have to." Erin stopped massaging for a moment and Noah turned around.

"I don't understand," he said.

"Tocalazine is a very unstable drug in any solution except dextrose. If it's mixed in anything except dextrose it's completely deactivated."

"What about the other drugs used in the study?" he asked.

"They're all mixed in saline, so it wasn't too difficult to find out which drug or drugs each woman received."

"And?" Noah asked impatiently, as if he felt left in the dark.

"The only women who received Tocalazine were from out of the country . . . and they were never enrolled in the official FDA study."

"How did you find that out?" he asked.

"I spent some time in Medical Records checking the IV solutions used to prepare the drugs. It didn't take too long to figure out. It was then a simple enough matter to check things out against the anonymous report I received on the Tocalazine experiments at my hotel."

Noah took a deep breath, removed his reading glasses and asked, "Did you ever figure out who sent the report?"

Erin took his glasses and dropped them into his shirt pocket. "Well, I have no way of being totally certain but I assume it was John Freeman. It seems he was just about ready to go to the FDA and spill everything."

"Where do you come in?" Noah asked slowly.

"I guess he sent me a copy as a hedge in case anything happened to him."

"I just can't believe any of this," Noah said.

"I'm afraid it's all true," Erin said, continuing to knead his shoulders with just the right amount of pressure.

There were a few moments of silence. Erin could feel Noah's muscles continue to relax but she knew his mind was working overtime.

"How does the Pitressin in Sarah Allen's IV tie in to all this?"

"I assume there was a foul-up in the pharmacy and she accidentally got Tocalazine. Leigh must have found out about it fairly quickly and taken care of the problem."

"What makes you think so?"

"Because if Sarah Allen went to term and gave birth to a deformed infant, Leigh would have been faced with the certainty of answering a lot of embarrassing FDA questions about birth defects in women receiving Tocalazine."

"Are you suggesting that the Pitressin was intentionally added to Mrs. Allen's IV to induce an abortion?"

"I certainly am. I can't think of any other reason for there to be Pitressin in her IV."

Noah was grim-faced. In addition to her romantic interest in him, Erin truly respected him as a physician. She could almost sense his embarrassment for his unethical, self-serving colleagues.

"I . . . I guess we all owe you a lot, Erin," was all he could manage.

"I saw Claire this morning," Erin mentioned, not dwelling on his compliment and assuming he would be more comfortable on different ground. "She looks great. Is it true she's going home tomorrow?"

"I don't see why not. By the way, how are you and Alex getting along?"

"We had a long talk. Everything's fine but I told him no more deals unless they're in writing."

"Now you're getting smart," Noah commended her. "It's a big, bad world out there, Erin. A trusting, reserved girl like yourself has to take every precaution when dealing with all those devious men out there."

She stopped rubbing for a moment and sharply pinched the back of his neck. He sat forward and thanked her for the massage.

"What about you?" she asked. "What are you going to do?"

"Well, I had an interesting call yesterday. It seems Georgetown University wants to start a fetal surgery program and they're looking for just the right person to head it up."

Erin leaned around until she was eye to eye with him. "Georgetown, as in Washington, DC?"

"Is there another one?" he asked.

"C'mon, I'm serious."

"Well, Marc Archer was in here this morning. He wants me to stay on and try to rebuild things. He thinks in time we can put this whole thing behind us."

"Is that what you want?" Erin asked.

"I don't know, I have my life's blood in this place. It's a tough decision."

She kissed him briefly on his forehead. "Well, you know what my vote's going to be. I think you'd love Washington."

"Actually, I'm kind of excited about Georgetown's offer," he confessed.

Erin looked around the room slowly, and then with her most seductive eyes, asked, "I was just wondering if you've ever done anything nasty in your office? I mean, we could close the door and—"

Noah stood up quickly, twisting his head as he did so to avoid colliding with hers. "Do I have to remind you that I have a prestigious position at this hospital and feel compelled to behave accordingly."

"I see. How about later after everyone's gone?"

"Not a chance," he insisted, pointing to the door. She leaned over and whispered something in his ear that made his complexion turn red. "Are you serious?" he asked in disbelief. "You'd really do that?" She leaned over and added something to her suggestion that gave him pause to think. "In that case, I may be forced to reconsider."

Epilogue

The uneventful birth of Matthew Weaver took place on Monday, January tenth at the Medical College of Virginia in Richmond. As a precaution, he was observed in the neonatal intensive care unit for the first three days of his life, and much to the delight of everyone caring for him, he thrived as any normal newborn.

"That's the best-looking godson a girl could ask for," Erin told Claire, who held Matthew cradled tightly against her chest. Alex and Noah smiled and then took a couple of steps back to allow Erin the exclusive. "I've never seen so much hair on a baby in my life," she added as both she and Claire stared at the baby.

"The nurse said I can give him a bath tomorrow," Claire mentioned. Matthew weighed just over seven pounds, had a cherubic face and was as pink as they come. Claire turned to Noah and said, "There isn't a single scar on him. Just like you promised."

"Even if there were, it wouldn't make a difference. That's the healthiest kid I've ever seen," he answered.

Mattie Johnson, an elderly nurses' aide, came through the

door pushing a bassinet. She ambled across the room and stopped at the foot of Claire's bed. She was fifty pounds over-weight and cast an ominous presence as she peered over the top of her tiny reading glasses. "How about getting some rest, Mrs. Weaver. I'll take care of Matthew for a while. As soon as you've had a nice nap, I'll bring him right back."

"Go ahead, Claire," Erin encouraged. "You look ex-hausted." Claire looked down at Matthew, kissed him on the forehead and reluctantly surrendered him to the nurses' aide, who carefully bundled him in a soft blue blanket and then placed him in the bassinet.

"It's time for us to go," Erin informed Claire after sneak-ing a peak at the new gold watch Noah had given her for Christmas.

"You've only been here for a little while," Claire protested.

"A little while? It's been over two hours. We'll be back in the morning." When Erin walked over to kiss Alex good-bye, he had already shaken Noah's hand and thanked him for the hundredth time.

"We'll see you both tomorrow," Alex reminded them.

Ten minutes later Erin and Noah were in their rental head-ing back to the hotel. It was a cold evening and Erin kept test-ing the air as it came out of the vents, praying for it to warm up.

"I've never seen Claire happier," she told him with a shiver as she rubbed her hands together. "And thank God the airline didn't lay Alex off. That was a real gift from heaven."

"Things really turned out well," he agreed. "By the way, have you heard any more about your story. When's it going to be published?"

"Herb and I have had several meetings. It's a touchy topic. He's having second thoughts about publishing it in the *AMA News*. I think he's leaning toward allowing me to sell it inde-pendently."

"Wow, I guess I didn't expect that," Noah said and then let out a short whistle.

"We both feel the *AMA News* might not be the best place for it."

Noah thought for a moment and then asked, "But he's not saying you shouldn't publish it?"

"Absolutely not. As far as we're concerned, this is important public information. I promise you, the story will be published within the next six months."

"Does that mean you'll be leaving the *AMA News* with lofty ambitions of becoming an investigative reporter?"

"Of course not, I love my job." She turned to him and placed her hand behind his neck.

"Did you ever hear anything about Carter St. John?" Noah asked.

"Actually I spoke with John Fredericks yesterday."

"The agent from the FDA?"

"That's the one. Actually, they haven't turned up too much on St. John other than he's a tough businessman. If you can believe it, the investigation is focusing on his wife, Susan. She's the one who actually hired Leigh Sierra. Evidently, Susan was a major player in Neotech."

"You're kidding," he said.

"The FDA thinks she was the mastermind and up to her phoney little eyelashes in the entire scam," Erin said. "They're pretty sure she was getting the money for the patient bribes from the institute's charitable foundation. It seems that a lot of the patients from Latin America came to Miami without any added incentive, but when they encountered one who balked, Susan was Johnny-on-the-spot with a little extra financial persuasion."

"What are the legal implications of that?" he asked.

"Well, there are very strict laws governing the financial activities of charitable organizations in the state of Florida. A lot of people donated substantial sums of money that they believed were going toward worthwhile projects at the institute."

"And you're saying it wasn't," he said.

"Some of it probably was, but John Fredericks said their financial experts have pretty much determined the charitable foundation's accounting records were falsified."

"Which means what?" Noah asked.

"Well, the law's pretty clear. A charitable organization's books are open to public review. I'm afraid Neotech and Susan St. John will be facing a host of criminal charges for forging and misrepresenting accounting records."

Noah just shook his head. "I'm speechless. I always thought I was dealing with honorable people."

"Never mind them. What about you, Noah? You haven't been very talkative about your plans."

He shrugged. "I was waiting for you to ask."

"So it's mind games we're playing now. Okay, what did you decide?"

"I called Georgetown today," he said without turning in her direction.

"And?"

"I accepted the position. I start February first."

Erin was now the one who was speechless. She had cautioned herself against getting her hopes up and had just about talked herself into the reality that Noah would stay on in Miami. For the past few months, they had each exhausted their vacation time commuting between Washington and Miami. Their relationship had grown and each had come to share an equal dependency on the other. They were best friends first and then lovers. "You start February first," she finally muttered.

"That's right."

"And you'll be living in the Washington area?"

"Well, considering I'll be working in Georgetown, it might be a tad inconvenient to live in New York," he explained, purposefully trying to be as nonchalant about the whole thing as possible. "In fact, I put down a deposit on a condo."

"Really?" she asked, going along with his aloof attitude. "How interesting. Which one?"

"That high-rise down by the river. You remember . . . the one with the *to-die-for* view."

"Wasn't that the one I said I'd give my firstborn to live in?" she asked.

"I think so. How long will it take you to sell your place?"

She looked down at her watch. "What time is it now?"

Noah finally broke down and shared an uncontrollable laugh with Erin. In the next moment, he pulled over and kissed the woman he loved until the windows fogged over.